CHRISTINA T.

THEIR
RIGID
RULES

48
FOURTEEN

FOURTEEN PUBLISHING TRADE PAPERBACK

BOOKS BY
christina thompson

THE CHEMICAL ATTRACTION SERIES

Their Rigid Rules
The Kindred Code
Chemical Attraction
Chemical Reaction

THEIR RIGID RULES

Their Rigid Rules. Copyright © 2014 by Christina Thompson.

First edition published 2014.
Second edition published 2017.

Excerpt from *The Kindred Code*, by Christina Thompson. Copyright © 2017 by Christina Thompson.

Edited by Matthew Brennan and Break Through Author. Cover by Ampersand Book Covers, www.ampersandbookcovers. com. Interior Book Design by Break Through Author, http:// www.breakthroughauthor.com.

ISBN-13: 978-1-937546-32-8
ISBN-10: 1937546-32-2

To Kraig, my one and only love.
Every story I write is a love letter to you.

CHAPTER
one

SATURDAY

THE COLD DRIZZLE OF THE November morning didn't faze him. Stuart Morgan had other concerns, such as tardiness for his weekend seminar. Irritated by his newly acquired sidekick, Stuart lengthened his stride toward the Hyde Building on Western Michigan University's campus. He hoped Reese Forester's shortness of breath would stop him from talking. Instead, the short and balding Jack Russell terrier yipped and nipped at his heels.

"Who would threaten to kill a history professor? It's not like I'm Indiana Jones," Stuart replied, carrying his briefcase in one hand and the soggy campus map in the other.

"The university hired me to look into it," Reese said, doubling his steps to keep up. "This is a serious threat, and you're surrounded by students, one of which who may be involved." He ogled the females with backpacks hurrying along the maze of wet sidewalks. "Hot young women ripe for plucking," he mumbled.

Ignoring the comment, Stuart checked the saturated paper again. "I wish you'd take the weekend off. I'm not on Michigan's campus. I'm a visiting professor. Nothing's going to happen." After yanking on the door to enter the four-story brick building, he flipped the deteriorating map over for directions to the second-floor lecture hall.

Breathing heavily, Reese placed his hand over the flimsy paper, tearing it in half. "This is the perfect place to follow through and you know it. Stuart, humor me and let me do my job."

Wadding up the wet paper, Stuart sighed and pitched the ball into the trash. "I'm not going to put my life on hold because of an unsubstantiated threat. For all we know, I gave a low grade to a student who decided to write a nasty letter," he replied, running a hand through his damp, blond hair. He flung the excess water in Reese's direction.

"Thanks," Reese said, sidestepping the splatter. "And it's not just one. There are a dozen vicious letters. No offense, but you really don't have a life. I've read your profile."

"That may be, but I like it the way it is. I was a Marine. I can protect myself." Taking the steps two at a time, he chuckled as Reese huffed behind him.

"Yeah, let's talk about that. Who'd you piss off while stationed in Afghanistan, Lieutenant Morgan?" Reese asked.

Wincing at the remark, he stopped next to the lecture hall door. "Don't call me that. It was a while ago, and if you haven't noticed, I'm a pretty nice guy."

"You're kinda pissing me off," Reese replied, out of breath.

Stuart smirked. "Fine. Call my former C.O., General Daniel Bingaman. He'll tell you how boring I was."

"I already know you're boring. You teach history," Reese said as tired students shuffled past them to find their seats.

"And you get to enjoy my lecture." Stuart smiled.

"I'll be observing your students closely, if I'm lucky, maybe even intimately."

"Aren't you old enough to be their father?"
"I work the big brother angle. Besides, you and I are only eight years older than that group." Reese wiped the sweat and rain back from his brow, into his thinning black hair. Dismissing Stuart, he slowly climbed the steps to a spot at the top of the tiered-seating lecture hall.

Before walking through the doorway, Stuart slipped off his Navy peacoat, shook it out, and scanned the room. Forty students had registered for the four-weekend course. He hated teaching weekends, especially during football season. And the two and a half hour drive to Kalamazoo from Ann Arbor irked him even more. He grumbled silently about the disruptions to his boring yet pleasant life until he spotted a young woman in a Michigan cap. Stunned by her smile, he stared. A single ray of sun parted the clouds of his abysmal day. Her genuine laughter made her hazel eyes sparkle as she joked with her friend.

An overwhelming urge to speak with her tugged at him. Blinking it away, he frowned. He never had that kind of reaction toward a student. He had his rigid rules as a young professional. Maybe the commotion of the death threat had affected him more than he thought. He sighed again and took his place to start the class.

AT SEVEN-FORTY IN THE MORNING, Taylor Valentine, holding a large coffee, slid behind the hard desk. She unzipped her backpack and pulled out a fresh notebook. Arriving early, she and her best friend, Eva O'Sullivan, sat in the second of the five rows off to the side—not the hated, front row middle.

The tiered lecture hall could seat about fifty students. In the front, a laminate waist-high table had a stool and dry erase board behind it. Taylor watched as zombie-like students filled the room. They probably wondered why they were here for four weekends of history, too.

"I still can't believe I let you talk me into this Civil War seminar," Taylor said.

"Oh, please," Eva replied. "You need the history credits, and the plan is to graduate before the holidays. Would you rather have an early class Monday through Friday for a whole semester?"

"But it's Saturday. I'm supposed to be watching football. I have a bet with Joe against State. He won't pay when he loses, but it'll be fun to tease him about it," she said as she sipped her warm coffee.

Eva grinned. "He'd expect you to pay. You're too responsible and reliable."

Laughing, Taylor rolled her eyes and let it go. Eva

was right, but was that so bad? Why should she struggle against her vanilla tendencies? Her plan and rules for her life reinforced those traits.

Swallowing the last of her coffee, she observed the group. Everyone appeared hung-over from various Friday night parties. Like her, many wore some kind of hat to cover their hair. They must have rolled out of bed ten minutes ago, too. While she waited, she pushed a strand of her dull, light brown hair away from her lightly powdered face and tightened her ponytail under her favorite Michigan cap. Eva sipped her green tea and tapped her pen on her notebook.

As always, Eva had her makeup perfectly applied. Her curly auburn hair hung below her shoulders and her Irish spitfire attitude magnified her petite frame. If Eva had an opinion on a subject, everyone knew it whether they wanted to or not. Although Taylor took a more subtle approach in their discussions, she admired her friend's tenacity.

As the group tried to get comfortable for the long day ahead, they waited for the professor to walk through the door. Instead, they watched Cindy Carter glide into class in all her attention-grabbing glory. In a dark green dress with matching heels, she gracefully sat in the front row middle. She opened her leather briefcase and pulled out her pad and pen. She looked rather virginal with her long, blond hair tied loosely with a white ribbon—a wolf in sheep's clothing.

Cindy lived on the same dormitory floor as they did. From two doors down, they could hear her vocal escapades. Eva said the main reason her rich daddy sent her to college was to find a husband. Cindy wasn't that bright, but with a model's body, she could easily get a degree in Flirting.

Before Taylor had a chance to ask Eva why Cindy was so purely dressed, she faced them. "Do you know anything about this visiting professor? I heard he's single and quite charming," Cindy said.

"I haven't heard a thing," Taylor replied, now knowing Cindy was working her way up the food chain to unsuspecting professors.

"I heard he has a PhD in Civil War History," Eva replied.

"He's probably been to those reenactments. Yikes," Taylor said, wrinkling her nose.

Eva grinned. "Stop it. You might actually learn something interesting."

"Well, I don't care what he has to say. I hope he's nice to look at," Cindy replied.

"How do you expect to pass the course?" Taylor asked.

"Better yet, do you know anything about the war?" Eva added.

"Of course I do." Since Cindy faced them, she didn't see the instructor walk into the room from the side door.

He wasn't just nice to look at, he was striking. He had lost the battle trying to smooth out his wavy, blond hair and looked taller than Taylor's six-foot height. His defined biceps tightened against his pale blue dress shirt. *Boxers or briefs*, she wondered as she checked out the rest of his muscular physique.

He set his briefcase quietly on the table and listened to the group chatter. Eva, a history fanatic, took this chance to ask Cindy if she knew who won. Taylor saw the professor raise his eyebrow as he shuffled some papers. He tried unsuccessfully not to look.

"We did," Cindy replied. "We always win. Don't we?"

The other forty or so students quieted, realizing the professor wanted to start. Eva took the opportunity to stick it to Cindy a little more. "Then who did we defeat?"

Not waiting for an answer, the professor began, "Okay, class. I can already tell I have my work cut out for me. We're all thrilled to be here, so let's get started. I expect a thoughtful, five-page essay on any part of the Civil War to be turned in the third weekend of class." Handing out the syllabus, he continued. "You will also take an essay exam on the fourth Saturday."

The class collectively moaned, and Taylor would have, too, if he hadn't been standing right in front of her. She reached for the class outline.

"I like the hat," he whispered, holding her gaze.

Wow! And she liked those sexy baby blues. Between the scent of his cologne and his penetrating stare, she felt faint. The room became a sauna, making it difficult to breathe. She gawked at him like a moron. As he moved on, the wave of heat followed him. She could breathe again. *How weird.* That's never happened before. She blushed as Eva smiled at her.

He spoke above the groans. "I'm going to move quickly through the material, so we can get out by noon."

While he took attendance, Taylor perked up. She could still catch kickoff if she was lucky. She and Eva were meeting Joe at Johnny's Bar to watch the Michigan-Michigan State game on the big screen. She hoped he remembered to get a good table in front.

She listened and took notes all morning. Dr.

Morgan's commanding voice spoke passionately about the different battle strategies. The people of that time sprang to life. For the last half hour, she continued to check her watch. Dr. Morgan started to wrap up his lecture.

He, too, kept looking at the clock at the back of the room. As she closed her notebook filled with messy writing she hoped she could decipher later, Dr. Morgan made a fatal error.

"Any questions?" he asked.

Taylor glared at anyone she thought might and saw the back of Cindy's hand go up. *Damn her.* She'd ring her neck for making her late.

"Dr. Morgan, I have a couple." Cindy used a sickly sweet, baby voice, trying to be sexy. It sounded like a whine to Taylor, but knowing what guys liked wasn't her forte.

"Yes?" he said, sounding half-annoyed.

"Why did they wear those drab blue and gray uniforms?"

He gave a brief explanation as he gathered his papers and stuffed them into his briefcase. Taylor pictured herself slapping Cindy upside the head, and she liked it.

"Why would we fight each other and not work together for the unity of our country?" Cindy continued, practicing her pageant questions and answers for the upcoming show. Our mouths dropped open.

"We'll cover that tomorrow," he replied, before walking out the door.

"Gee, Cindy, what did you think we've been discussing since eight this morning?" Eva asked as they headed for the exit.

"What do you mean? Isn't he cute? I bet he has tenure and money in the bank," Cindy replied.

Taylor agreed. *Handsome and a hard-core body. I could definitely get lost in his sky blue eyes*, she thought, as Eva caught up to her. "Joe had better have saved us a table," Taylor said.

"If he did, I'll buy the beer for the entire first half," Eva replied.

Taylor groaned and walked faster. She knew he'd forget, but she could hope. Joe Roberts became her first real friend in grade school. From different backgrounds, they didn't quite fit in, so they looked out for each other. He protected her from bullies, and she kept him out of trouble with the teachers. Unreliable, he occasionally came through.

As they walked into the crowded bar, Taylor realized this wasn't one of those rare times. Looking around, she didn't see Joe. She couldn't even see the two big screens somewhere off to the left, hidden behind the standing crowd. Moving closer, she checked the score on her tiptoes. Relieved that it was only two minutes into the game and no score, she turned to Eva.

"I'll find you later!" Eva yelled.

Johnny tended to the bar behind the long counter on the right. He motioned Taylor over. The gray-haired pudgy man in his mid-fifties acted the father figure with them. He knew she loved Michigan football. She had watched every game for the last four years in his bar.

He pointed to an old seventeen-inch Zenith at the end of the counter. "I pulled that out of my office for you. It's thanks for helping with my sciatica."

She smiled. She had finally talked him into letting her massage his lower back and hip at the chiropractor's office. Finding relief after the first session, he actually cried. She works on his hip every two weeks and gets free Cokes as a bonus.

She and Eva had gone through the intensive massage program the summer after high school for extra spending money. Starting college, they had decided to keep their jobs secret. Horny college guys did not need to know that they were massage therapists.

After taking the remote from his hand, she leaned over the bar and kissed his cheek. "I love you."

Johnny laughed, and she moved toward the other end of the bar. He had even saved them three stools. She took the reserved sign off hers and tossed her bag and jacket on the floor under it. She angled the TV. Nobody seemed to notice. Johnny gave her a beer, and she settled down to watch and yell. It was an important game for the state of Michigan—bragging rights were on the line.

Her dad had shared football with her. If she wanted to hang out with him, she'd join him in the den to watch the Big Ten Saturday afternoons. As an only child born to a couple in their forties, they didn't have much in common, but her dad liked talking about the plays and players. That had been their thing in the Fall. He had died of a stroke three weeks before high school graduation. Her mom had died a week later. Taylor believed it was from a broken heart.

After sipping her beer, she was about to yell at the referee for missing a holding call when she felt a tap on the shoulder. "The game's on," she said, not turning from the TV.

She heard a voice asking for the seat. Eva was somewhere, and Joe was nowhere. Shrugging, she reached over and pulled the sign off the stool. Not taking her eyes off the set, she watched one of the linemen miss his block. She winced as Michigan's quarterback got sacked. The coach took a time out, and they went to commercial. Turning, she chugged her beer and swallowed, hard.

"Professor Morgan, what are you doing here?" she asked as she sucked in air to breathe.

Smiling, he picked up his mug and gestured to the TV before taking a swig.

"Please say you're not a State fan," she said, pulling at her sweatshirt from the unbearable heat. Was she over the heating duct? She'd have to tell Johnny to turn down the temperature.

"Are you kidding? I'm hoping Michigan will get a Rose Bowl bid this year."

She laughed. "I think you checked the clock as much as I did."

Eva joined them. "Dr. Morgan, what are you doing here?"

"Shush," they said, turning back to the game.

"Johnny, bring us a pitcher," Eva said. "This is going to make class tomorrow even more interesting."

Taylor groaned as Michigan's kicker missed a twenty-yard field goal. A couple of guys a few stools down yelled at the TV screen above the bar. They wanted to beat the crap out of him for missing the kick. She stood up.

"Hey!" Taylor yelled at the guys. "His dad just died; cut him some slack. He'll get the next one. Besides, he made the earlier three points to keep us in the game." The men laughed at her but calmed down. Embarrassed by her outburst, she sat back on her stool then sipped her beer.

"Do you know the kicker?" Dr. Morgan asked.

"Only what I've read online," she replied. "It irks me when people trash and threaten the players. Like he wanted to miss that field goal? Come on," Taylor replied.

"Do you always come to the player's defense?" he asked. For some reason, his tone changed. How had the conversation gone from lighthearted to serious?

"When I can," she said with a frown. "Nobody's perfect. We all make mistakes."

Eva laughed. "Taylor's the most empathetic person I know. I think she secretly feels people's hidden pain. She's constantly stopping me from smacking idiots."

Taylor shrugged as Dr. Morgan stared at her. She wouldn't apologize for giving people the benefit of the doubt.

During halftime, Taylor and Dr. Morgan went round and round about who was the best player and what plays would work. He seemed surprised by her knowledge of the game and agreed with most of her assessments. He liked the coach's strategy and the team's tactics. She thought it was a very history professor thing to say. Without looking, she knew Eva rolled her eyes for the eighty-seventh time next to her. Eva and Joe constantly teased her about her passion for football. It was more out of love for her dad. When she watched, she always sensed him nearby.

Dr. Morgan raised his eyebrow. "What? You don't like football?"

"No, no, that's not it," Eva said, holding up her hand. "Guys in tight pants, what's not to like? Honestly, though, by your professional manner in class today, I couldn't picture you at a bar drinking beer and yelling at the TV."

"Am I that stuffy?"

"I found lecture fascinating, but you seemed irritated," Eva replied.

"Yeah, well, I insulted the university president telling him there is no way Notre Dame's Lou Holtz was a better coach than Michigan's Bo Schembechler. As a result I'm teaching weekend classes," he said with a sigh.

Laughing, Taylor leaned back. Her stool slid out from under her. Lightning quick, Dr. Morgan slipped his arms around her waist to prevent her from falling on the floor. He held her against him nose to nose. Smelling his cologne, feeling his hard body, and staring into those sexy blue eyes, she blushed. Her ears burned. She thought she'd burst into flames and had a hard time breathing again. She shouldn't like her professor's arms around her, but she did.

"Thanks," she whispered, biting her bottom lip. "I'll be back in a few minutes." She tried not to stumble to the bathroom.

FROWNING, STUART STARED AT TAYLOR as she walked away. "She's the one?" he mumbled, picking up her stool.

He knew he shouldn't have cut the class short, but he didn't want to miss kickoff. He needed some kind of normalcy to his disrupted routine. It had taken an extra fifteen minutes to talk Reese into letting him watch the game in peace. When he had entered the bar, he couldn't believe his luck. She was sitting alone by the small TV.

He enjoyed talking football with this sexy, young woman who was into it as much as he was. Her tenderness and compassion intrigued him. Could she really feel someone's pain? He wondered if she could feel his, because his mood lightened just being around her. The pressure against his chest lessened, allowing him to take deeper breaths.

Putting his self-control to the test, he had resisted the urge to touch her until she slipped off her stool. Without thinking, he wrapped his arms around her. His body jolted with an electric shock. His parents believed in the chemistry of love at first sight. *This wasn't it, was it?*

He slowly turned toward the bar to sip his beer. What the hell was the matter with him? He shook his head. He was mistaken. This was lust. It had been a while. He pushed his beer away and rubbed his hand through his hair. This was not the best time for anything, and she was his student for God's sake. He felt drawn to her nonetheless.

"She's the one what?" Eva asked, moving to sit on Taylor's stool.

He jumped. "Huh?" He tried to shake off the zap but couldn't.

Eva's eyes narrowed. "She's the one what?" she demanded.

He sighed. "I'm her professor. I'm not supposed to like her, but I do," he said quietly.

Eva laughed. He didn't think it was funny. He had a big problem—his resolve weakened.

TAYLOR WALKED TOWARD THE END of the bar and saw Eva in her seat next to the professor. She grimaced at her sudden twinge of jealousy. Talking to people, especially guys, came easy to Eva. Once, she had Eva teach her how to flirt. It came off embarrassingly fake. As a result, she left the hair twisting and eyelash fluttering to the pros, like Eva and Cindy. Taylor loved Eva like a sister so why would she care that men liked her better? She had her plan, and she's only talking football, and, jeez, he's her professor.

She sat on the other stool closest to the TV. Looking back at her, Eva grinned. Frowning, Taylor switched their beer mugs and averted her eyes to hide her hurt feelings.

Eva laughed. "Settle down," she whispered to her. "I'm going to give Joe hell for making us watch on this tiny screen. He just walked in." She leaned closer. "He's all yours."

Stunned, she choked on her mouthful of beer. Was she that easy to read? *Sips from now on. Don't make a fool of yourself in front of your professor.*

Dr. Morgan moved to Eva's stool to be closer— to her or to the TV? God, she needed to calm down. Blowing out a breath, she pushed her mug away.

She tried to focus on the game. "I hope the coach told special teams to stay in their lanes. I don't want to get burned again like last week," she said.

"Hey, you want another pitcher?" Johnny asked, already grabbing the empty one.

"Coke for me. I have class tomorrow, and the professor has me taking a ton of notes," she replied with a smirk.

"Make it two," Dr. Morgan said to him. He grinned and leaned toward her ear. "I heard he likes giving essay tests, too."

She smiled at the intimacy. His warm breath on her ear made her body rigid with awareness. She didn't dare lose herself in his gaze. After the game, she grabbed her bag and jacket. Dr. Morgan followed her out the door. She zipped her jacket against the chilly afternoon. All of the leaves had turned brown and created a wet, slippery layer across the sidewalk. She walked with care.

"Are you on campus?" he asked beside her.

"Yeah, Burke's Hall. Where are you staying?"

"The guest apartments for visitor speakers and professors who want to stay on campus."

"I'm going that way, too," she said, secretly happy to be with him a little longer.

CHAPTER

two

SUNDAY

NEEDING COFFEE AFTER ANOTHER RESTLESS night, Stuart stopped at the student union for breakfast on the way to the Hyde Building. He left his car parked at the visitor apartment, so he could enjoy the sunny fifty degrees. Only a few students milled about. He'd rather be in bed, too. His mind jumped to wanting Taylor Valentine in his bed. God, it had to be lust. He never had any interest in his students, even though many tried to entice him. This was different. She didn't pursue him. They talked football and enjoyed the game. He wanted what he couldn't have, plain and simple. He knew he'd get burned, but she tempted him to light the match anyway.

While eating half of his bagel with cream cheese, he juggled the other half, his coffee, and his briefcase. Hurrying, he took a shortcut among a dozen cars scattered throughout the parking lot. When his cell rang, he set his coffee on the trunk of a rusted Chevy.

He unclipped his cell from his belt, and the bagel landed face down on the pavement.

"Damn," he said into the phone as he leaned down to pick up the gritty mess.

"Not a morning person, Doc?" Reese asked.

Before he could answer, a shot rang out. Stuart dropped to the ground and looked around the car's bumper. His coffee tipped over and splattered next to him.

"Reese, where are you? I'm getting shot at in the student parking lot," he said, hearing another shot then screeching tires.

"Shit, I'll be right there."

After taking a deep breath, he peeked above the trunk. Thick white exhaust followed the exiting car. He couldn't see the make, model, or license plate. Pushing thoughts of war to the back of his mind, he brushed the dirt off his black slacks. His peacoat and white dress shirt had smears of gritty cream cheese and stains of coffee.

"Are you all right?" Reese asked, huffing next to him.

"Yeah, someone took two shots at me," he said, picking up the cup with a bullet hole in the center. "I gotta go back to my car for a clean shirt."

"Jesus, what the hell are you doing walking around campus?"

"I get your point." After dumping the bagel in the trash, he handed Reese the empty coffee cup and headed back to his car. "I'll drive back. Are you going to call campus security about the hole in the Chevy's trunk?"

"Yeah. Did you see anything?" Reese asked.

"No. Do you think he followed me to Kalamazoo

from Ann Arbor?"

Reese scanned the area as they walked. "Yes. Last night, I received the report on those letters from Detective Larsen. The cops think they were written by a female from this area."

"From Kalamazoo? Who?" He popped open the trunk to his dark blue Mustang and pulled out a gray t-shirt from his overnight bag.

"When was the last time you taught a class here?"

"Last year."

"That's about the time the letters started," Reese stated.

After tossing his coat in the trunk, he unbuttoned his ruined shirt and put on the gray tee. "So you think it's a student?" he asked, tucking the t-shirt into his black dress pants.

"I'll get the class list and check out a few other leads," Reese said, getting into the car.

Stuart drove past the rusted Chevy and parked in the employee section closest to the Hyde building. "This seems so absurd. Why would a female student want to kill me over a class she attended last year?"

"Maybe she's in this class, too. Any chance she's a spurned lover?"

He glared. "I've never had a relationship with a student."

"Are you sure that's the answer you want to give me? I saw you walking with a hotty after the game yesterday. Personally, I would have chosen the fiery redhead."

Stuart stood next to his car door and looked over at him. "You're following me?"

Reese leaned his elbows on the vinyl roof. "It's my job. Listen, Stuart. I don't care who you're doing. Just don't lie to me. I'm trying to keep you safe."

"I get that, Reese. I repeat. I have never been in a relationship with a student."

"But you'd like one with Taylor Valentine."

"It's not like that."

Reese grinned. "Of course not. She's different, right? Did you ever think she's working her wiles, so she can kill you up close and personal?"

Stuart wanted to take a swing at him. Instead, he laughed. "Her wiles? How old are you? Fifty? Go find the shooter."

"Oh, I will," he replied. "I'll clean this up first. I'm not looking forward to your lecture. I hated history in high school and still do."

BACK FOR THE EARLY MORNING class, Taylor's arms were full with her jacket, backpack, and another large coffee. She had washed her hair and left her hat in the room. She even wore some lip-gloss. He was handsome and charming.

Even though they had some things in common, could she really compete with the likes of Cindy Carter? Speaking of the Barbie Doll, she strolled in wearing heels and a football jersey as a dress. Taylor almost dropped her coffee.

"Hey, Cindy," Eva said, sitting down in the same seat as yesterday. "What's with the jersey?"

Cindy smiled sweetly. "I heard Professor Morgan loves football."

"He does but not that team." Eva laughed at the Michigan State jersey.

"Football's football," Cindy replied, turning back around.

Taylor figured she could check her off the list as competition. Whoa! What was she thinking? It was only a game and a short walk.

Eva leaned over. "Nice lip gloss, and don't worry about Cindy."

God, it's scary when Eva does that. "Am I that obvious? Please say I'm not turning into her," she whispered back.

"Not a chance. Yesterday was the first time I saw you relaxed around a guy." Eva nodded toward the door. "This should be good."

Dr. Morgan set his scuffed briefcase on the table and looked around the room. He cringed at Cindy's State jersey. She and Eva stifled a laugh. During the breaks, Cindy monopolized him. He ignored her outrageous advances and seemed oblivious to her obscene suggestions. Why didn't Cindy just strip down and give him a lap dance? It would have been less apparent.

Taylor smiled when he looked her way. He acknowledged her with eye contact. That was good, right? He looked very fine in his tight gray t-shirt. It accentuated those stunning blue eyes. She fought against staring.

She scrambled to write everything down and hoped she could read her chicken scratch later. Eva jotted down only a few words. With an eidetic memory, Eva never forgot a thing.

Taylor observed sophomore Lindsay Brant with thick pink streaks in her black hair. She lived on the floor below them. She, too, wrote only a few words in her notebook. Glancing over Cindy's shoulder, Taylor saw heart-shaped teddy bears with Cupid's arrows on her notebook.

Eva raised her hand. "Dr. Morgan, why are the name references different? For example, the North referred to it as the *Battle of Bull Run* while the South called it *Manassas*."

That was a great question. Why couldn't she impress him with a question like that? Probably because the Civil War was gobble-de-gook to her.

"I'm glad someone caught the references. Although some battles shared the same name, such as *Gettysburg*, the South had a tendency to name these incidents after towns, buildings, or railroad crossings. The North named the battles after the closest geographical feature like creeks, rivers, or peaks …"

Well, if she couldn't come up with a good question, she may as well stay close to Eva and have her excellence through association. After class, they stuffed their notebooks into their bags. Dr. Morgan came over and said he appreciated their attentiveness.

When Eva and the rest quickly left to catch a nap before another week of classes, he blocked her way. "Same bar stool next week?" he whispered a few inches from her.

Blushing, she smiled. "Will we get out early?"

"Possibly." When he grinned, she thought her legs would give out.

"That's exciting," Eva said as they walked back to their dorm room. "A covert meeting in a darkened bar."

"Oh, I didn't think of that. It doesn't matter, does it? I mean, it's the game at a bar, not a date, right?"

"I guess it's how you look at it. He asked you out to a bar, didn't he?" Eva said.

"Well, yeah, to watch the game. That doesn't count. Besides there are rules about dating your professor," she said, suddenly bummed. "As gorgeous as he is, I can't break the rules. It's giving me an ulcer just thinking about it. I follow the straight and narrow."

"You need to lighten up. He's a guest professor, and who'll know?" Eva said.

"Yeah, just my luck, I bend the rules, and there goes my education. I have my plan. You know how important that is to me. Besides, I don't even know him."

"We'll see about that."

IN THE EMPTY CLASSROOM, STUART shuffled his papers and absently jammed them into his briefcase. He had asked Taylor to watch the game with him next week. He couldn't help himself. Taylor had brightened his weekend. He liked the distraction from the chaos. He sighed as Reese strolled down the steps to the front desk.

"What'd you find out?" Stuart asked.

Reese sat in the front row middle and wobbled in the unbalanced desk chair. "It seems as if I had you pegged all wrong, Doc. You really aren't as boring as you say. Women fawn over you." He did a mocking version of Cindy Carter, wrapping her finger around her hair while batting her eyelashes.

"That's annoying," he replied. "What'd you find

out?"

Reese tilted the desk chair back. "This is what I don't understand. Three hot young women in this class clamored for your attention. You ignored them and kept a close eye on Taylor Valentine. What do you see in her?"

"I thought you didn't care."

Reese laughed. "So she does interest you?"

Ignoring the question, he clicked his briefcase shut. "Go home, Reese. I'll see you tomorrow."

"Bright and early," he replied, following him out the door.

Before heading back to Ann Arbor, he drove up the circular driveway to a colonial-style home. After stopping in front, he jumped out and rang the doorbell.

"Stuart, you're just in time for dinner," Doris said, standing back to let him in. Younger by a couple years, she had a slim, enhanced figure with a sophisticated style in her clothes and home décor.

"I can't stay. Where is he?"

"Have a seat, and I'll find him."

Instead, he paced across the marble tile next to the door. Seeing him coming down the wide hallway, Stuart met him halfway. "Why are you doing this to me? Reese is driving me nuts."

Bob steered him into the more inviting living room with burgundy wallpaper and an abundance of pillows tossed on the sofas and chairs. "It's for your own good. When you told me about the letters, I had to do something because you hadn't. This is serious."

"So serious that someone shot at me this morning," he replied, rubbing his hands through his hair. That brought back unwanted memories from his time as a

Marine.

"Did Reese find him?" Bob asked, pushing an olive green pillow aside before sitting on the sofa.

Stuart paced. "The police believe a woman from this area wrote the letters. Reese has it in his head that it's a student."

"He knows what he's doing. I trust him. That's why I hired him. Stay for dinner, and we'll talk it out."

"I have reports to grade. You tell Reese to back off around my students."

"I think you should start carrying your gun," Bob replied.

Shaking his head, he slammed the door on the way out. He refused to carry a gun ever again.

BEFORE TAYLOR ENTERED HER AND Eva's dorm room, she heard the thumping of heavy boots down the hall. Without looking, she smiled. Joe Roberts slid through her door before it fully opened. He yanked her in and quickly closed it.

The room had enough space for two twin beds and two desks. They had stuffed their dressers into the four-foot-square, walk-in closet for a little more breathing room. Even though they had to use the floor's communal bathrooms and showers, every room had a small sink and mirror by the door. Tossing her keys on her desk, she smiled at the two photos on her desk. One was her mother and father's wedding photo and the other was her, Joe, and Eva—the first time she had laughed since her parents' deaths. Joe was cradling Eva in his arms while Taylor rode on his back. Taken at College Freshmen Orientation, it was the beginning of their next adventure together. Her best friends were her family.

Eyeing Joe, she set her backpack on the floor by her bed. After dropping his jean jacket on her desk chair, he stretched out on Eva's tiny bed. It dipped under his weight. Her dark-haired, green-eyed hunk of a friend practically lived in their room. Many of their floor mates speculated until Eva set them straight. They seemed relieved that he was like a brother. They wanted to chase after him. What those young women didn't know was that Joe did the pursuing. He had a nasty habit of enjoying the chase more than the catch. He bored easily, which didn't bode well for the women on campus.

"Who are you hiding from?" she asked, shoving his boots off Eva's comforter.

"Nobody. I just wanted to hang out."

"So you don't mind if I open the door," she said.

"I do mind."

Frowning, she folded her arms and leaned against the closet door. "I'm not helping you again."

"Please," he begged, "just one more time."

"You're a jerk. You said that three times ago. Do it yourself."

He jumped from the bed and took her hand. "Taylor, pleeaase. You know I hate hurting them."

"Then why do you? Jeez, Joe, if I didn't know the real you, I'd hate your guts," she said, slapping his hands away.

He sighed. "That's the thing. I keep searching for that one. I haven't found her yet."

"Well, slow down. You need to improve your karma. You'll find her when you're supposed to," she replied.

He stepped toward her, and she hugged him. "Your mom used to say that," he said, squeezing her. "You're right, it's just—" Before he could finish, someone knocked. He got down on one knee and silently begged. After pushing him over, she cracked open the door.

"Um, hi," the freckled freshman said. "I'm looking for Joe Roberts. I was told he stayed in this room."

"Joey's not here yet. Can I help you with something?" She pinched Joe in the arm as he stood behind the door.

"Are you his sister?" the young woman asked. Her doe eyes blinked up at her.

Taylor twisted Joe's skin. "Excuse me, but how do you know my husband?"

"Oh, um, from class. Never mind." With tears in her eyes, she raced for the stairwell.

Taylor slowly shut the door. Leaving her hands on it, she sighed then turned back around. Rubbing his arm, Joe was leaning on the windowsill across the room. She didn't like hurting those girls either. Angry at him for involving her and disappointed in herself for appeasing him, she threw her pocket dictionary at him. He dodged it.

"Consider that our divorce," she said.

He picked up the paperback and set it on her bed. "I'm sorry," he said, kissing her cheek. "I'll make it up to you."

"Go away. I have to study."

CHAPTER
three

WEDNESDAY

LATE GETTING OUT OF BIOCHEM, Taylor hustled across campus. She'd make it to the chiropractor's office in time for her first massage patient of the afternoon. Without stopping, she unzipped a side pocket on her backpack and pulled out a granola bar. Lunch on the move. She didn't mind though.

Massage therapy was hard work, but she loved her job. When a person came in with pain and left without it, it was a satisfying high. That's the best part. The physical part wasn't so bad as long as she stretched her hands, wrists, and arms before she started. That workout and the walking on campus kept her in shape.

However, she has developed certain rules over the four years. She doesn't talk about her personal life with her clients. Most don't even ask. She never hangs out with them. Those who want to socialize generally want free massages. As bad as those rules seem, it was safer and more comfortable for her. To most, she was a pair of hands and a sounding board. She wasn't a true people person like Eva, who worked at the local gym, but Taylor laughed at their jokes, listened, and did her job. Most of the time, it worked.

Entering the one-story, gray, chiropractic building, she waved at her first client in the waiting room. "I'll be with you in two minutes, Loren."

He nodded, and she walked down the dark panel hallway. Dr. Ken Spencer had four treatment rooms in the front section with an office and breakroom midway down the hall. Quiet and secluded at the end, her modified storage room had a velvety green curtain covering shelves of supplies. She had enough room to walk around her table without touching the wall or curtain.

Being tall had its advantages, but this wasn't one of them. A huge picture hung on the opposite wall to the shelves. The image of the ocean waves, crashing against a rocky cliff, drove her crazy. Dr. Spencer had picked it out. She thought it was too big for the room. Many of her clients chose ocean sounds from her collection of relaxation music. When she stared at the picture too long, she could swear the room swayed. It made her seasick.

She quickly put clean sheets on the table for her client. Nerdy, Loren Johnson had his black hair neatly trimmed into a fifty's slick-back. This George McFly looked older than his forty-three years. He taught math at WMU. He came every week since she started. As his two-for, she massaged his back and listened to his problems. She never gave advice. Heck, she never got a word in edgewise.

"How's your back today?" she asked once they

were in her room.

"It's sore, like usual."

"Go ahead and get comfortable. I'll be right back."

"I can undress while you're here. I don't mind," he said, unbuttoning his plaid shirt.

"But I do." She walked around the other side of the table and shut the door behind her.

During the massage, she got the lowdown on his ungrateful teenage son, his bitch of an ex-wife, and the stresses of teaching math to idiot students. He must have forgotten she had him for a couple math classes during her freshman year. After the session, he opened the door while she waited in the hallway.

"When are you going to marry me?" Loren asked again for the umpteenth time.

She laughed. "I'm not ready to settle down," she replied, making a strong effort not to roll her eyes.

He chuckled and said he'd be back next week.

Her next client, Chris Simmons, was new to her. In his mid-twenties, his flabby middle mismatched his muscular arms. As a WMU graduate student anxious over his thesis, he had tension and needed his neck and shoulders massaged. She explained what to expect. As a rule, the more a person understood, the easier her job. Most were able to enjoy a massage once they knew what she was doing.

He seemed satisfied with her explanation, so she left for him to get undressed. She returned and started the damn ocean music again. He was nervous as she worked. Occasionally, she asked about the pressure and if she worked in the right area. By the end of the session, he became very vocal with moans and groans. She thought it was a bit weird, but he wasn't the first to *ooh* and *aah* through a massage.

He cleared his throat. "How much for a little more?"

"Excuse me?"

"I'd like the Happy Ending. I'm a great tipper," he replied, touching his now hard penis.

"We are done. The receptionist will check you out," she said, scrambling for the door. She heard a click and a chuckle as she shut the door behind her.

At the front desk, she told Betty not to reschedule him. She thought she wouldn't run into problems of the sexual nature; she worked at a frickin' chiropractic office. At the gym, Eva easily dealt with the sex talk and laughed it off. Taylor had received requests for dates and marriage proposals. It made her uncomfortable. She knew she didn't handle it well, but she shouldn't have to handle it at all.

Biting her hangnail, she waited in the breakroom. Peeking out the door, she watched Chris slide his cell phone into his coat pocket. At three o'clock, she met her last client of the day. She introduced herself to Reese Forester; he was short with thinning hair. She thought maybe he colored it. It seemed too dark for his complexion.

He wanted his back massaged. After giving her spiel on what to expect, she left the room. Returning, she saw the grip of his handgun sticking out from under his flannel shirt left on the chair. She cringed at the gun and hit play on the ocean music. She planned on breaking the disc after the session.

"So how long have you worked here?" Reese asked, face down on the table.

"Almost four years," she replied, kneading his back

with her almond oil. "Is this pressure okay?"

"It feels awesome. My back's been killing me lately, doing a lot of fast walking." He moaned. "Oh, yeah, this feels great, better than sex," he mumbled. "This is just a chiropractor's office?"

Wincing, she paused for a second before continuing. She didn't need any more of this today. Between his gun on the chair and his wicked sense of humor, she was even more uncomfortable being so far away from the reception area and other people.

"Are you married?" he asked.

"No."

"Your boyfriend must adore you then," he said with a chuckle.

"Yeah." She should have kept her mouth shut, but maybe knowing she had a boyfriend, he'd leave her the hell alone.

"He doesn't mind you massaging other men? I'd be extremely jealous."

Jeez, what's with the personal questions today? She changed the subject by asking about the pressure of the massage. He tried again to ask questions. She dodged them. By the end of the session, she was mentally drained.

Afterward, Reese opened the door with a huge grin. "How serious is this boyfriend?"

She smiled politely and pointed down the hall to the front desk. "Betty will check you out."

"How about dinner to discuss why your boyfriend should be jealous?"

"Hey, Baby," Joe said, walking toward them.

"Hi, Honey," she said, grabbing his hand. She pulled him closer.

Joe looked at their joined hands. "I thought I'd walk you home."

She leaned up and gave him a peck on the lips. "You're the sweetest boyfriend ever."

Reese frowned. "I'll see you next week."

While she stripped the dirty sheets off her table, Joe stared at Reese at the reception counter. "I just saved you, didn't I?"

"I need to hurry up and graduate. Nobody takes me serious here."

"You're a hot coed. What man wouldn't enjoy getting rubbed by you?"

She glared and made sure he saw her wipe her mouth from their kiss.

"Hey, that's not nice," he said, laughing. "Come along, Girlfriend. You can massage me at home." Carrying her backpack, he held her hand as they crossed the street and walked toward Burke's Hall. He lived two levels above them on the men's floor. "You don't want to date any of the guys you meet there?"

She sighed. "I don't want to get hurt."

Joe put his arm around her waist and pulled her closer. "I won't let that happen."

IN HIS TINY OFFICE AT the University of Michigan, Stuart collapsed into his chair behind his cluttered desk. He had taught two morning classes, each with seventy-five students, and he had another two courses this afternoon. He preferred to read the essays himself, but this semester he needed the help of his two graduate students. Many had written too much historical bullshit to pad their five-page essays into ten, thinking it would impress him.

Thanks to Reese's paranoia, he racked his brain. He couldn't think of anyone who would want him dead. With the nightmares of his past, he slept shitty and had no appetite. He refused to carry his gun. He'd let someone else be in charge for a change.

Restless, he thought he'd hit the gym before his next class. Grabbing his duffle bag, he headed for the door. The history department's secretary blocked his way. Uber-organized, Kay Miller supported the history professors. Their young, elf-like assistant helped with class scheduling, faculty meetings, and students. She wore latex gloves and held a letter.

"Is that another one?"

She nodded. "My prints won't be on this one. I was careful."

She reached into her skirt pocket and pulled out another pair for him. He returned to his desk chair. Kay remained standing and watched him carefully open it. The other handwritten letters rambled for a full page. This one had writing on the centerline:

I'll get to you and the ones you love.
Tit for tat.

"What's it say?" Kay asked, trying to read it upside down.

He peeled off his gloves. "That bitch is threatening my family now."

"I'll call Detective Larsen and Mr. Forester." She quickly left the room.

He sat back. These letters have been coming on and off for a year. Most were graphic, but this one was to the point and scared him the most. Who would do this? What did this person think he did? He'd call his parents and sister later. They lived in Arizona, so he thought they were safe. With his duffle in hand, he met Kay at her outer office desk.

"I've left a voicemail for both," she said. "I'll call you if they arrive before you get back, and I'll lock your door until they get here."

"Thank you." Walking out of the reception area, he turned back. "Kay, will you find Chase and Markus? Let them know that they can teach this afternoon's classes. I have a feeling I won't be available."

"Yes, Sir, but I think their heads will explode. Dr. Morgan, please, be careful," she replied before he shut the outer department door.

Thirty minutes later, while bench pressing, he saw his distraught graduate students rushing toward him. He smiled for the first time all week.

"Professor Morgan, you must be joking," Markus said, yanking on the neck of his worn Coors t-shirt.

Chase shifted from foot to foot. "We've never taught your class before."

"You have to do it at some point," Stuart replied, using his shirt to wipe the sweat from his face.

"We're not prepared," Markus said, readjusting his shirt to look more professional. Nodding, Chase sat at the weight machine next to him and bounced his knee.

"Breathe, guys. I'm not torturing you on purpose. Listen; tell the class they have an extra week on their essays. Make sure they keep it to only five pages. Let them ask questions on how we grade them. They'll eat that up and think you're giving away big secrets."

Seeing the relief on their faces made him laugh. He waved them away and answered his ringing cell. Kay informed him that Detective Larsen waited with another man.

"Did you get a hold of Reese?" he asked, walking toward the locker room.

"No, and I left three messages."

"Thank you. I'll be back in fifteen minutes."

Ann Arbor Detective Greg Larsen and FBI Division Director Peter Bingaman from Detroit discussed their next steps. Apparently, Reese asked his former commanding officer, General Daniel Bingaman, about his military background. After hearing about the threats, the General asked his brother for a favor, which now involved the FBI. Having been drilled many times about the letters, he half-listened to their discussion and graded the essays, stacked high on his desk.

IN THE LATE EVENING, TAYLOR lay across her dorm room bed and heard Joe, clomping in his heavy boots down the hallway. Majoring in law enforcement, he wanted to become a FBI agent. She kept telling him he couldn't spy on anyone being that loud. She waited for him to come through her open door, but he stomped past to the small lounge next door. Eva liked to study with the TV on. It was something they didn't have in common. Curious, she shut her notebook and tiptoed to the door.

"I got that info," Joe said quietly. This was her second clue that something was going on. Joe did most things loudly.

"What's it say?" Eva asked.

"It's impressive. He was a lieutenant and an expert marksman in the Marines. He received the Legion of Merit. It's awarded for exceptional leadership on the battlefield."

Extremely curious, Taylor stepped into the doorway. "What's going on?"

Both jumped at the same time. For a split second, Joe hesitated. "We were talking about class."

"Yeah, which class?" Taylor asked, folding her arms.

"Umm, ceramics. I wanted to make you a vase for Christmas. Now you've wrecked the surprise."

"Yeah, okay, you do that. Now, who are you talking about?"

"Damn, you're nosy," Joe replied.

"And you need to work on your BS skills. Jeez, ceramics class? What am I? Stupid?" she retorted with her hands on her hips.

Eva laughed. "Okay. Okay." She closed the folder on her lap and handed it to her. "You're not going to like it. We only did it to protect you," she replied, standing next to Joe, who towered over her. "It's about our weekend class and that … situation."

"You told him?" she asked, looking at Joe.

"Not everything," Eva replied.

"Why wouldn't you tell me everything?" he asked.

Ignoring him, Eva continued, "He's got the best connections around."

Well, that cheered up Joe. With a big goofy smile, he nodded. She still didn't understand. She opened the folder. The top line read *Stuart L. Morgan, Single*. It dawned on her what this was. She slapped the folder shut.

"Do you think he's like you, Joe, that you need to have him checked out?" she asked.

"Like me?" he asked. "We don't know this guy. He could be some psycho, hitting on coeds."

"You think I'm that freckled freshman?" she asked, raising her voice.

"No, I don't."

"Do you want to know the real reason I don't date? You're my role model, Joe. Do you think I want to get hurt like your long list of conquests?"

With an open mouth, he stared at her. "I wouldn't hurt you. I'm protecting you. You and Eva are family."

Eva smiled. "I think you made your point, Taylor. Can we get back to the folder?"

"What?" he asked, looking at Eva then at her.

Dismissing him, she shoved the folder back at Eva. "I don't want to know what's in here."

"Are you mad at me?" he asked.

"How about I read it and let you know?" Eva asked as they ignored him.

She was torn. Sure, she wanted to know. What if she didn't like the information, or worse, what if she did? Curiosity kills.

"Okay," she finally said. "Just give me the highlights. Ever been married?"

"No," Eva replied.

"Criminal record?"

"No."

"That's enough."

"You guys suck," Joe said. "I spent a lot of time on that."

"You're a big doofus," Eva said, pushing him toward the door. "Get out and keep your mouth shut."

"Fine, but I've got my sights set on him now," he said, before leaving.

"Oh great," Taylor said as Eva turned back from the lounge door. "He better not embarrass me."

"Of course he will. You're mad at me for checking him out, aren't you?"

"No, I'm curious, too, but what's bothering you about him?"

"If you do fall for this guy, I want him to be good enough for you," Eva said.

Yeah, she could easily fall for him. Giving Eva a hug, she considered her life's plan. She still had a long list of structured steps to check off before she could think about romance. She needed to stay focused.

IN THE DARK OFFICE LIT by his desk lamp, Stuart graded essays. Kay and the other professors had gone home hours ago. Knowing he wouldn't sleep, he continued to read them. Since this threat now crossed state lines, the FBI alerted the local police in Scottsdale about the possible threat against the Morgan family. He had called his dad, who lectured him on safety. His father had been right—he needed to be more cautious.

Hearing the door rattle in the outer reception area, he slid his desk drawer open and retrieved his U.S. Government-Issued Beretta M-9. He clicked off the desk light and slowly worked his way to his door. Carefully stepping over the scattered papers, he listened. As he stood next to the door, someone turned the knob. He aimed his handgun at the shadow's head.

"Don't move," Stuart said.

"It's about time you took some precautions."

He lowered his gun. "Reese, where the hell have you been?" he asked, flipping on the fluorescent light. The brightness stabbed him between the eyes. Moaning, he returned to his desk.

"I've been in Kalamazoo checking out students," Reese said, sitting across from him. "I already heard about the letter. Anything jump out at you?"

"She's threatening my family now," he replied, rubbing the bridge of his nose. "Have you learned anything new?"

"Yes and no. I've compared former Michigan students with Kalamazoo ties to your current list. Nothing. Now, Bob wants me to focus solely on the Kazoo crowd."

He snorted. "Yeah, Bob's been a big help," he replied.

"He also wants me as your bodyguard because you're distracted. If you have an issue with that, take it up with him. He pays my bills," Reese said, stretching out his legs.

"Just give me some space."

Reese smiled. "Right, to work your magic. I do have info on that particular student."

He sighed. "What student?" He knew exactly which student. His distraction.

"The perky B-cup with long legs."

"Taylor Valentine couldn't possibly be part of this threat."

"It seems as if your girlfriend has another boyfriend. I met him. Tall, dark, and handsome. They make quite the couple."

He slapped an essay on the desk. "Why would I care? It seems as if I have enough on my plate right now than to get tangled in some triangle."

Reese followed him to his apartment. Once inside, Stuart slammed the door. The only thing he had looked forward to in his upended life was watching football with that beautiful woman. He thought … well, it didn't matter what he thought. She had only talked a friendly game of football. He had hoped for more. He sighed. *It's better this way.*

CHAPTER
four

TAYLOR WAS DRESSED BEFORE EVA and had even asked to use her blush. On the way to class, Eva enjoyed teasing her about her crush. In the lecture hall, they sat in the same seats as before. With pink-streaked hair, Lindsay sat behind Cindy, who reapplied her blood red lipstick and pulled out her teddy bear notepad.

Again, Taylor sipped her coffee and watched the hung-over students trudge through the door. Last night, their dorm had gotten an early start drinking in the hallways for the anticipated victory over their MAC rival, Central Michigan. This afternoon, WMU students would pack the bars again to hopefully celebrate the win. She'd be focusing on Michigan football.

Eva chuckled at Cindy's tight, low-cut blouse. "She's looking desperate now."

Taylor bit her lower lip. "She has more cleavage than you and me put together. What if he likes that better?"

"Buy a padded, push-up bra," Eva replied.

Laughing, Taylor lifted her cup to take a drink. When she glanced at the door, she abruptly stopped the cup midway. Her hand sloshed coffee onto her desk. As she used a napkin to wipe it up, Reese Forester grinned directly at her and took a seat two rows behind them. Her body froze.

"What's the matter with you?" Eva asked.

"There's a creepy guy here who's also a new client."

"Where?" Eva asked, looking around the room.

She casually pointed behind her. "Was he here last week?"

Eva nodded. "It's probably a coincidence."

She hoped so. A few minutes later, she watched Dr. Morgan enter. In a business-like manner, he began lecture before he set his coffee on the table. She thought he'd smile at her or look her way. Instead, he spoke to the space twelve inches above the students' heads.

She scrambled again to take notes. In the back of her mind, she wondered if they were still going to watch the game together. He mentioned nothing about getting out early. She figured a week was a lot of time to forget. Extremely disappointed, she sighed at the disappearing possibilities.

Uncomfortable with the weird grunts, snorts, and wheezes from Reese behind her and the ambivalence of Dr. Morgan in front of her, she sat rigidly. This wasn't what she expected. She knew the course would be hard, but she had hoped to have fun afterward and maybe even try to flirt a little.

Eva leaned close to her. "Talk to him during our break."

She shook her head. "So I can embarrass myself?

No."

"Don't be stupid. I'll run interference with Cindy," Eva replied.

"I am stupid for thinking he was remotely interested," she said, before looking away. Why did that bother her so much?

When Dr. Morgan suggested a fifteen-minute break, Taylor bolted toward the door. In the bathroom, she splashed water on her face and scrubbed off the blush. *It was bound to happen. Just a buddy to watch a game with.* That happened frequently with guys. She usually didn't mind. She focused on school. She had promised her parents that she'd graduate from college.

Eva and Joe had made the same promise to them. Growing up, Eva and Joe hung out at her house. They had problems at each of theirs. Since the start of third grade, they did their homework together every day after school. They had received lectures about the importance of an education. Her dad had joked that he really had three kids, but he meant it. Her parents' life insurances paid for college for all three of them. Joe, Eva, and Taylor planned to stay together to make sure they followed through.

Taylor dried her face and headed for the vending machines. As she dropped her coins into the slot, she felt a tap on her shoulder. She jumped. She expected Reese. Instead, she found a young woman with long feathered bangs, frowning and pouting her lips at the same time.

"Um, I'm sorry to bother you, but are you Taylor Valentine?"

Bending over, she grabbed the Coke. "Yeah, can I help you?"

"Well, I'm hoping you can." She looked around

with her head tilted down as if afraid. "Dr. Spenser, um, suggested I talk to you about massage for my headaches. I'm taking this class, too, and, um, I thought I recognized you from his office."

She smiled at the thin, young woman. "Sure, we still have time on our break. Let's sit over here," she said, pointing to a nearby bench. "I've worked with many people with headaches. Are these migraines?"

"The doctor called them tension headaches from, um, stress."

"How long have you had them?"

"A year. Prescription drugs haven't helped, so I thought I'd try to be proactive. Do you think you can help?"

"Yes," she replied, standing.

"Do you have a card with your office number and hours?" the woman asked as she glanced around.

"I have a few in my bag by my desk."

This was good. She needed to keep her mind on work and school. With a few minutes left in their break, she retrieved a card from her backpack. To avoid tripping over books and bags, she kept her head down as she moved toward the woman across the room. Raising it, she saw that the woman was sitting next to Reese. At least, he moved away from her and Eva.

Taylor quickly handed the woman the card while he grinned his smarmy smile. *Coincidence or not, that guy's disturbing. Was he carrying his gun on campus?* She thought there were rules about that. With the rest of the class in their seats, she blushed as Dr. Morgan watched her return to her desk.

STUART HAD CALLED FOR A break and had watched Taylor Valentine fly out the door. He sighed as he shuffled his papers. Irritated with Reese's constant hovering, he wanted to concentrate on teaching. Luckily, he knew this lecture without his notes. Still, Taylor had drawn his attention without even trying. She wore makeup this week, but he preferred her without. She was a natural beauty unlike Miss Carter, who looked semi-plastic.

He ached for Taylor to smile at him. Instead, she sat tensely. His mood continued to darken when he thought of that boyfriend kissing her, touching her, making love to her. Swallowing a growl, he tried to focus on what Cindy Carter said as he moved back behind the lecture table. He kept as much distance from her as possible.

"What?" he asked, getting a headache from her high-pitched whine.

As she screeched more nonsense, Eva walked up to them. "Cindy, you have something in your teeth." Without a word, Cindy covered her mouth and left the room. "I deserve an A for that," Eva said, smiling.

"Yes, you do," he replied, slowly sitting on the stool.

"Are you going to Johnny's after class? Taylor'll be there."

"Her boyfriend, too?" he asked, without looking at her. He absently flipped through his binder of lecture notes.

"She doesn't have a boyfriend."

His head snapped up from the pages. "What? Are you sure?"

"We've lived together in the same dorm room for

four years. Yeah, I'm sure." She grinned. "Is that why you're in a sour mood?"

No use denying it. "Partly," he replied.

Eva laughed. "We'll see you at the bar. You can buy the first pitcher."

He nodded then smiled to himself. He still had a chance with her—she didn't have a boyfriend. He glared at Reese, who had moved to the back of the room and now read a newspaper. He did not trust that guy. He couldn't figure out why Bob recommended him.

Before he started class again, he grabbed another coffee from the vending machine. He spotted Taylor talking with another Cindy type. Amber Peppers came on to him during the first break last week. She had actually trapped him in the men's room. Cringing, he quickly turned away. He had strict rules about his students, especially the female ones. *Never alone and document everything.* Those rules had saved his integrity more than a few times. A couple other students cornered him with legitimate Civil War questions that he enjoyed answering—a refreshing relief.

Back in the lecture hall, Stuart watched Taylor hand Amber a note. She looked at Reese as if she knew him. *Damn rules.* He wanted her alone. Somehow, he finished his lecture and the group left by noon. He dreaded his chat with Reese.

"You going to that bar again?" Reese asked, following him out the door.

"Yeah, you have a problem with that?" he asked, increasing his stride with a smirk.

"I'll be there," Reese replied, trying to keep up.

Stuart stopped. "As long as it's far from me."

"Not a problem." He laughed. "You are up for a love

triangle. It should be fun to watch."

ON THE SAME BAR STOOL, Taylor watched the Michigan Wolverines take on Minnesota's Golden Gophers. She ignored the loud cheers from WMU students, who surrounded the larger TV screens. She and Dr. Morgan talked about football again and each other. She didn't think it would have turned out so well. At half time, Eva got a call and took off. Taylor didn't mind. She liked sitting close to him although she had a hard time concentrating on the game. Her mind went blank when his baby blues looked at her. She hoped she didn't babble.

During a timeout, she left for the restroom. She couldn't remember the last time she had this much fun with a guy. As she stepped out of the bathroom, someone yanked her arm from behind.

"It's good to know you cheat on your boyfriend," he said next to her ear.

With a sharp inhale, she tensed. Her body trembled. Her voice didn't work as she recognized Reese. He released her arm, and she hurried back to her stool. She shouldn't have lied. Dr. Morgan reached for her hand as she bent over to grab her jacket and bag.

"Taylor, what's the matter?"

"I need to leave," she said, watching Reese drink his beer at the far end of the bar.

"Leave?" His hands surrounded hers.

She nodded and blinked back tears. "There's a man

at the other end of the bar. I think he wants to hurt me."

He looked around her and glared at the man. "Why would you think that?"

"He grabbed my arm by the bathroom. He's in your class. Last week, I met him at my job."

Dr. Morgan sat up straight and squeezed her hands a little too hard. "He just now grabbed your arm? What did he say?"

She stared at her hands in his, and he quickly lessened the pressure. She liked the warmth. "He said it was good to know I cheat on my boyfriend." She took a breath. "I'm a massage therapist at a chiropractic office. He came in for a session and made some suggestive comments. He really creeped me out." She calmed her breathing so she wouldn't hyperventilate. She blew out the rest of the breath and slowly inhaled. "When my friend Joe walked in, I kissed him to imply he was my boyfriend. I had hoped Reese would leave me alone. He carries a gun."

Dr. Morgan's jaw clenched. "Don't worry. When the game's over, I'll walk you home."

She nodded. She knew she didn't do anything to provoke Reese. She had her rules. Dr. Morgan put his arm on the back of her stool. His nearness comforted her, but she wished he'd move closer.

Neither of them paid much attention to the game. Every time she caught a glimpse of Reese, he either grinned or winked at her. Finally, Dr. Morgan suggested leaving before the crowd. She nodded and grabbed her jacket and backpack. Reese leered at them as they passed.

"Looks like you win, Doc," he said, laughing.

Dr. Morgan walked over and punched him in the

jaw. Reese fell off his stool and continued to laugh. "You and I will discuss this later," Dr. Morgan seethed.

With the immediate group staring, he escorted her out the door. She hugged her body as they walked down the sidewalk. She ignored the overcast and windy afternoon. Dr. Morgan kept his hand at her mid-back. Intently scanning the area, he lightly brushed her jacket. She wanted him to hug her.

"Do you know him?" she asked.

Carrying her backpack, he hesitated as they climbed the steps to her building. "We've met," he replied. "I'm sorry this happened. I'll make sure he doesn't bother you again." He held the lobby door open for her.

She took her bag. "But he has a gun," she whispered.

"I'll be fine."

She walked past the reception desk to the security door for access to the dorm floors. Before she unlocked it, she gaped at Dr. Morgan as he got into Reese Forester's sedan. She hurried up the stairwell and passed her floor. On the fourth, she walked around the guys, lingering outside their rooms. She rarely visited the men's floor. It smelled like sweaty bodies, stale beer, and a hint of some kind of funky smoke.

She knocked on Joe's door. He had a single occupancy room for privacy. He wanted his space. She knew why he wanted it although he learned early on that the ladies shouldn't know where his room was located. She jiggled his locked doorknob while the group smiled. They knew he wouldn't open the door for just anybody. Joe Roberts had quite the reputation.

"Joey, it's me. Let me in," she said, knocking again.

The door immediately opened to his sparse room. He had a twin bed, a desk with neatly stacked books, and a dresser that held a small TV, a PlayStation, video games, and the same photo from Freshman Orientation.

She dropped her coat and bag on the floor. "Joey, I don't know what to do."

He opened his arms, and she rushed to him. "Calm down and tell me what's going on," he said, letting her wipe her eyes on his shirt. He sat her in his desk chair and rolled it next to his bed where he sat and waited.

"Do you remember that guy from my work last Wednesday?"

"Yeah, what about him?"

"He's also in my weekend class. I think he's been following me. He grabbed my arm at the bar today, and he carries a gun. Joey, I'm afraid."

"Start from the beginning," Joe said, leaning on his elbows to hold her hands.

She explained about Reese's comments in her massage room, seeing his gun, why she thought having a boyfriend would make things better, Reese grabbing her at the bar, Dr. Morgan punching him, and then seeing them leave in the same car.

"So Morgan knows the guy?" he asked, sitting back on his bed.

"He said they met. I don't understand what's going on. What else was in your background report?"

"Nothing on Morgan. What's the other guy's name? I'll check into it."

"Reese Forester. He must be a WMU student to be in the class. He's older though. I've never seen him around before," she replied. "Oh God, he's scheduled for a massage Wednesday. What am I supposed to do? He didn't actually threaten or hurt me."

"Just cancel the appointment," he said, standing to

pace.

"I'll have Betty do it. He's my last client, so I'll make sure I'm gone in case he shows up."

"I have class until three. Stay there until I come for you. If he shows up, I'll have a nice little chat with him."

"Joey, I just want him to leave me alone."

"You're no fun at all," he replied, grinning.

"I can trust you?" she asked, pushing his chair back by his desk.

"With this, yes." Joe lifted his shirt and dabbed the tear off her cheek. "Nobody's gonna hurt my girlfriend."

Smiling, she kissed his cheek as he opened his door. In the crowded hall, she stepped around ogling drunks while Joe tucked in his shirt. "Thanks, Baby!" He grinned and blew her a kiss. "Visit me anytime!"

The guys chuckled at his innuendo. She smiled at him from the end of the hallway. "I've seen Little Joey. More like Tiny Joey if you ask me," she said to the few guys next to her. They roared with laughter as Joe stormed after her. With a squeal, she ran.

IN THE CIRCULAR DRIVE IN front of Taylor's building, Reese pushed open the passenger door from his driver's seat. "Get in, Doc. We need to talk," Reese said.

Holding his temper in check, he sat down. "You have no right to harass her."

"She's playing you, and that makes her my prime suspect."

"Why? Because she has a boyfriend? She told me what happened Wednesday. You're disgusting to hit on her during a massage."

Reese laughed. "You should get one. She's good. That's the best my back has felt in a long time."

He clenched his jaw again. "Well, the boyfriend is only a friend. She didn't want some old lecher thinking she was single."

"That's what she wants you to believe," Reese stated, parking beside Stuart's Mustang.

"That's enough," he demanded, before slamming his car door shut.

Returning to Bob's home, Stuart pounded on his door. While he waited, Reese joined him. Doris answered with a smile.

"Hey, Dorie, Bobby around?" Reese asked, stepping in front of Stuart.

"He's in the den," she replied. "Are you both staying for dinner?"

"You bet," Reese replied.

Stuart shook his head and rubbed the tension in his jaw. After stalking down the hallway to the heavy oak door, he walked in without knocking. The room had a high ceiling, but the thick wood trim made it seem small. Bob hung up his phone from behind his large oak desk. He gestured for them to sit.

"You hired your brother-in-law?" Stuart asked.

"I trust him," Bob replied.

"Well, he's a sleazy shit," he said, sitting across from Bob. Reese silently took the other chair.

"What happened?" Bob asked.

Stuart shared his student's harassment story. After finishing his tale, he said, "He's taking advantage of a student, and I don't like it."

"Why do you suspect her?" Bob asked.

Reese sat back with his arms folded. "For a couple reasons. First, she has a quarter of a million dollars in a savings account."

"What the hell does that have to do with the threats?" Stuart demanded.

"It's unusual for a student to have that kind of dough."

"What's the other reason?" Bob asked.

"She's trying to get close to him, so she can make her move," Reese replied.

"That's bullshit. We've been watching football at the bar. How am I being played?"

Reese smiled. "What woman likes football? She's seen that you don't respond to direct seduction. She's using Michigan football, which seems to be your weakness."

Stuart sat forward and rubbed his hand through his hair. "Good God, that's all you've got on her? Bob, this is ridiculous. He isn't helping. She's not the threat. You either tell him to focus on other options or fire him." He stood in front of the desk. "It's as simple as that."

"Stuart, sit down," Bob demanded. Stuart folded his arms instead. "Reese, do you have other suspects?"

"She's my target."

"Target? She's a college senior. She saw your gun and was genuinely scared. What kind of angle are you working, Reese?" he asked before he sat back down in the chair.

Bob leaned forward. "Look at other options. I trust Stuart's instincts. If he says she's not the one, I believe him."

"And I think his lust for this young woman—"

Stuart jumped up again. "Leave it alone. If you come anywhere close to her or me again, I'll shoot you. You've read my profile. I won't miss my mark." He stormed to the den's door and turned back. "You are not welcome in my class or as my so-called bodyguard. Enough is enough." He retraced his steps to the front door.

Doris stopped him. "Please, stay for dinner. Bob's only trying to help. He's worried."

"No thanks, Doris. I wouldn't be good company," he said.

"Stuart, my brother can be a horse's ass, but he is good at his job."

He squeezed her hand. "Once this chaos settles, we'll get together."

CHAPTER
five

SUNDAY

SITTING ON HER BED, TAYLOR watched Eva pack her bag for another long day of class. Taylor should have told her about the incidences yesterday, but it would have made Eva angry. Her sister typically tries to be helpful by taking over. Most of the time, it was easier to let her. With a sigh, Taylor grabbed her baseball cap and followed.

"Why are you wearing a hat and no makeup?" Eva asked in the stairwell.

"I'm tired."

"You didn't say much about the bar last night," she continued.

"He walked me home."

Eva grinned. "Any kissing?" she asked, pushing open the security door to the lobby.

"No, there are rules about that," she mumbled.

"Your rules are too convenient. You need to get out more," Eva replied.

Wearing his flannel-lined jean jacket and green skullcap, Joe stood at the greeter's desk. The cute sophomore smiled up at him as he leaned over the counter to talk to her. His finger gently caressed the back of her hand. *What a flirt.* He saw them and dismissed the greeter.

"Hey, I thought I'd walk my favorite ladies to their class," he said as the young woman frowned.

"Are you just getting in?" Eva asked.

"No, I have a few things to do this morning," he replied.

Taylor urged them toward the door. "Come on. I don't want to be late."

Eva stopped outside. "What things do you have to do on a Sunday morning? You're never up this early. What's going on?"

Joe looked at Taylor while she shook her head from behind Eva. "Jeez, I'm just trying to be nice," he said.

Turning, Eva caught Taylor shaking her head. "You have until the end of our walk to tell me the truth. Don't lie. You know I can tell."

It was no use keeping it from her. Walking into the cold wind, Joe explained what had happened and that he planned to check out Reese Forester.

After she grilled Joe, Eva narrowed her eyes on her. "Why wouldn't you tell me?"

"I wanted to, but you always take over," Taylor said.

"I do not," Eva protested.

Joe laughed. "Yes, you do. All the time."

"You'll demand answers and get in everyone's face," Taylor added.

"Don't you want to know?" Eva asked, unaffected by the criticism.

"I don't need the drama right now. This is our last semester until graduation. I'm not going to screw that up."

Joe and Eva laughed at her outburst. "Boy, you really do need to lighten up," Joe said. She groaned and walked faster. They quickly caught up to her and linked their arms in hers, taking up the entire width of the sidewalk. "So if Taylor's the boring, straight arrow and Eva's the pit bull, what's that make me?"

"The player," they replied.

"I'd prefer tall, dark, and lethal," he said, making karate chop moves with his hands.

Taylor and Eva rolled their eyes as they neared their class. The Hyde building had two other classes on Saturdays, but on the Sunday their seminar was the only one in session making the area desolate of students.

"Do you want me to stick around?" Joe asked.

"I think we'll be fine, but it's good to know you have your lethal moves if we need them," Eva replied.

He grinned and moved like Elvis. "That's right, lil' ladies, I'll take care of ya. Thank you, thank you very much."

Without a word, she and Eva turned and walked away. Joe and Eva had distracted her for a little while, and she loved them for it. As she pulled at the building's door, she felt a dread in her gut. She could handle Eva and Joe's teasing, but Reese spewed mean sarcasm. She wasn't sure she could take any more of it. They quickly found their seats and waited.

"I don't see him," Eva whispered, looking for Reese.

"Good," she replied.

When Dr. Morgan walked in, she pulled the bill of her hat down to cover more of her face. She spent the morning listening to the Responsible Angelic Taylor on her right shoulder arguing with the Carefree Devilish Taylor on her left. Sure, she liked him. He was handsome, charming, sexy, a total gentleman, AND her professor. God, she couldn't turn off the noise.

WITH NO SIGN OF REESE, Stuart drove to class. As a precaution, he had strapped his gun to his lower leg under his dress pants. He knew the dangers and had a bad feeling about today. Distant memories of shouting men and heavy fire rushed to the forefront. He visualized a target on his back as he walked down the empty pathways. He relaxed slightly, climbing the stairs to the second-floor lecture hall.

Entering the classroom, he found his distraction hidden under her hat. Then he saw Cindy, wearing a white tank top and miniskirt … in the middle of November. He shook his head. *When would she give up?* He glanced at Taylor again as he set his briefcase on the table. She gave him no hint of her mindset. A little eye contact would ease his.

While he lectured the morning away, he watched Taylor take notes with her head down. Next to her, Eva gave him the stink eye. *Not a good sign.* He really needed to talk with Taylor.

"Dr. Morgan, are you okay?" a student asked.

He looked around as his students stared. Thoughts of Taylor Valentine disrupted his class. He had stopped talking all together. He sighed. "I need caffeine. Let's take a break."

He slowly sat on the stool and watched the group quickly leave the room. Taylor, one of the first. He ran his hands through his hair and stared at his notes on the table. What the hell was wrong with him? He looked across the table at Eva, who was frowning.

"She saw you get into his car," she stated, before leaving.

"Shit," he mumbled.

In the hallway, he scanned the students, who wandered between the vending machines and the restrooms. He spotted Taylor sipping from a bottle of Coke. She saw him and turned away. *Damn it. You're blowing it, Morgan, you idiot.*

He casually trapped her down a side hall. "Taylor," he whispered, "I can explain."

Under her visor, she tilted her head up at him. Her eyelashes were so long and her lips perfect. He wanted to kiss her. He lowered his head and then realized where they were. What was he thinking? He stopped a few inches from her lips. God, he was so close. She smelled like lilacs.

"Dr. Morgan, there you are," Cindy said behind him.

Ignoring her, he stood back and looked for any understanding in Taylor's face.

"Excuse me," Taylor said, stepping around him.

Cindy grabbed his bicep to stop him. "You seem a little stressed. Is there something I can do for you?" she asked, pressing her breasts against his arm.

"No," he replied firmly. He'd be doing a lot of documenting tonight.

He needed something strong but settled for a Coke.

After taking a deep swig, he returned to the lecture hall.
The students waited. He shuffled his notes to figure out
where he left off. On half a sheet of paper, he read the
note:

I need to see you at next break, room three-
twelve. T.V.

Knowing he would get his chance to talk with her,
he focused on history and checked the clock constantly.
At noon, he called for a half hour lunch break. He
gathered his notes as the group scattered. Some left the
building, but most crashed in the lounge on the first
floor. With the note in his pocket, he took the steps two
at a time to the third floor. In the back corner of the
building, he opened the door to a computer lab.

"Taylor?"

He must have beaten her to the room. A locked
cage stored hard drives while monitors were in another.
The twelve desk chairs around the long table looked
ergonomic. He could use a new one. He heard a popping
noise at the door and saw smoke seeping from under
another locked cabinet. As he pushed on the door to
leave, the fire alarm sounded. Unable to open the door,
he saw wood shims wedged between the door and
frame. The sprinklers weren't working and heavy smoke

filled the room. He slammed his shoulder against the metal door then yanked on the handle hoping to loosen the shims. They wouldn't budge. He rushed to the sealed windows and pulled on the iron bars.

Covering his nose and mouth with his shirt, he stumbled back to the door. He couldn't see through the dense smoke. In a sudden panic, he flashed to a haze-filled firefight from his tour with the Marines. He could taste the metallic grit of the blood-stained sand from years ago. As he coughed, he pulled out his gun, hidden at his ankle, and shot out the glass slit in the door. Smog filtered out. He reached out to dislodge the shims but couldn't reach them. On his knees, he shot the windows, clearing more of the smoke. Able to see slightly better, he searched for another way out.

"Stuart!"

He coughed. "In here!"

Within seconds, the door swung open. Reese grabbed him by the shirt and dragged him into the now clouded hallway. "I bet you're glad I don't listen," Reese said, dragging him toward the stairwell.

As the door shut behind them, they heard the firefighters racing toward Room three-twelve. Coughing, he cleared his lungs of smoke while Reese led him to the ground-level floor. Once outside, Reese sat him on a bench at the back of the building away from the chaos in the front. The cold air helped his breathing and calmed his anxiety.

"What the hell were you doing up there?" Reese asked. "Someone obstructed the door on purpose."

As he took in deep breaths, he thought about the answer to that question. Not wanting to make Taylor look worse in Reese's eyes, he asked his own, "How'd you find me?"

Reese leaned back and crossed his arms. "I knew something was wrong when your letter writer slashed all four of my tires. By the time I got over here, students were running from the building, and you were nowhere to be found."

With a sore throat, Stuart could only nod.

AT THEIR LUNCH BREAK, TAYLOR had nibbled on a granola bar and looked over her notes. She added phrases to her scribble to make them more understandable. Most of the morning, she had kept her head down to avoid Dr. Morgan's glances. She had listened to his voice but hadn't heard a word he said. Instead, her thoughts focused on the two of them talking and laughing at the bar last night. She had enjoyed his attention until the incident with Reese. She had finally looked up from her blank page when he silently stared at the back wall. For a full minute, the group waited then scattered when he called for a break.

He had cornered her down a side hall in an alcove and said he could explain. Eva had stepped in again. He had leaned in close to her face to whisper something. Intoxicated by his closeness, she had been tempted to kiss him. When Cindy interrupted, the Responsible Taylor quickly left. She almost made a fool of herself.

As the students waited for Dr. Morgan to return and start class again, they heard the fire alarm. Everyone grabbed their backpacks and hurried out the door.

Standing in the cold, the crowd watched the fire trucks approach. She searched for Dr. Morgan and spotted Reese Forester, stalking toward her.

"Where's Morgan?" he demanded.

"I haven't seen him since we broke for lunch," she replied.

"Damn it." He stormed past her and ran into the building.

The firemen entered soon after. Twenty minutes later, they exited without Dr. Morgan and Reese. She bit her thumbnail while Eva worked her way over to her. She knew Eva'd have answers.

"Where was the fire?" Taylor asked. "Was anyone hurt?"

"It apparently started on the third floor in a computer lab. They think a hard drive overheated and started to smoke," Eva replied.

"Have you seen Dr. Morgan? He's not with the group," she asked. "Reese saw the smoke and ran into the building."

"I haven't seen him. Do you think Reese did this?" Eva asked.

"I don't know."

Wanting more answers, Eva moved closer to the firemen while Taylor walked toward the side of the building to see the damage for herself. The rest of the students left for the day. She saw Dr. Morgan, coughing, with Reese sitting beside him. She stopped and turned back.

"Taylor, wait," he yelled hoarsely. He said something to Reese and joined her.

"Are you okay? I didn't see you come out with the class."

"I'll be fine," he whispered, pulling a note from his

pocket. "Did you leave this for me?"

She looked at it, and her jaw dropped. "No, that's not my writing." He nodded and returned it to his pocket. "I don't understand," she said.

He glared at Reese, who approached him with his gun drawn. He pulled out a card with his office phone number. "I have to leave now. Will you call me and let me explain?"

Stunned, she nodded and watched Reese usher him away. *Why wouldn't he explain it now? Was Reese forcing him to leave?* With a sigh, she stuffed the number into the front pocket of her jeans and waited for Eva.

"There's some weird stuff going on around here," Eva said as they walked back to the dorms. "Someone shot out the door and windows. Did you find Dr. Morgan?"

She nodded and told her what he said. They'd discuss it with Joe. He had a knack with puzzles. Returning to their room, they found Joe waiting for them inside. While they sat across their beds, Joe paced between them. Eva filled him in on the fire in the computer lab, its bullet holes in the windows and door, on Dr. Morgan and Reese behind the building, and on the note that Taylor had allegedly left for him.

Listening to the rehash, Taylor bit her thumbnail again. With every word, he quickened his pace and mumbled about not protecting her enough. For some reason, Eva smiled and watched him. He didn't say anything for a while.

"Joey, are you mad at me?" Taylor asked, pulling her pillow onto her lap.

"Yeah, I'm pissed. This is some mess you've gotten yourself into," he replied.

"Me? What did I do?"

"You're flirting with your professor at the bar and at class. What's the matter with you?"

With her mouth open, she stared at him then looked at Eva. She didn't think she flirted although she considered trying. Feeling the tears in her eyes, she buried her face in her pillow.

"What's wrong with flirting?" Eva asked him. "You can't go an hour without hitting on a woman. Fess up. You're really pissed that Taylor's interested in a guy."

Taylor looked up as Joe glared. "He's her professor! It's wrong," he replied, scratching the back of his neck.

"Who do you think you are? The sex police?" Eva asked, leaning back.

Taylor's eyes widened. "Sex! Jeez, we watched a couple of football games. That's it."

Joe turned on her. "That is not it. Reese Forester is not a student. He's a private investigator."

With her mouth open, Taylor stared in shock.

"Working for whom?" Eva asked.

"I have no frickin' idea," he replied, falling into her desk chair.

Taylor's head spun. *How much more confusing could this get?* "Can we just call Dr. Morgan?" she asked, handing him the business card.

Joe glared at the card then at her. "No, you're not calling him. We don't know who hired Forester. He's obviously checking into you."

"What?"

He folded his arms. "Did he interrogate you during his massage? How many times have I told you to keep your backpack and ID out of your treatment room? Mera, that ditsy teller at our bank, told me someone asked about the balance in your account. She described Reese. How do you think he got your account number?"

She opened her mouth but couldn't speak.

"And why was it so important to know if you have a boyfriend? Why would he grab your arm at the bar?" With each question, Joe raised his voice until he was shouting. "And why is Morgan getting into Forester's car? Is Forester working for him or against him? And why would someone leave Morgan a note and sign your initials? There are too many unanswered questions!"

"What should I do?" Taylor asked, hugging the pillow tighter.

"Until I get those answers, stay away from Morgan," he replied.

Eva jumped from the bed and stood level with Joe in the chair. "Wait a minute. Taylor hasn't done anything wrong. They were only watching the game when Reese grabbed her arm. I would think you'd be happy that Dr. Morgan made sure she got home safely."

"What are Morgan and Forester up to?" he demanded.

"I don't know, but she can't stay away from him. We need the credits from his class to graduate," Eva replied.

After Joe stormed from the room, Taylor slid sideways from a sitting position on her bed to a fetal one. She didn't understand anything. What was she missing? She closed her eyes and fought against a nagging headache. Eva tossed a blanket over her and left the room. Eva knew when to leave her alone. It took her longer to process information than it did for them. Even though she didn't know the answers to Joe's questions, she did know one thing. She needed to stick with her life plan. Any minor deviation was obviously a mistake.

CHAPTER
six

WEDNESDAY

AT SEVEN-THIRTY IN THE MORNING, Stuart sat behind his office desk. Reese stretched out in the chair across from him. After Sunday's incident, he had no choice but to let Reese tag along. Bob had helped clean up that smoking mess in the computer lab and had given him hell. Stuart had heard *I told you so* from Reese every other minute since Sunday. He had hoped Reese had Thanksgiving plans for tomorrow, so he could relax in peace. Unfortunately, his bodyguard informed him that he would be spending the day watching the Detroit Lions with him. *Oh, joy.*

The university and FBI strongly suggested canceling his other classes as a precaution. With a tenuous relationship with the university president, Stuart thought the president was happy at the chance for a reprimand by concealing the letters. The bastard's had it in for him since Stuart started teaching.

Stuart had arranged for his graduate students to

teach his U of M ones. He promised them season tickets to the basketball games for all the extra help. It seemed to ease their distress.

The FBI wanted him to continue teaching at Western to flush out the suspect. They agreed with Reese that a student might be involved. They wanted to keep the lead alive and hopefully him as well. He fought against adding his opinion on strategy and tactics during their investigation. His night sweats had gotten worse over the last six months. The Feds were the professionals and knew what they were doing, but he still found it hard to relax.

He should have told Reese about the note. Because of Reese's damn gloating, he held back. Taylor didn't need the additional attention from Reese or the FBI, but she was a part of this now. He had hoped she would have called and understood why she hadn't. He freaked her out, and he needed to fix it. He had looked up her cell number and had started to dial a couple of times. He had debated between calling her to warn her of the possible danger and waiting until Saturday to do it in person. He had no idea how he would explain. He barely knew her, yet she could be in harm's way because he liked her. By bending his rules, he created a major mess.

Stuart finally leaned forward and handed the note to Reese. "You asked me before why I was in that room. That's why."

"She gave this to you?" Reese asked, standing. "Why the hell wouldn't you tell me this?"

"Because you already have her convicted." Before he could continue, his desk phone rang. "Yes, Kay?"

"Director Bingaman is here."

"Thank you." Stuart met him at the door and shook

his hand. "Any news on the fire?"

In a black suit and tie, the seasoned director, with a few strands of white in his black hair, joined them. He started with the mini-bomb. "A component of the device was old and defective; it created the smoke. Otherwise, it would have taken out the corner of the building."

"Jesus, who did you piss off?" Reese asked.

Peter continued, "My brother and I are reviewing your service record again. He's rather fond of you and your military tactics. You've saved the lives of many Marines."

Stuart looked away and thought about all the men he didn't save. Some tactician he was. His medals meant nothing. He sighed and tried to focus while Reese handed Peter the note.

"She gave this to you?" Peter asked.

Stuart shook his head. "I found it on my desk after the first break. When I showed it to her after the incident, she said she didn't write it. I believe her."

"That may be, but she's part of this now," Reese said.

"I know that, and that's why I'm telling you about it. This stalker could have seen us watching the game or walking on campus."

Peter nodded. "The last letter did say *Tit for Tat*. She's in danger. You should have informed us of this sooner."

"I know. I screwed up," he replied, running his hand through his already messy hair. "I need to see her."

"I don't think that's a good idea right now. I'll assign someone to watch over her," Peter said.

"I'll go. She's working today. I have an appointment with her this afternoon," Reese said, smiling.

Stuart glared. "I think you can explain the situation

without getting a massage."

"Settle down. She already canceled my appointment. I'll go early to interrogate her."

"Reese," Stuart said, clenching his jaw.

"God, you have no sense of humor."

"Well, it's a little hard when someone's trying to kill me for no apparent reason," he said, folding his arms.

"Fair enough," Reese said, picking up his jacket.

"How much trouble am I getting her into? I should be the one to explain it."

"It's too dangerous," Peter said.

"Taylor needs to hear it from me."

"You still want a shot at her?" Reese asked.

"Not *at* her, I want a shot *with* her."

Eva had been right; Taylor had an empathetic way about her. Could she really take his pain away? At the very least, she was distracting him from it.

"Will she give you a chance once she finds out you put her in danger?" Reese asked.

Stuart followed them to the door. "I'd like to find out in person."

Reese continued to the outer office while Peter stopped and faced him. "You stay. I'll go with him. I won't let him blow it for you." Peter gave instructions to an agent, who took up residence in his outer office.

TAYLOR RACED THROUGH CAMPUS AFTER BioChem. Once again, she found Loren Johnson waiting for her. Like last week and the weeks before that, she listened to him vent during his massage. He liked to bitch about his life. Since she had known him, he had never taken any initiative to make changes.

Lingering outside her room afterward, Loren thanked her for the session. "You'll be graduating soon. Marry me, and I'll take care of you."

She smiled. "I'm not ready to settle down," she repeated yet again.

She placed her hand on his shoulder, gently pushing him toward Betty's counter. Taking the subtle hint, he said *goodbye*. She readied her room for her next new patient, Amber Peppers. She thought she might be the timid woman from class. She was right.

At the front desk, Taylor greeted Amber and led her to the massage room. After explaining what to expect, she left to let Amber undress and get on the table. During a massage, she usually doesn't initiate conversations with clients. She prefers to let them meditate. But Amber had a hard time relaxing even when she reassured her that it wouldn't hurt. This seemed to be an exception to her rule.

"You mentioned that you've had these headaches for a year. Were you in an accident?" she asked as she massaged her upper back.

"No, stress from my family," Amber replied.

"Have you thought about talking to someone about it? Professionally, I mean?"

Amber sighed. "Yeah, and my therapist says I need to let go. I guess I'm not ready yet."

For a half hour, Taylor massaged her head, neck, and upper back. Afterward, Amber opened the door with tears in her eyes. She lowered her head to hide them.

"The massage felt good. I don't know why I'm crying," Amber said, sniffing her nose.

Taylor took her hand and gave it a gentle squeeze. "Massage works to relax the body. It also taps into the mind and spirit. We call what you experienced an *emotional release*. I'm not a doctor, but it seems as if this is a great first step for you."

"You think so?"

She nodded. "I think it's important to discuss it with your therapist."

"Can I come back next week?"

"Sure, we can schedule right now."

Happy to be helpful, Taylor returned to her room. Done for the day, she'd study until Joe picked her up. After straightening the room, she took out her notebook. She hoped to find a topic for her essay. It would be easier if she was interested in the people instead of the overall battles. She imagined being in the midst of the war, brothers fighting brothers, mothers worrying about their husbands and sons, and women learning to survive with their men away.

Half an hour later, she heard a commotion in the reception area. Peeking out the door, she saw Reese. He demanded to see her. Betty told him she wasn't there, but he saw her. Afraid of his aggression, Taylor grabbed her bag and coat then ran out the side exit. *How stupid was that?* She now stood alone in the wide alley between the chiropractic office and a thrift shop. Next to the picnic table between the buildings, she checked around the empty front corner. Before she could cross the street, he grabbed her arm and yanked her back against the building.

"You're not going anywhere," Reese said, tugging

her toward the picnic table.

Before she could scream, Joe shoved Reese, who let her go and took a swing. Ducking, Joe hooked his leg, and Reese landed face down. With a knee between Reese's shoulder blades, Joe patted him down. She hugged herself when they spotted Reese's gun.

"Stop right there," an older man in a black suit said behind them.

As the man walked toward them, Joe quickly aimed Reese's gun at him. "I want to know what the hell is going on," Joe demanded.

"I'm going to reach for my ID," the man said calmly.

Seeing Director Bingaman's FBI badge, Joe handed him the gun but didn't move his knee off Reese. "Why is this Slimy Dick accosting my sister?" Joe demanded.

Reese spit dirt and wet, brown leaves from his lips. "I am a licensed professional," he mumbled.

"You keep telling that to your mother," Joe said, ramming his knee deeper into him as he stood.

Director Bingaman smiled. "Have a seat, and I'll explain."

Joe sat on the damp picnic tabletop, propping his feet on the bench. He motioned for Taylor to join him. While Reese brushed off the dirt, Joe put his arm around her.

"First, I'd like to know where you learned that move to take him down," the Director said.

"The school of hard knocks," Joe replied, grinning at Reese.

"You own a gun?" he continued.

"Yes, and I have a permit," Joe replied.

"How'd you know Reese is a PI?" he asked, putting the gun in his jacket pocket.

"I may not be a licensed professional, but I know how to do a background check," Joe said. "Can we get back to this ass and why he's harassing my sister?"

"Taylor Valentine is an only child," Reese said, smugly.

"I have a brother and sister," she whispered. "Blood means nothing; love is everything."

Director Bingaman nodded. "We are here to protect you, Ms. Valentine."

"Protect me from what?"

"From who is the question," Reese corrected, folding his arms.

"Stuart Morgan?" Joe asked. "I already checked him out."

"Apparently not good enough," Reese answered.

The Director sighed. "Reese, go sit in the car." Before Reese could object, Director Bingaman stopped him. "Now!"

Joe pulled her closer as Reese walked away. "I don't like that guy," Joe said.

"That's the general consensus, but you'll need to trust me," the Director said. "Dr. Morgan has received death threats. Someone has already tried to kill him twice on Western's campus."

Taylor sat up straight. "Who would want to hurt him?"

"We're trying to figure that out."

"That fire last Sunday was meant for him," Joe stated.

"Not a fire, a defective bomb. I'm telling you, so you know how serious this is."

"Was he hurt?" she whispered. She remembered him coughing.

"No, he's fine and worried about you, Ms. Valentine."

"Me?"

"The latest letter threatened him and those close to him. You have been seen together at the local bar as well as walking on campus."

"She hardly knows him," Joe replied.

"This person may not know that," Director Bingaman replied.

Joe stood and paced. "Taylor told me about the note Morgan showed her. This person lured him away using my sister," he said, tapping his thumbnail on his front teeth. "Is it someone from the class?"

"It looks that way," he replied.

"Joey, I don't understand."

"That professor you like so much is putting you in danger. That's why I didn't want you calling him." He turned on Director Bingaman. "What the hell are you going to do about it?"

The Director folded his arms. "I have assigned someone to watch Ms. Valentine until it's safe."

"It had better not be Forester," Joe said. "I'll protect my sister."

"That's not going to happen," Bingaman replied.

"You gonna stop me?"

She stepped toward her brother and placed her hand on his forearm. "Please, don't lose your temper."

Joe immediately calmed. "I want in."

Director Bingaman smiled. "What's your major?"

"Law enforcement. I can help with this."

"How?"

"Give me the class list. I'll check them out," he replied with his hands on his hips.

"You don't think we've done that?"

Joe smiled. "You haven't got him yet."

Bingaman snorted. "Her. We believe it's a woman."

Thinking that Joe enjoyed the danger too much, she stepped between them. "I'd like to know why class hasn't been canceled, especially if Dr. Morgan and I are at risk."

"He isn't teaching his U of M classes," the Director replied.

Joe moved her out of his way and stepped toward the Director. "Is my sister your bait?"

"Not exactly. But we do need to draw this woman out," he replied.

"No way!" Joe yelled.

Director Bingaman sighed. "Ms. Valentine, may I speak with you alone?" She nodded, and Joe stormed away. He headed in Reese Forester's direction. Sitting on the picnic table, she waited. The Director joined her.

"You will be protected."

She hugged her abdomen. "How long do you think it will take?"

"We aren't sure. We have a two-week window before the seminar is over."

She blew out a breath. "I'll help any way I can, but I have a favor to ask."

"I'm listening."

"Give Joe something to do. If you don't, he'll go off on his own. My brother is intelligent and street smart. I think you'll be surprised by how helpful he can be," she said, watching Joe and Reese argue.

Director Bingaman observed the same interaction. "What makes you think I can trust him?"

She smiled. "In fifth grade, Joe taped a drug

dealer's confession of selling pot on the playground. The guy had worked in the lunchroom and had easy access to students. Because of Joe, the police took down four other guys who dealt drugs to area elementary schools. He's wanted to be an agent ever since. He won't ruin this chance to help."

He nodded and whistled for Joe to join them. "Since you're an insider on campus, I'll let you look at the list." He pulled out a sheet of paper from the inside of his jacket pocket. "You report directly to me with anything unusual."

Joe smiled. "Yes, Sir."

He gave Joe his business card. "Don't make me regret this. Your career hinges on it." He turned back to her. "You won't know an agent's following you, but he'll be there."

"You mean the guy who's been waiting at the bus stop?" Joe asked, stuffing the paper into his front pocket.

"Okay, Smartass, how'd you know?" Director Bingaman asked, saluting the agent, who quickly averted his eyes.

Joe grinned. "Two buses have stopped already, and he's still sitting there."

"Anything minor, I want to know. Do NOT engage."

Joe nodded, grinning like a teen with the keys to Dad's car. On the way back to their dormitory, Taylor asked him, "Are you happy that I'm in danger?"

"No, of course not," he replied.

"Then you can tell Eva about that discussion."

Joe's grin dissolved as she slipped her hand into his. When did her world get turned upside down? She strayed briefly from her strict plan and look at what happened. *Back to it.* She had the rules and the plan to make her life easier. Life is structure, her parents had said.

CHAPTER
seven

SATURDAY

WITH REESE SKULKING BEHIND HIM somewhere, Stuart strolled toward the Hyde Building. As he neared the entrance, he saw a young woman flagging him down. He remembered her black hair and bright pink streaks from his class but couldn't recall her name. She had sat in the center of the room, three rows high. With an angry look on her face, she rushed toward him.

"What can I do for you?" he asked.

"You can apologize to my brother," she demanded, brushing a pink strand from her face.

"Who's your brother?" he asked, setting his coffee and briefcase on the nearby bench.

"Brandon Brant. I'm his sister, Lindsay." She seemed upset that he didn't already know this information.

"The same Brandon Brant who played Michigan basketball?"

She stuck her hands into the front of her sweatshirt pockets. "Yeah, he *played* basketball. You failed him, and now he's off the team. Thanks to you, he can't go pro."

"I'm sorry it happened, but that wasn't my fault," he said, leaning down to pick up his things. "He failed his other classes as well."

She glared. "Don't walk away from me!"

She withdrew a two-inch knife from her front pocket and jabbed it at him. Easily dodging it, he dropped his coffee and briefcase. Before she could lunge again, he grabbed her wrist. While she fought him, he simply turned her away. She struggled as Reese came running toward them and took the knife. Since he temporarily worked with the FBI, Reese cuffed her hands behind her back. She continued to kick and scream. Was this the same woman who shot at him and almost blew up a building?

Stuart picked up his empty coffee cup and briefcase. "I'm glad she didn't have her gun this time."

Reese frowned. "I'll call Peter and take her in. Smile, Doc. It's over."

Stuart did smile. It was over. He wouldn't have to put Taylor through any more danger. He dropped his cup in the trash. Even though he needed the caffeine, he needed Taylor's smile more. Peter said she agreed to help. Hoping they would still meet at Johnny's bar after class, he hurried down the hallway. With the huge obstacle removed, he would actively pursue Taylor Valentine.

ON THE THIRD SATURDAY OF the seminar, Joe walked Eva and Taylor to class again. He looked for the undercover agent and easily spotted him, dressed like a student. He smirked at the man's sideways baseball cap and baggy jeans. Instead of a tirade, Eva had told her that her life was finally getting interesting. On Thursday, over Thanksgiving dinner in the cafeteria, they had each promised to take every precaution. Joe had already checked off over half the names on the list. He would run the rest today and call the Director later. He loved his new assignment.

Trying to forget about the dangers, Taylor focused on class. She frantically filled her notebook and noticed Cindy flirting with the professor during the breaks. Taylor couldn't get close to him. He did look her way a few times but not long enough for her to smile back.

Eva leaned toward her. "Stop frowning. It's not attractive. What do you think he's going to do? Constantly stare at you?"

How does Eva do that? Was she talking aloud? "What if he changed his mind about watching the game?" she whispered back.

"He may not be watching you, but he is watching the clock."

Dr. Morgan finally closed his binder and packed his briefcase. "Okay, class, tomorrow is Gettysburg, and your essays are due. I hope you're not waiting until the last minute. Our class concludes next Saturday with the final essay exam."

Taylor smiled. He didn't even wait for questions. But before he reached the door, Cindy jumped in front of him. Taylor and Eva hurried past. Like the last two weekends, everyone crowded around the big screens.

Taylor enjoyed hogging the smaller set at the end of the bar. She caught the remote from Johnny while Eva circled the bar. Eva always took this approach, called it *checking out the scene*. Taylor took the reserved sign off the stool and blew Johnny a kiss. He set a pitcher and a mug next to her. After thanking him, she glanced around but didn't see the agent assigned to her.

The game started and still no professor. As she watched Michigan play, she checked the clock every few minutes. She started to worry. After she refilled her mug, Dr. Morgan grabbed the beer from her hand, chugged it, and waved for another one from Johnny.

She smiled. "Is everything okay?"

"Yeah, no more worries. Our threat is over. Although ... somebody told Cindy that I like football. It took me forever to get away."

"Cindy's determined all right. Her mind is made up," Taylor replied.

"It sure is, Professor," Eva said, pulling a stool closer to the bar, "and she just walked in."

"Aw, shit," he said. *Shit was right*. Taylor was really looking forward to this. "Maybe she won't see—" he said.

Cindy bumped her way through the crowd. "Dr. Morgan, there you are. I almost lost you."

With the timeout over, they turned back to the game and tried to ignore her. Cindy rambled about his class and her lawyer dad. She even suggested leaving for a walk on campus.

"Cindy!" Eva yelled over the crowd. "We're watching the game! Shut the hell up!"

Professor Morgan leaned toward Taylor. "I'll give Eva an A if she can keep her gagged."

His warm breath on her ear gave her goose bumps. It made it impossible to focus on the game. They reached halftime with a strong lead. She left for the bathroom while Cindy continued to yammer. Returning, she saw Eva next to Dr. Morgan. She was too far away to hear all but the end of their conversation.

"I'll take care of her. Just go," Eva said.

Go? He was leaving? Cindy, that bitch, I'd like to slap the tan right off her.

"Hey, you're back," Professor Morgan said. "Grab your coat and bag. I can't watch this with her jabbering in my ear. We'll find some other place to watch the game."

She looked at Eva who nodded. "Out the back?" Taylor suggested.

They stood in the brutally cold wind behind the bar. "We've got ten minutes. There's only one place I know," he said.

He slung her backpack over his shoulder and grabbed her hand. She matched his long stride. His hand sent a wave of heat throughout her body. With that armor, she hardly noticed the weather.

"My visitor apartment is the closest, and it's quiet."

She hesitated. "Won't you get into trouble having a student there?"

"Who'll know? It's Saturday," he said, picking up the pace.

Professor Morgan set her bag by the door and flipped on the set. The room was only a few feet bigger than her dorm room. It did have its own bathroom instead of a communal one, which was definitely a perk. With a few generic garden pictures, the room felt like a mix between a dorm and a hotel room. In the corner, she saw a small kitchenette with a sink and cube refrigerator. There was a small table with one chair by the TV and a twin bed and dresser on the other side of the room.

"Boy, they don't skimp on luxury for you guys, do they?"

"It's like being back in college, plus it's close to the lecture hall. Have a seat. I've got a couple of Cokes in the fridge."

The bed or the chair? She took the chair. It looked safer, and she was feeling a bit nervous. Sensing her distress, the professor jumped back into the game by yelling at the ref for a holding call. She, of course, started her own rant, encouraging the players as if they could hear her. Their defense played the best they had all season. She loved it when they were aggressive.

They became more animated as the plays went on. They yelled louder when Michigan ran the ball toward the end zone. Their arms flew above their heads to help the referee indicate the touchdown. Their high-five ended in a hug. She let go; he didn't.

Staring into his smoldering blue eyes, she held her breath. He had a hand at her back, holding her close. He pushed her hair from her face with his other and lowered his lips to hers. It shocked her to her toes. The warm feather-light kiss made her want to faint from the intensity.

"I've wanted to do that for a while," he whispered, cupping her face.

Dazed, she gaped blankly at him then remembered to breathe. She didn't know what to say. Before she could say anything, there was a BAM, BAM, BAM on the door. They jumped apart.

"Morgan, what's going on?" a man's voice barked on the other side of the door.

"Oh my God. Oh my God," she repeated, hugging her abdomen. "What do I do?"

"Just a minute," he yelled. He lowered his voice, "Grab your bag and jacket and go into the bathroom. I'll get rid of him." He sounded calm while she was about to pee her pants. He gently pushed her into the bathroom and closed the door. "What are you doing here? I'm right in the middle of the game," he said to the man at the door.

"I heard a lot of yelling. Are you okay?"

Oh my God, not only was it someone from school, it was Dean Brady. She recognized his voice from various student functions. She didn't know exactly what the rules were about kissing your professor, but there probably were some. *Wow,* she thought, touching her fingers to her lips. *That kiss was dreamy.* She had kissed guys before, even Joe, but she could honestly say she had never been kissed like that. Her whole body awakened with awareness over the exciting possibilities.

"I'm watching the game. Of course I was yelling. And by the way, I don't appreciate having to teach while being threatened," Dr. Morgan said.

"I heard that's over, and you're watching the game now. So what's the problem?" the Dean replied.

"Well, actually, I'm not watching the game. I'm talking to you."

"I promised my wife I'd mention the faculty function coming up," the Dean said as they continued talking.

What was she doing here? Her heart pounded in her throat. They could get into big trouble. As much as she liked where this was going, she couldn't mess up graduation. Who would know, he says. All the Dean had to do was open the bathroom door. Putting on her jacket, she heard the door shut hard. She waited a full minute before peeking out.

"I'm sorry about that. He's been dogging me for weeks about going to some dull dinner party," Dr. Morgan said.

She stepped out of the bathroom. "I gotta go."

"What about the game?"

"Sorry," she mumbled as she turned the knob.

After looking around the area, she picked up the pace. *Where to now?* Not back to the bar, she'd have to explain herself to Eva. She headed toward her dorm room. A block later, she stopped and pulled out her phone to tune in the game. Her hands were shaking while she slipped in the ear buds. Commentator Jim Brandstatter was saying something, but she wasn't paying attention. Luckily, her legs knew the way because her mind wandered and her eyes saw nothing.

STUART GROANED AT THE CLOSED door. What the hell was the matter with him? He spooked her again, and now she's gone. *Damn interruptions.* Finally alone with her, he couldn't resist any longer. He had moved a strand of soft, honey brown hair away from her face. He was desperate to taste her. Her satin lips had quivered, and he had become instantly aroused.

He grabbed his coat and slammed the door behind

him. He had to find her. *Then what? Apologize? Explain?* What he really wanted to do was kiss her again. So much for his rigid rules.

In the crowded bar, he scanned the room. Michigan still played on the big screen. Not bothering to check the score, he spotted Eva by the pool tables in the backroom. She smiled until she saw him alone.

"Where's Taylor?" she asked, leaning on a pool stick that was as tall as she was.

He rubbed his hand over his head. "She didn't come back here?"

"No, I haven't seen her since you left together. What happened?"

"I blew it." He turned away and slowly walked back to the apartment. He'd try to talk to her tomorrow although he had no idea what he would say.

Peter Bingaman met him on the sidewalk by the apartment. "Where have you been?"

"Out," he replied as he opened the door.

Peter followed him inside. "We need to talk. There's a problem."

"Now what?" he asked, sitting on the corner of the bed. He vigorously rubbed his hands through his hair. What else could possibly go wrong in his life?

Peter leaned against the door. "Lindsay Brant's not the one."

"What do you mean? She came after me with a knife."

"She wanted to hurt you, but she didn't write the letters. I have someone researching the students from your class. He lives on campus and says Lindsay only recently found out about her brother. She also has absolutely no knowledge of explosives."

"So where does that leave us? I'm still putting Taylor in danger?"

"We'll reassign someone to her first thing tomorrow morning. I called Reese, and he'll be keeping an eye on you."

"Thanks a lot," he replied. "Is the agent any good?"

"He knows what he's doing," Peter replied. "You really care about this young woman?"

He sighed. "From the moment I saw her, I knew she was the one."

"Love at first sight? You're sure?"

"It hit me like a bolt of lightning," he replied as he remembered catching her from the stool and their recent kiss.

"I wish you well with that, my friend," Peter said, opening the door.

"Do me a favor. Keep her safe. My future children depend on it."

Peter laughed. "I wish I knew about your Lighting Bolt Theory before I married. It would have saved me the heartache."

Stuart locked the door and thought about his own heartache if something happened to Taylor. To protect her, he'd have to take a more commanding role in this investigation. He prayed he would make the right decisions this time.

KEEPING THE LIGHTS OFF, TAYLOR plopped onto her bed. She lay there, staring at nothing, half-listening to the game, and thinking about that kiss. Did she blow her only chance with this guy? She did leave in a panic. What the hell was the matter with her? Was she socially inept? To calm herself down, she focused back on the game. It was over, and she had no idea what the final score was. *Damn it!* She wiped her eyes when she heard a key in the door lock.

Eva flipped on the light. "There you are. Professor Morgan came looking for you at the bar."

She squinted in the light. "He did?"

"Yeah, he looked totally bummed. He wouldn't say a word, except that he blew it."

"He said that? I'm the one who messed up."

"Okay," Eva said, sitting next to her, "from the beginning." Taylor started with him holding her hand, the visitor apartment, the game, the kiss, and the Dean. "Wow. That's extreme." Eva smiled.

"Well, what am I supposed to do now? I didn't leave because of the kiss. I left, so I wouldn't get us in trouble with Dean Brady. I think I should drop his class."

"No, you are not," Eva said firmly. "You already have your essay done, so the hardest part is over. If you don't want to face him in class, talk to him tonight."

"I can't do that. What will he think?"

"He'll think you care. Go. It's dark."

After touching up her make-up and brushing her teeth, she grabbed her heavy coat. Through the sputtering sleet, she worked up the nerve. What was she thinking? *Just do it,* her inner voice said. *If you don't, you'll regret it.* She finally knocked lightly on his door. In a t-shirt and sweats, he held a twenty-dollar bill in his hand.

"Hi," she whispered. She thought she might pass

out seeing his flat abs through his tight shirt.

"Hi," he said, smiling. "Come on in. I just ordered a pizza."

"Sorry I left so abruptly earlier." There, she got that part out before the nervousness set in. Smelling fresh soap, she walked past him and saw a damp towel lying on the floor. She was lightheaded.

"Can you stay for pizza?"

"Sure. I missed dinner." God, she was so lame.

"Great." He went to the refrigerator for a couple more Cokes. "I'm sorry I kissed you earlier," he said with his back to her.

Feeling a bit bolder, she sat in the chair. "Actually … I kind of liked that part."

"Really? Why did you leave? I thought we were having a good time," he said, handing her the can.

"Well, yeah, until the Dean of all people pounded on the door like he could see right through it."

"Oh that." He sat on the corner of the bed. "Bob and I grew up together. He's always giving me grief about going to Michigan and staying there. He went to Michigan State."

"You're kidding?"

"For the past few weekends, he's invited me over to have dinner. His wife's got it in her head that I need to be set up." He chuckled. "If she only knew I had a woman hiding in my bathroom."

"Yeah, your student," she said, blushing.

He shrugged. "How do you think Bob met his wife?"

Someone knocked on the door and yelled, "Gino's Pizza."

They ate the pizza, drank the rest of his Cokes, and

talked about their families. She brought up her parents but focused mostly on Joe and Eva. He told her about growing up with the Dean and briefly mentioned the Marines.

Dismissing that topic, he took a deep breath. "You're not out of danger yet," he said.

She sighed. "I'm confident Director Bingaman will find this person."

"I'm glad you are. I want to strangle Reese."

As she laughed, she glanced at the clock on the dresser and did a double take. "Two-twenty-three, that can't be right. Is it?"

"Yeah, can you believe it? I didn't think I could talk so long."

"Have you ever sat through your class?" She grinned. "I gotta get out of here. Do you know how many questions Eva will have for me? I won't get any sleep unless it's during your lecture." She grabbed her coat from the back of the chair and turned toward the door.

"Then don't go," he said quietly.

"I don't know." She weakened. He stood way too close and smelled way too good.

"I understand. I'll walk you home." He sounded disappointed, which, for some reason, thrilled her.

She opened the door to heavy sleet. "Oh boy, maybe I should stay," she mumbled.

"Yes." He turned her around and kissed her again.

Her mind went numb, but her body vibrated. She leaned against his chest to steady herself. He tugged at her coat. They stripped off their clothes as they worked their way to his bed.

Later, in a sleepy content daze, she whispered, "Did

Michigan win?"

"I don't know," he replied as she drifted off to sleep.

CHAPTER
eight

SUNDAY

ON HER SIDE, TAYLOR AWOKE with a warm comforting arm draped over her waist and deep breathing in her hair. She took a mental picture, hoping to remember the contentment for the rest of her life. She caught a glimpse of the watch on his arm and lifted her head to get a better look. She jumped up, and Dr. Morgan promptly fell off the side of the bed.

"Oh my God! We have less than an hour to get to class." She hunted for her scattered clothes then sat in the chair to put on her boots.

"What's your hurry? Class won't start until I'm there," he said.

On the floor, half-covered in the sheet, he looked all sexy like a blond god wrapped in a toga. He had no right to be so gorgeous.

"I can picture it now. We walk into class together with major bed head, wearing the same clothes as yesterday."

"We will be walking together until you're assigned another agent. Besides, do you think anyone would even notice?" he asked, leaning his elbow on the mattress.

"What class have you been teaching? Both Cindy and Reese would definitely notice. I couldn't handle that. I'll see you in class," she said, already opening the door.

"Taylor, wait. Not by yourself," he said, scrambling to get up. She quickly shut the door. "Be careful! And don't be late!" he yelled through the door.

It was a gloomy morning. Taylor set a swift pace, but the slippery sidewalks slowed her down in some spots. If she sent Eva ahead to save her seat, she could take a quick shower. With her keys in her hand, she hustled down the hall to her door. She saw the note on their memo board:

I want details.
Saving your spot with large coffee.

She loved that girl. She was out the door in less than twenty minutes with her hair in a ponytail, a warmer coat, and a backpack. Satisfied that she would be on time, she now hoped to beat him there.

STUART STARED AT THE CLOSED door. He smiled. She was the one. Now he needed to convince her of it. Wanting to be first to class, he quickly showered. When he opened the door, he found Reese on his doorstep.

"How long have you been waiting out here?"

"Long enough," Reese replied, grinning from ear to ear.

He glared and stepped past him. "Not one word."

"How about a few words?"

"Leave it alone."

Ignoring the demand, Reese continued, "How was it? Does she get a passing grade?"

He stopped. "When this is over, I'm going to kick your ass."

Reese laughed as they walked toward the cars. The cold sleet had left a thin sheet of ice across the sidewalk and parking lot. Stuart carefully walked through a mist of his own breath. Ahead of him, Reese slid on the black ice between their cars and landed on his back with a thud. Having the wind knocked out of him, he lay on the ground for a full minute.

"Wow, you really are good at your job. You saved me from that slick spot," Stuart said, smiling.

Reese groaned and turned on his side to get up. Glancing under the Mustang, he stopped. "I think we better take my car to class."

"Why?"

"Yours is leaking." Reese touched the pool of fluid under the car and smelled his fingers. "Someone cut your brake line."

"Shit," Stuart replied, helping him stand.

"You're right though. I am damn good at my job. I deserve a medal."

AS TAYLOR WALKED INTO THE quietly packed classroom, Dr. Morgan stood behind the desk with his notes. He sipped his coffee and smiled smugly. Already feeling self-conscious, she hurried to her seat while the entire class watched. She hated being the center of attention.

It stemmed from the turmoil after her parents' deaths. Thinking back to the media, lawyers, doctors, and those so-called friends with her best interest in mind, she winced and tried to calm the sudden ache in her heart. Eva waited until she settled in then handed her the cup of coffee. Taylor took a deep breath and slowly blew it out.

"He got here less than a minute ago," Eva whispered.

"Let's pick up where we left off yesterday," Professor Morgan began.

"I want details," Eva said under her breath.

"Later," she replied, reaching in her bag for her notebook.

She had a hard time concentrating on her notes. Each time he looked at her, she felt the heat in her face. Did everyone in class know what they did? Remembering how his hands felt on her skin and the passion of his kisses caused her to shiver. When she thought of her breasts against his soft, blond, chest hair, her nipples hardened. She shifted in her chair, which about sent her to the ceiling. She moaned aloud. God, what was the matter with her? She tried to focus, but she couldn't stop staring at his lips and his hands. This class was agony. She snapped out of it when he said they could take a break.

"Was it that good? You've hardly taken any notes, and he's trying hard not to look over here. Let's go for a walk," Eva said, standing.

"Yeah," she whispered.

"Well?" Eva said as they walked into the empty bathroom.

"Well what?"

"I bring you coffee, save you a seat, and all I get is a *well what*?" Eva asked from the next stall.

"You were right. It was a misunderstanding. I am falling for this guy."

"Falling for what guy?" a voice asked from the other stall.

"None of your business, Cindy," Eva said.

Taylor flushed and walked to the sink. When would she stop talking and start thinking? She headed for the door with Eva at her side.

"After class, I want full disclosure," Eva demanded.

"Fine, just not here," she replied, walking into the classroom.

"I'll accept essays now. Please bring them down," Dr. Morgan said to the group as he waited for the rest of class to file back in.

Taylor reached into her bag for her blue folder. Eva and a few others handed her theirs as well. She walked the reports down to the front desk. Being so close to him again, she felt a static electricity. Her hair stood on end. Could everyone tell they were naked together only a few hours ago?

He smiled. "If you don't stop staring and blushing, I'm not going to be able to concentrate on my lecture," he whispered. "And stop squirming. It's making me hard."

Mortified, her face burned. "Sorry," she squeaked before retreating.

After the break, the full class waited. Professor Morgan sat on his stool and flipped through the stack of essays in various colored folders. He picked one up, turned to a page, read it, and set it aside. With the sixth report, he flipped to a page and read it for a minute. Meanwhile, the whole room fidgeted.

Closing the blue folder, he looked at the cover. "Taylor, I'd like to talk to you after class." He slid the pile to the side, sighed, and resumed the lecture.

Her jaw dropped as all eyes zeroed in on her. *What the hell was wrong with her essay?* Gripping the desk, she started to hyperventilate. Eva passed her a note:

Brilliant acting.

Looking at her, Taylor mouthed, "What?"

Eva pretended to get into her bag. "You are so dense. It's an excuse to talk to you."

"Oh," she said as Eva rolled her eyes.

Taylor was able to concentrate enough to take a few

more notes throughout lecture, but she was definitely going to need Eva's for the exam.

"Next Saturday, I'll answer questions for the first hour. You'll have the next two to finish the exam. It will consist of essay questions. I expect thoughtful answers, no BS."

Rats, she thought, as she put her pen and notebook into her bag, waiting for the students to leave. She received a few sympathetic looks. In front, Cindy talked to Dr. Morgan. With only the three of them left in the room, Taylor slowly stepped down to the lecture table.

"Well, if you change your mind, I'll see you there." In a huff, Cindy shut the door hard behind her.

"Hello," he said when Taylor turned back from the door. "I'm sorry if I embarrassed you. I was trying to figure out how to talk to you before I left for the week."

"I didn't understand until Eva gave me this." She handed him her note.

"She's going to get that A yet. I want to see you again. Will you have dinner with me next Saturday?"

"I'd like that," she replied, suddenly feeling shy.

"And no more blushing. I thought maybe you were thinking about last night."

"I couldn't get any redder after your earlier comment."

"I was just having a little fun. It was nice that you were thinking about me." He grinned. "You made me want to take you on top of this table."

Sliding her finger along his jaw to his chin, she lightly kissed his lips. "And I would have let you."

At the door, she turned. His elbow rested on the table with his head on his hand and a shocked look on his face. That made up for the whole day. What had gotten into her? She was shameless.

WITH AN ARM FULL OF essays and his briefcase, Stuart walked toward Reese in the employee parking area. "What happened to my car?"

"It's being towed. The Feds want to look it over. Maybe they'll come up with a fingerprint on the line. In the meantime, we get to visit all the way to Ann Arbor. Anything new with you, Doc?"

Without a word, Stuart reclined his seat. Dismissing Reese, he closed his eyes and folded his arms. With Taylor's warm body next to him, he let himself sleep deeply. Those few hours were restful. He couldn't remember the last time he slept without waking in the middle of the night drenched in sweat. Some would call it post-traumatic stress. History was full of stories about the side effects of war. He knew from his studies as well as his personal accounts.

Pushing those thoughts away, he longed for more of Taylor's passionate lovemaking. He remembered everything. The curve of her hips ... the sweet taste of her neck ... the light touch of her roaming hands ... the low moans from her throat ... her dreamy gaze ... and the tight pull he felt as he entered her. Fully aroused, he sat up in his seat. Reese, thank God, kept his mouth shut.

EVA SAT ACROSS THE BED with her back against the wall. "What took you so long? Sit down," she demanded, pointing to the other bed.

"I'm tired. Can I take a nap first? Let's get something to eat." Taylor laughed as she took off her coat.

Eva looked like she was going to hurt her. After Taylor gave her rendition of the last twelve hours, she took a deep breath and waited for the verdict.

"Clarify some things for me. You used protection?" Eva asked.

She nodded and frowned. What did it mean to have them so handy?

Before she could ask, Eva continued, "And what did he say when you told him you were a virgin?"

"Oh God." She sighed. "I didn't tell him. When was I supposed to bring that up? Right in the middle of being ravished? *Oh, by the way, Dr. Morgan, I'm a virgin.*"

Eva laughed. "You called him *Dr. Morgan*?"

"No! I didn't say any of that. I'm not experienced. It just happened. I was nervous enough."

"Was it awkward or uncomfortable?" Eva asked with all seriousness.

"No, it was fast-paced and exciting." Her face turned red as she remembered.

"You are not telling me everything," Eva said, leaning toward her. "Your face was on fire after you dropped the essays off. What did he say?"

"Jeez, what are you? A detective? I told Joe that you'd make a better agent than he would. Where is he? Boy, I'm hungry." Changing the subject was not going to work. Eva waited. She'd be a whiz in the interrogation room. "It's embarrassing," Taylor said while Eva stared. "Fine! He said he wasn't going to be able to concentrate on the lecture if I kept staring and blushing. There. Are you happy now?" She threw up her hands.

"You two are so funny. I can't wait to see what happens next," Eva said, laughing.

CHAPTER
nine

WEDNESDAY

IN THE EMPTY HISTORY DEPARTMENT by seven, Stuart flipped on the light and made a fresh pot of coffee at the counter behind Kay's desk. While the coffee percolated, Reese found the couch in the outer office and stretched out. In his small room, Stuart stepped around piles of essays, folders, and binders. He had started to feel as if he was the guilty party. Reese and Peter interrogated him for the last few days. Reese had actually accused him of hiding information.

Apart from his feelings for Taylor Valentine, his life had become an open book. He wasn't exactly sure about his feelings for her. The chemistry was unmistakable, but how could he care about her in such a short amount of time? She confused the hell out of him and took him out of his element. He liked his rules and order.

He leaned back in his chair and propped his feet on the corner of the desk. He had planned a romantic evening for her this Saturday and had already put most of his scheme into motion. The rest would be handled this morning. He wanted to be protective of her safety.

She took her education seriously, as she should. If he disrupted that in any way, he would never forgive himself. He was already stomping all over his rules. *Should he risk everything he had accomplished?* It would make things difficult for both of them, possibly even dangerous.

"Dr. Morgan, you're here early," Kay Miller said, holding his favorite *Go Blue* coffee mug. He had been so distracted he had forgotten to fill it earlier.

"Yeah, I'm helping the guys as much as I can. How are they doing?"

She handed him the mug filled with steaming coffee and smiled. "Other than they each carry a bottle of Tums, they're fine."

He laughed. "Before they arrive, I'll put a dent in this pile of essays. Don't let Reese irritate you too much."

"Yes, Sir. You're in an awfully good mood for being threatened," she said.

"I've met someone." Any time he thought of Taylor, he grinned.

Kay's smile faltered. Her lips tightened. "I'll let you know when Chase and Markus arrive," she said, before shutting the door, hard.

Leaning back, he sipped his piping hot coffee. He jumped at the knock on the door. Glancing at the clock, he flinched. An hour had passed, and he hadn't read a single essay. Sheesh, he needed to call his dad and hear his Lightning Bolt Theory again. He had become a lovesick dodo.

"Come in," he yelled as he sat up in his chair. He laughed at the sight of his students in their disheveled clothes. "Have either of you slept lately?"

"Not much," Markus replied, moving a stack of essays from a chair.

"That pile is graded and so are those," Stuart said, pointing to the window ledge.

"What about these?" Chase asked, picking up a stack of forty from the other chair.

"Those are from the Kalamazoo seminar. I want you and Markus to grade them."

Chase sat down with the pile on his lap. "But I thought you were doing it since we're teaching."

"The plan has changed slightly."

"What now?" Markus demanded.

Stuart abruptly stood. His chair rolled backward, crashing into his file cabinet making a large dent. "I've had enough of the whining. Do you want to graduate the master's program or not?"

Stunned at the outburst, they nodded.

"Then suck it up and do your work. I think I've babied you two long enough. Not only will you teach my classes for the next month, you will grade the Kalamazoo essays and write their exam," he said, leaning his fists on his desk. "Do you have a problem with that?"

"No, Sir," they replied. Their bloodshot eyes were as wide as he'd ever seen them.

"Good," he said, pointing to the door.

They scrambled from their seats with the essays. Stuart sighed and retrieved his chair while Kay frowned from the doorway. He wiggled his finger for her and pointed at the chair across from him. She sat stiffly on the edge. He opened his desk drawer and pulled out three thick binders.

"In an hour, call them and give them these," he

said, plopping the binders on the desk in front of her.

"What are they?" she whispered.

"My lecture notes for those classes."

She smiled. "You weren't really mad, were you?"

"I'm tired of the disorder. I like my unexciting life," he said, picking up his empty mug. He sighed and set it back down.

"I should remind them that they could be working for Dr. Jeffers. He has his grad students teaching all of his classes as well as washing his car, running his errands, and babysitting his seven-year-old twin boys," she said, taking his empty mug.

He laughed. "Thank you, Kay." She left then returned with a full one.

ONCE AGAIN, TAYLOR RAN LATE from BioChem. Dr. Lee let his students get him off topic. His latest rant on pharmaceutical companies and their lack of safety procedures in drug testing kept the class from leaving on time. As interesting as it was, she had to work. A few students walked out. She could never be that rude.

After the Déjà Vu massage session with Loren Johnson, she turned down his marriage proposal again. He really needed to get a new life. She had two more clients before greeting Amber Peppers, who walked with slouched shoulders. Her long, feathered hair hung over her ears and fell forward into her eyes. During the session, Amber didn't say much. Taylor hesitated to ask about her therapy session. If Amber wanted her to know, she'd say so.

Listening to ocean music, Taylor mentally pinched herself for not chucking the CD earlier. She massaged her shoulders and neck. Even though Amber's muscles were still tight, her breathing started to deepen. *Progress*, she thought, as she ended the session.

Amber opened the door. "I'd like to come back next week," she said, wiping her eyes with her hoodie sleeve.

"I have next week off for exams, but Betty will schedule you for whatever time is convenient after that."

Amber nodded and walked away. Taylor hummed as she straightened her room. After daydreaming for the past few days, she had to hurry back to the dorms to finish her neurobiology paper. Final exams were fast approaching, too. Not only was she worried about her studies, she also stressed over the threat that surrounded her and Dr. Morgan.

Joe had reassured her with his joking nature, but her anxieties took over. She had her rules and her life plan. Indirect death threats were not part of it. The steps were college, graduation, and career, with romance far into the future. Her parents drilled that into her brain since kindergarten.

After grabbing her backpack from under the massage table, she shut her door. As she walked down the hall, she saw Joe talking to Amber outside the front door. Amber didn't need to get mixed up with him. By the time Taylor said *goodbye* to Betty and stepped out the door, Amber had left and Joe was leaning against the building.

"You're done early," she said, slipping her arm through his for the added warmth.

Joe saluted the observing agent in the tan sedan.

"Has he been close to you?"

"I haven't paid attention. I'm panicking over exams," she said as they walked across campus. "You weren't hitting on Amber, were you?"

Joe stopped. "No way, that type is dangerous."

Freezing in the cold wind, she tugged him forward. "What type?"

"She's like Cindy, slutty and unstable. They're likely to cry rape, fake a pregnancy, or get pregnant on purpose to trap you into marriage."

"Amber is not like Cindy," she replied. "She's shy."

"Are you talking about the woman I was just talking to?" Joe asked.

"Yeah," she replied, confused that he would say such a thing.

"I heard she broke up a marriage because the guy wouldn't go out with her. She's bad news," he said.

"What did you say to her?"

"I said nothing. She hit on me. I was waiting for my wife," he said with a grin.

She laughed. "Maybe she'll try to break us up."

"Not a chance, Baby. Although … it sounds like I have competition now. Eva told me about you and the Doc. You love him?"

She frowned. "How naive do you think I am? I had sex. It was bound to happen someday." She looked up at him. "What's the problem? You have sex all the time, and you don't love any of them."

He grimaced. "It's not all the time, and it's different for you."

She laughed. "Are you jealous?"

He hesitated. "Maybe I am. If you fall in love with this guy, where does that leave me? We've been together a long time."

"What are you talking about? We're not romantic. I'm your sister."

"I know. It's just—"

"Joey, I love you. That won't ever change. Besides, you're jumping too far ahead. I have my plan. You know that." They stopped in front of their building.

He laughed and hugged her tight. "I love you, too."

"Good, now let me go, so I can study."

"You, study. I need to find your bodyguard. What a dolt. There are hundreds of students in this dormitory who are possible threats, and he's somewhere out here."

She kissed his cheek. "Be nice. He could be your boss someday."

"I'll keep that in mind," he said, looking around.

She smiled as he stalked toward the sedan. Joe had found his calling.

ENTERING MARIO'S SPORTS BAR WITH Reese tagging along, Stuart found Peter at a back table. He took the chair against the wall while Reese sat with his back to the crowd. At least during this interrogation, he could eat. He needed a cold beer. Having been a regular for years, he ordered lasagna without looking at the menu. After draining half his bottle, he sat back and waited for the discussion to begin.

"We still have Lindsay Brant. She admitted to wanting to stab you. She denies the letters, the shooting, and the bomb. We had her in custody when your brakes were cut," Peter said.

"She was upset over her brother. I get that," Stuart replied.

"You believe her story?" Reese asked, downing his whiskey shot.

"Yeah, we had help checking her out," Peter replied.

"From Taylor's boyfriend, Joe?" Reese replied, smiling. "You trust that guy?"

Peter nodded. "He's a natural. He's also checking the rest of the students on the list."

With the arrival of their meal, the conversation shifted away from Taylor's so-called boyfriend. Once again, they scrutinized every minor scuffle of Stuart's military history, even after he left. His former squad had encountered hostiles and another Marine had died. Stuart had nothing to do with that. He had left two days prior. One soldier he wasn't responsible for killing.

"Was the dead Marine married?" Reese asked.

"Just his elderly parents in Florida," Peter said.

"I'd like to know when I'll get my car back," Stuart asked.

"A few more days," Peter said, eating the last of his ravioli. He answered his phone on the first ring. "Bingaman," he said. "Okay, give me the two names." He took a pen from the pocket of his breast suit jacket and wrote them in his mini-notebook. "I'll check into it further. That's it. You're done." He smiled as he listened. "Joe, leave him alone and let the agent do his job … Fine, stay close to her and only OBSERVE." He slipped his cell into the inside pocket of his jacket and laughed. "This kid has a bright future as long as he doesn't piss off any more of my agents."

Stuart wasn't sure he would like Joe, who seemed to

care about Taylor a little too much. How close were they really? Boy, he sounded jealous. "What are the names?" he asked, pushing those other thoughts aside.

"Cindy Carter and Amber Peppers," Peter replied. Stuart groaned and Reese laughed. "You know them?"

"They've both flirted with the Doc in very aggressive ways. I thought they were just wild, crazy chicks," Reese said.

"What makes Taylor's friend suggest those two?" Stuart asked.

"He said their behavior doesn't gel, and they're unstable," Peter replied.

"I'd agree with that assessment," Stuart said.

"I'll look deeper into their background and see what comes up. In the meantime, stay alert here in Ann Arbor. This woman seems to be upping her game," Peter said.

"I've got it covered," Reese replied, pushing the bill toward him.

While Peter grabbed it, Stuart reached for his phone. "Yes, Kay."

"Dr. Morgan, I found another letter. I must have missed it earlier."

"Does it have a postmark?"

"No, Sir. It has a woman's cursive writing," she replied.

"What makes you think it's from her?" he asked as the men stared at him.

"The writing on the envelope says *To the Dead Doctor and his Lacerated Lover.*"

The blood drained from his face. "We'll be right there," he whispered. Before Stuart hung up, Peter had already waved down their waitress.

Back in Stuart's office on campus, Peter carefully opened the letter and bagged the envelope. Stuart unfolded the sheet of computer paper with the same cursive writing.

You don't deserve happiness.
I'll make you suffer like I've suffered.

Peter slid the letter into a clear plastic bag. "We'll dust it, and I'll alert the agent watching Taylor."

Reese looked at the letter. "Call the boyfriend, too. He seems to keep a close watch over her."

Peter nodded and gathered the evidence. "We'll bring both women in if we have to."

"What the hell did I do?" Stuart mumbled.

TAYLOR STUDIED HARD … OR AS hard as she could without thinking about Dr. Morgan kissing and touching her. It helped that she and Eva had quizzed each other earlier. She had a good understanding of the politics and people during that time, but she wasn't sure about writing essay answers. As she caught up on her reading for her other classes, she heard stomping footsteps. Immediately alarmed, she jumped from her bed.

Before she could check it out, Eva came running into the room. "I … gotta tell you … what I … just heard … but don't … freak out."

She hated it when Eva said stuff like that. While she waited for Eva's breathing to slow, her heart rate and blood pressure went up.

Eva dropped her coat on the floor and sprawled out on her bed. "I ran all the way from the library."

"You ran across campus to tell me some gossip that you don't want me to freak out about?" Taylor shut the door and paced the four steps. "Get on with it!"

"Cindy's been boasting that she's invited to the big faculty function at the Dean's house this Saturday night."

"Yeah, and?" she asked, biting her hangnail. She didn't like where this was going. He would not do this to her, not even as a joke.

"She's going with her dad, whose second wife is friends with the Dean's wife."

She stopped pacing. "Oh no, she's the set-up, isn't she?" She was ticked that Dr. Morgan didn't even warn her. And why was she still referring to him as Dr. Morgan? She had sex with the guy.

"I think so," Eva said. "Cindy was saying that a number of Western's faculty members were attending, including your very own Dr. Morgan."

"He didn't give me any details about dinner. Tell me, Detective. What do you make of it?" She could hear the angst in her own voice. "I don't need this before an exam. I could cancel dinner, but there's no way I'm letting Cindy get her claws in him."

"That's the spirit," Eva said, clapping her hands together. "Let's think this through. Why would he want to flaunt you? He doesn't seem the type to do that. And there's still the chance he could get into trouble for bedding a student."

"Are you sure he's going?" she asked, ignoring her comment.

"The Dean's wife told Cindy's stepmom he was going to be there."

"I guess we'll find out Saturday."

As exhausted as she was, Taylor didn't get much sleep. She kept going through different scenarios, and they all ended badly—well, except for her either slapping or punching Cindy Carter in the face. She liked that part.

CHAPTER
ten

TAYLOR WOKE WITH A SENSE of apprehension. After a week to think things through, she started wondering if she could have been a fling? Was she reading too much into it? And why would she care? She had to remind herself of her plan.

In heavy coats and boots, she and Eva plodded to class in the inch of snow that covered the sidewalk in early December. They didn't say much. Eva sensed her sullen mood, and Taylor stayed quiet, so Eva could focus on the exam. They automatically found their seats and waited. Ten minutes late, Dr. Morgan sauntered in with a stack of exams and his coffee. He placed the exams on the desk and scanned the room.

She caught his eye and held it briefly. Was it possible for him to look sexier? Breathing became difficult again as she thought of him naked and kissing her. Now she was dizzy. Her mind went blank. She couldn't remember anything. *Focus, damn it!*

"Okay, let's have your questions," he said, sitting on the stool.

Cindy raised her hand. "Dr. Morgan, I heard you're going to the Dean's dinner party tonight. Is it black tie? My invitation didn't say."

What the hell kind of question was that right before an exam and in front of forty students? That punch in the face may become reality yet. Dr. Morgan immediately looked up at her. She raised her eyebrows. She'd like to know the answer, too. His mouth opened, but nothing came out.

Eva came to his rescue. "Cindy, we're here to take an exam. Let's stay on topic."

Dr. Morgan recovered and asked for relevant questions. She thought Eva earned herself an A+ for the class. Taylor wasn't letting him off that easily. She kept a straight face. He looked a bit unnerved, which she thought he deserved.

When the questions stopped, he sighed. "There's been a change of plans with the exam." He passed them to the front row, and they passed them back. "You have only one essay question with the rest multiple choice. You have two hours. Good luck."

Well, it was a relief to have only one essay. It surprised her, considering the talk of an exam with many hard essay questions. Many students finished within thirty minutes, including Eva and Amber. After another fifteen minutes, she decided she'd done the best she could. He watched her the whole time, increasing the pressure. What was going on in his head? Even if they weren't going to dinner, she still wanted him to kiss her again.

After slipping on her coat, she put her test face

down on his desk. Looking bored, he winked and slid his business card across the table. She palmed it, smiled, and walked out the door.

"What took you so long?" Eva asked, standing in the hallway.

"I wanted to be sure of my answers," she replied, flipping the card over.

Same bar stool!

"You still don't know what's going on for dinner," Eva said, glancing at the note.

"I know, but for now my exam is over, and I need a nap."

"Yeah, you may be up late," Eva said.

Taylor smiled.

After an hour and a half snooze, she took a long hot shower, shaving her legs and pits. She plucked a few eyebrows and put on a bit of face powder. She figured she'd add more once she knew where they were going. She painted her toenails and trimmed her hangnails. Humming to their classic rock radio station, she felt ready for anything.

Standing in their closet, Eva held up a black spaghetti-strap dress. "I think you should wear this later for dinner. It's sexy, dressy, and classic short, not slutty short. It'll show off your long legs. You'll be a knockout wherever you go."

Not knowing much about fashion, she left those decisions to Eva. Taylor owned one pair of basic black pumps for emergencies such as this. Shoe shopping for a size eleven had neither been fun nor a priority, no matter how hard Eva tried to dress her up. Like Joe, Taylor preferred to wear jeans.

"He's not going to know what hit him. I guarantee it," Eva said.

"Are you going down to Johnny's, too?"

"Oh yeah, I want to know what was up with his exam, among other things."

"Let's go now, and we'll split some nachos."

By the time Taylor pushed the empty plate away, Eva was *checking out the scene*. Taylor grabbed the remote and angled the TV toward her stool. Michigan had only two games left in the season. She hoped for a Rose Bowl bid with her fingers crossed.

Seeing Eva flit around the room made her smile. Eva could flirt, kiss, and schmooze with anybody. Taylor could not although lately she'd been bolder than ever before. Eva was finally rubbing off on her.

IN THE BAR, REESE TOOK off toward the pool tables, and Stuart looked around for the agent assigned to Taylor. In the crowd, he didn't see him, but he did spot Taylor. He couldn't get to her quick enough.

"Hey, you," he whispered in her ear. She smelled like a bouquet of fresh lilacs. He really had missed her.

"What are you smiling about?"

"Eva has such a knack with people. She's graceful without even trying."

"Well, I like your passionate flair," he whispered in her ear again. When she shivered, he smiled.

"Dr. Morgan, are you trying to get on my good side?"

"Why, yes, I am, and stop calling me *doctor*. I am not your instructor anymore. By the way, is the flattery working?"

She nodded and kissed his cheek. He brushed against her frequently. An electrical current zapped him each time. He needed her closeness as much as he needed air to breathe. The intensity shocked him. He forgot about the game. He didn't even realize it was a commercial break until she excused herself.

"I need her in my life," he mumbled as he watched her walk away.

"You think so, huh?" Eva said, suddenly standing next to him. She put her hands on her hips. "Do you know how stressed she is about this threat? She's worried about you, and we're worried about her getting hurt."

He leaned back to widen the gap. "I'm trying to keep her safe until the person is caught. That's why she has an agent watching her."

"Hurt by you," Eva said, stepping closer.

"Me? I don't want to hurt her," he replied, leaning farther back on the stool.

She shook her finger in his face. "What about this other business about the Dean's party? Flaunting her about. That's just mean. Are you trying to get her expelled from school? Because that's what'll happen."

"You wait just a damn minute," he said, standing

over her. "I care about her, and I'm going to explain about that damn party when I get the chance. I will protect her."

Un-intimidated, Eva didn't budge from her spot. She tilted her head back and jutted out her chin. "Yeah, we'll see how well she's protected when you move on to your next admiring virgin."

RETURNING FROM THE RESTROOM, TAYLOR saw Eva confronting Stuart, who looked upset. She suspected Eva was grilling him about the exam.

"I didn't know," he said, looking down at his hands as he slowly sat on the stool.

"So why change the exam?" Taylor asked, bumping her hip into him just to be nearer.

"It's my prerogative to design the exam any way I want," he replied quietly.

Eva dismissed the questioning. "Johnny, we need another pitcher!"

Standing next to him, Taylor bit her lower lip. "Do you still want to have dinner later?" she asked, afraid of the answer.

He took her hand and a deep breath. "I made reservations at Holly's Bistro on South Westnage, but I have to make an appearance at that gathering. I've been avoiding Bob for the last few weekends. I thought maybe we could have dinner then later, toward the end of the night, stop by briefly."

"You won't mind being with your student at a

faculty function?"

"Who's going to know you're my former student?" he asked, looking hopeful.

"Have you forgotten your buddy, Cindy, will be there? She'll pitch a fit if I show up on your arm."

"A little cat fight would liven up the party for sure," he said with a chuckle. His hands pulled her hips closer. "I'm not opposed to begging."

Smiling, she put her hands lightly on his chest and kissed him. She pulled back a couple of inches, which she found extremely hard to do. "Okay, I've wanted to slap Cindy for the longest time." He hugged her as the entire bar abruptly cheered.

Eva yelled above the noise, "Do you guys even care that Michigan scored?"

They watched the replay of the touchdown. Michigan would play the tough Ohio State next week. At least it was a home game. That usually helped. After confirming their date, they hurried away in different directions.

STUART WALKED OUT OF THE bar, still stunned at Eva's revelation. He had no idea. He assumed—well, that's what he got for assuming. She trusted him, and he should have paid better attention. For as much as he liked the idea that she was his alone, he wondered if he was too rough with her. The guilt hit him on the head like a defensive end blindsiding a quarterback.

"She's pretty brave to be kissing her professor in a

crowded bar," Reese said, catching up to him. "Someone might turn her in."

Ignoring Reese again, he thought about his plans for the night. He'd make a few minor adjustments. He would make this an amazing night for her, as a woman's first time should be, not sex in some crappy student apartment with a lout who only thought of himself. He looked at his watch. He had a couple hours.

"I know you and Agent Martin will be following us tonight, but can you do me a favor and stay out of sight?" he asked, sitting in Reese's passenger seat.

"What's in it for me?"

"What do you want?"

"Details," Reese replied, grinning.

"That ain't going to happen. If you screw this up in any way, I'll tell Doris how you wrecked my romantic night with this woman."

Reese cringed. "Jeez, Doc, playing hardball? Fine. I'll observe from a distance."

He eyed him. "What's the catch?"

"I want to critique your romantic evening, and you have to sit and take it."

Stuart wanted to thump him. Instead, he nodded. "Under one condition. I'll take the harassment in the car on the way back to Ann Arbor on Sunday. Once there, that's it, no more."

"Deal," Reese replied. "I can always drive super-slow."

He glared. "Cindy will be at Bob's party. Keep an eye on her. I don't want anything ruining this night."

"You got it, Romeo. Do me a favor then. Keep your gun handy, especially if you want us out of sight."

WITH SEVEN O'CLOCK RESERVATIONS, TAYLOR planned to meet Stuart in the dorm lobby at six-thirty. Eva had helped her zip up her black dress and touch up her makeup as if she were getting ready for her first grown-up date. Most dates were casual, in groups shooting pool or the movie sort, not a black tie party. Down in the lobby, she set her coat and purse on the bench next to the front desk. A sophomore greeter stared as he checked IDs and made calls for guests. She glared, and he quickly averted his eyes.

She wanted to be a little early for the extra practice walking in heels. She couldn't remember the last time she wore them, and she had to dig deep in her underwear drawer for a decent pair of nylons. She didn't have a strapless bra, but she really didn't need one.

She paced and glowered at the greeter as he talked on the phone. Turning, she saw Stuart in the doorway. She caught her breath. He wore a black tuxedo with a bow tie, vest, and overcoat. *Wow.* He looked as handsome as a model from GQ magazine. Her first thought was to run her fingers through his neatly combed hair to set it free again.

"You look fantastic," he said, rushing toward her.

The greeter waved down some of the guys coming from the security door. They leaned on the desk and watched while Stuart helped her with her black wool coat. He smelled delicious. Between his cologne and that look, she wanted to skip dinner and go back to his guest apartment.

As they walked toward the front door, she heard someone behind them. "Taylor's smokin'."

Stuart, not missing a beat, turned back. "Yeah, she is, and she's with me tonight."

"Good night, boys," she replied over her shoulder.

Stuart escorted her down the few steps to a sleek black car. "I hired a driver for the night. I want to concentrate on you."

"That's thoughtful," she replied while he opened the door for her. Seeing the guys standing at the window watching them, she hiked up her dress a little higher and provocatively swung her legs into the car.

"You're a tease," Stuart said. He saluted the growing crowd and walked around the car. Inside, he nodded at the driver. "After this little scene, I have a feeling I'll have major competition for your affection."

"I guess I shouldn't have done that. I forget how fast gossip spreads, especially something juicy like being with my professor." She saw the driver's eyebrows lift as he looked in the rearview mirror.

"Nobody even saw me."

"You're sweet," she replied, smoothing down her dress.

He casually reached for her hand. The wave of heat climbed her arm and slid right to her groin. She wanted to straddle him in the back seat and kiss him while the driver watched. The thought inflamed her face. As they talked, her mind drifted toward other wicked activities.

At Holly's Bistro, the candlelit booths along the wall had high backs for privacy. She felt as if they were the only ones there. They drank wine and ate prime rib, which melted in her mouth. Dorm food would never be the same. The conversation continued to flirt comfortably, often tinged with hints of later.

"Eva said they have a piano player," she said, looking around.

"Tonight, they have a guitarist. He's supposed to start soon."

As if he heard them, a hippy with a guitar came from somewhere and sat on a stool next to a microphone. There was no introduction. He just started playing a James Taylor tune, adding to the already romantic mood.

Stuart laid his napkin beside his plate. "Let's dance."

"They have a dance floor?" she asked, looking at the singer.

Stuart pointed to a small open area where two other couples danced. She took his offered hand, and he led her to the dance floor He sensed her discomfort at seeing the others in proper dance position.

"Just follow my lead," he whispered.

She liked not being in charge. She didn't have to pretend to be someone she clearly wasn't. It seemed as if she had known Stuart longer than a month. Being around him was exciting, yet comfortable … and safe. She hadn't felt that since before her parents died. Was Stuart filling that void in her heart?

They danced through two songs before returning to their table. Their plates were cleared and replaced with two pieces of cheesecake with drizzled chocolate and two empty coffee cups on saucers. The server quickly filled their cups. Sipping hers, she asked if they could take the dessert with them since she was full from dinner.

"Certainly," he said. "Are you having a good time?"

"This has been wonderful. You are so sweet to do

all of this."

"It's my pleasure," he said, taking her hand. "I enjoy your company — brainy and sexy."

Uncomfortable with the compliment, she excused herself to the ladies' room. Nobody had ever called her *sexy*. She liked that. It made her fearless and ready to take on the faculty crowd. She washed her hands, popped in a cinnamon candy, and reapplied her lipstick with a new confidence.

Smiling, Stuart watched her walk back to the table. He had the desserts boxed and the bill paid. Standing, he helped her with her coat. "Are you ready for a quick side trip?"

"Sure, and then to the Dean's?"

"The function is the side trip. I have more planned for you tonight."

"Ooh, I hope it's naughty," she said, picking up the dessert boxes.

"Oh, it is." He chuckled and gave her a light swat on the rump to get her moving toward the door.

As the wine wore off, she started to feel a little panicky. The driver pulled over on the street past the Dean's mansion because the whole circular drive was still full, three-cars-wide.

"I thought you said everyone would be gone by now," she said, wringing her hands.

"Don't worry. I'll stay right next to you."

Arm in arm, they walked up the path to the front door. The house lights were on in every room. Through the windows, she could see several small groups conversing. Everyone held drinks in their hands. *I could really use one of those about now*, she thought, stepping up to the door.

"I promise this will be quick," he said.

Stuart planted a deep, lingering kiss on her that made her head spin. He grinned. He must know the effect he had on her. Making her weak-kneed wasn't fair. He opened the door and walked in. The staff person jumped, surprised they didn't knock. He took their coats as Stuart asked where the host was.

"He's in the library, down the hall, second room on the left."

"Thanks," Stuart replied, reaching for her hand, which she gladly gave to him.

Along the wide corridor, three different groups stopped talking and watched them pass. He dropped her hand and put his arm around her waist. Her tension eased slightly.

"They're jealous that I'm with such a beauty," he whispered.

They turned into the library doorway. The large room had leather couches, a heavy wood coffee table, and a sideboard with many types of alcohol that called her name. Books filled every wall from the cathedral ceiling to the floor except for that six-foot-long sideboard.

She cringed when five groups of four paused their discussions and stared. While looking for a place to hide, she groaned when she spotted creepy Loren Johnson in a group. She tried to slide behind Stuart.

On the far side of the room, Dean Brady smiled. "Stuart, there you are," he said, walking toward them.

Stuart gave her waist a squeeze and gently maneuvered her back to his side. "Smile, Darlin'."

Dean Brady shook his hand. "Doris was wondering if you were coming."

"Bob, I'd like you to meet my girlfriend, Taylor."

Wait, she was his girlfriend?

"Taylor, so nice to meet you." He gave her hand a gentle grasp. He was very different from the uptight guy she'd seen around campus. Wearing a black tuxedo, he was shorter than she expected.

"Hello," she replied shyly.

"Stuart, watch out for Doris. She has a firm agenda."

"We won't be staying. We have other plans." Her face flushed again.

"Before you leave, I need to get with you about a couple of things," the Dean said.

Taking the hint of wanting privacy, she asked where to find the ladies' room. Before she left, he kissed her cheek.

"I'll be right here," he said.

She wanted to leave an impression since the whole room ogled them. She seductively slid her hand from his bicep to his fingers. He growled in her ear giving her goose bumps. Man, she was getting the hang of this flirty stuff.

When she came out of the bathroom, Loren Johnson grabbed her upper arm and yanked her down an empty side hall. She lost her shoe. He squeezed her arm hard and held her against him.

"What are you doing here?" he demanded.

Frowning, she peeled his fingers off her arm and stepped back. "I am here as a guest. Don't worry. I won't tell anyone that you're a client," she replied as she tried to move around him.

He blocked her way. "Who did you come with?" he asked, angrily.

Not wanting to answer, she was suddenly isolated and afraid.

"Is there a problem here?" Reese asked, standing behind Loren. He twirled her shoe on his index finger. Dressed in a navy blue suit and tie, he didn't look nearly as annoying as he did when he wore flannel and jeans.

Loren glared. "No."

She took the shoe and quickly slipped it back on. "Thank you," she whispered as she passed him.

"Taylor," Reese said, turning toward her, "where's your agent?"

She stopped. "I haven't seen him today."

Reese nodded and turned back to Loren. She took a moment to gather herself. During her four years as a massage therapist, she had found that some clients didn't want anyone to know they received massages. She didn't think it was a big deal, but she always respected their privacy. It upset her that Loren felt he had to hurt her to make his point. She rubbed her arm as she entered the library.

She returned in time to see Cindy put her hand on Stuart's forearm as he held his drink. She thought about her face-slapping scenario. In a long, slinky, black halter dress with a slit to the hip, Cindy talked to Stuart and the Dean. *Here you go, Taylor. Don't embarrass yourself or your new boyfriend.* Smiling, she walked around to Stuart's other side.

"Hi, Cindy. How are you?" Not waiting for her answer, she took Stuart's drink, subtly letting Cindy's hand fall from his arm. She flashed him a devious smile and thanked him for holding it for her. He raised an eyebrow and grinned.

"Taylor, what are you doing here?" Cindy demanded.

"What do you mean? I'm here with Stuart," she

replied. On cue, he put his arm around her.

"Cindy, you know Taylor?" the Dean asked.

"We were students in Professor Morgan's seminar," Cindy said, raising her voice. Now, not only were the closest groups listening, the whole room seemed to take a few steps closer.

"That's right. I *was* his student."

"I know she's been seeing him before this. Isn't there some law against that?" Cindy practically screeched now.

Stuart was about to say something, but the Dean stopped him. "Oh boy, I think we should discuss this in private and let our other guests enjoy the gathering. Cindy, Taylor, Stuart, please follow me."

Taking the drink from her hand, Stuart set it aside and smiled. *He took pleasure in this?* She knew if she strayed from her plan, it would get her into trouble. She needed to think things through. Romance was too far down on her list.

Resisting the urge to chew her lower lip, she glanced at the group as they left the library. She got the feeling that the guests were disappointed rather than relieved, but what did she know? They followed the Dean farther down the hall to a door on the right. At the Dean's heels, Cindy yapped in his ear.

Taylor thought about making a run for it, but Stuart's hand on her back pushed her forward. He probably knew she wanted to bolt. Before they entered, the Dean asked three other guests to leave the room.

While they waited, Stuart grinned and whispered, "I kinda like women fighting over me."

Taylor elbowed him in the abdomen then followed Cindy and the Dean. When she turned to see what damage she had done, he had the nerve to continue grinning. Shaking her head, she took the chair the Dean offered. Cindy flipped her long blond hair off her shoulder and glared at her from her seat on the couch across from her. Dean Brady didn't even look at Stuart.

The smaller den had oak trim like the library with a small couch, two leather chairs, heavy desk and high-backed chair and more bookshelves on two of the walls. She eyed the sideboard with alcohol decanters. By the door, a fireplace held a small, glowing fire. It started to die down, but for some reason, it still felt warm in the room. Stuart stood by the fire while the Dean settled behind his desk.

"Dean Brady, this is not proper. What's the university's stand in this matter?" Cindy demanded. Her voice was definitely a whine and not very ladylike. She was asking about proper? She would have been in his bed in a second. Cindy was pissed that she beat her to it.

Taylor couldn't believe it. She was more of a slut than Cindy was. She cringed at the thought. She certainly didn't see that coming.

Standing, the Dean reached for a huge binder on a shelf to his right. She heard him mumble something about giving his wife an earful. Pretending confidence, Taylor placed her hands on her lap and crossed her legs. *Talk about being in the principal's office.* She was there only once in third grade for punching a boy who pulled her hair. Maybe there'd be more hair pulling tonight.

In his tuxedo, Stuart leaned on the mantle. Her mother would have said he looked dashing. Taylor would have agreed with her. He showed no nervousness whatsoever. Did he even care what happened to her education? Sitting, the Dean flipped open to a page.

He looked at Stuart and sighed. "Cindy, there are codes of conduct about WMU students and faculty fraternizing but nothing about visiting professors and their weekend seminars. Without the specific wording, there is nothing I can do." The Dean had his friend's back.

Taylor relaxed until Cindy opened her mouth. "Drop her from the class. She had an unfair advantage. That's cheating," Cindy demanded.

All right, enough is enough. "Excuse me," Taylor interrupted. "I worked hard in that class."

"Yeah, on your knees," Cindy retorted.

Calming herself before she spoke, she directed her statement to the Dean. "First of all, she has no proof."

"Are you denying it? I saw you at the bar with him," Cindy replied with a smile.

"Yes, and you were there, too, with about fifty other people who were watching a football game." Although she kept an even tone to her voice, she was a wreck inside. All of her hard work for a college education was slipping away. She started to panic.

Cindy glared. "What about your comment in the women's bathroom about falling for a guy?"

Taylor saw Stuart raise an eyebrow. He quickly hid his smile. Her panic became annoyance at Cindy and her big mouth. She wanted to yank out her hair. The thought of giving her a bald spot made her smile.

"I don't know what you're referring to. Again, do you have someone who can corroborate that?"

"Eva O'Sullivan," Cindy replied with another smug smile.

Taylor gave her a surprised look. "My best friend?

Really? Are you sure?" *Not only was she a slut, she was a big fat liar, too.* Cindy's long talons dug into the leather couch cushion as Taylor turned back to the Dean. "Dean Brady, I need the credits to graduate on time. I will not drop this course. I have done nothing wrong."

"If I may interject for a moment," Stuart said.

Yeah, you had better, Buddy.

"I had only two means for grading the class. My assistants at Michigan are grading the essays. Those same assistants wrote and faxed over today's exam right before the class started. I was ten minutes late making copies. They have the only answer key to grade the exams. This is part of their graduate work. As you can see, there will be no compromise in Taylor's essay and exam grade."

Her mouth opened. *He saw this coming?* They turned to the Dean, who leaned back in his chair.

He steepled his fingers as he spoke. "I conclude that with a passing grade for the class, Taylor will receive credit. I see no reason to believe there has been a compromise in the grading process."

"That's bullshit!" Cindy yelled, jumping to her feet. Her heel stepped on her gown, causing more cleavage to show. Her boob almost popped out.

"Enough!" the Dean said. "That language is unbecoming."

"This isn't the end of this!" Cindy screamed, pointing a finger at her.

Taylor stood and towered over her. "This does end here or you can ask your daddy what *defamation of character* means."

Cindy slammed the door so hard that Stuart had to catch a knick-knack from falling off the mantle. Taylor blew out a long breath and sank into the chair.

Stuart rushed to her. "I am so sorry to put you through that," he said, kneeling beside her. He held her shaking hands.

The Dean walked over to the decanters and poured three glasses of something. After handing one to her and the other to Stuart, he took a hard swallow from the third. "Boy, you stood up to that brat. Firm and calm, I like that."

Absently, she took a gulp of the liquid. She gasped at the burn. "Sorry about disrupting your party."

"I was hoping for a cat fight." Stuart laughed.

"It crossed my mind," she replied, taking a sip this time.

"Well, Stuart, I wasn't sure what you were up to, but I'm glad you learned from my mistakes. You're still the best tactician around," he said with a chuckle. "I need to get back to my guests and have a chat with my wife."

"Thanks, Bob. We'll be out shortly," he said. The Dean left, and Stuart turned back to her. "I didn't think it would go that far. I had to let it play out here, so it wouldn't put your status in question with graduation around the corner."

"Why didn't you tell me?"

"I wanted to, but I couldn't compromise the situation by having you know prior events."

Suddenly, she was exhausted. This wasn't quite how she pictured the evening. He did care about her education and took the necessary precautions to protect her. How lucky was she to have such a considerate boyfriend? Could she make room for him in her plan? She honestly didn't know.

"How long have you had this planned, Mr.

Tactician?"

He grinned. "Are you sure you want to know?"

She nodded.

"From the time it took us to walk from Johnny's bar to the visitor apartments that first Saturday after the game."

"You did not," she protested.

"The overall plan, yes. Details came later," he said as he set her glass on the coffee table. "Taylor, I'm crazy about you. I don't want to ruin this good thing between us."

She took his face in her hands. "Thank you," she said.

It was all she could say. He touched her deeply, but the timing messed with her plan. He confused the hell out of her. Still on his knees, he leaned forward and kissed her. She absorbed as much of him as she could. She didn't know if it was the liquor or the passion making her dizzy again. He slowly pulled away, and she sat back panting.

"If we don't leave now, I'm going to have my way with you on Bob's desk," he said.

After taking a few minutes to compose themselves, they walked back into the library where the Dean talked with a few others she didn't recognize. Again, everyone turned. She would never get used to that. From a corner group, Loren shot daggers at her. She slipped her arm into Stuart's, and they headed toward the sideboard. Taking a sip of her fresh drink, still not knowing what it was but needing it, she watched the Dean work his way over to them.

"Hello, you two. I had a chat with my wife, and she's looking for you, Taylor."

"Uh-oh," Taylor said, glancing at Stuart for some support.

"She wants to meet the woman who makes Stuart act so boldly."

"Oh, it seems to work both ways. I think it's all the Civil War talk about fighting and standing up for one's beliefs."

Both men laughed. "I deserve a raise," Stuart said.

"Not at this university with the commotion you've caused." The Dean chuckled. "We haven't been this lively in a long while."

"Come on, Darling. Thanks, Bob, and please, tell Doris no more firm agendas."

The same man handed them their coats. How he remembered which one was hers she didn't know. As Stuart helped her slip on her coat, she saw Reese talking on his phone and walking toward them. Stuart looked at him, too, and quickly ushered her out the door.

CHAPTER
eleven

AFTER THE DEAN'S PARTY, STUART helped her into the warm car and nodded at the driver. Taylor blew out a breath and stared out the window, distracted by her thoughts about a completely different set of consequences that could have happened tonight.

He tensely gripped her hand. "Taylor, are you upset that I planned for this?"

She looked back at him and smiled. "It's rather reassuring knowing I'm not the only one who likes to plan ahead. We could have gotten into some serious trouble." He relaxed slightly. "Is everything okay? I saw Reese earlier. He didn't look happy. And you're carrying your gun."

"It's a precaution. Reese talked to you? He promised he'd back off tonight."

"He actually came to my rescue. A professor, who's also a client, cornered me. I think he was bothered that I might talk to people about his treatment."

"Did he hurt you?"

"Reese helped me slip away and asked if I'd seen Agent Martin."

Stuart put his arm around her. "I don't want to think about that. You are my focus tonight."

Smiling, she leaned into him. His warmth sheltered her. She wanted to forget the outside world. "What's next in your grand plan?"

"I enjoyed dancing with you earlier. How about a few more?"

"That sounds wonderful."

Their chauffeur turned into the drive of the downtown Radisson Hotel and waited his turn to stop in front of the entrance. "The hotel bar has a band. Okay with you?" Stuart asked.

"Sure, I've been here a few times."

He raised an eyebrow. "Oh, yeah?"

"Dancing at the bar," she said with a giggle. "Who's the band?"

"The Feds. I heard they're pretty good."

"Yeah, I heard that, too," she replied. She had heard that from Joe, who happened to be the band's drummer. She chuckled to herself. Knowing Joe, this night would continue to be interesting.

After they checked their coats, she excused herself to the ladies' room. Between the drinking and the cold air, she really had to go. She snagged her nylons, pulling them up, and chucked them with no regrets. Coming out of the bathroom, she saw Joe talking to a couple of women in the lobby. Seeing her, he dismissed the women and rushed to meet her.

"Whoa, Taylor. Are you looking hot for me?" he asked, checking her over.

"I'm here with my date. He seems to think your band's good."

"Very funny."

"Don't embarrass me," she said, knowing he would.

"Where's Agent Martin?" he asked, looking around.

"I don't know. I saw Reese earlier, so I suspect he's around here somewhere."

Joe nodded and folded his arms. "I was with that group of guys at the front windows watching you get into the car. They gave a collective *wow*. Do you understand what you've done? Those guys have a new opinion of you. You've wrecked four years of my hard work."

"What do you mean?"

He sighed. "Eva left a message on my cell. Cindy's on your dorm floor and is pissed. What's up with that?"

Taylor explained about Cindy outing them as a couple and her threat that it wasn't over. Joe swore and ran a hand through his dark brown hair. He got in her face.

"You need to be careful around her," he said, clenching his teeth.

"Why?" she asked, taking a step back from his angry stance.

"I told you before she's not stable."

"You think she's the one threatening Stuart?" she asked, hugging herself.

He immediately relaxed his posture. "I don't know. The Director's checking into it. In the meantime, go have some fun."

She smiled. "Joey, behave." She kissed his cheek. She knew him too well not to expect some mischief.

From the doorway, she looked through the crowd and saw Stuart at the bar with his back to her. She liked this place. The band set up on a stage to the far right next to the designated dance floor. The area wasn't huge but was big enough to move around on. The middle tables were packed. That would stroke Joe's ego. On the left side, the bar's counter stretched the full length of the wall. It was a step up from the tables with a three-foot space for the stools. It overlooked the crowd and had a great view of the band.

Stuart talked with the bartender, who looked her way and nodded. As she met him, Stuart spun his stool around and grinned. He helped her up to sit next to him. She sighed as she adjusted her short dress. She liked stools. Watching football, she sat on stools all the time. These even had backs, which are the most comfortable stools to have. However, dresses and stools do not go together. She tried very hard not to flash anyone as she attempted to sit down gracefully.

"What's going on?" she asked, gesturing toward the bartender, who had moved off to make drinks for someone else.

"He was getting our drinks when he looks up and says, 'Whoa.' So I say, 'Black dress.' He nods, and I tell him you're with me."

"Jeez, is my dress that short and that tight?"

"You truly fascinate me. You're beautiful, yet you don't even realize it."

Ignoring the comment, she smiled and sipped her wine. The band came to the stage, so she swiveled around to listen. Since her stool seat was at eye level of those sitting at the tables, she felt self-conscious and exposed without her nylons. *Who would have guessed nylons were a protective force?* She crossed her legs and hoped everyone kept their eyes on the band.

Ogling her, Joe banged on the drums and mouthed, "Yeah, Baby."

She grinned and mouthed back, "Jealous?"

He looked taken aback at her question. Then he smiled. It was wide and menacing. *Oh God, what was he going to do?* She was about to fill Stuart in on the Joe situation, but he looked smug with his arm around her.

Feeling a bit ticked for reasons too complicated for her to sort out right then, she changed her mind and listened to the band play only fast rock classics. Becoming more and more uncomfortable on the stool, she crossed her legs back and forth. Joe leered. Stuart leaned over and asked if she was okay.

"Yeah, this stool isn't comfortable for a woman playing dress up," she replied, spinning her seat to the bar to take a drink.

He laughed. "You're getting quite the looks from the band members."

"Well, you may like me being stared at, but frankly, I don't. I'll be back in a few minutes."

She hopped off the stool and straightened her dress. She tried not to stagger. Was she turning into a mean drunk? She sat in the stall to get her head straight. It wasn't Stuart; it was just this dress. Was she really that different dressed up? She had been more daring. Was that out of character for her? God, she didn't know anything anymore.

She could feel herself start to tear up, so she hurried to wash her hands and check her makeup. She frowned at her reflection; she looked the same. As a group of women came in, she hurried out the door. She figured it was a break for the band, not a good time to leave Stuart alone.

She paused in the doorway. Stuart sat to the right of her empty stool with the drummer to the left of it. Having no idea what would happen next, she hurried over. Putting her hand on Stuart's shoulder, she kissed his cheek.

"I'm sorry for the outburst. I don't like the attention," she said.

"I'm sorry, too. I enjoy having an attractive woman on my arm, so I hope you don't mind my attention."

She laughed. "You know just what to say." She wrapped her arms around his neck and kissed him. He obliged and pulled her closer. *Man, he's a good kisser.*

"Let's get out of here," he whispered.

It took a moment to come to her senses. "Oh no, we haven't danced yet, and you owe me at least two."

"Whatever you want," he replied, looking over her shoulder. "I'll be right back."

Attempting to sit again, she watched him leave. *Boy, he's handsome in a tuxedo.* She couldn't believe he was with her. She had to be dreaming.

STUART RUSHED TO THE LOBBY. Reese had tried to get his attention for the last ten minutes. He could tell by his face that something was wrong.

Reese held up his hands. "I know I'm not supposed to interfere, but you need to know what's going on."

Before Reese could continue, Peter Bingaman entered the hotel lobby from outside.

His gut tightened. "What?" Stuart demanded.

"Agent Martin's dead. We found him in his car in front of Taylor's dormitory. He's been dead since early this morning," Peter replied.

"Shot in the temple," Reese added.

"Shit," he mumbled. *Taylor had been in danger all day?*

"It looks like the focus may be on Taylor now," Peter said.

"Have you checked out Cindy Carter's background?" Stuart explained the events at Bob's party. "I don't want her anywhere near Taylor."

Peter nodded. "I'm taking over for Agent Martin."

"She's not leaving my sight until I can explain it to her," Stuart replied.

"Where is she?" Reese asked. "Is it really safe to leave her alone? Half the men in there are trying to peek under her dress every time she crosses her legs."

Without a word, he turned on his heels.

AFTER WATCHING STUART LEAVE, SHE spun her stool around to face the bar. She sipped her drink. "Why don't you kiss me like that?" Joe asked.

"You don't call me *beautiful* or take me to black tie functions."

"If that's all it takes, let's go," he replied, putting his arm on the back of her stool.

"Joey, please don't start anything. He likes me," she pleaded.

"You know I can't say no to you. Now, give me

a little sugar." Leaning toward her, he made smooch noises.

"No way, Buddy. Back off," she said, mockingly.

At that precise moment, Stuart returned and stood behind Joe. Before she could explain, he shoved Joe's arm from her stool. "She said, 'Back off.'" He sounded calm and in charge. It gave her goose bumps.

"Stuart. Really. It's okay," she said.

"Yeah, Stu, it's okay," Joe mocked. She stared at Joe. Did he want a fight?

"No, it's not. This lady's with me."

Joe stood. Out of nowhere, the other four band members surrounded Stuart. Joe looked over Stuart's tuxedo. "And just what are you going to do about it, James Bond?" Joe asked, raising his voice.

The whole bar got very quiet. Once again, they were the center of attention. Although Joe and Stuart had the same height and physical build, they were polar opposites. Stuart's blond hair and calming nature contrasted Joe's dark hair and quick anger. Stuart flexed his hand ready to throw a punch. *How did this get out of control so quickly?*

Hopping off her stool, she squeezed between them and put her palms on Stuart's chest. She felt his strong heartbeat under his shirt and vest. His heat distracted her. She blinked to focus.

"Honey," she whispered, "as much as having two men fighting over me is appealing, you may remember an earlier situation." She stepped aside. "I'd like you to meet my pain-in-the-ass friend, Joe Roberts."

Scowling at each other, neither made any move to shake hands. She thought she heard them growl. Joe's gang moved within a foot of Stuart. The silent crowd waited for a fight while the manager worked his way toward them from across the room.

She sighed. "Don't you guys have another set?" She shooed the band members away, and they left as if scolded by their mother. She faced her brother. "Joey, play some slow songs."

"Anything for you, Baby." Joe tilted her chin upward. Before she could react, he kissed her on the lips for the count of three Mississippis. Then, glaring at Stuart, he snarled, "You and I will talk later." As Joe returned to the stage, he put his arm around the manager's shoulder to reassure him.

Stuart sat and faced the crowd. She couldn't tell if he was mad or not. *Why would Joe do that? He promised. If Joe messes this up for me, he's a dead man.* She stepped between Stuart's knees.

"I should have warned you he'd do something stupid like that. But like you said earlier, it's nice being fought over," she said, trying to lighten the mood.

"I did say that, didn't I?" He smiled. "You are turning me inside out."

"And you, my knight, make me feel very sexy." She leaned closer and slid her hands up his thighs. "Did you know I'm wearing only two articles of clothing? I'd like to take them off soon."

"You like torturing me, don't you?" He held up his hands, indicating she won. "Okay, two slow dances."

She turned around and leaned back against his chest. He wrapped his arms around her waist and set his chin on her shoulder. This felt so much better than sitting on some damn stool.

"We'd like to dedicate this set to my favorite gal, Taylor," Joe said, back on stage.

Joe grinned and blew her a kiss. She wanted to grab that kiss, throw it to the floor, and stomp on it. *I'll make him pay*, she thought, as the whole crowd turned and looked at her. The band started with ZZ Top's "Legs." Laughter filled the room, of course, at her expense. The band then played "Long Cool Woman in a Black Dress" by the Hollies.

"Oh, these guys are hilarious," Stuart said in her ear.

"They are good though," she replied.

"Yeah," he said, nibbling her ear, "I'll admit that."

"Oof, you need to stop."

The way he made her feel, she'd strip naked right here if he asked. Having sex once had turned her into a trollop, and she liked it.

"I will if you stop grinding your hips into me," he whispered.

The crowd roared with laughter as the band sang Roy Orbison's "Pretty Woman," The Troggs' "Wild Thing," and Jimi Hendrix's "Foxy Lady." After a few more dirty looks from Taylor, Joe said they were going to slow it down.

"Thank God," Stuart said. They made it to the dance floor as the band played "Something" by the Beatles. "This is what I've been waiting for." He held her tight, cheek to cheek.

"He's not going to play another slow one for a while."

Stuart chuckled. "I'm surprised he's playing this one."

"I say you give him a salute and we take off. There's cheesecake waiting for me in the car. Dessert before or after dessert?"

"No argument from me."

As the song winded down, she took Stuart's hand and led him off the dance floor. She turned in time to see Joe's laugh slide into a glare. She thought he'd jump over the stage at them. She looked at Stuart who smiled innocently.

"What did you do?" she asked in the lobby.

"I saluted like you said."

"What else?"

"I flashed him this." In his hand, he held a hotel key card.

She giggled. "You are so bad."

"And you, my darling, have tortured me long enough. Come with me." He hustled her into the open elevator. After pushing the button, he kissed her before the doors fully shut. They quickly found the room. "Alone at last," he said, holding the door open.

With the room lit by a single lamp, she noticed a huge vase full of red roses and champagne on the table with two glasses. "You're pretty sure of yourself," she said, slipping off her shoes and scrunching her toes in the carpet. She smelled the roses.

Stuart tossed his tuxedo jacket over the back of the chair and laid his gun in its holster on the table. He opened the bottle. "I was here last night." He nodded toward his suitcase in the corner before handing her a glass. "It seems that our friend Cindy found out where I've been staying and talked someone into opening the apartment. Campus security tipped me off saying that my girlfriend, wink wink, was waiting for me inside. At first, I thought it was you, but I saw Cindy through the half-opened curtain. I turned around and checked in here." He gave his rendition as he slipped off his shoes and unbuttoned his vest.

"That bitch. If I would have known …"

He chuckled. "Having a king-sized bed with you in it did cross my mind when I checked in. You bogart the bed, you know. I didn't want to end up shoved on the floor in the morning."

"What? I did not … Oh, I did."

He took her glass and set it aside. "I think you have two items of clothing that require removal," he said in a low voice.

The desire in his eyes made her swoon. She forgot her name; she forgot to breathe. With a tender kiss, he wrapped her up in his arms. Her hands craved the heat through his shirt. His mouth found her ear then her neck. It sent an electric shock down her spine. He slowly unzipped the back of her dress. She started to pant and moaned in his ear. The arousal was almost unbearable. She didn't dare move. Was she dreaming?

He moved his fingers up her exposed back gently pushing the thin straps of her dress off her shoulders. He stepped away just enough to let the dress fall to the floor. She slowly unbuttoned his shirt. She pushed his shirtsleeves down his arms and felt his sculpted biceps. *A chiseled Adonis*. Her raw emotions quickened at his perfection. Her hands slid to his soft chest hair.

He moaned. "Do you have any idea what you do to me?"

He had this power over her body. Did she have the same power over him? She daringly slid her hands through his blond locks and pulled him closer. Her naked breasts pressed against him. She sighed with pleasure. This was a wonderful dream.

After gently laying her down, he kissed her lips.

Her fingers dug into his shoulder while her body quivered. She arched to his caressing hand as moans left her mouth. His hand slid agonizingly lower to the top of her black bikinis. He slipped his finger under her waistband and gave it a slight tug. His mouth found her taut nipple.

"Please," she begged.

"Please what, Taylor?" he whispered, leisurely tasting the other.

"Please, don't..." she panted, barely getting the words out. She gripped his shoulders harder.

"Please, don't what, Taylor?" he hoarsely asked again, yanking a little more on her waistband.

"Please, don't make me wait," she cried out. Before she knew it, he entered her and a wave of intense tremors overtook her body. She lost complete coherency to pure bliss.

CHAPTER
twelve

SUNDAY

IN THE DARK HOTEL ROOM, Taylor blinked a few times to see if her eyes were actually open. Barely breathing and not wanting to break the spell of a fantastic dream, she quietly sighed. Behind her, she heard soft snoring then faced the noise. She still couldn't see, so she slowly reached out and found a warm, muscular arm. She wasn't dreaming. Silent tears soaked her pillow. Tears of joy, tears of relief, or tears of love, she wasn't sure which.

She listened to his breathing change to a deep sigh. She carefully pulled her hand away to wipe the wetness from her face. The bed shifted weight. His voice grew closer.

"Taylor," he whispered, "are you okay?"

"Yeah," she replied, trying not to sniff her nose.

"No, you're not. You're crying. Did I hurt you? What's wrong?"

"I'm fine. I'll be right back."

She felt her way to the bathroom. She shut the door and flipped on the light. Getting an instant headache from the bright light, she looked at her naked self with smeared mascara, red nose and eyes, and witchy hair.

Thank God, it was dark in there. She washed her hands and scrubbed the makeup off her face. She checked out the rest of her nakedness and remembered being thoroughly caressed and tasted. Her face flushed again. She was such a slut.

Pulling herself together, she switched off the light. Before opening the door, she waited for her eyes to adjust. In the now lit room, Stuart, in his gray boxer briefs, sat at the foot of the bed with his elbows on his knees. He looked up as she took a step toward him. He jumped to his feet. She realized she cared deeply for this handsome man.

"I'm okay, really."

He hugged her. "You're trembling. Let's get back under the covers." He led her to the bed and propped the pillows against the headboard.

She pulled the sheet to her chin. "I'm okay, really," she repeated. "I've never … well … I've never …"

"You've never been with anyone before me," he said, finishing her sentence.

"Oh my God! I'm that bad at it that you could tell?" Horrified, she tugged the sheet higher to cover her face.

"Hell no! I got reamed by your roommate for not figuring it out before."

She moaned. "How humiliating," she whispered, pulling the sheet over her head. She slid her body farther down the bed.

He dragged the sheet over his head and slouched down closer to her. "Why didn't you tell me before?" he asked under their pup tent.

"What was I supposed to say? 'Hey, Dr. Morgan, want to have sex with your virgin student?'"

"You would have called me *Dr. Morgan*?" he asked with a laugh.

She groaned again. "No, that's why I didn't say anything."

"I see your point, but why are you upset now?"

"Our first date has been rather heated from the Dean's house to the bar to … well … you know. It's intense with you. Is it always supposed to be that way?" she whispered.

"With me, of course." He laughed. "The chemistry between us is amazing, wouldn't you say?"

"I have nothing to compare you to," she replied with a giggle.

He hugged her under the covers. "Trust me, it is."

"I do trust you."

"Good, then let's order breakfast."

Wearing one of the hotel's robes, she hid in the bathroom until the attendant left. She was still embarrassed, knowing that a whole bar full of people knew Stuart had a hotel room key for their stay.

"Coast is clear!" Stuart yelled.

He looked adorable in the hotel's other tight fitting robe. Taking a bite of a bagel, she curled up in one of the two oversized chairs next to the food cart. The attendant had brought a variety of food with plenty of coffee.

"So … about last night," she started.

"Yes?" Raising an eyebrow, he grinned.

"Before that. In the bar." She flushed. "What would you have done if I hadn't stepped in?"

"Haven't I taught you anything in my class? If

you take out the top officer, or in this case the head ringleader, the group will crumble. I was a Marine. I'll fight if I have to," he said, taking some scrambled eggs. "What's Joe's beef with me besides this obvious threat?"

She sighed. "Joe has been my protector since third grade. We met in the principal's office."

He laughed. "I can see Joe there, but not you."

She smiled. "Jimmy Timmerman yanked my braid at recess, so I punched him in the stomach. He barfed all over Brenda Langston who tattled. Anyway, I'm sitting next to Joe crying my eyes out. He's calmly waiting as if being in the office was part of going to school. He asked me what I was in for then said I did the right thing sticking up for myself. Boys are not supposed to hurt girls, he stated. He proceeded to tell the principal the same thing. Mr. Reed told us to go back to class. Much later, I learned that Joe's dad beat him and his mom on a constant basis."

"Wow, that's heavy."

"I told my parents what had happened. They encouraged Joe to come over to our house after school. They took Eva under their wing, too. Eva grew up in a household where her mother didn't give a damn about her. Her mom's boyfriends gave her more attention, and she never met her father. We grew up as a family. With my parents gone, we watch out for each other."

"That makes a lot more sense now. They really love you."

"Yeah, what's not to love?" she replied, hovering over the food cart. She picked up a chunk of honeydew melon and sucked the piece into her mouth.

"You're right."

"I'm right about what?" she asked, choosing a

strawberry.

"I'm agreeing with you," he replied, watching her pick at the fruit. Confused, she looked at him. He sighed. "I said, 'They really love you.' Then you said, 'What's not to love.'"

"Yeah, I was being sarcastic," she replied. She popped a large green grape into her mouth.

"I love you, too."

She swallowed the grape whole and croaked out. "What?"

"I love you," he said a bit more tensely.

She turned her back to him. "You mean, *love you love you* or *love you like a buddy to watch football*?"

"Well, I think we've established that you're not my buddy, so I would say the *love you love you* kind."

She looked over her shoulder. "I think I love you, too."

Grinning, he motioned her to his lap. "You think you love me? Is it *love me love me* or *love me like your professor*?"

She sat with him. "I've never been in love before. Can you love someone this soon?" she asked as he wrapped his arms around her waist.

"Who's to say how soon you can fall in love?" He turned her sideways on his lap, so he could see her face.

She leaned against the cushioned arm of the large chair and propped her legs over the other side. "What will people think?"

"Who cares? After what we went through last night, people are going to believe what they want," he said, tucking a strand of her hair behind her ear.

"Yeah, like Cindy." She told him about her conversation with Joe telling her to stay away from her.

"We need to talk about this threat that surrounds us," he said, holding her hand. "Someone killed Agent Martin yesterday morning. Peter and Reese informed me last night."

"Oh my God," she replied as she sat up.

He kept her from standing. "The FBI will be talking to Cindy and Amber today."

"They think one of them could be a killer?"

"I don't know. What I do know is you still need to be protected. Peter will be at your side from now on. He wants us to observe the questioning and thinks we may be able to help. Are you okay with that?"

She nodded. "This seems so surreal."

"I know. I'm not going to let anything happen to you. I promise."

"I don't want anything to happen to you either."

She leaned her head against his shoulder. She could stay like this forever. He held her, and she snuggled tightly against him.

Finally, he sighed. "As much as I'd like to keep you in this room all day, we need to meet with Peter at the Kalamazoo Police Station."

"Will I have time to change?"

He nodded. "We still have the car service available."

After she survived the embarrassment of walking through the hotel lobby to retrieve their coats, the driver strapped her vase of roses to the front seat and drove them to her dorm. Stuart stopped her from getting out of the car.

"I want to see you next weekend," he said.

"How are you going to top our first date?"

"Oh, I think I can," he said smugly. He pulled something from his tuxedo coat pocket.

She looked at the plain white envelope. "There is no way you can top last night. It was the most romantic date ever."

"I think I can," he repeated. "Open it."

Having no idea what he could possibly be up to, she peeled back the seal to look inside. "Oh my God! When did you get these? Are these for real?"

He laughed. "We're going to the Big House."

She tackled him. They had tickets to the Michigan-Ohio State game, one of the biggest rivalries in college football. She had never been to a home game. She hiked up her dress and straddled him.

He grinned. "I thought it would be a reward for getting through exams this coming week and a distraction from the threats," he replied, rubbing her naked thighs.

"Thank you. You're the best lover I've ever had."

She ran her fingers through his hair and kissed him. He slid his hands under her dress to pull her hips closer then deepened the kiss for a moment.

"Our driver is watching in the rearview mirror," he whispered in her ear.

"Oh," she said, blushing. She quickly scooted off him and straightened her dress.

He leaned closer to her. "I'll meet you in the lobby after I make a call."

She gave him a quick peck on the cheek and retrieved her flowers and boxes of cheesecake. She had thought the walk of shame through the hotel lobby was bad, but the dorm lobby was worse. Half a dozen guys turned from the information desk. Not knowing how much they knew, she smiled, walked to the security door, and juggled her keys to get in. As she entered the stairwell, someone yelled her name.

Kevin, the lead singer of The Feds, grinned as the group started to leave. "Taylor, I enjoyed singing to you last night."

Oh God, they all knew. She realized that the next few weeks were going to be full of embarrassment if she let it. "Stuart wanted to thank you. Your music got me so worked up, and he reaped all the benefit."

Laughing, she went up the stairs, proud of herself for not blushing. When she walked into their room, she found Eva lying across her bed, studying. Eva shut her book and took one of the cheesecake boxes.

"What's the rumor mill say?" Taylor asked as she found a clean pair of jeans and sweatshirt.

Eva lifted the lid and ogled the dessert. "When Cindy started bad mouthing you, I threatened her, and she shut up. That won't be the last though," she said, using her fingers to take a bite. Closing her eyes, she savored the mouthful. "The other thing is the wild bar portion of your night. You've created a frenzy with every guy here, and it's pissing Cindy off even more."

"Uh-oh, I ran into a few guys on the way up."

She quickly filled her in on her romantic date, the dead agent, and having to go to the police station. "How am I ever going to concentrate on exams? My head is still spinning thinking about last night and next weekend. Then there's this death threat. This isn't part of my plan."

"Well, I think your perfect plan sucks," Eva replied, dropping the empty box on the floor.

"How can you say that? That plan has helped me stay focused on what's important," she said, tugging on her black winter boots.

"I know it's important, but it's not written in stone.

Life is about change and taking chances," Eva replied.

"I've always played by the rules."

Eva rolled her eyes. "By bending them, you found a terrific guy who just told you he loves you. Jeez, Taylor, life's too short."

"Any more clichés you want to throw at me?" she asked, folding her arms. "How about *live life to the fullest* or *when you least expect it*?"

Eva laughed. "I like the one your mom always said—*the Chemistry of Love at First Sight*. It's Joe's favorite, too."

She slowly sat on her bed. "It was for me, the moment I saw his blue eyes. Electricity shot through me when he caught me from falling off that stool. Mom would have said it was chemistry, wouldn't she?" She suddenly missed her parents more than she ever had.

Eva hurried to her. "Yeah, I loved those stories she told us," she said, hugging her. "Well, if it happened to you, there's hope for me, right?"

Taylor wiped her eyes and nodded. "When you least expect it."

"You deserve to be happy so no more worries. Joe and I have your back."

Taylor kissed her cheek then grabbed her heavy coat.

STUART WATCHED TAYLOR ENTER THE dormitory with her arms full. As she disappeared, he dialed his cell. "We're running a little late."

"Why? Were you up late?" Reese asked.

"As a matter of fact, we were. Did you find them?"

"I can't wait for the drive home," Reese said, laughing.

"Yeah, yeah, me either. Did you find them?" he asked again.

"Cindy Carter is in an interrogation room. She's waiting for her bigwig lawyer dad. The Feds are still looking for Amber Peppers. She gave a bogus address to WMU when she signed up for your class."

"Does Peter think Amber's the one?" Stuart asked.

"He's been tightlipped. He wants to find out what Cindy knows first," Reese replied. "How much longer are you going to be?"

"Twenty minutes," he replied as he got out of the car.

He slid his cell back into his pocket and readjusted his gun in his shoulder holster. Wearing jeans, a black t-shirt, and his tuxedo jacket, he entered the building and sat on a bench. In the quiet area, he stretched out his legs and leaned his head back against the wall.

After a rough start, they had an incredible night. He couldn't get enough of her openness and passion. When her tentative touch became more daring, he lost all control. Infatuation combined with love. It doesn't get any better than that. She trusted him, and he would never betray that.

He wanted to spend the rest of the day with her, but he knew that wouldn't be the case. She had exams next week, and he needed to finish his semester as well. He dreaded the drive. Reese would have a lot of material to cover.

He observed half-asleep students in their lounge

pants and slippers wandering around. Seeing Taylor, he stood to greet her. She had been crying. Her eyes were red. Did he miss something? She had only been gone a short while.

"What's the matter?" he asked in the middle of the lobby. Students shuffled slowly past them. Looking at his feet, she shook her head. "Please, tell me," he said, lifting her chin.

"My parents would have loved you, too," she whispered.

He kissed the tear on her cheek. They returned to the car. At the station, he tipped the driver and sent him on his way. They were quickly escorted to an observation room where Joe and Reese waited. Joe hugged her and kept his arm around her waist.

Stuart hesitated in the doorway. Reese turned from the glass window and watched his reaction. With a sigh, Stuart set his suitcase next to the door and stood on the other side of Taylor. Joe was smart to be wary of him. Stuart had put her in danger. He understood Joe's protectiveness and cut him some slack, for now. However, he would kick Joe's ass if he ever tried to kiss Taylor on the lips again.

"Joe, this is Stuart Morgan," Reese said, grinning.

Without taking his eyes off Cindy in the other room, Joe snorted. "Yeah, we've met."

"Joey, be nice," Taylor said, taking a step toward the observation window, letting Joe's arm drop from around her waist. At the table, Cindy filed her nails with an Emery board.

Joe looked at Taylor then glared at him. "Why should I be nice? Someone killed a Federal agent, and you're next on the list."

"You think I want this?" Stuart asked, glaring back.

"I think you're a selfish bastard to involve my sister," Joe replied.

"Well, I'm in love with your sister, so deal with it!"

Joe glanced at Taylor. Ignoring them, she stepped closer to the window. "Fine, I'll deal with it!" Joe replied through his clenched jaw.

"Fine," Stuart said, ending the standoff.

Grinning, Reese watched the heated exchange. "Damn, I'm disappointed. You're both packing. I was hoping for a duel at ten paces or something," he said, leaning on the window frame.

"With Reese in the middle," Taylor said. He and Joe nodded at the suggestion.

"What the hell did I do? I saved you from that nerdy professor," Reese said. "Did you tell them that he yanked you right out of your shoe and left a bright red mark on your arm? I'm the frickin' hero here."

"Which professor?" Stuart and Joe asked at the same time.

Taylor sighed. "It's not a big deal."

When the interrogation room door opened, the group turned their attention to Director Bingaman who entered with Stanley Carter, the lawyer daddy. Reese tapped the intercom to hear the discussion. "Is my daughter under arrest, Director?" Stanley asked.

"No, we're hoping for some information."

"Daddy, I already told them that I didn't know Dr. Morgan before and that you drop me off at class every Saturday and Sunday," Cindy said in her high-pitched whine.

Stuart saw Joe and Reese also cringe at her voice.

"I thought you lived on the second floor of Burke's

Hall," Peter said, opening the brown folder in front of him.

"Except for Saturday and Sunday nights," her father replied.

Peter nodded. "Have you ever fired a weapon, Ms. Carter?"

"No, she has not nor do we own one."

"Do you know how to make a bomb, Ms. Carter?"

Cindy looked at her dad. "Um, no?"

Her dad put his hand over hers to stop her from answering anything else. "What are you getting at, Director?"

"I have a two-year-old police report from a fire in your garage," Peter said.

"That fire was an accident!" Cindy screeched.

"No, Ma'am, it was not. The fire marshal stated it was arson. Someone made a Molotov cocktail and threw it against the garage wall."

"Damn," Joe said, "I knew she was unstable, but holy shit."

"It was never proven who did it," Stanley stated.

Peter nodded again. "How do you know Amber Peppers?"

She looked at her father, who nodded for her to answer. "We have two classes together."

"Does she live on campus?"

She shook her head. "She lives in some crap apartment on Burdick Street."

"What's the name of the building?" Peter asked.

"How would I know? You wouldn't catch me in that neighborhood."

"I understand you made quite a scene at Dean Brady's party last night."

Cindy glared at him. "I was supposed to be Dr. Morgan's date. Mrs. Brady, the Dean's wife, set it up, but Taylor Valentine ruined that. The tramp. She acts all high and mighty, but she's nothing more than an orphaned whore. We're supposed to feel sorry for her because her parents are dead. Well, she pretends to be all virginal, but I know that bitch and Joe Roberts have done it. She's the only girl he lets into his room. I heard she earns her money for college by massaging men. Ha. More like blowing men."

Taylor stiffened at the comments. Stuart and Joe immediately stepped closer to her. Peter sat back and let Cindy rant while her dad tried to stop her.

Twirling her long blond hair around her finger, she pouted. "Daddy, I'm of class and money. Why would he want to be with her and not me?"

"Because you're a Crazy, Fire-Loving, Barbie Doll," Reese replied. Covering her mouth, Taylor stifled a laugh as Cindy's dad told her to be quiet.

"Ms. Carter, would you submit a sample of your handwriting?" Peter asked.

"No, she will not," her dad replied, moving his chair back. "We have nothing more to say."

While the group waited for Peter, Stuart squeezed her hand. "Are you okay?"

Taylor nodded. "Couldn't the FBI look at all the student's handwriting from the essay on your exam?"

"That's a great idea. The tests are property of the school," he replied, putting his arm around her before Joe did.

"That's definitely a start," Peter said, shutting the door behind him. "Any other thoughts?"

"Does her alibi for everything check out?" Joe

asked, crossing his arms.

"For the first shooting, yes. For the bomb, the cut brakes, and Agent Martin's death, her alibi is her father."

"Amber has seen Taylor for massage," Joe stated.

Stuart pulled her closer. He couldn't believe Amber was that close to Taylor. If Amber's the one, she had easily infiltrated their lives by posing as a massage patient. He wanted to make Taylor stay with him until they found her. If he demanded it, would she? He doubted it, especially if Joe had a say in the decision.

"On the intake form, her address stated the town of Parchment not Burdick Street in downtown Kalamazoo," she replied.

"Where in Parchment?" Reese asked.

She shook her head. "I don't remember."

"We'll check her paperwork on file at the chiropractor's office," Peter replied. "Good, what else?"

"You're the Fed. Why don't you know what else?" Reese asked.

"I'm smart enough to bring in different perspectives," Peter said.

"Is Amber Peppers her real name?" Joe asked.

"When she signed up for the class, she used a social security number. We're checking her background that way."

"I don't remember her in any of my classes," Taylor said.

Peter nodded. "I've got guys working on that, too."

Running out of questions and answers, Peter leaned against the door. "Okay, this is what we're going to do. Stuart and Reese are going back to Ann Arbor. Taylor, I'm afraid you're stuck with me. I'll escort you back to your dormitory and pick you up in the morning."

"I'm staying with her," Joe said, looking at Stuart.

Knowing she wouldn't leave school, Stuart nodded. He trusted Taylor. What would they have if he didn't?

"Sharing a bed?" Reese asked.

"Why not? Didn't you hear? I'm the campus whore," Taylor replied, walking toward the door.

Peter stepped out of her way and let her leave but stopped the rest from following. "Joe, I want Taylor and her roommate staying in your room. I'll stay down the hall in the empty one. I already cleared it with the school. Any questions?"

"No, just a suggestion," Joe said. "I'd bring disinfectant and your own bedding. That room is covered in DNA."

"You're kidding me?" Peter said, frowning.

"A woman could get pregnant just standing in there."

"God, that is disgusting," Peter said as Reese laughed.

Stuart left the room and found Taylor on a bench by the entrance. "I am so sorry to put you through this," he said.

She smiled. "You're worth it," she replied, touching the side of his face with her fingers.

"I'll be back on Friday to pick you up. Don't worry. With Joe, the pit bull, watching over you, you'll be safe. Besides, he's been looking out for you since third grade."

She smiled. "Eva's the pit bull. Joe's the player."

He laughed. "And what do they call you?"

"I'm the uptight goody-two shoes."

"You are my Passionate Princess, and I am your Adoring Knight."

"Oh my God," Reese said behind him. "You have

a PhD in Civil War History and teach at a prestigious university, yet you spout that sappy stuff."

"I need a barf bag," Joe added. "That lovey-dovey line actually works?"

Stuart groaned while Taylor nodded. "What do you two know about women?" she asked. "Joey, you've never had a steady girlfriend, and I suspect Reese hasn't either."

Stuart chuckled as they walked away without another word. He kissed her one last time then started the slow walk to Reese's car. He tossed his luggage in the back seat and waited in the front.

"So," Reese said, backing out of his parking spot, "where should I start?"

"You can say whatever you want about me. Leave Taylor out of it."

"How can I leave her out? She's the best part," Reese replied.

"Not a bad word about her."

Reese shrugged as he drove toward the interstate. "Pretty slick planning to protect Taylor from having to drop the class."

"I was a boy scout. I like to be prepared."

"Learned from Bob's mistake with my sister, smart," Reese replied. "Joe set you up nicely. He gets points for that."

"He loves her like a sister," Stuart stated.

"Pete and I had a good laugh over the clash and the music selection. I was hoping for a fight."

"I bet you were."

"You got the last laugh though. I saw you flaunt your hotel card. Funny stuff," Reese said.

"I can play, too," he replied, reclining his seat to

stretch out.

"Joe seemed pissed for the rest of the night. Are you sure it's just a brother-sister thing? He kissed her like he was re-staking his claim."

Stuart sighed. He thought that, too. "I understand why he's protective. I'm glad he is."

"Do you think you'll ever get along with him?"

He closed his eyes and smiled. "Sure, I like Joe. He has good instincts. I understand he dropped you to the ground and made you kiss the dirt. Are we done?"

"How was the sex? I bet she's wild in bed. Did she give you a special massage?"

He opened one eye and turned to face him. "We're done."

CHAPTER
thirteen

WEDNESDAY

JOE GUARDED THE SHOWER STALLS on the men's floor while Taylor and Eva washed. Taylor wished this threat would end, so she could feel clean again. Disgusted by the gross hygiene habits of these guys, Eva confronted them. Each denied he was the culprit.

Director Bingaman kept his word and never let Taylor out of his sight. His only breaks were when she was locked in Joe's dorm room. All three of them slept in his small space. She and Eva shared the bed, and Joe found a mattress for the floor. He enjoyed the rumors about them being a threesome. Taylor gave up on her uptight image. Since her date with Stuart, her so-called angelic reputation slid down the crap-covered toilets in the guys' bathroom. It bothered her, but she told herself it shouldn't matter. She'd be graduating soon. She'd stick with her plan as much as she could.

After their showers, they returned to Joe's room. She had her BioChem exam today and her last test for

Analytical Statistics tomorrow. Eva and Joe quickly left for their classes while she waited for Director Bingaman to lock his dorm room door. He had allowed her and Eva to call him *Peter* but had reamed Joe when he tried. She smiled. Joe worked hard to impress Peter, who kept him on his toes with *what if* scenarios. Joe loved having a private tutor.

Peter picked her up promptly at nine-thirty and drove her in his Cadillac Escalade to the student union for breakfast before her exam. He wouldn't allow her to walk anywhere, which was fine with her. December's weather had turned nastier with its cold sleet. In a brown suit and overcoat, he wore his gun and badge for all to see, much different from Agent Martin's surveillance from afar. Peter wanted everyone to know that a Federal agency protected her. When anyone asked why, he sternly shook his head and told them to mind their own business.

At a corner table in the student union, he watched the crowd while they ate. "I have a daughter who's a freshman in college. Over Christmas break, she's going to get a lecture on safety."

She swallowed the last of her bran muffin. "What kind of safety?"

He sipped his coffee. "The guys on that floor work all kinds of conniving angles to get with the women."

She laughed. "You didn't do that when you were in college?"

"That was different," he replied, gathering their trash.

"Yeah, okay," she said, rolling her eyes as she stood to leave.

"These guys seem more underhanded than I ever

was."

"Well, I'd like to think the women are wise to their schemes."

"Are you trying to make me feel better?" he asked, escorting her out of the building and into the cold overcast day.

"Did it work?"

"No," he said, scanning the wet and slippery sidewalks.

At the same time, they spotted Cindy, stalking toward them as if she had a purpose. It was too late to turn away. Wearing an expensive black leather jacket that formed to her body and matching dress boots, she stopped in front of them.

"So you've moved on from professors to Federal agents? I'll see if Dr. Morgan needs consoling," Cindy said.

Taylor smiled. "I'll ask him if he wants your skanky type of consoling when I see him this weekend. I doubt it though. He seems quite content."

"You'll pay for taking him away from me," Cindy said, striking out her hand to slap her.

Peter stepped between them and stopped her hand. "Is that a threat, Ms. Carter? If it is, it's enough to arrest you for harassing Ms. Valentine and Dr. Morgan."

Cindy glared and yanked her arm away. "He's out of your league, Bitch. You'll bore him soon enough," she replied, before spinning on her heels.

Per Peter's orders, Taylor walked quickly to his SUV. Not a problem, as the wind slipped through even the tiniest openings of her heavy winter coat.

"Are you ready for this exam?" he asked, buckling his seatbelt.

She sighed. "I hope so. It's been a little tough concentrating lately."

"You've been a good sport about all of this. Stay away from that girl. She may not be Stuart's stalker, but she has it in for you. Joe was right. She's unstable."

"Do you think Joe will make a good agent?"

"One of the best," he replied. "He'll do well."

"If he gets in. He sent in his application months ago and hasn't heard back. He won't admit it, but he's worried." She watched Peter nod. "You know about his father and mother?"

He glanced at her. "You mean the crooked ex-cop who's still in jail for getting his female contact killed? And his mother who died from a drug overdose when he started his senior year in high school? Yeah, I'm aware of them."

Turning her body toward him, she bit her thumbnail. "Will that keep him from getting in?"

"It may have been an issue, but it's not anymore," he replied.

"What do you mean?"

"I like to be thorough with those helping the FBI, so our lawyers don't have issues down the road. I vetted him. Joe's worked hard to get away from that negativity. He's never even gotten a damn parking ticket," Peter said with a chuckle. "I made a call and a recommendation. I won't let his parents take away what he's accomplished." He smiled at her. "I have his acceptance letter in my breast pocket. If he can cut it at Quantico, I'll make him an offer to work for me."

"Oh, Peter," she said, tearing up. "You won't be disappointed. Thank you." She wiped her eyes. "I guess some really great things have come out of this mess."

"Do me a favor and keep it a secret. I want to put him through his paces a little longer."

She nodded. "I hope you work him really hard."

"Oh, I plan to," he replied, parking in the employee lot.

In class, he sat next to her in the top row, far back corner. Knowing the exam could take a while, he opened his laptop to check his email and work on the case. She sat with her four pencils and waited. Dr. Lee continued to frown at them as he passed the exam to each individual. Peter ignored him until Dr. Lee cleared his throat.

"He's not allowed in here," Lee said, handing her the thick booklet. "Are you trying to cheat?"

"No," she replied quickly, "he, um—"

Peter moved his suit coat away from his gun and thrust his badge toward Dr. Lee's face. "These give me permission to stay."

"What is the meaning of this?" Dr. Lee whispered as the other students focused on their booklets.

"Ms. Valentine is under my protection. I will not be leaving, and I have no idea how I would help her cheat on a Biochemistry exam. If you have any more concerns, I suggest you call Dean Robert Brady."

"I think I will," he replied with a harrumph.

Dr. Lee returned to the front desk and pulled out his cell phone. She flipped through the fifteen-page exam and moaned. She wanted to cry. At the end of the two hours, she handed her test to Dr. Lee who nodded at Director Bingaman behind her.

"How'd you do?" Peter asked in the hall.

"I didn't ace it, but I think I'll pass," she replied. "Any chance we can meet Joe and Eva at Johnny's for a beer."

He laughed. "Yeah. I glanced at some of the questions. It looked like a foreign language to me."

On a Wednesday afternoon, they had the pick of any table in the place. Johnny waved at her from behind the bar while Peter chose a table in the corner. Once happy with the seating arrangements, he ordered a coke for him and a bottle of Miller for her. While they waited for Eva and Joe, she picked at the label.

"Will things ever return to normal?" she asked.

"What's your definition of normal?" he asked, watching a couple of men sitting at the bar.

"I'm not sure anymore. I'll graduate and look for a job. That's part of my plan."

"What's your plan?"

She shook her head. "Eva and Joe make fun of it because it's orderly. They think it's too convenient."

"Nothing wrong with that," he replied.

"I hear a *but* coming," she said, putting her elbows on the table.

"Not from me. I like having a plan even if it changes. My nine-year-old daughter wants to be a rock star's wife."

She laughed. "That's sort of a plan. Do you miss your wife and family?"

He sighed. "My wife and I are separated."

"I'm sorry you have to be here."

"I miss being in the field. Except for my repulsive room, this is a vacation away from the screaming matches. Makes me wish I knew about Stuart's Love at First Sight Theory before I got married."

"What?" she asked, pushing her half-empty bottle toward the middle of the table.

"Damn," he mumbled, "me and my big mouth."

"Peter. Please," she begged.

"Stuart said he fell hard the moment he saw you. It hit him like a bolt of lightning." She covered her mouth as Peter sat forward. "Are you upset over that?"

She shook her head. "I felt the same way," she whispered.

He laughed. "I'm such a sucker for happily ever after."

"Me, too," she replied, smiling.

Joe joined them. "How could you start drinking without me?"

She wiped her eye. "How'd your exams go?"

"Aced all three today," he replied, smugly. He sat next to Peter with his back against the wall.

"What classes did you have?" Peter asked, leaning back in his chair. He looked relaxed, but he scanned the room constantly.

She smiled. "He had Ceramics, Social Dance, and Fencing."

"Hey, I took my hardest classes earlier," he said, imitating Peter's form. "Besides, I may have to go undercover someday, and those classes may come in handy." Peter laughed and shook his head.

"Yeah, undercover as a ceramics teacher," Taylor teased.

Joe nodded. "To bust the drug dealer who's combining the clay with cocaine to get through customs."

"And the fencing and dancing?" Peter asked.

Joe grinned. "I might have to dance with my female contact before saving her from pirates."

"Is Joe telling his undercover stories again?" Eva asked, standing beside the table.

Taylor nodded. "How'd your exams go?"

"Glad they're over," Eva said, plopping into the chair. "It's been four days now. Why haven't you found Amber yet?"

Peter waved the waitress over and sighed. "She's smart enough to stay off the radar. No paper trail, nothing."

"Who would teach her something like that?" Joe asked after they ordered lunch.

Peter nodded. "Go on," he said, sipping his second Coke.

"Well, it's something you'd have to learn—how not to get caught when on the run, how to shoot a gun, how to cut a brake line, how to assemble a bomb. These aren't things you just know how to do."

"Very good, what else?" Peter asked the group.

"She could have learned some of it from books, the internet, or a boyfriend, husband, father, fiancé," Eva added.

"How about someone with a military background?" Taylor offered. "Could that be a connection?"

"Reese, my brother, and I have been over Stuart's military history," Peter replied.

Joe snorted. "I don't like Reese."

"I don't care for his sarcasm, but he helped me when I needed it at the Dean's party," Taylor replied, absently rubbing her arm again.

Joe reluctantly nodded as the waitress brought their burgers. Mentally exhausted from exams and threats, they quietly ate. Peter bought saying it was a productive working lunch. They returned to Joe's room to brainstorm, nap, and study for tomorrow.

AFTER LUNCH, STUART SAT BEHIND his desk and graded the last essay of the semester's classes. With his door open, he saw Reese snoozing on the couch in the outer room. Kay complained twice that he snored too loud. *Some bodyguard,* he thought. He expected Markus and Chase to stop in with the forty graded exams from Kalamazoo. They had taken them to their apartment to grade in the evenings. He anxiously waited to compare the handwriting with the vicious letters.

He had called Taylor twice to wish her well on her exams. He would have liked to talk to her all night, but Reese was listening to his side of the call. Stuart suspected Joe and Eva were listening on her end. Taylor loved him. His heart beat only for her, but he worried about her reaction to the stress. The idea gnawed at him.

He thought about his own stress and his reactions to it—like reliving that Afghan firefight over and over. The numbness, hopelessness, nightmares, and cold sweats continued to plague him. He couldn't put her through the same thing.

Peter had given him updates on Monday and Tuesday. She had no outward threat against her. Peter also told him about the rumors and innuendos surrounding her reputation. Everyone now knew that she dated her professor while in his class and that she worked as a massage therapist. Knowing it upset Taylor, Cindy spun tales of Taylor's sexual expertise as some madam in a massage brothel. Many guys scheduled sessions at the chiropractic office causing her to quit.

All of this tension because of him. It made him nuts he couldn't be there to comfort her and make it right. She never even brought it up when he talked to her. God, what was he doing to her?

"Kay!" he yelled. "Find Chase and Markus now!"

He shoved his chair back, causing a loud bang and a bigger dent in the file cabinet. With his hands on top of his head, he stood in the middle of his cluttered office.

"What's the problem?" Reese asked from the doorway.

"You know what the frickin' problem is!"

"Whoa. Doc. Settle down."

Stuart shoved a pile of essays onto the floor. "You settle the hell down. I need some air." With his coat in his hand, he stalked past him and stood next to Kay's desk. "If they're not here in thirty minutes, I'll fail them and fire you!" He slammed the outer door behind him.

Reese ran to catch up and grabbed his arm. "Stuart. Calm down. This isn't helping."

He shoved Reese against the wall and put his forearm against his neck. Reese gasped for air while he seethed. "Don't tell me what to do! Just frickin' find her! I want my life back!" He released him and set a fast pace to the gym.

Stuart lifted weights and punched the heavy weight bag until his hands became numb. After a long shower, he jammed his sweaty workout clothes back into his locker. He knew he needed to apologize to Kay and probably to Reese, too, but he didn't feel like it. With a heavy heart, he left the gym. Reese was leaning against the building waiting for him.

"You feel any better?" Reese asked, zipping his heavy coat to his neck, as he stepped into the wind.

"No," he said, walking back to the office.

"You made Kay cry," Reese said.

"What about you? Did I make you cry?"

"Nah, I'm tougher than you think. You need to apologize to her."

He stopped. "Are you telling me what to do?"

"No, just making a suggestion. Here. This might help," Reese said, handing him a yellow rose wrapped in plastic. "I stopped at the convenience store next door."

He sighed and took the flower. "Just when I want to shoot you, you do something nice."

"I'm complicated."

When they entered the outer office, Kay sat stiffly in her chair. "They were here, and then they left," she said quickly. "They put the essays on your chair."

"Thank you, and I'm sorry," he said, handing her the flower.

She smelled it. "I understand, Dr. Morgan," she replied, before frowning. "Please, don't be mad, but another letter came. I, um, I wasn't thinking and opened it." With tears in her eyes, she waited.

"Where is it?" he asked quietly.

"On your desk. I know Director Bingaman said not to touch them, but—"

"Kay, it's all right. I'll explain it to him. Why don't you take the rest of the afternoon off?"

She nodded while Reese entered his office ahead of him and used two pencil erasers to hold the letter open. "Damn."

"What now?" Stuart asked. He moved the exams from his chair to the corner of his desk next to the pile that Kay had picked up for him. Using the pencil erasers, Reese turned it around to face him.

Enjoy your happiness while you can. I am patiently waiting to pounce. You will feel my pain. She won't love you once we're finished with her.

The bile rose in his throat. "She has help now," he whispered as he looked at the envelope.

Addressed to Dr. Morgan, it had a Kalamazoo postmark. The return address had no name, just Burdick Street. He remembered that at the police station Cindy had said Amber lived on Burdick Street. He held it up to Reese who filled in Peter on his cell.

"That bitch is toying with us," Stuart said.

Reese left the room while still on the phone. That couldn't be good. Stuart sat back in his chair and sorted through the stack. He flipped to the last page of Amber's exam. Without reading the content, he put the letter next to the exam. The handwriting looked close. Then, he saw her last sentence on the test.

Yes, I'm the one. You'll both die.

"Reese!"

Off his cell, Reese read where he pointed. "Well, we're on the right track," Reese said, putting the exam in a clear plastic bag. "Her prints may give us a real name and background. I can't imagine her not having a criminal record."

"Let's go," Stuart said, shoving his chair under his desk.

"Where?"

"Kalamazoo. Taylor's the target. We'll gather the troops. Amber will try to distract them and grab her. I will not let that happen."

Reese held up his hand to stop him. "Peter doesn't want you there. He said one target per city."

"He expects me to wait for something bad to happen? You call him back!"

CHAPTER
fourteen

IN THE MORNING, PETER LET her return to her room for clean clothes. He stood outside with his badge prominently displayed, scaring half the women on the floor and intriguing the others. Taylor had heard that some of the sophomores went gaga for the daddy-figure with a gun. All week, they had taken turns, knocking on his door throughout the night. He had dismissed them and turned into a grouch from the lack of sleep. She had teased him about being a player like Joe.

Smiling, she stretched out on her bed. She didn't think she'd miss it so much. She was proud of herself for getting through her exams without a total meltdown. Peter had upped her security after they confirmed that Amber was the one threatening them. He and Joe never let her out of their sight for a second. Peter had other agents hunting Amber down. Her skills put them to the test.

Taylor had taken her last exam with Peter by her

side yesterday. He mumbled about feeling stupid. With school over, she could finally concentrate on Stuart before diving in to the next part of her plan. He would be picking her up around lunch today. She couldn't wait to hug and kiss him. To be alone with him at his apartment sounded heavenly. Dorm life wasn't as fun as it used to be.

"Taylor!" Peter yelled. "I'm coming in!" The door flew open. She hopped up from the bed while he raced to the window. With his cell in one hand, he pushed the curtain aside with the other to look at the area below.

"What's going on?" she asked, wrapping her arms around her abdomen.

"My agent saw her walking through the student parking lot next to the building."

"Did he catch her?"

"No, but she can't get far on foot," he replied. "I'm going to help him. Are you okay with that?"

"Of course, find her and end this."

"Don't leave the secured part of this building."

She nodded. "Peter, please find her before she gets away."

He hesitated for a second then rushed for the exit. She blew out a breath and answered her ringing cell.

"What time are you leaving?" Eva asked.

"I'm not sure. Peter just left. They're chasing after Amber now."

"I'll be there after I finish this test. It should only take an hour."

"Well, I'll be doing laundry for this weekend."

She'd keep her word to Peter. The basement was a part of the secure area. She put her laundry basket, full from a week's worth of dirty clothes, down on the floor.

After tossing her liquid Gain and a baggy full of quarters on top of the clothes, she grabbed her keys and stuck them into the pocket of her well-worn jeans. Heading down the hall and hoping for a few open washers, she passed Cindy. They ignored each other. Fine by her, she had better things to think about.

Taylor didn't bring any reading material. She deserved time for contemplation. Humming, she took the stairwell to the basement. After unlocking the main hallway entrance, she walked to the third door and peeked through the slit to the empty laundry room. *Great*. She could use three washers at once and finish in no time.

Using her key again, she held the door open with one foot and slid the basket inside with the other. The gray cement room had five sets of washers and dryers around the walls with a couple of utility chairs and two six-foot long tables in the center of the room.

Letting the door slam shut, she set her basket on a table and opened three washers. Forty minutes went quickly while she thought about graduation, Stuart, and the next steps in her plan. As she carefully set the folded piles into her basket, she heard a key in the lock. Four unfamiliar men walked into the room. She thought she knew all the guys in their dormitory.

"Hi, guys. The room's all yours," she said, picking up the basket.

"You're not leavin," the beefiest one said. His mammoth chest stretched his black t-shirt to the point of ripping.

"What?" She was alone in a locked room with four men, and they had nothing pertaining to laundry. In a cold sweat, she shuddered.

"We're here to teach you a lesson," the same guy said. If he were green, he'd be the Hulk. His three greasy minions weren't big, but they looked strong. The thick-necked Hulk leaned back against the only exit while the other three slowly surrounded her.

"What lesson?" Her shaking hands set the basket back on the table.

The big guy did all the talking. "A lesson of what happens when you flaunt your body."

She forced a smile. "Oh, yeah?" Brushing her hair from her face, she sauntered toward him. "I bet there are a few things I could teach you." She hoped she sounded seductive.

He grinned. "Like what?"

She placed her hands on his massive chest and smiled up at him. "How about this?"

Using all the strength she could muster, she kneed him in the groin. His eyes bulged, and he fell over moaning. She quickly reached for the door handle, but the other three yanked her back. She let out a scream so loud she scared herself.

They slammed her onto the table, knocking the air from her lungs. Gulping for a breath, she hit one in the stomach. He let go, and she struggled against the others. She kicked, punched, and shrieked. One held her arms above her head. The others tugged at her jeans. They ripped.

What were they going to do? She knew, but would they kill her, too? *Stuart, where are you? I need you.* Her throat became raw from screaming. Would anyone even hear her?

One of them growled, "Shut her up."

A hand squeezed her neck while another covered

her mouth and nose. Her mind screamed, then stopped.

AFTER GETTING HIS CAR BACK, Stuart made Reese follow in his own. He wanted to be alone with Taylor and not let Reese torture her with his insane questioning about their date night. He found a spot close to the building and hurried toward the lobby. Eva joined him. Before she said a word, they saw Joe race out of the stairwell and through the security door toward them.

"Where's Taylor?" Joe demanded by the front desk. "She left her phone in her room," he said, holding it.

Stuart's chest tightened. "I don't know. I just got here."

"I got off my cell with the Director. He's chasing Amber and left her in her room," Joe replied.

"Well, I talked to her an hour ago, and she said she was going to do laundry," Eva replied.

"Shit," Joe said, turning to look at the nervous greeter behind the desk.

Stuart read Joe's mind. "Eva, call security. Joe, where's the laundry room?"

Joe led him back through the security door and down to the basement level. They froze at the sound of a curdling scream. Joe used his key in the stairwell for the basement hallway and struggled with the door.

Stuart followed him down the corridor. Through the slit, they saw Taylor motionless on the table with three guys surrounding her. Joe scrambled to get his key in the lock. One of the guys said she was dead. Stuart flashed back to combat. *Wounded men shouting. Others lying dead. Gunfire tearing through his ears.* His mouth went dry. He was dizzy and could feel the pounding in his chest.

"Something's jammed inside it," Joe said as his hands shook.

Stuart pinched the bridge of his nose to clear his mind. Taylor needed him. "On the count of three, we'll break the damn door down," he said, willing himself to breathe.

As one, they broke through. They got in a few swings before the guys scattered out the door. His concern lay with Taylor. He rushed to her and checked her pulse.

"Joe, it's faint. Call nine-one-one."

Seeing red marks around her neck, his mind raced with murderous scenarios. He was pretty sure Joe would be his accomplice. While they waited for an ambulance, he monitored her pulse and breathing.

He gently whispered "I love you" in her ear. He was anything but serene. As he begged God to save her, he condemned those bastards to hell.

TAYLOR HEARD A DISTANT VOICE calling. She couldn't quite make it out. It sounded like Stuart, but this Stuart sounded upset; not her Stuart, who was always calm and confident.

"Taylor, please, wake up," this Stuart said. "Guys, she's coming around."

She opened her eyes and swallowed. The saliva sizzled against her dry throat.

"Hey, Darlin'. How you feelin'?"

Her voice wouldn't work. As she tried to get her bearings, she slowly looked around. Her freshly folded piles were scattered all over the filthy floor. When she saw the Hulk sprawled out in the midst of her clothes, she shivered.

"Do you remember?" Stuart asked, helping her sit up. He put his coat over her shoulders.

She could only nod as Joe and a security guard searched the cement floor by the door for something. He looked over and smiled.

"You like being the center of attention, don't you?" Joe said.

"No," she whispered.

She sat in the chair Stuart offered. She hurt all over. Her arm felt heavy as she moved her hair from her face. Did she run a marathon? She was so tired.

"How did those guys get in?" Joe asked.

She swallowed again, even that hurt. "They walked in while I was trying to leave."

"What did they say?" Stuart asked, pulling his chair closer to hold her hand.

"They said I flaunt my body. I don't do that, do I?"

Stuart put his arm around her. "No, Honey, you're not like that. You've done nothing wrong."

She looked down at her shredded jeans. "What did they do to me?" She cried. "I kicked and screamed. One of them put a hand around my neck and mouth. I don't remember after that." She hugged herself and rocked back and forth.

"Taylor, it's okay. Really," Stuart said.

"I don't know how long I was out."

He knelt beside her, so she could see his face. "Darling, when you stopped screaming, Joe and I were at the door. Part of someone's key was broken off in the lock. You were only out a short time."

"How'd you find me?"

While the security guard talked on his two-way radio, Joe said, "We heard your big mouth screaming. Then the screams stopped." He paused for a moment to clear his throat. "When we heard the words 'she's dead,' we went nuts and broke down the door, in one try I might add."

Stuart continued, "We hurried to you and didn't even see the big guy until he tried to get up. Joe clocked him good."

"Excuse me," the guard said, after getting off his radio. "The EMTs are here and want to check you out upstairs. I'll stay with this guy until the police can get him."

Stuart and Joe helped her to the door. She had gotten very stiff. She kissed them both on the cheek. "My heroes. I love you both."

"But me more, right, Taylor?" Joe asked, grinning.

Before she took the second step, Stuart swept her up and carried her the rest of the way. "I want you checked out now."

In the lobby, security guards talked with students, others looked on, two EMTs rushed through the door, and police officers tried to establish some order. With Reese supervising outside, more officers handcuffed and stuffed the three guys into a police car. Eva ran to her as Stuart set her on her feet. Taylor held his arm to steady herself. She needed his warmth. Even with his coat, she trembled.

"Taylor, did you let those guys in the door?" Joe asked.

"No, they had a key," she whispered.

"Someone gave them a key. Someone knew where Taylor was. Someone with an axe to grind," Eva said.

Taylor gasped and pulled Stuart closer. She told them about passing Cindy on the way to the laundry room.

"Miss, I'd like to get you checked out now," the paramedic said.

"Where the hell are the Feds?" Joe yelled.

"Eva, stay with her," Stuart said. "Honey, I'll be right back. I need to make a phone call."

"And I need to chat with our greeter," Joe said.

After checking her out, the EMT left for the basement while Eva talked to a police officer. Taylor went over to where Stuart yelled into his cell. She still wore his warm coat that smelled like his cologne. Comforted by it, she pulled it tighter around her. She cringed as students stared and whispered. Her ears were ringing from the gossip.

"Get over here now!" Hanging up, Stuart reached for her hand.

"Who was that?"

"Bob needs to be here, especially if Cindy had something to do with this. Peter's on his way."

Joe's voice got louder as he yanked the greeter up and over the top of the counter. "You will tell the Feds all of that!" he yelled, hauling him toward the door.

While a security guard tried to break up the crowd, the other two brought up the staggering Hulk in handcuffs from the basement. He was still in pain.

Good. She slid behind Stuart who looked confused.

"You said that if you took out the head ringleader the rest would crumble. Not so," Taylor whispered.

"You gave us enough time to find you. What did you do?" he asked.

"I sack-tapped him with my knee." Joe had taught her the self-defense technique at the start of college. He also made her swear never to do it to him.

"That's my girl," he said, hugging her.

Walking in, Peter flashed his badge and reestablished a ranking order. At his side, Joe filled him in, quickly talking with his hands. Peter nodded and commanded the room. Stuart waved Joe over to them.

"I'm taking Taylor to her room. She doesn't need this crowd gawking," Stuart told him.

Joe nodded while Eva returned from talking to a few of the students. "I'm going with you," Eva said.

On their dorm floor, Cindy stepped out of her room and pulled her door shut. She blocked their way. "Taylor, you look a fright. Gee, Professor, you really ought to train your whore better," she said, looking her up and down. "Are you bored with her yet?"

Taylor slapped Cindy so hard her head snapped to the side. "Bitch," Taylor bit out, "you will go to jail for this." Taylor's body started to shake with anger and anxiety.

Cindy glowered at her for a second before turning to Eva. "What is she talking about?" she asked in a sweet, innocent voice.

"Cindy, you forgot to lock your door," Eva said, just as sweet.

"No, I didn't," she cooed.

Eva turned the knob and pushed open her door.

"You know, Stuart, the key that those guys used broke off in the lock. They found the other piece in one of the guy's pockets, so it'll be easy to trace the serial numbers to the original owner."

Cindy's face paled, emphasizing the bright red handprint. "But Amber said it would work."

Fuming, Stuart gently pushed Eva and Taylor to their room to avoid a fistfight. He quickly called Peter. He tried hard to keep an even tone to his voice, but his knuckles turned white from gripping his phone. Taylor thought for sure his cell would crumble to dust. He kept his back to her throughout the call. After hanging up, he took a few deep breaths before calmly turning around.

Eva, the mother hen, took over. "I'll get your clothes from downstairs while you take a hot shower. Stuart, you stand guard."

They watched her leave. "I still want you to come with me to my apartment," he said.

"I don't want to stay here," she mumbled.

Stuart checked the shower stalls and gave the all clear. She told him he could wait in the room. He refused and stood outside the shower door. The hot water eased some of the tension. Exhausted, she slowly slipped on her brown terry cloth robe and towel dried her hair. Stuart carefully guided her back to the room where five more men waited. For so many people in one small space, it was very quiet. Having already packed Taylor's suitcase, Eva ushered her through the maze of men to sit on the bed.

"Taylor, can we go over what happened?" Peter whispered. He seemed even more upset than she was. Usually impeccably dressed, he had loosened his tie. His suit jacket lay across her desk chair, and his unsnapped gun holster angled awkwardly against his hip.

She hoped he didn't blame himself. It was her fault for being so stupid, for not thinking things through. Joe would lecture her for sure. He frequently did when it came to safety. *Don't walk alone on campus at night. Don't open your door to anyone. Stay on the defense.* Eva typically rolled her eyes at him, but they followed all of his rules. Stuart would probably lecture her, too.

She sighed and nodded slowly. The Dean, Joe, and another agent she didn't recognize sat on Eva's bed across from them. The mattress dipped, almost touching the floor. Reese leaned against the closet door while Stuart positioned himself by the other. Peter knelt beside her and held her hand. The other agent took notes while Eva brushed her hair.

Taylor told them everything she knew. She started with Cindy in the hallway, the guys in the laundry room, and things going dark. Stuart looked composed, but he clenched his fists throughout her story. Eva took her turn, ending with Cindy's unlocked door, her pale face, and Amber's apparent role. Joe and Stuart also told their version.

With all the facts, the men stepped into the hallway to discuss the next step. Taylor, Eva, and Joe hugged and renewed their promise. They would graduate together and stay close forever. After they left, she found a stack of clothes on her dresser that Eva had set out for her to wear. She shut the closet door and changed into the sweats and t-shirt. In the full-length mirror on the door, she looked at the red marks on her neck. She could have died today. After tugging the light bulb chain, she sat in the dark and pulled her knees to her chin. She squeezed her eyes shut. This wasn't part of her plan.

IN THE EMPTY HALLWAY, THE men formed a tight circle and put their heads together. "That bitch set Cindy up," Reese said.

Stuart seethed. "Her dad had better not get her out of this."

Peter looked at his agent. "I want more men on this. That schemer pulled us away, so Cindy could get to Taylor." The agent nodded. "Arrest Cindy Carter and throw her ass in jail."

Joe and Eva joined the group. "She's changing," Eva said. "She doesn't look good."

Stuart groaned. "She's coming with me to Ann Arbor," he said, waiting for Joe to fight him on it.

Joe nodded sadly. "I'm going to mill around to see what else turns up."

"I'll help you, Joey," Eva whispered.

Leaving for the lobby, Eva reached for Joe's hand. Peter and his agent left in the other direction. Bob and Reese waited in the hall while Stuart entered her room.

Not seeing her by the bed, he opened the dark closet and found her huddled in the corner. What had he done? His heart wrenched in pain at what he had put her through. He crawled to her as she stared past him.

"Come on, Darling. Let's get your boots and coat," he whispered. He pulled her along. Numbly, she followed. In the hall, Reese took the suitcase from him. "I need to get her away from here," Stuart said.

"Let me go down first, and I'll draw the crowd away

from you," Bob said.

"I'll follow you back and watch the apartment," Reese added.

He nodded and escorted her to his car without incident. Reese put the suitcase in the trunk while Stuart helped her sit in the front.

"Can I rest for a little while?" she mumbled.

He covered her with his coat. "Yes, my love," he whispered.

He had turned this vibrant young woman into a walking zombie. She not only loved and trusted him, she put her life in danger because of him. Joe was right. He was a selfish bastard. As he drove, he thought about almost losing her. He could still lose her. She could easily leave him. He silently pleaded for her to stay. If she'd let him, he'd spend a lifetime making it up to her.

"HEY DARLIN'," STUART WHISPERED. "LET'S get out and stretch."

Taylor sat up to look around. On the way to Ann Arbor, they had stopped at a roadside rest area. Standing stiffly, she gave him his coat, and they walked toward the restrooms. She pushed her memories of earlier to the back of her mind. Stuart made it easier for her. He had a knack for calming her panic that bubbled so close to the surface.

By the time they pulled into the parking lot of his apartment, they were laughing and teasing again. She looked forward to seeing his home. He guided her down the first floor hallway to a door on the right. His two-bedroom apartment had an open floor plan. She could see the living room straight ahead and the kitchen with dining area to the right. Opposite the front door, a slider faced the back of his building with three doors to the left of the living room. He pointed out that the first door nearest the front was his bedroom, the middle door the bathroom, and the last door his office.

While he put her suitcase in his bedroom, she went exploring. She wandered into his living area with white walls and two small tan leather loveseats with a coffee table between them. No TV. Stuart returned and sat on a stool by the kitchen counter. On his coffee table, she spotted newspapers and a college football magazine. *Not surprising.* She peeked out his slider's heavy drapes. A bare, three-foot square patio was next to a narrow alley by a brick warehouse. *It wasn't much of a view.*

She fixed the curtains and turned back around. His round table had only two plain wooden chairs. The small kitchenette with a u-shaped counter opened to the large room. Stuart quietly watched her. He had only a couple of cupboards with a refrigerator and microwave. The countertops were bare except for an empty dish drainer.

He put his elbows on the counter. "Interesting?" he asked.

"Very," she replied, looking at the outside of his refrigerator.

It, too, was bare except for a University of Michigan calendar magnet right in the middle. She opened the door to find cans of Coke, six bottles of Miller Lite, and the basic staples found in most refrigerators: butter, ketchup, mayo, and a half-empty gallon of milk. She shut the door and smiled, saying nothing. In his freezer, she found some Swanson pot pies, a couple Hungry Man TV dinners, and two ice cube trays. Both trays had only a couple of cubes. Smiling again, she took out the trays and emptied them. After refilling both, she carefully set them back in the freezer.

"You are very funny," he said.

She enjoyed this. It helped her relax. He made no further comment, so she continued her quest of Stuart's living habits. She opened his first cupboard to find glasses, plates, and bowls all in sets of four.

Still not commenting, she opened the second cupboard. This one surprised her. It contained six different boxes of cereal upside down on the bottom shelf. They ranged from Cocoa Krispies to healthy granola. She pulled out the Fruit Loops and gave the box a shake.

Smiling, she pointed to the prize on the box. "You take them out right away, don't you?"

Laughing, he nodded and said it was easier to get to the prize from the bottom. He had been doing it since he was a kid. It had become a habit even without a prize. Looking around the large room, she didn't see any Christmas decorations, plants, pictures, or paintings on the wall. It was clean and plain.

She leaned on the counter across from him. "Do you even live here?"

He laughed. "In these rooms, no. Most of the time, I'm in my office or bedroom."

She kissed his nose. "I can see you spending a lot of time in your office but in your bedroom? It makes me wonder."

"Makes you wonder what?"

"It makes me wonder who you're spending

time with in your bedroom," she replied jokingly, but there was a hint of concern. She knew he had been in relationships and dated other women.

"A bit of jealousy?"

"Yes."

She backed away and walked toward his office door. She could have lied, but it bothered her. How was she compared to them? Yeah, that bugged her.

This room definitely had that lived-in look. Piles of papers and reports cluttered his desk. He had four bookcases. Two held textbooks and binders, she guessed for all his class lecture notes. Military books about the Civil War as well as WWI, WWII, and the Korean War lined another. Sci-fi books packed the fourth bookcase. She noticed many were by the same authors—Robert Jordan, David Eddings, and Stephen King.

She smiled. "Are you a Sci-Fi nerd?"

"I prefer the term *geek*."

Taking a closer look at his messy desk, she found a couple of framed photos next to his computer. A studio picture of an older couple was obviously his parents. Stuart had the same brilliant blue eyes as his mom and his dad's smile.

"You and your dad have the same sense of humor?"

He chuckled. "Yeah, it drives my mom nuts."

She set that one down and picked up the other. This one was a similar studio picture of a younger couple with two young boys.

"Your sister?"

"That's Mary with her husband, Dewayne. Jake's seven and Riley's five," he replied, still leaning against the doorframe.

She set that picture down then kissed him lightly

as she walked past. Leaving the bathroom for another time, she walked to his bedroom. She had no idea what to expect.

"Okay, lover boy, let's check out your inner sanctum."

Just inside, she stopped. The walls were the same plain white. In light oak, his nightstand, dresser, and huge cabinet matched. His bed stood out in the room. A rustic patterned comforter with matching bed skirt, pillow shams, and various pillows looked masculine and very romantic. The bed was probably the nicest part of his apartment. Was this his approach to get women into his bed? He said he loved her, and she believed him. Her head told her those women were before he met her, but her heart wondered how many others had been romanced in this beautifully made bed.

She turned away from it. She didn't want to think of that now. Taking a deep breath, she tried to get her emotions in check. After everything that had happened today, she didn't want her mind to wander too much into his romantic past. Stuart watched her. His eyes narrowed, his expression less amused. She quickly asked about the huge cabinet opposite the bed.

"Open it," he replied.

She pulled on the center cabinet doors to find a large flat-screen TV. The two side cabinets were full of movies—westerns, action, sci-fi, and comedies. The bottom drawer surprised her. She found video games and units with controller accessories.

She laughed. "You and Joe have more in common than you think. It's an addiction with him. Don't let him see those. He'll want to move in."

"Do you play?"

"I beat Joe once. He didn't talk to me for a week, so I'm not allowed to play anymore." She closed his drawer and checked out his movies again. From behind, he wrapped his arms around her waist. She sighed and relaxed against him.

"I thought tonight we would order in and watch some movies."

"That sounds perfect," she whispered.

In the bathroom, she took the opportunity to look in his medicine cabinet. She returned as he set up the bedroom with drinks and plates on a couple of trays from his closet.

"You find my fungal ointment in there?" He laughed.

"Nope, but I haven't checked out your nightstand yet."

"Only condoms in there."

For her or for all the other women he brought home? "How about this one?" she asked, switching the topic. "*The Philadelphia Story* is my favorite Cary Grant movie. I haven't seen it in years. My parents loved it, too."

"Great," he replied as the intercom buzzed. She jumped on the bed and propped up the pillows while Stuart talked to the pizza guy.

"Not your usual one person order, Professor. You got company?" he asked, looking around.

"That is none of your business, Randy." Stuart tried to block him from seeing the bedroom. Too late, the guy saw her moving the pillows around on the bed. She gave him a little wave.

Randy stammered. "Oh, wow, okay then, enjoy your night."

Shaking his head, Stuart, carrying their pizza and salads, walked back into the room.

"Let's see how quickly the rumors fly on this campus," she said as he set the boxes down on the trays. "You don't have any Cindys around here, do you?" She tried to sound light but failed.

He rushed to comfort her. He held her until something poked her back. She wiped her eyes and pulled out a pillow with a Sears's price tag. He ripped it off. "I thought I got all of these."

"What do you mean?" she asked.

"Well, I bought the whole bed set and pillows last week. The woman said it was romantic but masculine. I thought you'd like it."

She hugged him fiercely. "I do. I love it, and I love you."

"Good. Let's eat."

She enjoyed the pizza and movies. It was just what she needed. Stretched out next to him, she laid her head on his chest. His hand gently caressed her shoulder. She flinched. After pulling up her sleeve, she saw all the bruises. Flashing back to the struggle, she cried again.

"Every time I see my neck I think about almost dying today. I was so afraid. I prayed that you'd find me."

"Thank God I did," he said, gently hugging her. "When you stopped screaming, my heart skipped beats. Seeing you not moving and that guy's hand around your neck, my heart stopped altogether. I thought I'd lose my mind when one of them said you were dead." He stopped for a moment. "I vowed that if I could get to you in time I would protect you for as long as you'd let me."

On top of Stuart's new bedding, she fell asleep with his arms wrapped tightly around her.

CHAPTER
fifteen

SATURDAY

"HEY, YOU STILL FEEL LIKE going to the game? We can always watch it on TV," Stuart said, lying next to her on top of the comforter.

She abruptly sat up. "Are you nuts? We're going."

Wearing blue scarves, hats, and mittens, they walked down the shoveled sidewalks. In the sunny thirty-degree weather, Reese trailed after them from a distance. With an hour and a half until kickoff, traffic lined the streets. Tailgaters were out in full force. Wonderful smells of spicy chili, burgers, and steaks filled the air. Grilled ribs made her mouth water. With the promise of junk food in the stadium, they continued the walk. Excitement filled the air. She heard Michigan's and Ohio's fight songs along the way with a lot of friendly, and not so friendly, ribbing.

At the major intersection next to the stadium, a traffic cop on a podium with a megaphone directed cars and pedestrians. He poked fun at Ohio State fans.

It was all chaotically organized. Venders were selling programs, foam Wolverine claws, and cold weather gear.

Her mouth dropped in the entryway, which opened into the huge sunken arena. They looked down onto the field. An awesome sight. The crowd poured in. On the field, players on both teams stretched, and the kickers practiced punts, testing the wind direction.

Their bench seats were below the press box midway down. Across from them, the players, coaches, and marching band used the tunnel to get onto the field. In the stands, fans surrounded it hoping to touch their favorite players. Airplanes with advertising banners were already flying around the stadium. Seeing the band high-stepping gave her goose bumps. When they started the Michigan fight song, the crowd sang with fists in the air.

The stadium collectively cheered every offensive down and every defensive stop. They were on their feet most of the time. Stuart clearly enjoyed the game, yelling as much as she was. They finally knew they were winning when Michigan intercepted a pass and ran it in for a touchdown. The crowd went berserk. Stuart grabbed her face and tenderly kissed her, so different from the emotion of the game.

The postgame fascinated her, too. While fans ran onto the field, the camera crews were all over it, interviewing senior players and coaches. The band played as the crowd dispersed. While standing, she and Stuart watched everything at once. Everyone in their section left for the field or somewhere warmer, leaving them alone in the stands.

Stuart held her hand and went down on one knee. "Taylor, I can't wait any longer," he said. "Marry me. Be my wife."

"Oh, Stuart," she whispered.

From his pocket, he pulled out an antique diamond ring. "My life means nothing unless you're part of it."

"Where did you get this?"

"My grandmother," he replied.

Nodding, she held out her left hand. She loved him with all of her heart. She trusted him to save her, and he did. He slipped the ring on her finger and engulfed her in a hug.

"Let's celebrate. I want the whole world to know," he said. Reese waited outside the stadium and followed them as they walked arm-in-arm back to his apartment. "Are you up for dinner at my local hangout?"

"Sounds good. I'm starving," she replied.

"We'll stop at the apartment first. I'll make sure we can get in."

She washed her face and hands, reapplied her makeup, and smoothed down her hair. Hat head was almost as bad as bed head. *I can't wait to tell Eva and Joe,* she thought, as she admired her ring.

"That was odd," Stuart said, setting down his cell phone.

"What was?"

"I talked to the owner Mario of this Italian sports bar down the street. I'm a regular, so I asked if he could reserve me a table. He said, 'Of course, for you and friend to celebrate.' But I didn't say anything about you."

"Maybe he thinks to celebrate Michigan's win."

"That could be."

Once again, Reese trailed them as they walked the two blocks to the restaurant. Mario met Stuart at the door and steered them past a number of people waiting in line.

"Come. Come. Best table for you and fiancée. I bring bottle of wine on house," he replied, before leaving.

"What's going on? People are staring and smiling at us. Is my hair sticking up again?" she asked.

"Oh, no," Stuart said, looking over her shoulder. "Remember when I said I wanted the whole world to know? We're on SportsCenter. Look." He pointed to the big screen behind her.

By the angle, it looked as if a cameraman from the field saw Stuart on one knee proposing and caught it on film.

"Oh my God. I look horrible. My nose is so red from the cold and crying," she replied.

"Thank God you can't read my lips from that angle," he said, laughing. "How could I live down being so sappy? Reese and Joe would have a field day."

"It was romantic and sweet," she replied as Mario poured them each a glass. "I think you've topped our first date."

During their dinner, two professors and three students came over to congratulate them. Reese left them alone but scowled from his seat at the bar. She didn't understand why he was so upset although she thought maybe he was still mad that Stuart didn't have a third ticket. Reese could have bought one, but he didn't want to pay from his own pocket.

Walking back to the apartment, she observed, "It's never dull with you. I thought history professors were supposed to be boring."

"Apparently not," he replied. "Now, before I turn my phone back on, how many messages will there be?"

On his couch, he showed her that he had eight. He

put it on speaker. The first message from Eva and Joe said that she left her cell in their dorm room and that they're always the last to know. Three other messages were from Stuart's colleagues and one from a woman named Kay, who didn't sound happy for them. Taylor made a mental note to ask about her later.

His sister, Mary, called to warn him that he made their mom cry. Stuart laughed. Taylor wasn't sure it was all that funny. His mom cried and carried on about something in the next message. Before Taylor could ask for a translation, Stuart deleted her message halfway through. She bit her lip. The Dean left the last one. He gave his congrats and said Doris was jealous of their romance. Then he turned serious, saying there were developments and to call him. That sobered them instantly.

"Everything will work out," Stuart said. "You call Eva and fill her in. I don't want her mad at me. I'll call Bob and my parents." He kissed her cheek as he left for his office. She used his house phone that sat on the kitchen counter.

"Hey, I saw the rock. It's antique, isn't it?" Eva asked.

"You could tell?"

"The clip runs with all the football updates. We tried to read your lips," Eva said, laughing.

"And could you?"

"No, so fill me in."

She sighed with relief. She summed up her proposal and asked for the news. Cindy's dad is claiming mental breakdown due to stress from finals and graduation. The Dean expelled her, and criminal charges are pending. Cindy's dad will try to commit her instead. All those guys will go to jail.

"I just want it to be over," Taylor said.

"I know, Babe. Hang in there. I'm your maid of honor, right?" Eva asked.

"Of course, but we haven't talked about any of that yet."

"I'm buying a bunch of brides' magazines, so we can go over them when you get back."

After talking to Eva, she put her ear to Stuart's office door. She could tell Stuart wasn't happy talking to Bob. She went to his bedroom to change but couldn't find any pajamas. Apparently, Eva didn't think she needed any. She snooped in his dresser and found a gray t-shirt with a big Michigan winged helmet on it.

Before putting on the shirt and clean undies, she took a quick shower. Through the mist, she saw darker bruises on her neck and arms. She was beat up. After drying her hair, she listened at his office door again. This time, he sounded calmer, and she heard him laugh a couple of times. It must be his parents, a good sign. She worried over his mom's message and the fact he deleted it. She'd have to ask before she stressed over it too much.

Hearing the banging on the front door, she peeked through the tiny security hole. An angry Reese stared back. *Did he enter the main lobby door with someone?* She cracked the door.

"Let me in. Now," he demanded, pushing the door open.

AFTER KISSING TAYLOR'S CHEEK, STUART dialed his cell and sat on the papers covering his desk. Bob told him about her daddy committing Cindy to get out of jail time. The agent had lost Amber by the library. Bob also said Peter would stay in Kalamazoo to head up the search. Stuart set his cell aside. He would wear his gun all the time. Amber was a murderer. If she came near them, he wouldn't hesitate to kill her. He slid the drawer open and set his gun on the desk next to him. He dialed his parents. *Better now than later.* His mom answered on the first ring.

"Oh, Stuart, we couldn't believe it when we saw you on the television and proposing, no less. I didn't even know you were dating anyone. Your sister and I have been gushing over the romance of it."

He laughed. "I didn't plan to have it broadcast."

"She's adorable. When can we meet her? What's she like? How'd you meet?"

"It's a long story, Mom."

"Well, at least give me her name." She turned away from the phone and spoke to someone else. "John, it's Stuart. I'm asking him right now," she said in the background.

He shook his head and smiled. "Her name's Taylor, Mom," he said as he heard the phone shift hands.

"Son, it's Dad. You made the rest of us look bad. Who can top a romantic proposal on television? Was it like I said?"

He laughed again. "Yeah, Dad, like a bolt of lightning. My hair stood on end."

"Did she feel it, too?"

Stuart stared at his bookcase. He didn't know. Less

enthused, he answered, "Well, she accepted." He heard muffled voices again.

"Stuart, it's Mom."

"Her name's Taylor," he repeated.

"She's not pregnant, is she? You don't have to get married. I mean, you love her, right?"

"No, Mother, she's not pregnant. And, yes, I love her." He made sure they used protection each time.

"John, she's not pregnant," she yelled at her husband. "Have you set a date?"

"Jeez, it's only been a few hours."

"Stuart, it's Dad again. You better warn her that your mother will want granddaughters."

"Okay, Dad," he replied, smiling at the thought.

His dad lowered his voice. "The police check in with me every day about any suspicious behavior. Are you safe, Son?"

"The FBI's involved, and we're protected."

"The FBI?" he whispered. "Who's we? Is she in danger, too?"

"Dad, don't worry. It's being handled. We'll talk again in a few days."

"Okay, Son, take care of yourself and your love."

He blew out a breath. He'd let his mom calm down about the idea of more grandkids before he'd let Taylor anywhere near the phone. Hearing the pounding on the outside door, he jumped with his gun. He flung open his office door and found Reese staring at Taylor, who wore his t-shirt.

She relocked the door and stretched up to hook the higher chain. The shirt rode up and showed a hint of her pink bikinis. Boy, he loved those long legs. His shirt looked fantastic on her, too. He quickly realized he wasn't the only one checking her out.

"Reese, what the hell is going on?"

Taylor jumped and turned toward them. The bruises had darkened on her legs and arms. The pain in his heart returned. When she pulled the shirt down to cover more of her thighs, it tightened over her breasts. They gaped at her hard nipples in the cold room. Reese grinned until Stuart shoved him.

Remembering why he was there, Reese became angry again. "I can't believe you two!"

He walked around Reese and blocked him from ogling his fiancée. "What?"

"I just got off the phone with Peter. Cindy is literally yanking out her hair and foaming at the mouth. I didn't think you could make a death threat worse, but you did."

"I don't understand," Taylor said, snatching the blanket off the back of the couch.

"Cindy saw your romantic proposal. Hell, everybody's seen it. Anyway, it pushed her over the edge. I think her dad's right to lock her up in the loony bin."

Shivering, Taylor sat on the couch and covered herself with a blanket. "How angry will Amber get?"

"Yeah, good question," Reese replied. "You two couldn't downplay this love stuff, at least for now, could you?"

Stuart set his gun on the coffee table and folded his arms. "You think we planned that? We were all alone in the stands."

"Well, it's done now, and Peter's pissed."

"At us?" Taylor asked.

"He's livid that he hasn't found Amber yet," Reese said, sitting across from her. He grinned at her bare feet, and she quickly covered them, too.

"Well, you're not staying with us," Stuart stated.

"I'll sleep on the couch," Reese replied, bouncing on it to test the comfort.

"No way, go sleep in your car."

"The wind chill is dropping. It's already starting to snow."

"I don't care," he replied.

Reese looked at Taylor. "He needs the extra protection. You don't want to become a widowed fiancée, do you?"

"Damn it, Reese! That's uncalled for," he replied as Taylor bit her thumbnail.

Without a word, she left the blanket on the couch and shut the bedroom door. A second later, she threw out a pillow that landed by the front door.

"Looks like I get to stay," Reese replied, smiling. "I hope the walls are thin. I filed an image of her in that shirt in my Rolodex. It'll come in handy on those lonely nights," he said, stretching out his legs.

"Taylor and I will compromise." He picked up the pillow and opened the front door. "The hallway is heated and close enough." He grinned as Reese grabbed the blanket and took the pillow. "Sleep well, my friend," Stuart said, closing the door behind him.

AFTER TOSSING OUT A PILLOW, Taylor flipped on the TV. She knew Reese played dirty, but it worked. She had finally met her one. There wouldn't be another. She needed to protect him the best she could. Whatever it took. She lobbed the extra pillows off the bed and pulled back the comforter. Her legs felt sensuous against the crisp white sheets. Hearing the shower, she propped herself against the headboard and watched their proposal on ESPN and ESPN2.

With a towel around his waist and damp wavy hair, Stuart stood in the doorway. "He's sleeping in the hallway."

Smiling, she bent her knees to her chin and patted the spot next to her. He dropped his towel and walked to her. She caught her breath at the dark blond hair on his chest, abdomen, and lower. She must have built up an outstanding amount of karma from previous lives to be with such a magnificent god. She felt unworthy, a mere mortal.

"See what you do to me," he said, pointing. She blushed. "I don't think you need this shirt." He slipped it over her head. "Do these still hurt?"

"Touching is uncomfortable," she reluctantly replied. "I have an idea though. Let me do all the touching."

He grinned. "Oh yeah?"

"But you can't touch me at all."

"Not even a little?"

She shook her head and turned off the TV. She had the right amount of light to see, but it was dark enough to be bold. On her side, she leaned on her elbow an inch from his body heat. Starting at his head, she played with a loose curl by his ear. She slid her fingers along his clean-shaven face and down his neck to his opposite shoulder. On her knees, she kneaded his taut bicep and forearm. She reached for his hand. Her breasts grazed his chest. He groaned and watched her closely. Smiling, she continued to rub his hand, rough from the winter weather. She skimmed her fingers back up that arm and down the other one without breaking contact.

She loved the feel of his hard muscles and soft fur. Smelling his aftershave, she tenderly kissed his chest. She moved her hand lower to his flat abdomen and felt him clench the bottom sheet with his fists. Without touching any intimate areas, her fingers moved lower.

She slid her hand down his leg to his foot. Having to reach over his body to massage the other, she let her nipple glide ever so slightly across him.

"This is torture," he growled, breathing heavily.

Fascinated with his body, she tentatively stroked him. When she wrapped her fingers around him and gently squeezed, he groaned. She smiled at her power.

"Say it," he demanded.

She hovered over him on all fours. "Say what, Stuart?" *Payback would be so sweet.*

"Please, Taylor. I can't take it. I need to touch you," he begged.

She didn't hold out long at all. His gentleness made her melt. She forgot about … everything.

Much, much later, she cuddled against him. "Are we having a long engagement?" she asked.

"Engagement? What engagement?"

She smiled. "Do I need to turn on SportsCenter?"

"Oh, yeah, I remember now."

She looked at her ring. "This is beautiful."

"Do you want a long engagement?"

"I really don't know. Everything has been a blur." And what about her plan?

He caressed her hand as it lay on his chest. "I don't

want a long engagement. I want you with me now."

"I'm afraid to go back to the dorms," she whispered. The thought made her stomach ache.

"Then live here with me," he said, kissing her fingers.

"Do you want to live together for a while?" Would that fit her plan?

"I want to be your husband. Do you want a big wedding?"

"No, I don't have family except Joe and Eva. Do you?"

"My family's in Arizona. So, no."

"Then what? Courthouse? Vegas? Cruise?" she asked.

"What do you think about Las Vegas?"

"When?" she asked, biting her lip in the darkness. It was just a small change to her plan, right?

"Let's do it over my winter break. We can spend the holidays with my folks then go to Vegas. We'll even fly Eva and Joe out. What do you think?"

She thought for a moment. She loved him and wanted to be with him. What about her plan? She finally nodded and hugged him. She'd think it through later.

CHAPTER
sixteen

MONDAY

WHILE UNDER HEAVY GUNFIRE, STUART wiped the sweat and blood off his face and crawled toward Taylor's burned and battered body hidden behind the mutilated metal of the HMMWV. Inhaling sand and smoke and tasting metallic grit, he cradled her as her lifeless eyes stared back...

Drenched in sweat, Stuart abruptly sat up in bed and quickly checked on Taylor. Seeing her cocooned under the comforter, he blew out a breath and tried to calm his heartbeat. The last few mornings, he desperately reached for her to confirm her safety.

Stuart fought against puking. With the threat still looming, he would continue to remain overly protective. He didn't care his horrific dream of her was fictitious.

Letting her sleep, he slid out of bed. In the shower, he let the water wash the images away and contemplated their agenda for the day. He'd make a few phone calls to Peter and Bob this morning, but the rest of the time would be wide open.

He wouldn't mind hunkering down for another day of movies and Mario's delivery. Hell, he'd do it for the whole week. He planned to spend most of the time in his bedroom. Smiling, he thought of a strategy to get her to play him on his Xbox. He laughed. Video games and sex, was he sixteen?

After making a pot of coffee, he slid back under the comforter. In a t-shirt and sweats, he snuggled against her back and kissed her neck. She moaned and angled her head, so he had better access. He chuckled and kissed her shoulder. When she hummed, he worked his kisses up her neck to her ear. His warm breath caused her to shiver. He felt the goose bumps on her arm.

"Let's get married today," he whispered in her ear. He joked, but he really liked the idea.

She stretched out her legs and seductively rubbed her backside against him. "What?" she asked, still half asleep.

"I know a judge who went to Michigan," he replied, sliding his arm around her waist.

She stopped his hand from roaming under her shirt. "What's your hurry?"

"Why wait?"

She turned on her back and eyed him. "Because we need a license, and I'd like to graduate first. I have my plan, you know."

"I suppose Eva would want my head on a platter if we left her out."

She nodded. "She's already declared herself my maid of honor, and I'd like Joe to walk me down the aisle."

He tensed at Joe's name. Joe loved her and was

probably in love with her, although he wouldn't admit it. As much as he wanted to confront Taylor about it, he thought she needed to work it out with him. He wouldn't step in unless Joe got out of control.

"Then what should we do today?" he asked.

"Well, I need to call Eva and make sure she picks up my graduation gown for Saturday, and I should probably call Joe to check in. What about you?"

"I figure we'll cut Reese some slack and stay put again today. Mmm," he said, kissing her fingers. "What should we do?"

"Is food part of this plan?" she asked, sitting up and sliding away from him. "I have calls to make, and you want to call Peter, right?"

He nodded as she left the room for the bathroom. He felt her apprehension from the doorway. She had every right to feel anxious, especially after Friday's attack. She changed the subject every time he attempted to bring it up. He prayed the effects would be temporary for her. He'd be patient while she processed the trauma. Something else bothered her though, but he couldn't put his finger on it. *Yet.*

After changing into jeans, he slipped on his winter hikers. He'd give Reese a break and bolt the doors for the day. He peeked through the bathroom door to find Taylor in the shower. The room smelled like lilacs, his new favorite flower.

"I'll be right back. I'm going to talk to Reese for a second."

She pulled the shower curtain back to look out. "You'll tell me what's going on, right? You won't keep anything from me?"

He didn't want to share, but he nodded and shut

the door. He still worried about the amount of stress he put on her. Taylor puts up a good front, but she talks in her sleep. Well, she mumbles and wiggles in her sleep. He tried to decipher her gibberish to get the gist of her subconscious thoughts. *Joey, don't fight. Eva, I want it my way. Not out of order.* She begged with Joe and demanded with Eva. He didn't have a clue whom the last message was for, but she had whimpered about it. He needed to figure out what was *out of order* and fix it.

In the lobby, he checked his empty mail slot and glanced out the front doors. With two inches of snow on every surface, small snowflakes swirled in the parking lot between the three brick buildings of the apartment complex. The buildings created a u-shape with parking in the middle. His section created the connecting part of the three. He tried to distinguish Reese's snow-covered car in the two-thirds full lot. He found him in the front row.

As they stood next to the driver's side door, they watched an eighty-eight pale green Lincoln Continental plow through the snow toward them. He reached for his gun and realized he left it in the apartment. Reese had a hand on his as the extra-long boat slid into the spot next to them.

Reese leaned down to look through the passenger window and laughed. "Looks like you got company."

With an overstuffed backpack, Joe exited the car. "You saved me hours of pounding on doors."

"Why are you here?" Stuart demanded. His enjoyable day alone with his fiancée just hit a smart-assed snag.

Joe walked around the front of his car. "I brought Taylor a bag for the week," he said as the snow blew around them.

"I'll take it," he said, hoping to dismiss him.

Openly annoyed, Joe stopped. "Are you keeping me from seeing my sister?"

"I should, but I won't," he mumbled.

"What the hell does that mean?" Joe demanded, swinging the pack over his shoulder.

Before Stuart could argue, they watched three large fire trucks scream toward them. Each stopped in front of a building section. Firefighters jumped down from all sides as the alarm suddenly sounded in the buildings. He exchanged a look with Joe and Reese. Amber's name was psychically distributed.

They ran for Stuart's building. The firefighters blocked them from entering. In different stages of dress, his neighbors filed out while the firemen explained about a complex-wide gas leak. Nobody was allowed back inside. He and Joe looked for Taylor. Reese scanned the crowd for Amber. To add to the turmoil, someone cut the electricity. He prayed it was protocol for gas leaks.

"My fiancée is in there. She hasn't come out yet. Let me through to get her," Stuart demanded.

"Sorry, Sir. We have men pounding on doors," the firefighter replied, blocking them.

He ran his hands through his hair. "She was in the shower and may not have heard the noise."

"No entry. It's for your own safety."

"It's not mine I'm worried about," he muttered, before turning to Joe. "Behind this building is an alley. My apartment is on the first floor the fourth one from the south end. Meet us there." Joe nodded and took off. "Reese, go do what you do best so I can sneak by. Then, watch for Amber."

Reese stalked toward the Captain. Flailing his arms, he ranted about his bedridden grandmother in the other building. While the group of firefighters gathered, Stuart slipped through the doors as the last of the people ran out. Rushing down the empty hall, he scrambled for the right key. He burst through the door to a pitch-dark apartment. Silence filled the room.

"Taylor!"

"Don't move," she replied.

"It's me. Where are you?"

"I'm in the kitchen. Stay where you are," she said. "Do you keep a flashlight over here?"

"In the drawer with the pot holders," he said, moving through the darkness toward her voice. He banged into a chair. "Oww."

"I told you not to move." She flipped on the flashlight with her left and held his gun in her shaking right.

"Honey, please set my gun on the counter," he said, moving chairs and the coffee table out of his way. She had barricaded herself in his kitchen. He quickly grabbed his gun and tucked it behind his back. "Have you ever used one before?"

"No, and I didn't like touching it. What's happened?"

"Well, the first chance we get, you're getting a lesson on handling a gun. You left the safety on. The fire department says gas leak, but we're not taking any chances," he said, pulling her toward the bedroom. "I need you to grab anything you may need from the bathroom while I pack a few things. We only have a few minutes."

While she gathered their toiletries, he felt around in his closet for a duffle bag and blindly threw in clothes from his drawers. The alarms still blared as she added her armful to the bag. After taking the flashlight and large duffle, he worked his way to the slider.

"Where are we going?" she whispered behind him. She slipped on her coat.

"Far from here," he replied, pulling the curtain back a few inches. "When I say go, jump into Joe's car and keep your head down."

"Joe's here?"

Through the sliver of light from the gloomy morning, Stuart nodded. Joe's long tank barely fit between the warehouse and the building. When the car stopped, he pulled at the slider. After checking both ways to find the alley empty, he hurried her to the car. The slider's security lock latched behind them. He tossed the duffle in the back seat then Taylor. He joined Joe in the front.

"Let's go," Stuart said.

Joe gunned it forward until they saw a black van with dark windows ahead of them. "Shit," Joe said, slamming into reverse. As the van sped toward them, Joe looked behind him and floored it. "Hey, Babe, isn't this fun? Now get down." She sprawled out on the seat.

Stuart held his gun and watched the van gaining on them. "Does this beast go any faster?"

"Hang on." Joe spun a one-eighty out of the alley, missing another fire truck that slid to a halt and blocked the van from following. "I am so good," he said, checking his rearview mirror. "It's road trip time. While I waited to get out of the front parking lot, I called Peter. We're going to a safe house."

Stuart set his gun next to him and picked up Joe's. He checked his clip. "A Hardballer? I suppose you tell the ladies the gun's named after you?"

Taylor snorted behind them, which gave him the answer. Joe glared without a word and tucked it under the pristine white vinyl seat. "Where are we going, Joey?" Taylor asked, buckling her seatbelt.

Joe smiled at her in the rearview mirror. "The Director has a cabin on a lake near Saginaw. We'll hide out until things cool down."

"You mean until Saturday. We're not missing graduation," she replied. Joe nodded.

"Only if it's safe to go back," Stuart replied, glancing at her.

"No," she stated, crossing her arms.

"What do you mean 'no'? It may still be dangerous. We'll talk about it later," Stuart said.

"There's nothing to talk about. I will not miss graduation," she replied.

Stuart turned back around while Joe smirked. "We'll see," Stuart mumbled.

"I heard that," she replied.

Feeling her icy glare on the back of his head, he sighed. Joe crawled toward the highway. With the blowing snow causing brief whiteouts, it would take a few hours. Cars swerved and slid out of their way.

Creeping behind an orange snowplow, Joe clearly enjoyed Taylor's silent treatment, which annoyed the hell out of him.

"You'd think an Army tank like this would have better traction, so you could go faster," Stuart said. "It's quite the ride."

Joe smiled. "Thanks. I love my car. I am the tortoise. Slow and steady wins the race," he continued.

Taylor chuckled.

Stuart leaned forward and looked at the console. "Is this an eight-track player?"

"Yup, and it works. I've got Bobby Vinton, Tom Jones, and Neil Diamond."

Taylor laughed again. "Don't forget Elvis," she added.

Stuart crossed his arms. "Do you get a lot of action with this monster?"

Joe grinned again. "Plenty. Taylor and I have spent lots of time in the back seat."

Stuart looked back at Taylor. She shrugged, neither denying nor confirming Joe's comment. Seething, he glowered out the front window.

"What? No more pot shots at my car?" Joe asked.

Instead of answering, he dialed Reese's number.

WHILE SHE LISTENED TO STUART'S one-sided conversation, she thought back. When she heard the fire alarm, she started to panic, especially being alone in the apartment. As much as she wanted to run, she made herself stay. Remembering Stuart talk about the different defensive tactics in the seminar, she took his gun from the end table. The lights went out as she moved the furniture around. With the barricade fixed, she sat on the kitchen floor and waited. Listening to the alarm, the fire engines, and the shouting in the hall, she knew she had made the right decision to stay where she was.

Amber could have planned this. In the chaos, she could have easily slipped in and slipped out with no one the wiser. Taylor wasn't going to fall for her ploy again. She trusted Stuart to come for her. She thought he would have complimented her plan. She was proud of it. Instead, he tossed her in the car and told her she couldn't go to graduation. If he thought she'd sit by and let him order her around, he was sadly mistaken. If he pressed the issue, she'd have Joe take her. She wouldn't let Joe miss graduation either. They had worked too hard and had come too far to miss it. End of story.

Stuart also pissed her off with his mean comments about Joe's car, formerly her parents' car. After they died, she had given it to Joe. She didn't like to drive and figured he'd take her anywhere she had to be. She grew up with that music. Lame or not, it reminded her of happier times of home, a place gone forever.

She chuckled as Joe quoted her dad, who was a stickler about car safety, especially in the winter. All three of them knew how to change a tire, check the oil, jump a battery, and they knew all about the proper etiquette of winter driving. Joe should have at least two bags of kitty litter in his trunk. She couldn't help but laugh about her and Joe in the back seat. Her parents took them everywhere. Eva often joined them in the back seat, too. She'd share the joke with Stuart later. She was too upset now.

While she stewed, she listened. When she leaned forward to hear better, Stuart turned on the radio and adjusted the speakers in the back. He purposely kept her out of the discussion.

"You can count on a long engagement with that attitude, Mister," she said.

"What?" Stuart asked, looking back at her.

"You heard me," she replied, feeling the tears break

the surface.

"More problems in paradise?" Joe asked.

"Shut up," Stuart said as he faced the front. "Where the hell are we?"

"There's a map in the glove box," Joe said, glancing at her. He handed her the box of tissues.

She blew her nose and watched the tiny flakes layer the ground. She couldn't see farther than a quarter mile in any direction. They inched forward. Bored with their silence and the AM Spanish station, she pulled the sealed bag from under Stuart's seat. She took out a small plush blanket. After pushing the emergency kit on the floor behind Joe, she slipped off her boots. Using the duffle bag as a pillow, she curled up and closed her eyes. She listened.

She jumped when she felt the car slowly turn. "Are we there?" she asked, wiping the dry, crusted drool off her mouth.

Joe laughed. "I told you she'd eventually fall asleep after pretending for a while."

"Yeah, whatever," Stuart replied. "We have another hour on the back roads until we get to the cabin."

She pulled her legs under her body and stared out the window. The farther north they went, the more snow they came across. She estimated about six inches along the road. It didn't look like the snow would let up either. She wanted to ask about a weather report, but she stubbornly bit her tongue. The unplowed roads became less defined. Everyone else knew better than to go out into the blizzard. Joe stayed in the middle of the white space between the tree lines. The Lincoln's heavy frame kept them steady and centered.

"Peter said the first private road after the s-curve,"

Joe said as he focused on the area.

Stuart leaned forward and wiped the fog off the inside window. "Left or right side?"

"Uh, right, is that it?" Joe asked. "It looks like a driveway."

"I don't see a mailbox, so it must be a road. What now?" Stuart asked.

"We take the fork to the left. It's the only house on the small lake. He said it's isolated. He and his brother own over a hundred acres. I guess we'll be fine as long as nobody trailed us," Joe said.

"The weather will help cover any tracks," Stuart replied, pointing to a small house.

When Joe finally turned off the engine, the three of them blew out a breath. She slipped on her boots and stiffly stepped out into the cold. She had to pee. Her legs and back ached. Joe rubbed his back as well. Without a word, Stuart took the duffle bag. Joe handed her the one he had brought her and popped open the trunk. Smiling at the four bags of kitty litter, she watched him grab his bag.

Stuart glared. "You thought you were going to stay with us at the apartment?"

"Yup," Joe replied, slamming down the trunk.

She ignored them and climbed the three steps to the deck. She followed it around to the back of the house to a lovely view of the lake. She stood above the attached wooden ladder with two dozen steps that lowered to a walkway. It ended at the water thirty yards away. She turned back to see that the house was one story with a cathedral ceiling and huge windows overlooking the lake.

"I didn't have time to write it down. Shut up and let

me think," Joe said to Stuart, standing next to the side door. "I gotta get it on the first try."

Looking around Stuart, she saw Joe stare at a number pad that she assumed unlocked the door and security system. Stuart impatiently huffed a few times, to Joe's frustration.

"Can we just call Peter?" she asked.

"Did you see any cell towers?" Stuart asked, switching the duffle to the other hand.

She flinched at his sarcasm. It hurt.

"F-you, Stuart," Joe fumed. "Taylor, that was aimed at me, not you."

She walked away and heard Stuart swear. Ignoring them, she focused on her breathing. The fresh cold air calmed her down until she inhaled a large snowflake. Coughing, she started to gag and dry heaved over the side of the railing. Stuart dropped his bag and held her hair away from her face. She pushed him away. She didn't want him to see her retching.

"Ha, I got it," Joe yelled.

She rushed past them into the large room. She kicked off her boots and quickly scanned the area for the bathroom. She slammed the bathroom door behind her. Able to think straight now, she washed her hands and face. The bathroom was plain and manly with woodsy tones. Entering the great room, she realized that it wasn't plain at all. The pine walls had all sorts of pictures and mementos. Many were of the Bingaman brothers hunting, fishing, and drinking. She wandered through the cozy home.

Peter had a wall with his achievements and awards. She admired a picture of him and the President. *Impressive.* General Bingaman's wall also had awards and many pictures. She immediately recognized the General and Stuart in a couple. In the first one, General Bingaman awarded a medal to Stuart, who looked very handsome in his Marine uniform. She remembered from Joe's report that Stuart won an exceptional merit award for leadership in battle. She knew Stuart didn't like talking about that time in his life. She hoped he would open up to her someday. He slept rigidly as if ready for battle, always on his back, never moving. The second picture showed a close-up of them. While the General smiled, Stuart looked in pain.

"Did you see Peter with the President?" Joe asked, standing behind her.

She nodded and glanced at the closed bathroom door. Across the room in the corner was a small kitchen with only an eating counter with stools. Men must not think a dining table important. She loved her mom's large kitchen. Taylor, Joe, and Eva did everything there. They not only ate there, they did homework, played games, built school projects, and cried there after her parents died. *Wow, where did that come from?*

Joe checked out the large flat screen on the wall in front of a long couch. "Hey, they have a secured satellite connection with the phone hooked to the TV. Cool."

"They need to stay in contact with the military and FBI somehow," Stuart added. He glanced at his pictures with General Bingaman and quickly turned away. "Anybody hungry?"

"Starving," Joe said, dismissing the TV for food.

She shook her head. *Not after barfing*, she thought. On each side of the giant TV opposite of the view to the lake, she found doors. Before she opened the first one, she looked around. Peter had one couch facing the TV and another facing the view. She was glad they enjoyed nature, too.

Through the door, she found a large bedroom. This house looked deceptively tiny from the outside, but most of it was under the hill. The underground bedroom also had light pine walls with a rough log bed frame and matching dresser. She saw pictures of Peter's daughters on the dresser. Another flat screen took up the wall next to the door.

Her backpack and Stuart's duffle sat on top of the bed. Frowning, she tossed his into the great room and locked the door. She'd rather sleep alone. How could he take her for granted already? *How, you dolt? Because you give in to him, every time he kisses you.* Thinking about him now made her lightheaded. No wonder he thought he could walk all over her with his demands. She had no control of her thoughts or her body around him.

"Taylor, let me in, so we can talk," Stuart said, testing the knob.

"I'm tired."

"Come on, Honey. It's almost three. We never had breakfast or lunch."

"I'm not hungry."

Her stomach growled, but she didn't think he heard it. Food was the last thing on her mind. She worried about the threat, missing graduation, and the constant bickering of the two men she loved the most.

Stuart sighed. "I'll fix you something when you're ready."

She leaned on the door and listened to them go at it again.

"You're making it easy for me," Joe said.

"So you admit you're trying to cause a problem,"

Stuart replied.

"I don't think you're right for her."

"Oh? And you are? You've had your chance."

She walked away from the door. She couldn't take it anymore. *Why couldn't they get along?* Sitting on the bed, she spotted the satellite phone on its charger. She bit her lip and dialed Eva. After their forty-five minute discussion, she sobbed against Peter's fluffy pillow. She knew what had to be done, but could she do it without anyone getting hurt?

STUART PACED BETWEEN THE COUCHES from the door to the kitchen. "Maybe I can jimmy the lock to check on her."

Joe stretched out on the couch that faced the blank TV screen and bedroom doors. "It's only been an hour and a half. I'd give it thirty more minutes. Her bladder is a two-hour holding tank."

Stuart continued his set path. How had things gone so wrong? They went from getting married today to the silent treatment. Joe irked him by bringing up their history every chance he got—from the back seat of his monster car to knowing her bodily habits. He knew how important history was. Hell, he taught it. Joe and Taylor had a deep bond. He didn't want to break theirs, but he wanted one with her, too. Twenty-five minutes later, the bedroom door opened, and she rushed to the bathroom. Her eyes and nose were red from crying. His fault again.

"Told you," Joe said, laughing. "I know her better."

When she came out, she hurried back to Peter's room. Stuart followed and locked the door behind them. He leaned back against the door and crossed his arms.

"Please, don't do that," she whispered, wrapping her arms around her body.

"Do what?"

"Block the door. The Hulk did the same thing in the laundry room. I'm feeling trapped again." She sat on the edge of the bed and sobbed into her hands.

"Oh, God. Honey. I'm sorry," he said dropping his arms. He knelt beside her. "I don't want to hurt you."

"You said you wouldn't keep things from me, but you have."

He set the box of tissues next to her. "I don't want you to worry."

"But you promised."

"Joe's in love with you," he replied, trying to change the subject.

She sighed and shook her head. "Joe thinks I'm a China doll that can easily break. Obviously, you think the same."

He held her hand. "You are precious to me, but you're stronger than he gives you credit for."

"Like building that barricade?"

"You did pay attention in my class." He smiled. "You've been through some traumatic events in your life and have come out on top. However, I still have this fundamental need to protect you."

"If we get married, are you going to be as demanding as you were today?"

His heart stopped. *If?* He took a deep breath. "When it's necessary to protect you, then yes."

"I made smart choices today, but you think I'm brainless. Your demands aren't needed. I thought marriage meant equal partners. I won't be your subordinate, Lieutenant."

"I don't think that, and you're right."

What more could he say? For almost forty years, his parents discussed and decided things together. Boy, she had a lot to teach him. He sat next to her, and the bed creaked loudly. He grinned, and she shook her head.

"Oh, come on. Please? Just a little payback? He blatantly tortured me with images of the two of you making out in the back seat."

"About that," she said. "Joe implied. That car was my parents, and they drove us everywhere when we were kids."

"Why didn't you tell me? I spent the whole ride trying to get the image out of my head," he replied, relieved with the news.

"You made fun of my family car," she stated. "Will you stop provoking him?"

"After this, I won't start a thing." He bounced a little more on the bed. "Can I?"

She stood and smiled. "Have at it."

Laughing, he jumped in the middle and bounced on his knees. The squeaks and creaks echoed in the room. He kept a steady pace while Taylor folded her arms and waited.

"Can you moan a little?" he whispered.

"No, and I think you're giving yourself a little too much credit on the time," she said, grinning.

"How dare you!" He threw her on the bed next to him. "Let's stop pretending then." He tickled her, and she let out a screaming laugh. "That added just the right touch. Thank you, Darlin.'"

He stopped the bouncing and kissed her. He felt her body soften at his touch. Hoping they were back on the right track, he slid off the bed and helped her up. Before he unlocked the door, he kissed her again.

"I'll be out in a minute," she said.

Stuart pretended to tuck in his shirt as he walked out the door. Joe stood by the French doors at the back of the house.

"Are you done pretending?" Joe asked.

He grinned. "You think so? You'll never know, but you'll have an image in your head."

"Yeah, of you jumping on the bed."

Taylor joined him in the room and squeezed his hand. He looked down at her sly grin and laughed. She had tussled her hair as if they really had made love. He wanted to drag her sexy body back into the room. She slowly moved her hair from her face.

"What's for dinner? I'm suddenly ravenous," her soft voice intimately asked him.

Joe gnashed his teeth from across the room.

"Thank you," Stuart whispered in her ear.

CHAPTER
seventeen

TUESDAY

THE SUN SHIMMERED OFF THE ice-coated trees, creating a magical wonderland. Fairy tales were made of this splendor. Heavy snow piled two-feet high on the railing like thick icing on the top of a cake. She wanted to taste the sweetness.

Her protectors shouldn't have a problem letting her outside today. They were miles from anything. While Taylor daydreamed of cake, Stuart slipped his arms around her waist. She'd recognize the feel of him anywhere.

"It is pretty, isn't it?" he asked in her ear. "Fit for the Passionate Princess and her Adoring Knight." She smiled and leaned back against him. It made a fantastic dream. For about a second.

"Can we eat now?" Joe asked from the stool by the kitchen counter. "Stuart gets all the credit."

Stuart held her hand and led her to the other stool. She smelled eggs and groaned. She bit her tongue.

Grinning, Joe watched her.

"Ready?" Stuart asked before he lifted the napkin to show off his cooking skills.

She nodded and saw bacon with scrambled eggs on the plate. "I thought breakfast was always a box of cereal," she said, smiling. "This is thoughtful. Thank you."

"I've got skills," Stuart replied.

Stuart handed Joe a plate and joined them with his. Joe inhaled his food while she chewed her bacon. Across from them, Stuart ate while standing.

"You're not going to tell him, are you?" Joe asked with a smirk.

"Don't be an ass," she replied. "I will."

"What other bits of history between you two am I missing?" Stuart asked, slamming his fork on the counter.

"Taylor's allergic to eggs," Joe said, chuckling. "You don't know very much about her."

Stuart reached for her plate. "I'm sorry, Honey. I didn't know."

"It's not your fault," she said. "I do love bacon though."

Stuart handed her his bacon and scraped her eggs onto his plate. "What should we do today?" he asked as he raised an eyebrow.

She smiled. "Inside or outside?"

"Both," he replied, watching Joe roll his eyes.

"Let's make a snowman while Joey washes the dishes."

"Sounds like the perfect plan," Stuart said. "The dish soap's under the sink."

After Stuart left to change, she turned on her

brother. Before he said a word, she cut him off. "I've begged you not to argue with him. Now, I'm demanding it. It's not funny. It's hurtful. It all stops now."

"He can take it."

"Joey, it hurts me," she replied with tears in her eyes. "Are you trying to make me choose between the two of you?"

He flinched. "Could you?"

"If you're making me, I will. Either way, could you live with the decision?" Her heart ached as she watched him rub his hands over his face.

"No, I don't think I could," he whispered.

She kissed his cheek as she stood. "Come outside when you're done."

She found a box with winter hats, gloves, and scarves. Leave it to General Bingaman and Peter to be prepared. At the base of the steep steps, she started to roll a snowball. The heavy snow packed easily. Stuart worked on his own creation closer to the frozen lake.

By the time she set the head on the top, Joe clomped down the steps. Without a word, he walked down the dock toward Stuart and the water. She watched him closely to see if any barbs were exchanged. To her surprise, they actually seemed civilized.

She frowned at Joe's funk. Eva told her she'd have to make him ease up. Her eyes narrowed at Stuart's design. He had built a fort with four-foot-high sides. He was hoping for a fight? She growled. After their discussion, she knew Joe would be a sitting duck.

Taylor packed two snowballs. Her plan relied on timing. She lobbed the first one and hurled the second. She couldn't have planned it better. The lobbed one hit Joe at the back of his neck and sloshed down the inside of his jean jacket. He howled. Stuart roared as the second one nailed him on the side of the head. Instead of looking at her like she wanted, they turned on each other. For two seconds, they sized each other up. Then, World War III broke out. Apparently, her planning skills needed work.

For half an hour, they creamed each other with snowballs. Mostly they missed, but every fourth ball found its target. She heard them laugh and swear at each other as they took cover behind trees and bushes like a couple of big kids. Then, they abruptly stopped.

"What?" they said to each other.

"I didn't throw the first one," Joe said.

"Well, I didn't either," Stuart replied.

As one, they turned to look at her. *Uh-oh.* Her eyes widened in horror as they both scooped up snow and ran toward her. She scrambled for the steps. Halfway up, she grunted as a cluster of snowballs hit her in the back. The force pushed her against the ladder-like steps. She whacked her head, slipped, and fell backward onto the wooden walkway. The snow absorbed most of the impact, but her head hit a bare spot.

The next thing she knew, she lay on the bed, stripped of her wet clothes. She blinked as Stuart covered her with a blanket and called out to Joe. The sound reverberated in her throbbing head. Instead of cartoon stars dancing in a circle above her head, she had little Evas pointing her finger and telling her it was an idiotic idea. Taylor rubbed her head as the guys looked down at her. They geared up for a long lecture.

"Where am I?" she asked to dismiss the sermon.

They shared a glance. "We're at Peter's cabin. You don't remember?" Stuart asked. The bed creaked loudly when he sat next to her and took her hand.

She looked at Joe then Stuart. "Do I know you?"

"What?" Joe asked. He frowned at Stuart and they exchanged more glances.

"Tell us what you do remember?" Stuart asked.

"I remember that both of you throw too hard. What happened to not hurting girls, Joey?"

"Jesus, Taylor. That is so not funny." Joe almost said something else, but he thought better of it and left the room.

"It really wasn't funny," Stuart agreed.

"It was a little," she replied, sitting up. "Did you do anything perverse to my body when you undressed me?"

He grinned. "You will never know." As soon as her feet touched the floor, she felt dizzy. Stuart caught her from falling and lifted her back on the bed. "I think you should rest for a while. I promise to play nice."

She woke from her nap to a dim light in the dark room. Stuart had left the door open. She heard Joe whispering angrily at him. Her head pounded as she got up. She dressed but that was as far as she could go. She lay back down and listened.

"I'm not asking to take over. I'm asking you to let me help take care of her," Stuart said from the living room.

"You're the one who's endangered her the most," Joe replied.

"I know that, and I want to make amends."

"I've protected her my whole life. I love her, and I'm not giving her up."

"Not giving her up?" Stuart asked. "What does that even mean? You sound obsessed."

Joe growled. "I've been there and helped her through more shit than you will ever know."

"Yes, you have," Stuart said.

Joe pressed his point. "Where were you when her junior prom date bailed at the last minute?"

She smiled. Evan wasn't even a boy she liked. She just wanted to go and see what all the excitement was about. Juniors had invited Joe when he was a freshman and a sophomore. He tried to tell her it was boring, but she had cried in her peach prom dress. He borrowed a suit and danced only with her even though many other girls had asked him. When he spotted Evan and his new date across the room, Joe gave him a bloody nose, soaking Evan's tuxedo shirt. She happily spent the next two weeks in detention with Joe.

Joe continued. "Or where were you when she was too scared to drive after hitting a deer?"

Oh, that poor deer. She had hit it straight on and watched its loose fur poof like a powder puff when it hit the ground. After a month of not driving, Joe forced her to drive down the same road twenty times. She had called him every horrible name she could think of, even made up some new ones. He had her so distracted that she didn't even think about driving or the accident.

"Did you know that I broke the news to Taylor about her dad?" Joe's voice cracked. "It was the worst day of my life and the hardest thing I've ever had to do."

She would never forget that day either. She and Eva had gone shopping while Joe and her dad worked on the Lincoln. After Joe's mom died of an OD at the start of their senior year, Joe had stayed in their guest room and helped her dad whenever he needed it. When Dad had collapsed in the garage, Joe called for the ambulance and waited for her to return. It happened so quickly with her mom, too. Taylor barely remembered graduation. For weeks after, things were a blur. Eva was a tremendous help by getting her to focus on massage school, but Joe officially moved in and managed everything. She had spent many nights crying in his arms. He never took advantage of her although some nights she wished he would have to distract her from the pain. She and Joe had promised to be each other's family. *Blood means nothing; love is everything*, Joe had said. They had mourned the losses of both sets of parents from their lives. They had each other, and that was enough.

Stuart remained silent. In the other room, Taylor sobbed as Joe told the story. "As he lay dying, he asked me to watch over Taylor. I swore I would. I won't break my vow."

She never knew he made that promise. He had given up his life for her. *What a burden!* She sat up and quietly blew her nose. Even today, she had been so mean to him.

"It's a great responsibility," Stuart replied. "You haven't taken it lightly."

"Can you imagine how vulnerable she was our freshman year? Those guys would have used her, abused her, and left her to rot. Do you know how hard it was to keep them away from her for four years? I threatened, fought, even blackmailed to protect her. Then, she falls in love with the first guy who penetrates the shield I built up around her. Now look where we are. She is in more danger than I have ever imagined. I failed." Joe's voice cracked again. "I need some air."

Hearing the door slam shut, she burst into tears again. Stuart stood in the doorway. "You heard all that?"

She nodded and blew her nose.

"He's having a hard time letting go. If we're to have a chance, he'll need to back off a little."

"When he comes back, I'll talk to him," she whispered.

STUART HELPED TAYLOR TO THE couch in the living room. With only an hour left of daylight, she wanted to face the windows on the smaller sofa. He searched the kitchen while they waited for Joe to return.

He had to admit he had fun earlier in the snow. He and Joe worked off some steam, but a chill had run down his spine when he saw Taylor fall. She had lain motionless. They scrambled to get her into the house. Then, as they debated calling Peter for a helicopter, she woke up.

Joe obviously had a lot on his mind. Stuart had a feeling he wanted to let go but didn't know how. He hoped Taylor could get through to him.

Seeing Joe on the deck walking toward the side door, Stuart grabbed a can of WD-40 and shut the bedroom door. He now understood Joe and Taylor's relationship better than he had. God, he wanted this threat over. He wanted his life back.

Stuart quickly sprayed the creaking parts underneath the bed. The slightest movement in the night woke them. The noise had upset her even though nothing physical happened between them. Like a dummy, he forgot to pack any condoms. He thought about calling Peter on the satellite phone for an update. Instead, he eavesdropped. He turned the knob and cracked the door. Taylor pulled her legs underneath her body and propped her elbow on the back of the couch. Joe sighed and stripped off his outer gear.

"So you heard?" Joe asked, looking around the empty room.

She smiled. "You wanted me to."

"Yes and no," Joe replied, plopping down beside her. He tilted his head, resting it on the back of the couch, and watched the ceiling fan spin.

She rubbed the big goose egg on the back of her head. "You win."

In shock, Stuart stared through the crack. *No! It was not supposed to go like that.* Joe turned to her. He questioned her statement, too.

She continued. "I thought Stuart was my one. Maybe I'm wrong."

No! You're not wrong! I am the one! Every cell in his body wanted to rush into the room. He gripped the doorframe to stop himself. He didn't want to hear anymore, but he couldn't move. Joe gaped as well.

"Are you supposed to be my one, Joey? We've been through so much together. I've always thought of you as my best friend and brother. Our love is deep and strong. It's good and pure. Nobody could ever break that. That's why I'm wondering if you really are my one. You've heard Mom's stories about the chemistry of love and what it's supposed to be like. Is that us?"

Stuart couldn't breathe. He and Taylor had chemistry. She didn't feel it, too?

"Maybe that is us. I've loved you my whole life," Joe replied.

Stuart felt a knife slowly breach his ribs and pierce his heart when Taylor leaned over and kissed Joe. It wasn't a peck either. The pain froze him as if ice encased his body. Still, he couldn't turn away.

Taylor sat back. "What did you feel?"

"What do you mean?" Joe asked.

"Did you feel it?"

"What?"

"When Stuart first kissed me, my body jolted like I stepped on a live wire. Every kiss since has felt the same," she stated.

Stuart blinked as he tried to comprehend her meaning. Joe did the same. As it clicked for them both, Joe pulled her closer. He kissed her again to make sure. Stuart could only watch and hope.

With tears in her eyes, she searched his face. "I'm not your one, Joey. She's out there somewhere, waiting for you. She'll need you, and you'll need her. It will be the perfect fit, and your heart will expand from the joy of it."

"I can't leave you," Joe whispered.

"I couldn't bear it if you left my life, but you've fulfilled your promise. You're the one who cleared the way, so I could meet Stuart."

"Are you sure he's right for you?"

"You know he is," she replied with a smile. "I've watched you, and I've heard Reese's stories. Whenever Stuart barked out an order, you followed it. You knew about his military training and honors. Admit it. He is a good man, and you admire him."

Joe blew out a breath and finally nodded. "I'll deny it, and it doesn't mean I'm letting up on the sarcasm. If he's going to be part of this family, he'll have to take it.

And you make sure he knows that he owes me."

She launched herself at him. "Thank you, Joey."

Joe laughed and hugged her back. "I know you've been talking to Eva. She fights dirty, too."

Stuart held his breath for so long he gulped for air. Was his mind playing tricks on him? Taylor went from Joe winning and their kissing to chemistry of love and promises met. She still turned him inside out. His mind reeled as he tried to gain perspective on what had just happened.

That was the most impressive strategy he had ever witnessed. Her technique never once let Joe tap into his anger and defensiveness. She gently nudged him down a path of least resistance and let him work it out in his head. She helped him save face as if he had won. Joe had won. Stuart won, too. He found himself in awe of Taylor.

He knew she could hold her own, but she possessed a subtle strength that he hadn't seen before. She wielded a great power. He hadn't a chance, and he doubted he would want to fight against it. He backed away from the door and sat on the bed, feeling as if he experienced every possible emotion. Exhausted, he stretched out. The tension dissipated throughout the entire cabin.

With red eyes and nose, Taylor climbed up next to him. She laid her head on his chest. "I'm sorry if I hurt you," she whispered.

He kissed the top of her head. He wouldn't deny that he listened. "It killed me at first. Then I understood what you were doing. So you felt that bolt of lightning, too?"

"Every time," she whispered. "Stuart, there's something else we need to discuss." She lifted her head to look at him. "Joe and I need the closure. We want to attend graduation with Eva."

Before he could debate the subject, the satellite phone buzzed. Stuart jumped to answer it, dismissing the topic. Frowning, Taylor watched him.

"Stuart, is everything okay?" Peter asked.

"It is now. What's going on?"

"You've received another letter. Amber's peeved. She quoted your parents' and sister's addresses in Scottsdale. The gas leak ploy was definitely her doing. You played it right by getting out of there."

Stuart kicked his duffle bag, sending it across the hard wood floor. "Why is she doing this? What's being done? Has my family been notified?" Taylor hugged a pillow at his alarm. He reached for her hand. She hurried to him and wrapped her arms around his waist. He squeezed her.

"As a precaution, we've assigned agents. Your nephews are on their winter break, so they'll stay close to their parents," Peter replied calmly.

"What about Eva?" he asked, looking at the terror in Taylor's face.

"She hasn't been happy. She says I'm stalking her while she's working at the gym."

He whispered to Taylor that Eva was okay. "You're on the defensive. Any progress offensively?"

Peter groaned. "No, she's in hiding."

Taylor asked for the phone, and he reluctantly handed it to her. "Peter, when can we come home?" She listened and laughed. "Joe hasn't broken anything yet. He and I want to attend graduation on Saturday. It's important that all three of us are there together. Use us as bait if you need to."

Stuart shook his head and demanded the phone

back.

Taylor stepped away from him. "No, I mean it. I've done everything you've asked." She pressed her lips together in frustration. "Have I mentioned that you have a lovely getaway here? You have quite a few personal items ... In fact, I've been snooping around and found some boxes in your closet ... Joe would be most interested ... Yes, he would hold that over your head ... I swear Joe will never know ... Thank you." Smiling, she passed the phone back to Stuart.

"It looks like you're coming back for graduation," Peter said. "I'll get with Bob and make sure the place is locked down."

"I don't like it," he said as Taylor leaned against the closet door.

"If you marry her, you're never going to have it your way again. You know that, don't you?"

"I haven't had it my way yet," he replied. "After you talk to Bob, Joe and I will want to go over the plan."

"I'll make a conference call as soon as I can. Stuart, stay away from my boxes. They're in very fine condition and part of my retirement plan."

"Now I'm extremely curious." He placed the phone in the charger while Taylor blocked the closet.

"What are in the boxes?"

"I promised," she replied. "Eva's okay?"

"Peter's with her," he said, picking her up and moving her out of the way. "He said they were in very fine condition and for his retirement." Taylor thought that was hilarious and watched him from the bed. He found six large boxes full of comic books. "Wow, I never would have guessed it." He shut the closet door as Joe knocked.

"Come in," Taylor yelled.

Joe opened the door and wiggled his finger at her. She hopped off the bed and followed him to the window. They looked where he pointed. At the edge of the bright floodlights, along the water line, four deer nibbled at the bushes. While Stuart relayed Peter's conversation to Joe, Taylor watched the deer wander away.

During dinner, Stuart asked Joe about Taylor growing up. To her discomfort, he brought up every embarrassing moment. Taylor added her own versions as well as a few stories about Joe. All in all, it was a productive day.

CHAPTER
eighteen

WEDNESDAY

AFTER LUNCH, TAYLOR STOOD NEXT to the window. Another storm had gone through last night and added an extra six inches of snow. She couldn't see Joe's car anymore. Outside, the guys decided to hone up on their gun skills. She watched them line up paper cups and plates near the edge of the lake. Earlier, they had engaged in another snowball fight. They made her stay inside for that, too. Somehow it had become the two of them against her on anything that had to do with her safety. She smiled as they took aim. Stuart said something to Joe, who nodded and changed his stance slightly. She hoped she was witnessing the beginning of a friendship.

She scrounged in the freezer and found a whole chicken. She thought she'd cut it up and cook it for dinner. She used to help her mom cook, but that was over four years ago. She hoped she remembered a few things though. While she looked in the pantry for a side dish, the guys burst through the door.

"Of course I'm better. I've had years of practice," Stuart was saying.

"I suppose you learn faster when someone's shooting back," Joe replied.

Taylor lifted her head to see Stuart flinch then laugh. "Yeah, I guess you do."

"Did Stuart kick your butt?" she asked, setting a box of macaroni and cheese on the counter.

Joe nodded. "He hit the bull's eye every damn time. I want a rematch."

Stuart shrugged. "You're not much of a challenge."

Laughing, Joe left for the General's room while Stuart set his gun on the counter and sat on the stool.

"Do you want a session?" Stuart asked.

"Ooh, yeah," she replied with a grin. "You have condoms?"

He growled. "No, damn it."

She came around the counter and hugged him. "I'd still like the session," she whispered.

His cold lips found hers. She ran her hands through his damp hair while he moved his cool fingers under her shirt. Feeling the steam rise from their contact, she leaned her body closer to his.

"God, I'm not going to be able to stop myself if we continue this," he moaned.

As tempting as it was, she stepped back. She had no control and lost all ability to think when he kissed her like that. "Good point. From now on, you sleep with Joe in the General's room," she said, smiling.

"Like hell I will. I'll be the man and show the restraint," he said, mockingly pushing her away. She frowned and pulled her shirt up, pretending to wipe her eyes. She flashed him her bra. He jumped from his stool and backed away. "Stop that right now," he said.

As he moved toward their room, she followed him and stripped off her shirt. "Let's test that restraint."

He grabbed her around the waist, pulled her inside the bedroom, and shut the door with his foot. He kissed her neck and gently pushed her bra straps off her shoulders. She moaned as the electricity numbed her mind. He had her undressed and under the sheet in no time. She tugged at his jeans, but he gently held her arms above her head. With one hand holding hers, his other roamed the length of her body. She arched to his touch.

She wiggled to get free to undress him, but he slid his thigh over her leg to hold her still. His tongue found her breast. He watched her face as she writhed under his touch. His mouth covered hers before she could cry out. He brought her to such heights that her body trembled with emotion.

"Not so loud. I don't remember if I locked the door," Stuart whispered in her ear. He let go of her hands and watched her. She couldn't form words. Instead, she tried to catch her breath. "You were squirmy," he said.

"You're not nice," she whispered, lying on her side to face him.

He kissed her fingers and grinned. "What do you mean? You seemed happy."

She entangled her leg with his and caressed his muscular bicep. How could she be so lucky to have met such a sexy, gorgeous man? She kissed his chin. His gaze touched her soul. She loved him completely.

"I need you inside me," she whispered, moving closer.

He smiled and kissed her nose. "Are you trying to weaken my restraint?"

She nodded as he moved back to the edge of the bed. "Why won't you kiss me?" she asked, following his movements.

She positioned herself on top of him and misjudged the amount of space they had. They fell off the bed with a heavy thud. Naked, she straddled him and yanked at his jeans to get them off.

Joe banged on their door. "Can I come in?"

"No!" She scrambled for her clothes while Stuart laughed.

Joe jiggled the handle. "God, you left the door unlocked? You want me to walk in on you? Ugh, well finish up in there. The Director's calling in five minutes."

She dressed and smoothed down her hair while Stuart grinned from the bed. She blushed at her sorry display of seduction. He wasn't even tempted. He sent her to the moon, and she couldn't even get his pants off.

With a sigh, she turned away from the mirror. Was he bored with her already? Cindy had said as much. Taylor didn't know any sexual tricks. She quickly left the room and found Joe reading a comic book on the couch facing the TV. Peter would cancel their graduation if he saw it.

She snatched it away from him. "Where'd you get that?" she demanded.

"Hey, I borrowed them from the General's closet. He has a whole stack," he replied, snatching it back. "Besides, it gave me something to do while you were trying not to squeak the bed. It needs more oil."

"I'm sorry." She hurried to the bathroom.

"Why's she upset?" Joe asked Stuart.

"I honestly don't know," Stuart said as she shut the door.

Pushing her inexperience with sex out of her mind, she fixed her hair and quickly returned to the great room. Stuart pushed the button on the remote control to bring Peter's conference call on the large screen. She stood behind the guys as they sat on the couch. Peter greeted them and glared at the comic in Joe's hand. She shook her head as he stared accusingly at her.

"Peter, I hope you don't mind that we tapped into your food pantry, and Joe's been reading your brother's comics while in his room."

He nodded. "We have a woman who comes in to clean. She'll stock up for us. Thanks for the heads up."

"Your room will need the most cleaning," Joe said with a chuckle. "Add to the list more lube for the rusted springs on your bed."

Blushing, Taylor smacked him in the head and left for the kitchen.

"Hey, what did I miss?" Reese asked, standing next to Peter on screen. He leaned close to the camera, making his face take up the full screen. Afraid Reese would jump through the TV, Joe and Stuart leaned back against the couch. "Any threesomes, fist fights, or gun standoffs?" Reese asked.

Stuart smiled. "Well, there was kissing, target practice, and snowball fights. Do they count?"

"Damn, I miss all the fun," Reese said, backing away from the screen. "I want details."

"Yeah, that'll happen," Joe replied. "Is there going to be a problem with us attending graduation?"

Taylor stopped chopping the chicken and waited to hear the answer.

"No. We'll have part of a team watching Stuart and Taylor while the others will have pictures of Amber. Bob doesn't have a problem with the tighter security. With the Lieutenant Governor speaking at commencement, his people will also have their own security crew for him."

"Do you have the schedule and layout of the facility?" Stuart asked.

Peter pressed a button, and half the screen showed the design and set up for the ceremony. Stuart pointed out problem areas. When Joe asked for permission to bring his gun, Stuart confirmed Joe's accuracy and safety with his weapon. Peter agreed and said he liked the fact that Joe asked and didn't demand.

They planned for Saturday for a good two hours. Taylor waited until they wrapped things up before she put the chicken in the oven. With many of the roads buried under snow, Peter would send a helicopter for them Saturday morning. Peter and Joe would drive up after the thaw to dig out his car. She thought they would enjoy the drive for different reasons. They would give each other a hard time, but at least it wouldn't be about Peter's comics. Smiling that she got her way, she dumped the macaroni into the boiling water.

WHILE NAILING DOWN THE DETAILS, Stuart watched Taylor flit around the tiny kitchen. She had an anxious habit of biting her bottom lip. He didn't understand why fixing dinner made her fretful. Maybe it was listening to them talk strategy. He smiled as she stirred the macaroni. Her hips swayed with her arm as if dancing to a song in her head. God, he wanted to strip her naked again.

"Stuart, will that be a problem?" Peter asked for the second time.

"Uh, what?"

Joe rolled his eyes. "He's distracted."

Reese laughed. "Is she wearing that t-shirt again? Man, that image came in handy. It's number one in my Rolodex."

"What!" Joe growled.

Stuart leaned over to Joe while Reese laughed. "Let it go. We'll corner him later."

Joe smiled and nodded. Peter sighed. "Will being that far away from the graduates be a problem? I don't want you changing seats during the ceremony."

"No, Taylor may not be able to see me, but I'll be there for moral support," he said, glancing at her smiling face.

Truthfully, he didn't like it at all. He wanted to be closer, so he could protect her. Joe would be next to her and alert, but they were supposed to be able to relax and enjoy the procession instead of watching every face for Amber.

When would this end? He had told Joe to shoot to kill. As dangerous as Amber was, wounding her would only make the situation worse. He reminded Joe that she was a murderer and had given him some tips during their target practice. Joe soaked it in and asked for more. Stuart thought that once they resolved the threat, he and Joe could become good friends. He could think of him as a younger brother. He smiled. *Yeah, a smart-mouthed, pain-in-the-ass brother.* Nonetheless, Joe learned fast and cared about his sisters. He couldn't fault him for that. He admired Joe's dedication to his family.

"What?" Stuart asked again.

"Do you have anything else to add?" Peter asked as Joe and Reese snickered.

"How many will be in attendance?"

"There are about three hundred graduates and six hundred guests. It's by invitation only, so it should be slightly easier," Peter replied, ending the discussion. "All right, you'll be picked up at nine o'clock. Make sure you shovel a large enough space for landing."

He and Joe already cleared the deep snow from a space this morning, but they'd have to redo it each day until Saturday if any additional snow fell. He thought that the actual ceremony would be safe for Taylor. He worried about the before and after part. Anything could happen during that time.

"Dinner's ready," Taylor called out after they switched off the TV.

She set the baked chicken on the bar's counter. Joe forked a piece and spooned a large helping of macaroni and cheese on his plate. Joe cut into the chicken thigh and stared at it. From the other stool, Stuart looked at his breast piece. The chicken leaked bloody juice from its raw center. Stuart debated between eating just the outside and hurting her feelings. Before he could say anything, Joe made a face.

"What's the matter?" she asked.

"Nothing, it looks great." Stuart narrowed his eyes at Joe. When Taylor turned back to the stove, he whispered, "Don't make her cry."

"Why would it make her cry?" Joe asked.

"What's wrong?" she asked again.

"It still raw in the center," Joe replied, turning his plate to show her the blood. Stuart braced himself for the tears.

She leaned over to look. "Oh, is your piece raw, too?" Stuart nodded and watched her response. "Okay, I'll just put it in for another thirty minutes," she replied, putting the two pieces back on the pan. She slid it back into the oven. "I guess we'll eat in courses. That's sophisticated, right?"

He thought for sure she'd cry. Joe was right—he didn't know her at all. Now he felt like shit for not giving her enough credit. When would he ever figure her out? He had so much to learn about her. Maybe she was right; maybe they did need to slow things down.

"Is there something wrong with the macaroni?" she asked him.

"No, it's fine. I was just thinking that a long engagement might be better," Stuart replied absently.

She winced and stared at her plate. "I'll do better next time," she whispered. "I haven't had much practice."

"What? No. That's not what I meant," Stuart replied, sitting up straighter.

"That was mean and out of line," Joe said. "We've lived in the dorms for four years. We're not allowed to cook there."

"That's not what I meant," he said again.

Before he could continue, Taylor spoke, "Joey, would you mind watching the oven? My head's still hurting." After grabbing her coat and a hat, she quickly shut the door to the deck behind her.

"Dude, what's wrong with you?" Joe asked. "You're

the one who made her cry. She's trying."

He ran his hand through his hair. "I know that."

Watching her on the back deck, he sighed. What was he thinking? That was the dumbest thing he'd ever said. He didn't even want a long engagement. How could he explain? He wanted to hug her and take it back. He slipped on his coat and stood next to her. He took a deep breath as he thought about the right words.

"I'm not mad at you," she said, looking out at the frozen water. "I know I'm not wife material."

He couldn't believe that came out of her mouth. He turned her to face him. "Hey, my stupid comment had nothing to do with dinner. I haven't gotten a read on you yet. I think you're going to react one way, and you do the opposite."

"Are you bored with me?" she asked as her eyes pooled with tears.

"That will never happen. You have a lot to teach me, and it proves that we need to spend more quality time together. Alone. That's where the stupid long engagement comment came from."

"I feel so inadequate," she whispered, turning away.

He pulled her closer. "Why would you say that?"

"What kind of wife would I make? I can't cook. I'm inexperienced with sex. I can't even seduce you. You make me lose my mind, and I couldn't even get your pants off. The only thing I know how to do is laundry."

He laughed and kissed her forehead. "You will be my wife. I love you completely. As long as you love me back, nothing else matters. We'll learn to cook together. Why do you think Mario's restaurant is number one on my speed dial? You've seen what's in my freezer. And, for your information, you turn me on without even trying."

"What about earlier?" she asked, tilting her head up to look at him. She was doing it again, making him want her with those long lashes and lush lips.

"What about it? I was rock hard that whole time. Thank God I had my jeans on. If Joe hadn't interrupted, we would have been in big trouble, and we would have regretted it." He put a finger to her mouth to stop her from interrupting. "We would have regretted the unprotected part, not the great sex part. And don't for a minute think that was easy for me."

She slid her arms through his open coat and hugged him. "You're right. We need to spend more time together. I seem to be misreading you, too," she replied against his chest.

CHAPTER
n i n e t e e n

SATURDAY

WHILE THE GUYS SHOVELED THE area for the helicopter, Taylor cleaned and straightened the cottage. The past week went quickly. She missed Eva and talked to her one other time on Thursday. Their brief conversation eased her mind slightly. Peter had been watching over her as he worked the case. The two of them had packed up almost all of their stuff from their dorm room and put it in temporary storage. Eva said they'd finish their room and help Joe with his on Sunday.

Christmas was fast approaching and she hadn't done any shopping yet. She hated waiting until the last minute. She was also nervous about how far behind she was on her scheduled plan. She and Eva were supposed to find an apartment together. She had finished her resume but hadn't sent it out to employers yet. Stuart and the persistent danger sidetracked her. The unease of the unknown made her queasy.

Deep in thought, she jumped as the guys burst

through the door. With cold, red cheeks, they had remnants of snowballs on their jackets. Sweat dripped from under their wool hats.

"I just cleaned the bathroom," she said, putting her hands on her hips.

They stripped off their outer layers. "We had to get in one more snowball fight," Joe said, shaking his damp head like a wet dog.

"Why?" she asked.

"To see who gets in the shower first," Stuart replied, moving toward the bathroom door.

She sighed at the mess by the side door. She'd wait until the last minute to clean it up. Joe moved toward the couch to wait his turn. "Hold it," she said, stopping him. "You stand over there. I just cleaned over here."

"By the door? Sheesh. Peter's got a maid, you know."

"I know, but he was very generous to let us stay here. We've made a good friend. I want him to know how much we appreciate his help."

Joe reluctantly agreed. He watched Taylor straighten pillows as busy work. "Are you sure about graduation?" he finally asked. "We don't have to go. It's not that big a deal."

"Don't you start. We've worked hard. Amber will not take that away from us. She will not win," she replied, crossing her arms.

He laughed. "You're sounding more and more like Eva. Do you promise to follow orders?"

She hugged him and nodded against his sweaty chest. "I promise."

"Hey, what's going on?" Stuart asked from the bathroom doorway. In his tight gray t-shirt and jeans, he frowned. She caught her breath at the sight of her handsome fiancé. Would she always react that way to him? She hoped so.

"Looks like he caught us," Joe replied, grinning.

She pushed him away. "You smell." Stuart laughed.

An hour past the scheduled landing time, she began to pace, much to the guys' amusement. She finally told them to pick on each other again, instead of focusing on her. They agreed and started a round of friendly banter. To her surprise, she found it calming.

They heard the noise before they saw it. A huge military helicopter buzzed the lake and landed in the space by the road.

"Was that a Huey?" Joe asked, staring out the window.

Stuart nodded and grabbed their bags. He quickly led them up the shoveled path.

"If they're going all out, why not a Black Hawk?" Joe mocked, pushing her from behind to make her keep up.

Stuart sighed. "A Black Hawk is for the Army. A Huey transports Marines. Oorah," he said over his shoulder.

"*Semper Fi,*" Joe mumbled.

She shivered as they approached the menacing flying machine. The General and Peter were taking every precaution for their safety. She suddenly felt guilty about pushing the issue. Who was paying for this beast?

The pilot jumped down from the side door. "Lieutenant Morgan, welcome," he said, with a salute.

Stuart winced before he shook his hand. "Captain Baker, you've moved up in the world," he replied. He turned to her. "I used to let Baker carry my field equipment a long time ago. It's good to see you, Kyle.

This is the rest of your cargo—my fiancée, Taylor Valentine, and her brother, Joe Roberts."

"Ma'am, Sir," he replied, nodding to them. "General Bingaman sends his regards."

"So he's got you chauffeuring civilians?" Stuart asked, helping Taylor and Joe inside.

"I volunteered for the privilege," Baker replied, following them into the hold.

Stuart sighed again. "I'll fasten them in, Captain."

"Yes, Sir," he replied, before returning to the front.

As they quickly left the ground, Stuart closed his eyes and swayed with the motion. Joe enjoyed the ride and looked at everything at once. Taylor watched Stuart closely.

Joe leaned across her. "Why is a Captain saluting a former Lieutenant?"

With his eyes still closed, Stuart shrugged. "Probably force of habit. He used to be my Private."

"You've flown in these before?" Joe asked.

Stuart turned and looked at him. "Always under fire."

Frowning, Joe sat back. Taylor caught a glimpse of the pain similar to what she noticed in the picture with the General. Biting her lower lip, she reached for his hand to reassure him.

He smiled and leaned down to kiss her. "I'm fine. It's been a while. Leave it to the General to go all out." He nodded at Joe, who tried to see what the pilot was doing. "Do you think he'll stop giving me shit now?"

"I doubt it," she replied. "How long will it take? I don't see a bathroom on this flight."

He laughed. "An hour and a half tops. Are you okay?"

"A little intimidated. They think highly of you. Will you tell me about it?"

"Soon," he replied, sitting back.

The noise kept the conversation to a minimum. She read Joe's mind. He wanted details of Stuart's accomplishments. She wouldn't push the issue, but Joe would. She didn't think Stuart would comply. Holding her hand, Stuart kept his eyes open as if struggling to push away his memories. She knew what that felt like.

Trying to distract him during the trip, she caressed his thigh and kissed him every so often. As they landed at the Kalamazoo Airport, she asked if he would have condoms for tonight. Laughing, he nodded and said he would buy a case.

Her ears still hummed even after the pilot turned off the motor. Stuart helped her unbuckle and said the humming would subside in a few minutes. Captain Baker slid open the side door, and Joe jumped out first. Stuart joined him then lifted her down. He hugged her as Peter approached them.

"Thank you for your distraction," Stuart whispered.

"Please, be careful today," she replied.

"Uh, Sir, we need to proceed to the SUVs," Baker said, holding his automatic weapon at the ready.

Peter directed her and Joe to the first black SUV parked on the snowy tarmac and Stuart to the second. The third, holding a few agents, would follow. Peter wanted them split up for their protection. Stuart wrapped his arm around her as he ushered her to the car. With their bags, Joe walked with Captain Baker.

Joe talked low while the Captain shook his head. After tossing their bags in the back, Joe climbed into the car next to Taylor. Peter jumped in and drove his

Escalade with Eva in the front passenger seat.

"Did you miss me?" Eva asked.

Joe chuckled. "It was as if you were right there with us. Taylor's becoming a taller version of you."

Taylor nudged him and laughed. "I missed you. And Peter, too. Thank you again."

"How's the fishing in the summer?" Joe asked, leaning forward.

"You will never know," Peter replied.

Joe grinned. "Eva, did you know that the Director had his picture taken with the President? He has all kinds of photos and mementos on the wall but none of his wife at his little getaway."

"Does she even know about your cabin?" Eva asked.

"You three are becoming a big pain in my butt," Peter replied, glaring at the road.

They laughed at his discomfort. "It's a beautiful place," Taylor said. "Rustic and high tech."

"Romantic?" Eva asked.

"It could have been," she replied. "This time it was all snowball fights and target practice."

"Who won the target practice?" Peter asked, smiling at Joe in his rearview mirror.

"Who do you think? The guy doesn't miss," Joe stated. "So what did Stuart do to get the admiration of the General and warrant a ride in a Huey?"

"That's his story to tell. Good luck getting it out of him," Peter replied.

"Where are we going until the ceremony?" she asked before Joe pushed the issue any further.

"We're being sequestered in a room at the complex next to the auditorium," Eva replied. "We'll be separated until right before the procession starts."

That sounds safe, she thought, as she looked out her window. The nervousness set in as Peter's radio squawked. Other agents updated the director with their status. She had a feeling that Captain Baker would have liked to accompany them with his huge gun. She would have made room for him.

"Where will Stuart be?" Taylor asked.

"He, Reese, and a few agents will be at Bob's house until this shindig starts," Peter replied. "His wife has invited the whole group over for a private celebratory dinner afterward."

Their car and the agents' car stopped at a back door to the complex next to the empty parking lot. They had three hours of waiting. Another agent greeted them at the door and rushed them to a small dressing room. Eva had already picked out their clothes. They hung next to their black graduation gowns. She and Eva laughed at Joe's displeasure of dress pants, shirt, and tie. They'd tried forever to dress him up, but he loved his worn Levis and t-shirts. While she updated Eva with the highlights of the past week, she watched Joe and Peter in the corner. Joe nodded then slipped something into his ear.

With half an hour to go, Eva touched up her makeup while Joe messed with his gown. Eva berated Taylor for her constant frown. They renewed their promise to be there for each other always, which made her extremely happy. Lately, she had begun to worry about the three of them growing apart.

In their black gowns and caps with golden yellow tassels, they posed for pictures. Eva made the agent take several until there was a knock on the door. With one agent in front and another in back, they found their spot in the long line of graduates next to another long line of faculty. Taylor and Eva chatted excitedly, but Joe stood rigid and messed with his ear. He froze and stared at nothing.

He swore then whispered, "Please. No."

Instantly alarmed, Taylor grabbed his arm. "Joey, what's wrong?"

He snapped out of his stare. "I, uh, gotta hit the head."

Joe turned and ran through the crowd of professors. The bathroom was the other way. While Eva talked with the agents, Taylor followed him. As she worked her way through the mob, someone grabbed her arm.

Loren Johnson pulled her close to him. "Taylor, when will you be back at the chiropractic office?" he asked, harshly gripping her arm.

"Take your hand off me," she seethed. "I won't be back. I quit."

Unfazed by her irritation, he released his hand. "Will you let me know where you'll be working? I don't care about those rumors."

Wanting to get away from him, she nodded, but before she could run in Joe's direction, both agents blocked her. Without a word, they ushered her back in line next to Eva. As she searched for Joe, the faculty moved into the auditorium. Joe rejoined them when they reached the door. He scowled. Whatever had happened, he wasn't happy. She squeezed his hand, and he hugged her fiercely. Before she could ask, they stepped through the doorway as the orchestra played "Pomp and Circumstance."

WEARING BLACK SLACKS AND A royal blue dress shirt, Stuart paced the length of Bob's living room and waited for Peter to pick him up for the ceremony. He hated being away from Taylor. This set-up didn't feel right at all. He should have put his foot down, but he promised himself not to disrupt her life more than he already had. Bob and Reese reassured him about security. Bob would be with the other deans and would keep a close eye on Taylor, too. Reese and Peter would attach themselves to his hip, which annoyed him even more.

He thanked Doris again for inviting them to dinner later. She was dying to meet everyone and wanted to hear the first-hand accounts of the last month. Because of the commotion of the so-called illicit triangle, her party had become a hit. Stuart thought the assault on Taylor and the part that Cindy played had the faculty begging for another invite to her Christmas gathering next week. He and Taylor would be as far from Kalamazoo as possible. He was still hoping for Vegas, but that seemed impossible now. He growled and paced.

With his gun at his side and his heavier dress coat buttoned to the neck, he jumped into Peter's Escalade in Bob's circular drive. All the agents had com units. Reese and Joe had them, too, but they could only listen. He wished Joe could give him updates on Taylor's status, but only the agents could communicate about her.

Peter flew toward the auditorium and parked by the side door next to the parking lot. While they waited for the okay from the agents in the building, Stuart watched the latecomers circling the lot for an open parking spot.

He shook his head as a few stragglers refused to move on to the next lot farther from the auditorium. It wasn't as if a spot would magically open. The ceremony hadn't even started yet.

When Peter nodded, Stuart quickly headed for the door. He heard a shot and grunted in pain. The force against his back propelled his body through the doorway and onto the floor. All hell broke loose with men shouting over each other.

"Morgan's been hit. I repeat, Morgan's been hit," Peter yelled into his com unit. "The suspect is in a white minivan with dark windows. It left the east parking lot, heading west."

Moaning, Stuart rolled on to his back. Reese knelt beside him as the door slammed shut. Peter turned off his headset. "Did it hurt?" Reese asked.

"Hell yeah, it hurt," he replied, getting to his feet. He unbuttoned his coat and peeled off his bulletproof vest.

"Are you ready to play dead?" Peter asked. Stuart nodded as Reese stared. "We need an ambulance! Now!" Peter shouted into his com. "There's a lot of blood. He's dying." He turned away and anxiously yelled bogus demands.

"There's no blood," Reese said.

Stuart rolled his eyes and brushed the dust off his pants. "We thought she might be listening to the FBI frequency. She's been cleverly avoiding the FBI, so it's plausible."

"You can't be seen now," Reese replied.

Before Stuart could agree, Joe ran into the room. With his cap in his hand, he stopped in his tracks. Stuart saw the pain in Joe's eyes and realized what he thought.

He rushed to him. "Joe, I'm sorry. I'm fine. That was for Amber's benefit in case she was listening."

"Son of a bitch! Why the hell didn't someone give me a heads up?" Joe demanded.

Reese held up the vest with a bullet lodged in the center. "She just now took a shot."

Stuart continued. "I swear, Joe, it wasn't planned. We went with it."

Joe blew out a breath. "All I could think about was explaining another death to Taylor."

Stuart reached out and grasped his shoulders. "Man, I am so sorry. Did you tell her?"

"No, but she's gonna freak when she finds out," Joe said, tugging on the tassel of the cap.

"She doesn't need to know," he replied.

Joe narrowed his eyes. "I won't lie to her."

"I will tell her later, not you. You got that?"

"Is that a command, Lieutenant?" Joe fumed sarcastically.

Glaring, Stuart made a fist at the reference to his former rank. "It is. If you tell her, you will never see her again. I'll make sure of it."

As soon as he said it, he knew he would catch shit, but Joe would not undermine his relationship with Taylor again. Grinding his teeth, Joe barely held back his temper. He warped his cap with both hands. His body shook with anger.

Peter barked from the doorway, "Joe, get going! By God, you are going to graduate today!" As Joe refitted his cap to his head, Peter put his hand on Joe's chest and calmly added, "Keep your eyes open. My guys are pursuing the van, but she may have help. I need you to stay focused."

Joe angrily nodded and hurried away.

"You sure know how to push his buttons. Do you think he'll tell her?" Reese asked.

"I don't know," Stuart replied.

Reese was right—Joe would stay angry. Stuart couldn't blame him either. Thank God Amber went after him instead of Taylor, although she also wore a vest under her gown, as did Joe and Eva. Every precaution, Peter had said. Stuart paced in a small dressing room that had a video feed of the ceremony. While Peter coordinated the ambulance and the transporting of his dead body, Stuart watched the three students receive their diplomas. They were a close-knit group, and he envied them. He hoped they would let him in someday. Not likely if Joe had his way. After everything that had happened this past week, he knew he needed to apologize.

AFTER THE CEREMONY, AGENTS SHOVED Taylor, Joe, and Eva into another SUV. They barely had time to take off their gowns and put on their coats. She couldn't wait to take off the protective vest. Taylor watched Peter slam the doors to the back of an ambulance. With its flashing lights on and no siren, it left ahead of them.

"Was someone hurt?" Taylor asked. "I didn't notice anything during commencement." Joe looked out the other window and mumbled that someone would hurt later. The agents in the front seats glanced at each other.

Eva watched Peter get into an SUV next to theirs.

"If Peter shut the doors, it must be an agent or—" Eva leaned toward the agents. "Where's Stuart?"

Taylor suddenly wanted to vomit. "Is Stuart okay? Where is he? Joey, you know something. Tell me now," she demanded.

The agents tensed and waited for Joe's answer. Joe sighed as they watched campus security hold up traffic for them to leave first. "Stuart's fine and will meet us at the Dean's house," Joe mumbled as he clenched his hands into tight fists.

Taylor rubbed her nauseous stomach. Seeing the questioning look on Eva's face, she knew Eva would get straight answers later. The agents seemed to relax as Joe sat rigidly next to her. Parked in front of the Dean's house, the agents escorted them to the front door. Doris and Bob greeted them while Peter talked with his agents just outside. Stuart and Reese stood in the hallway next to the library and waited for the end of the introductions.

Only a few years older than Taylor, Doris reminded her of a young Martha Stewart, not only in looks but also in her holiday decorating style. The whole house looked as if it were straight out of Woman's Day magazine. Doris took their coats and made them feel welcome. After ushering them into the living room, Bob offered them something to drink. Doris left to put the final touches on dinner. Stuart and Reese held back until Peter shut the front door and nodded at them.

Within a blink, Stuart was at Taylor's side, helping her take off her vest. She wore her black spaghetti-strap dress. Since she hadn't been shopping in a while, Eva thought it was the only presentable thing in her closet.

She wrapped her arms tightly around his waist. He winced but hugged her back. Before she could ask anything, he kissed her. Again, she lost all thought and felt faint. Pulling back, he grinned, knowing exactly what he did to her.

"Can we finish a little business before dinner?" Peter asked.

"We should discuss this in private," Stuart said, taking the glass Bob held out for him.

Taylor folded her arms. "How much privacy do you need?"

"I just meant we wouldn't want to bore you with the details," Stuart replied, taking a gulp of his drink.

"No. What you really mean is you don't want to discuss it in front of me. Well, too bad. What are you hiding?"

He ran a hand through his hair, which clued her in that she was right. He sat on the loveseat and crossed his legs. Leaning on the frame of the doorway, Joe sneered. Their friendly banter from this morning had disappeared. Stuart and Joe glared at each other as if carrying on a telepathic conversation. Taylor sighed. She was glad Eva was there. She knew Eva would back her up—she wanted answers, too.

Peter sat in the leather chair in the corner. Bob and Reese took up residence on the long couch. Left standing in the middle of the room, Taylor stormed to the other chair next to Peter and sank into it. She glowered at everybody.

"Okay, well, this is what we know," Peter said, breaking the tension. "My team found the abandoned minivan off Sprinkle Road."

"Minivan?" Taylor asked. "You saw Amber in it?"

Stuart tensed as Peter continued. "Well, no."

"So what happened to point you in the direction of

this minivan?" Eva demanded.

"Any clues left in the van?" Stuart quickly asked.

"Yeah, they found a couple of things. The first was an airline ticket receipt with a time and date of a flight to Mexico."

"When?" Reese asked.

"Ten-thirty tonight. A team is staking out the airport now," Peter replied.

"Great, so it's over," Stuart said, downing the rest of his drink.

"What's the second thing?" Eva demanded.

Peter sighed. "They found a rifle and are running the prints. We'll know more in the morning."

"A rifle?" Taylor whispered, staring at Stuart. "Who was hurt?"

"Nobody," Peter replied.

"We saw you slam the ambulance doors shut," Eva said.

Peter glanced at Stuart as Doris walked back into the room. "Dinner's ready," Doris said.

Stuart jumped to his feet. "Great, I'm starved. Are stuffed mushrooms on the menu?" he asked, escorting Doris toward the dining room.

Peter, Bob, and Reese rushed after them. Eva hustled after Peter for answers while Taylor grabbed her brother's arm to stop him. "Joey, what's going on?"

"Can we eat? We're supposed to be celebrating."

She frowned at his deflection to the question. "How much more stress am I supposed to endure?"

He hugged her and whispered in her ear, "You are surrounded by new friends and family. This threat is almost over, and we finally graduated college. Your parents would be proud of all of us. Let's toast them

and have a good time. We deserve it. Don't you think?"
Smiling, she nodded. He wiped her cheek with his
thumb and kissed her forehead. "Let's get drunk."

She laughed, and they walked arm in arm into the
dining room. She took her seat next to Stuart. He eyed
Joe who sat across from them next to Eva. She scanned
the mountain of food on the table–poached salmon,
stuffed mushrooms, scalloped potatoes, and steamed
vegetables.

"Doris, everything looks delicious. Thank you for
inviting us," Taylor said, breaking the silent strain in the
room. She reached for Stuart's hand under the table. He
squeezed it enthusiastically.

Doris smiled and motioned for the group to dig in.
"It's my pleasure. I wanted to apologize to you and Stuart
personally for my blunder with that young woman." She
tensed as she waited for a response. At least she didn't
say the bitch's name.

Stuart answered for her. "Will you believe me now
when I say I do better on my own?"

"I have been informed by my husband that I will
never be allowed to set anyone up again. Although Joe,"
she said, turning to him, "I know a few ladies who would
enjoy your company."

"No, thank you. I'm not the settling-down type."

"I didn't think I was either," Stuart said, spinning
Taylor's engagement ring on her finger under the table.
"What about Reese?"

"No way. I've seen those women. Sorry, Sis, but
you suck at set-ups," Reese said, helping himself to the
salmon.

"Don't even look in my direction," Peter said,
holding up his hands.

As they ate dinner, Taylor thought about her life's plan. She had focused so much on school that she hadn't let herself think about anything else. Her perfect plan had changed, which made her uneasy. Eva and Joe thought it was a plan of convenience, but she considered it a memorial to her parents. She wanted them to be proud of all the choices she made in her life.

Before Doris rose to clear the table, she patted her husband's arm. "Dear, tell them our idea."

Bob smiled. "In honor of the newly engaged couple, we decided to have an early bachelor and bachelorette party."

"All right," Joe said, grinning. "Bring on the strippers."

"No strippers," she and Stuart replied.

Laughing, Bob continued. "In the den, I have a couple large screen TVs set up with all sorts of video games."

"You play, Stuart?" Joe asked, sitting up in his chair.

"I don't, but I'll give it a shot," he replied with a smirk.

"Oh, he plays. He beats me every damn time, and now it's payback," Bob said, rubbing his hands together. "I got the booze and a bunch of games."

"What do the ladies have planned?" Reese asked.

"We're going to the downtown Radisson Hotel Spa for manicures, pedicures, and massages," Doris said.

"That sounds wonderful. Do they have male masseurs?" Taylor asked, grinning.

"Oh, no you don't," Stuart said.

"I'll go with the ladies and keep a close eye on them," Reese said, grinning.

"No way," Joe and Stuart replied as the ladies

laughed.

"I believe I'll have the pleasure," Peter said.

"Ladies, we'll clear the table," Bob added.

"Thank you, Dear," Doris said, kissing his cheek.

Stuart pulled Taylor aside. "Be careful, and I'll see you when you get back."

"I'll be slick with massage oil. Will that be okay?" she whispered.

He growled. "I'm thinking maybe we should stay at the hotel."

"Whatever you want," she said.

"I want you," he said, pulling her even closer, "and I bought a big box of condoms that we'll use up later." She giggled and kissed him.

While Peter drove his Escalade, the women sat in back and chatted about the possible wedding plans for Vegas. "Are you okay sharing a room with Joe?" Taylor asked Eva.

"Room yes, bed no," Eva replied. "He promised nothing would happen no matter how drunk we got."

"Would that be weird?" Doris asked. "He is handsome."

"Very weird. He's our brother. He's cute and all, but he is not my type," Eva replied.

"What's your type?" Doris asked.

"Someone mature like Stuart, someone fun with a sense of humor like Stuart, and someone handsome with a good job … like Stuart," Eva said, grinning.

"Hey, he's mine."

"He's so into you." Eva laughed. "I want someone who's just as crazy about me as I am about him—like you and Stuart."

"He's out there somewhere," Taylor replied.

CHAPTER
twenty

BLITZED FROM THE ALCOHOL AND relaxed from the massages, the three women stumbled back to the SUV late Saturday night. Peter rolled his eyes and helped them into his car. As he drove, they giggled about nothing. Peter honked the horn twice in front of Bob's house. With their coats in hand, Stuart and Joe ran out the front door.

"I need some help. I am not carrying these drunken women into the house by myself," Peter said as he opened the back door to hear more screams of laughter.

Slipping on his coat, Stuart yelled for Bob to get his wife. He and Joe met Peter by the open door as Bob ran to stand beside them.

Doris slid out first and tugged on her husband's shirt. "Come along, Lover," she slurred. "Let's get naked."

"Game's over, guys," Bob said. He swept his wife up in his arms and carried her into the house.

Reese stepped forward and peeked into the car.

"Any soused broads in there for me?"

"I'm drunk but not that drunk. Joey, help me out," Eva said. Frowning, Reese returned to the house.

"Jeez, how much did you drink?" Joe asked, lifting her out by her waist like a toddler.

"We lost track," Eva replied, leaning against the side of the car. "I need some air. Joey, let's walk. It's not that far."

"Fine, as long as I don't have to carry you." Joe looked at Taylor, still in the car. She smiled and gave him a little wave. He grinned. "Have fun with that one," he said to Stuart. "Last time she was that lit, she wanted to bowl in the nude. She thought it would better her game because her clothes were too constricting. Before I realized what she was doing, she stripped off her shirt. I had to carry her out over my shoulder. It made the rest of the night very interesting," he said, amused by Stuart's glare. Joe pushed the point of their intimate moment further. "Remember, Taylor?"

She nodded and blushed. She had asked Joe what it felt like to have sex. He told her he'd discuss it with her when she was sober. Of course, she never ever brought it up again.

"Joey, come on before I have to pee," Eva said as she started to skate down the icy drive.

"Stay cautious," Peter yelled.

WHILE JOE CHASED AFTER EVA, Taylor removed her panties. Stuart watched her wiggle her finger at him.

Peter leaned on the hood and waited for the drama to settle. "Uh, Peter?" Stuart said.

"Get in, and I'll take you to the hotel." Peter sighed. "Just promise you won't leave the room. I'm tired. I've never heard women talk like those three. I know now what I'm doing wrong in my marriage."

With their bags still in the back, Stuart climbed in next to Taylor. "Have you been naughty without me?"

She shook her head then grinned. "I've never done it in the back of a car before," she whispered, pulling him on top of her.

"I know all the places you've done it. I've been with you, remember?"

"Do you think Peter will know if we have sex back here?" she whispered.

"Yes, I'll know," Peter replied from the front seat. "Cool it. I can't take any more sex talk." He kept his eyes on the road and mumbled, "Apparently, I haven't done anything right in bed either."

"I've been fantasizing about you all evening," Stuart said, kissing her neck.

She moaned and slid down onto the seat, hiking up her dress. "Take me."

"Oh God, we have to wait," he said, glancing up to see where they were.

"But I need you inside me," she whispered as she pulled her dress up more.

"Taylor, stop. You're making me crazy," he said.

Peter parked in the ramp across the street from the hotel. "Good God, we're here. Get the hell out of my car," Peter said, before standing to check the area. "I don't remember this being in my job description," he mumbled. "I need to get back behind my desk."

Stuart helped her out. The cold air started to sober her. He signed for two rooms across the hall from each other while Peter assessed the front lobby. He gave one key card to Peter and promised to stay put until morning.

"How was your video game tournament?" she asked as they walked through the lobby. She moved toward the music in the packed bar.

He steered her away. "Every time I'd start to win, they'd say stuff about you to distract me. It drove me nuts."

Peter ignored them and eyed the group next to the bar entrance. She stopped and swayed in front of the elevator. "What stuff? Should I be mad that they were talking about me?"

"No, Honey," he said, holding her steady. "This was their version of a bachelor party."

On the third floor, they found their room. Peter disappeared into his while he worked to open the door and keep her from falling over. He finally propped her against it.

"Do you want to tell me what they said?" she asked, loosening his belt. She tugged at his shirt.

He pushed the door open and grabbed her before she fell backward onto the floor. "Well, Bob said the spa had three massage therapists—two women and one guy. He said you chose the man. Joe said the young, buff guy loves rubbing hot pieces of ass. They tortured me with that vision." He guided her into the room.

"What else?" she asked, neither confirming nor denying the allegation.

Upset, he continued, "Joe mentioned he once walked in on you when you were naked. Bob and Reese wouldn't let that mental image drop either. It was like they planned to knock me off my game the whole night."

"Anything else?" she asked as she leaned against the wall across from the king-sized bed.

He groaned and set his gun on the side table. "Joe said he overheard you and Eva's discussion on your Victoria's Secret purchases a couple weeks ago. He'd think twice if he actually saw you in the lingerie. I got so pissed. It's a good thing you came back when you did," he said, watching her struggle to take off her coat.

"Do you want my version of these events?" she asked, tossing her coat toward the chair but missing it.

He sat at the foot of the bed a few feet from her. "I think so," he replied, ready to catch her if she started to tip over.

"If all those things are true, does it change your opinion of me?" she asked with her arms crossed.

"Of course not," he replied, slipping off his shoes, "but I'd like to hear what you have to say about them."

"First, I didn't get massaged by the guy. You said no. Eva and I both had the female therapists."

"Oh, really?" He grinned. "Does Bob know this? It would make me feel better if I told him."

"I don't know. The guy wasn't that young or that buff either. Doris said he was very professional. Joe has seen me totally naked. He purposely walked in on me in the bathroom. I had only a towel around me, so I flashed him."

"You did?" he asked, clenching his jaw. He wasn't sure he wanted to know any more, especially if Joe's carrying her shirtless out of bowling alleys. Yeah, Joe had protected her from other guys, but he was the one closest to her. Stuart hated his vivid imagination.

"Joe saw me naked when we were ten. Eva warned me he was going to do it and dared me to flash him," she said, smiling.

He laughed. "That bastard. I'll ring his neck."

"And about my lingerie, Joe may have thought he spied on us, but the guy has lead feet. We knew he was there. We indulged his fantasies a bit, which, again, was Eva's idea. He never saw any of our purchases."

Relieved, he blew out a breath.

"Besides," she said, unzipping her dress and letting it drop to the floor, "There's only one man I want to wear lingerie for." While he watched, she stepped toward the bed wearing only her thigh-high nylons and black heels.

"Wow," he said, already forgetting what they were just talking about, "you are so damn sexy."

She put her left foot on the bed between his legs. "I need some help."

He slipped off her shoe. As her toes rubbed his groin, he slowly rolled down her nylon, kneading her leg as he went. He kissed her inner thigh. She wobbly switched legs. He watched her face and slid down the other nylon. After setting her foot back on the floor, he glided his hands up the sides of her legs. Standing, he steadied her and kissed her hungrily.

"I want you," she whispered when he kissed her neck.

He laid her on her back. With her elbows propping her up, she watched him toss the jumbo pack of condoms on the bed and drop his clothes to the floor. Climbing onto the bed, he hovered above her, his hard member pressed against her.

"And I need you," he replied. Before they could continue, someone pounded on their door. "Don't move," he told her. He grabbed a hotel robe and his gun before cracking the door.

Disheveled, Peter stood before him. "Joe just called. Eva's in the hospital from a hit and run. He thinks it was Amber."

"Is she okay?" Taylor asked, jumping up. More alert and still naked, she scrambled for jeans and a sweatshirt from their luggage.

Peter averted his eyes. "Joe thinks she has a broken leg and wrist. She's still unconscious. I've got an agent meeting with the local LEOs now."

"Give us two minutes," Stuart said.

FROM A CORNER CHAIR IN the emergency waiting room, Joe rubbed his hands over his face. Ignoring the holiday decorations, Taylor ran to her brother while Stuart and Peter hurried after her. Joe stood and hugged her. "It happened so fast," Joe said.

"How is she?" she asked, squeezing him.

"I don't know. She hasn't woken up."

Peter pulled the corner chairs into a tight circle and motioned for them to sit. They leaned in and talked quietly so not to disturb the other visitors and patients.

"Start from the beginning," Peter said.

Joe rubbed his fingers over his brow and tried to focus. His voice didn't have his usual air of confidence, which unnerved her. "We were a block from our dorm. Eva acted all goofy and danced around ahead of me. I yelled for her to wait at the end of the sidewalk. She did.

She spiraled like a ballerina." He stared at his palms. "Out of nowhere, a car jumped the curb and clipped her leg with its front side bumper. I watched her bounce off the car and land on her head and shoulder."

Taylor covered her mouth to hold back her sobs.

"The car didn't stop?" Peter asked as he continually surveyed the waiting room.

Joe shook his head and held out his hand. He had written down a few numbers and letters on his palm. "I could only remember part of the license plate."

"Good," Peter replied, writing it down on his mini-notepad. "What did you do next?"

"I, uh, ran to her. She had a deep gash on her head, and her body angled oddly, bending where it shouldn't. I wanted to straighten her out. Instead, I put my wool cap against her head to stop the bleeding. I called nine-one-one then you."

Peter nodded. "What can you tell us about the car?"

Joe blew out a breath and calmed his shaky voice. "Uh, I think it was a late model Buick."

"What color?" Peter asked while she and Stuart remained quiet.

"It seemed to have a dull finish. It was patchy with rust primer and the exhaust pipe spewed heavy white smoke as it left."

"You're doing great, Joe," Peter replied. "Anything else you can remember?"

He shook his head then added sadly, "The doctor seems more worried more about her head injury than her broken bones and dislocated hip."

Peter nodded and stood with his cell phone. "All right, gang. I'll call Reese and have him stay with Bob. You three stay together."

"I want to sit with her," Taylor stated.

"I'll see if it's possible," Stuart said. He walked across the room to check with ER registration.

"It's my fault. I let my guard down," Joe said to her.

"This mess is not your fault, Joey," she said firmly.

Stuart returned. "She's not awake yet, but they'll allow one of you to sit with her."

"Go ahead," Joe mumbled.

Taylor followed the attendant down a corridor to a room. She walked through the doorway of the intensive care unit. Bandages covered Eva's temple, her left wrist, and her lower left leg. Monitors with attached wires bleeped. One screen showed her low blood pressure. Sitting beside her, Taylor took Eva's very cold hand in hers and gently massaged it.

"Hey, Evie, it's me. Wake up, Sis, so I know you're all right."

Taylor babbled on about this and that. She knew she rambled, but it helped calm her queasy stomach. Her own head started to ache. She struggled to keep her emotions in check. *No crying*, she told herself. The change in monitor beeps brought her eyes back to her sister's face.

Eva grimaced. "Taylor, it hurts."

She hit the call button and smiled. "Are you trying to take the attention away from me?"

"Yeah, I was jealous."

She squeezed Eva's fingers. "I guess I'll have to find you a man then."

"You know my type," Eva mumbled before closing her eyes again.

The nurse ran in and checked the monitors. "Was she talking coherently?" Taylor nodded. "We'll need to do more tests. I'll keep you updated."

Taylor kissed her sister's hand and left.

CHAPTER
twenty-one

SUNDAY

STANDING OUTSIDE EVA'S DOOR AT two in the morning, Taylor heard a commotion in the waiting room. She rushed toward the angry voice. Joe shouted at Stuart, who let him rant. Peter spoke low, trying to calm him. While the waiting room crowd watched, Joe clenched his hands and stepped closer.

"First, Taylor! Now you're trying to take Eva away, too," Joe growled. Stuart dropped his arms as Joe cocked his fist.

"Joey! Step away!" she yelled, approaching them.

Glancing at her, Joe moved even closer. With his face inches from Stuart's, he tapped Stuart's chest with two fingers. "This is your fault. Eva could die because of you."

Stuart remained unprovoked. "You're right."

"No, he's not. You want someone to blame. Blame that bitch," she said, stepping between them. She lowered her voice. "Joey, what's the matter with you?"

"Me? Him! If I don't play it the Lieutenant's way, he will keep you away from me!"

"I didn't mean it; but if you call me by that rank again, we'll have it out here and now," Stuart replied, not budging from their standoff, Taylor squished between them.

"Mean it or not, you still said it," Joe said, glaring.

"You two, come with me," Taylor demanded.

She walked to an alcove in the hallway. She hated the fact that people were leering at them and knew their business. Standing next to each other, they crossed their arms and waited. They were so much alike. *Why couldn't they see it?* Peter stood behind them, ready to break up a fistfight.

She looked at Stuart first. "After this past week, how could you say something like that?"

"I didn't mean it," Stuart repeated, "and I was going to apologize."

Joe snorted. "Yeah, right."

She glared at Joe and shook her finger at him to shut him up. "What makes you think he could do it?" Before he could answer, she turned back to Stuart. "And you, if you say anything like that to Joe again, even as a joke, you will have damaged our relationship beyond repair." Peter smiled from behind them while her anger escalated. "Stop acting like you're in eighth grade and grow up. My sister is lying in a hospital bed because of Amber. Why don't you focus on finding her instead of ripping into each other? It isn't helping!"

Upset that they hated each other, she did an about face and went to the vending machines. Her body shook from her outburst. She leaned on the wall and stared at the snacks. Her stomach tightened into a ball of nervous tension.

"Trying to decide on a snack?" Peter asked a few minutes later.

She clenched her jaw. "My purse is at the hotel."

He pulled out some change from his pocket. "What do you want?" She opened her mouth, and he quickly added, "From the vending machine, I mean."

"Water. My head's killing me."

He chuckled and handed her a bottle. "You deserve the headache with what you put me through earlier. Don't worry about those two. They'll work it out."

"How? They despise each other."

"Not really. They both feel responsible," he said, adding coins for his Coke.

"They didn't even ask how Eva was doing," she said, pinching her earlobe, so she wouldn't cry.

"Is she awake?"

She nodded. "For a little while. She even joked with me. They're running more tests to be safe."

"Let's sit and wait," Peter said. "I obviously need to motivate my agents."

She picked a lone chair away from the rest. They got the hint that she was still angry and upset. If she weren't so tired, she'd laugh at them. Joe and Stuart went out of their way to be nice to each other. Stuart bought Joe a Coke while Joe accepted his apology. They glanced at her while they talked about their video games. They tried to be civil. Peter growled non-stop into his cell. She hoped he was making some progress.

With her knees pulled to her chin, she dozed in her chair while the guys paced. The ER had a busy early morning, delaying Eva's tests. That meant she wasn't as serious as some of the others—at least that was comforting.

At seven, a nurse motioned them to an empty hallway. Eva had a concussion and needed to stay. The nurse showed them to her private room on the third floor. Taylor entered with the nurse while the guys hung back. Eva looked so frail and childlike without her usual pristine makeup. She was still beautiful but looked nothing like a fiery Irish pit bull.

"She's resting," the nurse said. "That's the best thing for her now."

"Can I stay?"

"I think it would be best to come back. We'll take good care of her."

She nodded and left the room. The men surrounded her. "We can visit later."

Peter posted a guard outside Eva's door. "Let's get some breakfast in the cafeteria then some sleep," he said.

Visitors, nurses, doctors, and other hospital employees with badges sat at various tables. Standing in a long line, she and Stuart observed a dad and his son in front of them. Using a cane, the dad limped with his leg in a knee brace. His grade-school-aged son held his other arm to offer support. Needing a distraction from her worries, she quietly followed Stuart and listened to their conversation.

"I know it's hard, David, but it's as important as your other subjects," the dad said, ruffling his son's loose curls that covered his ears.

"What's so important about history? How's it matter? It already happened," David said, stepping closer to the stack of trays next to the silverware.

Stuart turned to her and raised his eyebrow at the boy's comment. She smiled.

Leaning heavily on the cane, the dad patiently explained, "Do you remember your first rocket football game against Hopkins? You kept getting burned by their running back."

"Ugh, yeah," David replied, frowning, "but I did better the second time we played them."

"That's right. You learned his tendencies. History is like your memory. Those who don't remember history tend to repeat it."

Grinning, Stuart turned to her again. "I like this guy."

She chuckled and looked around him. David's dad had short hair that probably would be wavy like his son's if it was longer. His firm jaw line and manner suggested authority, but they joked like best friends.

"My physical therapy session is in the afternoon today. If you use that time to finish your assignments, we'll do something fun afterward," David's dad said, shifting his cane to grab his wallet.

David dutifully pushed the tray along the track. "Can I study in the big sunroom? It has a gigantic Christmas tree," he asked, setting the full plates on the tray.

"Sure, Son."

Before picking up the heavy tray, David eyed the group behind him. Taylor smiled back at the young boy while Peter and Joe drooling over the food. She set a plain donut on Stuart's tray and watched David and his dad walk side by side to an empty table.

Too tired to talk, she sat and listened to the plan they'd been over a hundred times. "Stay as a group and keep your eyes open." *Some plan. They needed a new one. This one wasn't working.* As Stuart talked about strategy,

Peter and Joe nodded intently.

She watched David and his father. They laughed even though the dad rubbed his leg under the table. David glanced at her a few times, most likely disturbed that she was staring. After her third sigh, she walked to refill her coffee cup. As she dumped in some creamer, David approached her.

"Are you safe?" he whispered as he looked over his shoulder at the men from her table.

"What do you mean?"

"That man at your table has a gun hidden under his coat. Does he want to hurt you? I can tell my dad. He's a cop."

She smiled. "He's allowed to carry one. We're visiting my sister. She was hit by a car."

"Is she going to be okay?" he asked. "I could make her a Get Well card. It gets boring around here."

"I think she would love a homemade card. Have you been here a while?"

"Six weeks. My dad's in rehab. We stay in the housing section until my dad can drive again," David said, giving his father a thumb's up.

"Did you see his gun or did your dad?" she asked, glancing at the men from her table. They had stopped talking and watched them.

"I did first and told my dad. He suggested I come and ask you to be sure."

"Thank you for your concern. It's a very responsible thing to do."

David stood taller and grinned proudly.

"Can I thank your dad, too?" she asked.

"Sure, maybe it'll cheer him up. His leg hurts a lot," he replied, leading her to his table.

She saw Joe stand. Frowning, she held up her hand to stop him from approaching.

LISTENING TO PETER AND JOE, Stuart silently sipped his coffee and watched Taylor leave to get more. Joe was right. All of this was his fault. He might have felt better if Joe had punched him. Taylor had been annoyed with both of them since the argument. He held no animosity toward Joe. Hell, he liked the guy and understood his frustration about Eva's accident and Taylor's safety.

"What's she doing?" Joe asked.

Stuart smiled as Taylor and David talked. He wanted a family and hoped she did, too. They hadn't talked much about it. He pictured her with their children. He desperately wanted that future with her.

"Where's she going?" Joe asked, standing to follow.

"She says stay put," Peter replied, watching them closely.

Ready to pounce if necessary, the three of them watched Taylor introduce herself to the man and his son. While she stood next to their table, she set her hand on David's shoulder and shook the dad's hand. She thanked them again and grinned as she returned to their table.

"What was that about?" Joe demanded.

"It seems that this group is exhausted and not paying attention. That young boy saw Peter's gun and asked if I needed assistance."

"Looks like you got made, Pete," Joe said.

"For the last time, it's Director Bingaman, unless you'd rather be friends and not work for me." He pulled a letter from his inside jacket pocket and handed it to Joe. "Congratulations."

Watching her brother read the letter, Taylor's grin slid to a frown. They waited for him to shout from the rooftop and say something cocky. He didn't. Joe remained quiet.

"You recommended me?" Joe finally asked, looking at Peter.

Peter shared a glance with Taylor. "I did," he replied. "You deserve it."

"Thank you," Joe said as he stared at the letter. "I won't let you down."

Stuart didn't understand the melancholy mood. The rest of them apparently did. Peter finally smiled. "I expect grateful ass kissing now."

Joe folded the letter and tucked it into his back pocket. "Yeah, you should kiss my ass and be grateful you found the best agent you'll ever have."

There it was. Joe's cocky attitude returned, and all was right with the world. Well, almost. While Taylor tried to blink away a tear, Peter chuckled. Looking around, Stuart's gut constricted in the packed cafeteria. He didn't feel safe here. Some people were eating standing up while others wandered around looking for an empty table. He had a hard time seeing around those closest to them.

"I think it's time to leave," Stuart said.

Joe stiffened, realizing the same thing. "I'll follow you and Taylor out while Director Bingaman leads you through the crowd."

"Joey, are you taking over now?"

"It's a good idea. Let's go," Peter replied.

Peter drove them to the hotel. Joe stayed with Peter across the hall from Stuart and Taylor. All of them dragged their feet to their rooms and collapsed into bed.

Taylor laid her head on Stuart's bare chest. "Tell me again that she'll be all right."

"She's tough, but she'll need your support as she heals," he replied, kissing the top of her head.

"I have a plan for that," she said, yawning.

Before he could ask her what she meant, her breathing deepened. He followed suit a few minutes later.

TAYLOR BOLTED UPRIGHT AS THE hotel phone rang. Next to her, Stuart reached for it. In his boxer briefs, he sat on the edge of the bed and muttered into it. She rubbed her temples and glanced at his muscular back and arms. She loved looking at his sculpted body. Blinking, she leaned closer and focused on a nasty bruise between his shoulder blades. He hung up and lay on his side facing her.

"We have an hour before Joe pounds on our door," he said.

"How'd you get the bruise on your back?"

He winced. "Yeah, we, uh, need to talk about that," he said, running his hand through his already messy hair. "Just remember that I'm fine."

She sat against the headboard and pulled the sheet to her chin. "I don't like how this story starts." She sighed.

"All right, give it to me straight. What happened?"

He told her about being shot and playing dead in the hopes that Amber would come out into the open. She stared in shock as she processed the information. This drama had unfolded while she had happily listened to flowery graduation speeches? How foolish. She shouldn't have insisted.

"Honey, it's just a bruise. I had on the vest," he said as he reached for her hand.

She pulled away. Angry tears blurred her vision. "Just a bruise? What if she aimed for your head? Would that have been just a bruise? God, you could have died, and it would have been my fault."

"That's crazy. It's Amber's fault, remember?"

"Well, this crazy bitch overreacted in Joe's car when you said no to attending graduation. To regain some kind of control, I demanded it, and you almost died."

Stuart smiled. "Does that mean I get to boss you around from now on?"

In his Michigan t-shirt, she jumped from the bed. "It's not funny. Why didn't you tell me when it happened? I should have worn one of those ear things."

He watched her fret by the window. "I'm glad you didn't. You wouldn't have liked what you heard. Peter played it up as if I was dead in case Amber was listening."

She stopped as she remembered the anguish on her brother's face. "Joe heard that you were shot?"

He nodded. "When he showed up, I tried to explain that it wasn't planned, but he was his usual angry self."

"Can you blame him? He came back so upset. His body shook."

He groaned and met her by the window. "Taylor, I swear I didn't mean it, but I wanted to be the one to tell you. I wanted you to see for yourself that I was okay. That's why I threatened him."

"Oh, Stuart, how awful. You knew how deep that would cut into him," she said, wiping her eyes with her hand. "Please, fix it. I need you and Joe to work it out. I want all of us to be a family."

He nodded. "I'll think of something."

"Thank you," she whispered against his chest.

AFTER AN HOUR, STUART OPENED the door for Joe and Peter while Taylor finished getting ready in the bathroom. Before he shut it, he saw two agents standing in the hallway. Joe sat in the plush chair and propped his feet on the corner of the made bed. Peter tossed three bulletproof vests next to Joe's feet.

"Joe already ordered lunch. I need to fill you in on the latest," Peter said, leaning against the wall.

"Taylor will be out in a few minutes. You'll be happy to know that I slept in that chair," Stuart said. Joe perked up at his little white lie—his Taylor-approved little white lie. "I think she lost her voice after the tirade."

Joe smiled. "Oh yeah?"

"You were right. We should have told her after the fact instead of waiting."

"Did she throw stuff?" Joe asked eagerly.

Sitting in the chair by the table, Stuart pointed to the small bottles of shampoo and lotion lying on the floor by the window. "I should have known she had good aim by those snowballs she threw at us," Stuart replied.

"Well, you gotta learn to duck and dodge. I'm a pro. My quick reflexes will help when I'm undercover," Joe replied, smiling.

Peter rolled his eyes. "You piss off Taylor so much that it enhanced your skills?"

Stuart laughed as Joe nodded. "I've been training my whole life to be a Fed."

"How are you at dodging bullets? Like mine if you piss me off?" Peter asked.

"What are you talking about? Who else is dodging bullets?" Taylor demanded as she stepped out of the bathroom. Her eyes narrowed on the three of them.

"I was telling Stuart that he needs to duck when you throw stuff," Joe replied, grinning.

She glared at him. "Do you want to start something?"

"No, not today," Joe replied as someone knocked on the door.

Peter motioned Taylor away from the door. With a hand on his gun, he answered it. "Yeah, we'll leave in a half hour," he said to the agents. He rolled in the room service cart with a pyramid of shiny metal trays with covers. Joe had ordered three burgers with fries and a chef salad. Taylor grabbed the salad and sat on the bed. "Is everybody on the same page?" Peter asked, setting his plate on the table.

Stuart nodded and glanced at Taylor. She listened and quietly munched a cucumber.

"All right, we traced the prints from the rifle to Roan LaRossa. My agents have him in an interrogation room at the Kalamazoo Police Station. He has a record for breaking and entering as well as assault and battery."

"I thought they'd find Amber's prints," Taylor said.

"The prints on the flight receipt are the same as those on Amber's exam from the seminar. We're going to find out what LaRossa's up to. I'm assuming he's working with Amber, unless Stuart separately offended this guy."

"I've never heard of him, but I've never heard of Amber Peppers either," he replied.

"The team staked out the airport last night, but she never showed," Peter said.

Joe swallowed his huge bite of burger. "Her supposed flight was about the same time Eva was hit?"

Peter nodded. "I want to know where the hell she is. You're all going with me. It's not the best idea, but none of you are leaving my sight. Once in that observation room, you will stay there. This may take a few hours."

"Taylor, you'll need to hit the head before we leave," Joe said, dipping his fry in ketchup.

"I'll hit you in the head," she mumbled.

Wearing their guns and vests under their winter coats, Stuart and Joe pressed against Taylor's side, barely giving her room to breathe. Peter and his agents surrounded them through the hotel lobby and out to the SUVs. With lights flashing, their convoy rushed toward the police station. Stuart and Joe picked Taylor up by her arms and practically ran to the building. The policemen, detectives, and staff watched in silence as the entourage of FBI agents shoved them into the small observation room.

"Does everyone know why we're here?" Taylor asked.

"No, but they will before we're done," Peter replied.

They looked through the one-way window. "That's

the guy?" Stuart asked.

"He looks like a greasy weasel," Joe said. The guy had a long thin schnoz with beady eyes that were set close together.

After Peter left for the interrogation room, an agent entered and leaned against the door with his arms crossed. Feeling Taylor stiffen, Stuart asked the agent to lean on the wall instead of the door. The agent shrugged and complied. Stuart pulled Taylor close. Even through the vest, he could feel her tremble. They stepped to the window as Peter entered the room. He introduced himself and sat in the chair across from the weasel.

"What does the Division Director of the FBI want with me?" Roan asked, leaning back in his chair.

"I want you for attempted murder," Peter replied.

"No way."

"You've got some explaining to do. Where should I start?" Peter opened his brown folder. "We have your prints on this rifle." He showed him an image of the rifle. "Do you have a permit?" He looked up while Roan silently folded his arms. "Didn't think so. That van was reported stolen from a car lot. How'd you come across it?" Roan remained quiet.

While Peter pressed about the rifle and the van, Joe tapped his thumb to his lips. "Why does the name LaRossa sound familiar?"

"You mean the LaRossa Dealerships. There are seven across the state," Taylor replied.

"Oh, yeah, I wonder if he's related to the owner, Sammy LaRossa," Joe asked. "I heard rumors that he's connected."

"To the mob?" Taylor asked.

Joe nodded, and Stuart shook his head. "Great, just

great," he mumbled.

After twenty minutes of watching Peter grill Roan, they watched another agent fly through their door. Stuart and Joe had their guns drawn before the door was fully shut. "What's going on?" Stuart demanded.

"Roan has a visitor, and it's not good," he replied, locking the door behind them.

"What the hell does that mean?" Joe asked with a glare.

The agent nodded at the one-way window. They turned back to see Peter greet his guest. A weathered man, with a black cowboy hat, black leather vest, black boots, and a silver belt buckle with *LAROSSA* stamped on it, entered the room. Roan smiled as if his savior had arrived.

"Hello, Peter. How are you?"

"Hello, Sammy. Come on in and have a seat. I've been waiting for you," Peter replied.

Stuart and Joe turned to the agents next to their door. "The Director knows Sammy?" Stuart asked.

"Yeah, the Director's been after him for years for illicit dealings, but Sammy's slick."

"Uh-oh," Joe said, glaring at Stuart. "What the hell did you do? And what have you gotten us into?"

Stuart moaned and turned back to the window. "I wish I knew."

"What has my nephew done this time?" Sammy asked, sitting next to Roan.

"He stole a minivan," Peter started.

"No, that's not true. I borrowed one from the Stadium Street lot," Roan replied.

"And the rifle?" Peter asked.

"It's not mine," Roan said.

"Your prints are all over it and on the trigger," Peter said, sliding the ballistics report and the fingerprint results to Sammy. While he looked it over, Peter took out Amber's WMU Student ID photo from the folder. He held it up to Roan. "Who's this?"

Roan shifted in his chair. "I don't know."

Sammy glanced at it and sighed. "What has Bebe gotten you into, Roan?"

Peter, as well as the rest of the group behind the window, waited for an explanation. They held their breath and watched.

"Bebe LaRossa is my niece and Roan's cousin. I haven't seen her in over a year. She's gone off the deep end. Before you ask, I have no idea why," Sammy said.

"Do you know Stuart Morgan?"

Sammy and Roan shook their heads.

"This woman is trying to kill him and has gotten Roan to help her. Where is she, Roan?" Peter demanded.

Roan shrugged. "I don't know what you're talking about."

"She also killed a Federal agent, so you are in deep shit. Do you understand that? Not to mention, you broke your probation. You will go to jail. For how long is up to you."

Shocked, Roan looked at his uncle for support. Sammy sat back and shook his head. "You tell them everything they want to know. I don't want trouble brought down on this family because of Psycho Bebe. Her mother was just as nuts."

"I want a deal," Roan said.

Peter slapped his hand on the table. "Screw you. I have you for attempted murder. Where is she?"

"I don't know. Alls I know is that she asked for my

help. Wednesday was the first time I heard from her in years. She said she wanted some guy dead. She had it all set up, and alls I had to do was aim at his heart."

"She specifically said 'his heart'?" Peter asked.

"Yeah, she was so angry. I don't mess with Bebe when she's that irate."

"How'd you know the guy would be at the graduation ceremony?"

"She told me where to be and what time Saturday afternoon. 'Easy as pie,' she said."

That confirmed she monitored the FBI chatter. He held Taylor's cold hand in his. He kissed her fingers to warm them. Behind the window, they stared in disbelief. He still had no idea who Bebe LaRossa was and why she wanted him dead.

"What did she want you to do next?" Peter asked.

"Leave the van close to the airport. That's it. I haven't talked to her since. That's all I know," he replied, looking at his uncle again.

"She set you up, Dumbass," Sammy said, sliding his chair back. "Peter, he's all yours."

Roan jumped up. "Uncle, I'm family. I need your help."

Sammy stood. "Okay, I'll help you. Director, he did borrow the minivan off the lot. My assistant made a mistake when she called the police about its disappearance. The rest is at your discretion."

Peter nodded and pushed his chair back to stand. "Do you know where Bebe is, Sammy?"

"Last I heard she had an apartment in Parchment," he replied.

"Uncle. Please," Roan begged.

"Roan, you're an idiot," he said, before dismissing

him.

"I hope you're not harboring her," Peter said. "I would hate to bring your name into this, especially when my agent is dead because of her."

At the door, Sammy turned back to the director. "You have my word. I won't impede your investigation. I want nothing to do with that girl."

Peter nodded and shook his hand. Collectively, the group let out a breath.

"Well?" Peter asked from the doorway. "Does her real name sound familiar, Stuart?"

He shook his head. "Does that even help?"

"Do you trust Sammy?" Joe asked.

Peter snorted. "No, but I believe him when he said he wants nothing to do with her. He doesn't need the added pressure from the FBI."

"Can we visit Eva now?" Taylor asked.

AT THE HOSPITAL BY THREE in the afternoon, she rushed toward Eva's room. Stuart, Joe, and Peter trailed her. She held her breath as she opened the door. She wanted to dismiss everything from this morning and focus on her sister. Seeing Eva sitting up, Taylor blew out her breath. She quickly tossed her winter coat and vest in the chair. She already told them she wouldn't wear it around Eva. Her sister didn't need to know about the LaRossa connection. The guys added theirs to the pile, much to Peter's dismay.

"You look much better," she said, reaching for her

hand while the guys stood at the foot of her bed.

Eva smiled. "I had a young visitor here an hour ago. He seemed to think I know something about math and history."

"Oh really?" she asked, feigning innocence.

"He asked if I'd help him in the atrium," Eva added.

"Help who?" Joe asked.

"It's *whom*," Peter replied. "I have to teach you grammar now?"

"Are you up to it?" she asked, ignoring them.

"The nurse said I could for a little while," Eva replied. "It might be a good diversion from my stiffness."

"Whom needs the help?" Joe asked.

"It's *who*," Stuart said.

Taylor turned to the guys and put her hands on her hips. "Listen up, Smartasses. I'm taking Eva to the atrium to visit with our new friend. You three, sit at a different table and don't make a scene." She turned back to Eva. "You should have seen them last night. A bunch of macho bullies."

"Hey," Joe said, "I was upset."

"Joey, go find a wheelchair. You two, outside," she demanded.

Eva laughed as they left. "You're turning into quite the pit bull."

"Are you going all goody-goody on me?"

"Not me. I like adventure."

After getting Eva situated in the wheelchair, Taylor pushed her slowly toward the first floor atrium with Stuart, Joe, and Peter surrounding them closely, and other agents following at a distance. In the hospital's sunroom, patients and guests visited at small tables.

Among the huge Christmas trees, poinsettias, and

other festive decorations, Taylor spotted David alone at a corner table with his book and papers. She parked Eva beside him and pointed the men to the next table.

David grinned. "You're not really sisters. I don't see any resemblance."

"You don't have to be related to be family," Eva replied. "So how'd the fractions go?"

David moaned and slid his practice sheet over to her. "Third grade math is stupid."

With her good arm, Eva looked over his work while Taylor sat back and enjoyed their interaction. David slid his chair closer and sat on his foot as Eva pointed to the numbers on the page. Thirty minutes later, David nodded and shoved the papers into his book.

"Are you getting excited about Christmas?" Taylor asked.

He nodded. "It'll be just Dad and me since Grandma and Grandpa are home."

"Are you going to get your dad something?" Taylor asked.

"I promised to be good for a full day, but it doesn't start yet," David replied with a sly grin.

"That'll be the best gift ever," his dad said from behind him.

"Eva's been helping me with my homework."

"Matt Connor, this is Eva O'Sullivan," Taylor said.

Matt took Eva's hand in his. "Thanks for keeping David company."

Eva stared at their joined hands. "Oh," she mumbled. She moved her gaze to his face and smiled.

David gathered his book, papers, and pencils. "We're going to see a movie today," he said to Eva. "Can I visit you later?" Eva nodded and gaped at Matt. David looked at his dad. "Isn't she pretty?"

Still holding her hand, Matt grinned. "She's mesmerizing."

"What's that mean?" David asked.

Not hearing the question, Matt continued, "May we both visit you later?"

With a flushed face, Eva nodded then watched them leave as the men joined their table.

"I've never seen you speechless," Joe said, laughing.

Putting her hand to her face, Eva slowly looked away from the door. "What?"

"I didn't see a ring on his finger," Peter mentioned.

"Oh, that's nice," Eva mumbled as the group chuckled.

Happy with herself, Taylor pushed Eva back to her room. She had a feeling her recovery would be miraculous. That handsome rugged man just zapped her like a thunderbolt of lightning. It didn't hurt that his son was adorable, too. Exhausted from the trip, Eva let Joe lift her onto the bed.

Taylor shooed the men out and covered her with a blanket. "We're leaving so you can rest. I'll see you in the morning since you'll have other company tonight," she said, fluffing her pillow.

Eva frowned. "Do I look all right? I haven't any of my makeup."

She laughed. "You're mesmerizing." She kissed her blushing cheek and started for the door.

"Taylor," Eva whispered with tears in her eyes, "thank you."

"Don't overdo it."

CHAPTER
twenty-two

STUART LAY ON HIS SIDE and watched Taylor sleep. He saw right through her scheme involving the Connors. She had smiled at Eva and Matt's first meeting. *Coincidence?* He'd like to think divine intervention had something to do with it.

"Why are you watching me sleep?"

"Just thinking," he replied, touching her cheek with the back of his finger.

She turned on her side. "About what?"

"My dad's theory on the Chemistry of Love at First Sight."

"Do you think Eva and Matt felt it?"

"It was pretty obvious." He chuckled. "It should speed up her recovery."

"That's my plan."

"How are you feeling today? Any more signs of a hangover?"

She shook her head. "At the spa, we gave Peter such

a hard time."

"Alcohol turned you into an uninhibited wild woman. I'll have to remember that."

She groaned. "It's a rare occurrence."

He laughed. "If you overdo it again, I want to be around to take advantage."

"I wasn't that bad, was I?" she asked, pulling the sheet to her nose.

"You begged me to take you in Peter's back seat while he was driving. I think your panties are still on the floor of his SUV."

"Oh no," she replied. "No wonder he hasn't looked me in the eye."

"When Reese finds out, he'll try to ply you with drinks, so he can watch. It's a good thing Peter was your driver."

She frowned. "I wanted to forget the bad stuff for a little while. I'm afraid for all of us. I don't understand why this Amber-Bebe person wants to hurt us."

"I don't either, but we'll find her," he said.

"When? After she's killed someone I love? I just found you. I'm not going to let her take you away."

"That's a double damn ditto. I know it doesn't seem like they're doing much, but Peter's furiously working with his people behind the scene. This is top priority since Agent Martin has been killed."

She shivered. "It's too bad it had to come to that," she replied, sitting on the edge of the bed.

He watched her dig around in their bag. How long could this go on? Eva lucked out this time. Would Taylor be next? He thought nothing could happen to them as long as they were together. He hoped to God he was right.

AFTER STOPPING AT THE GIFT shop, Joe and Stuart each carried a bouquet of flowers up to Eva's room. Joe grinned that he had beaten Stuart to the largest one. Taylor had a small bag with some foundation, lip gloss, and a hairbrush. Peter had a stack of magazines and held Eva's door open for them.

Sitting in her bed, Eva smiled. On her bedside table, she had an enormous flower arrangement. They must have just arrived because she still had the card in her hand. Joe frowned at his smaller one and set his on the windowsill. Taylor handed her the bag and looked at the card:

Truly Mesmerizing.

"There's no signature," Taylor said, smiling. "How was your visit?"

"Nice," Eva replied as the guys laughed.

Joe made a semi-circle with the chairs. Before he could give Eva a hard time about the huge vase of flowers, young David flew through the door. He stopped in his tracks, surprised to see so many people in her room.

He hurried to Eva. "Where's your security guy?"

Eva smiled. "He's taking a break since all my bodyguards are in here."

With his hand behind his back, David looked closer at the people in the room then turned back to her. "How long are they staying?" he whispered. "Dad and I want to visit you again."

Eva glanced at the grinning group. "I'd like that."

"I think Joe needs to do a background check," Taylor said.

David looked at Joe. "Are you a cop?"

"What makes you think that?" Joe asked.

"My dad does that."

"He's a police officer?" Peter asked.

David nodded. "That's why we're here. He was shot in the leg at work." Dismissing them, he faced Eva. "I made you something."

Eva took the card with her good hand while the group watched. "This is so sweet, David."

"It's a *Thank You* on the front. That's you helping me with my homework," he said, grinning. "The inside is a Christmas card. That's Dad holding your hand again."

"Again?" Joe asked, smiling.

Taylor laughed. "David, did you figure out what *mesmerizing* means?"

Eva sighed and blushed.

David grinned. "I think it means my dad likes her."

Eva turned a brighter pink.

"Have you ever played *Catch Him Kiss Him*?" David asked Eva.

Eva's eyes widened as the rest of them resisted the urge to laugh. "What?" Eva asked.

"It's a game my grandma and me play. She would

chase me then kiss me if I got caught. You and my dad could play," he encouraged.

Joe held back his laughter. "I don't think it'd be much of a game. I think Eva would simply let him win."

"You would?" David asked her. They could feel the heat of her face from across the room as she nodded. "Where's the fun in that?" David replied.

Not holding back any longer, the guys roared with laughter.

"David, does your dad know you're here?" Taylor asked, coming to Eva's rescue.

"Not exactly. Can we come back later?" After Eva nodded, he left as quickly as he came.

"I like that kid," Joe said, wiping his eyes for the third time.

WHILE THE GROUP LAUGHED AND teased each other, Stuart took a drink order. He and Peter left for the vending machines. He enjoyed their banter. Relaxed around her family, Taylor gave as good as she got. They knew how far they could take the mockery before it became prickly. He wanted to be part of that family bond. With his arms full of bottles of Coke, he waited while Peter answered his phone.

"Damn it," Peter said, sliding his cell into the breast pocket of his suit coat. "I need to meet with my team."

"Go," Stuart replied. "We'll stay in the room. I have my gun. Joe has his, too."

Peter nodded and headed for the elevator. Stuart

walked toward Eva's room at the end of the hallway. He glanced through an open doorway into what he thought was an empty room. Smiling at him, Amber aimed her gun at his chest. With his arms full, he couldn't react quick enough to get his gun from his side. She motioned him into the room. As he passed her, she slid out his weapon and shut the door.

"You're a tough guy to isolate," she said, motioning him farther into the room. She set his gun on the small table behind her.

He tossed the bottles onto the single bed and leaned on the windowsill across the room from her. "You win," he said, crossing his arms.

She glared. "This isn't about winning. It's about payback. You took from me, and I'm going to take from you. Give me your phone."

He tossed it onto the bed, too. "Please tell me what I've supposedly done to you."

Keeping one eye on him, she scrolled the numbers in his phone. "Supposedly? You killed my fiancé." She dialed then spoke into the phone. "Stuart and I are visiting, and we'd like you to join us. You have two minutes to knock on Room three-fifteen. Otherwise, I'll shoot him right through the heart." She tossed his cell back on the bed. "How much does she love you?"

He angrily stepped forward, but she shook her head. "Tell me who your fiancé was and get this over with," he demanded.

His whole future with Taylor crumbled. He knew they wouldn't let her in the room. They had no new strategy. They could do nothing more. He would die for her today. His only sorrow was knowing how wonderful his life would have been. If only his past would stay there.

AS THE BLOOD DRAINED FROM her face, Taylor set her phone on the tray. She started for the door while Joe and Eva watched her. "Hey, where are you going?" Joe asked.

Robotically, she answered, "Amber has Stuart in Room three-fifteen. If I don't go there in two minutes, she'll shoot him."

"Taylor, you can't go," Joe said, grabbing her arm to stop her.

"I have to," she said. "Maybe I can reason with her. I couldn't live with myself if I don't at least try. Joey, please."

"Shit," he said, releasing her. "Then do it my way." He took his gun from his ankle holster. "Turn around." He tucked it into the waistband of her jeans. "Make sure you face her, so she doesn't see this. Get in front of Stuart, and he'll do the rest." He quickly dialed Peter's number. "Where the hell are you? Amber has Stuart."

Taylor hurried to the third door from Eva's room. She knocked and entered before Peter returned to stop her. She saw Stuart across the room. His calm dissolved; he looked in pain. She quickly scanned his body for injuries. Seeing that he was unharmed, she let out a breath of relief.

"Taylor, please don't," he begged, taking a step toward her.

Amber kept him from advancing and laughed. "Shut the door. She must love you to put her life on the line," she said, aiming the gun at her.

Making sure she faced Amber, she reached behind her and pushed the door closed. "You're very smart to fool the FBI," Taylor said, slowly sliding sideways toward Stuart.

"Jonathan taught me well," Amber replied.

"Tell me about him," she said. "He's your love?"

"We were engaged. Then he left for Afghanistan," Amber replied. "I tried to get over his death, but it still hurts. He's the only one who understood me."

Even though she stared down Amber's gun, Stuart closeness gave her the confidence to continue calmly. "I imagine that it will always be painful, but we made some progress in our sessions."

Irritated, Amber absently aimed the gun around the room as she talked. "Not quick enough. I thought I'd give you a chance to save his life, but you failed to make me better."

"Things like this take time." She angled her body closer to Stuart. "Tell me what happened to Jonathan. Maybe I can still help."

Amber glared at Stuart and moved the gun back to him. "He was due to come home, but he got bumped by Lieutenant Morgan, who had priority. Two days later, a sniper shot Jon three hours before his scheduled departure. Even though it happened years ago, it still tears at my heart."

"Taylor, get behind me," Stuart growled under his breath.

Ignoring his demand, she moved in front of him and in line with Amber's gun. "That is horrible. I'm sorry that happened," she said, feeling Amber's pain, "but it isn't Stuart's fault."

The gun slid from her waistband.

"Morgan did it on purpose. He wanted him to stay longer," Amber said, wiping her face with her other hand.

"That's not true," she said, feeling Stuart's finger draw an arrow on her back to move left. "Stuart told me he took that flight because his dad had a heart attack and wasn't expected to live. Jonathan let him," she lied, hoping Amber would see Jon as a sacrificing hero.

"That's a lie!" Amber yelled.

"It's true," Stuart said, nudging her harder toward the side. He played along. "Private Gunderson gave up his seat, so I could hurry to my father's side before he died."

Amber shook her head. "Jon was coming home to me. He hated you. You had cited him for disorderly conduct four times. As punishment, he couldn't call or email. He despised you, and so do I," she said, raising her weapon.

Now or never. Taylor stepped to the left and out of Stuart's way. She heard two shots and felt a burning pain in her shoulder. Stuart caught her as she fell backward. Was her arm on fire? She saw blood everywhere. She looked into Stuart's distraught face and asked if it was her blood. Confused, she saw Peter and Joe rush into the room.

Stuart picked her up and carried her to a gurney in the hallway. "Why did you do this?" he asked as nurses and doctors surrounded her.

"Because I love you," she whispered as her eyes lost focus.

CHAPTER
twenty-three

AFTER WATCHING THEM WHEEL TAYLOR away, Stuart stared at the blood on his hands. Taylor's blood. Transported back in time, he found himself tending to a neck wound of a fellow soldier. Blood had stained his hands then, too. He started to shake and struggled to stay in the present. He turned to Peter, who checked on the now dead Amber. Stuart had shot her in the forehead, but not before she shot Taylor. God, more dead at his hands. Would Taylor forgive him? He needed her to take his pain away. She had already started to help his soul heal.

"How could you allow this?" Stuart asked, reeling from the idea of Taylor dying.

"I let her," Joe replied. "She wouldn't take no for an answer, and the Director wasn't there. We only had two minutes. It was me. I sent her in." Joe abruptly turned and rushed to the men's room.

Stuart and Peter found him puking in a stall. Taking a deep breath, Stuart washed the blood off his hands and prayed she'd be all right.

Peter leaned back on the sink. "Joe, she would have entered the room no matter what. You know that. By putting the gun in her waistband, you gave Stuart a way to end it. Your quick thinking saved them both."

Stuart dried his hands and left to track down information on Taylor's status. He hoped Joe had saved them both.

HEARING BLEEPS, TAYLOR TURNED HER head. Pain shot down her right arm as she remembered the incident. Her arm was bandaged and in a sling across her chest.

A nurse leaned over her. "Ms. Valentine?"

"Is Stuart safe?" she asked, groggily.

"He's outside the door. You just came out of surgery. They took out the bullet and repaired the damage. You and your baby are okay."

"Baby? What baby?"

"You're pregnant, Dear. Three weeks," the nurse replied, checking the IV in her left hand.

"Healthy?" she whispered. *Oh, please, be healthy.*

"Perfectly," the nurse replied.

Relieved, she blew out a breath. As she tried to organize her thoughts, her body trembled, sending a sharp pain down her arm. Oh my God, she was pregnant. How did that happen? She stared at the nurse, who checked her vitals on the monitor.

"Does Stuart know?" Taylor whispered. She saw her blood pressure numbers rise.

"We would never release that type of information without the patient's consent." The nurse smiled. "Is this news to you?"

"Yes," she whispered.

"Well, something good came out of this. Should I send in your fiancé?"

"No."

The nurse frowned. "Okay, I'll let him know that you want to rest."

She couldn't hold back the tears anymore. "Please, don't tell him about the baby."

The nurse patted her hand and nodded. "If you need anything, press the call button," she said, placing it under her left palm. "The pain medication will numb your arm and make you sleepy."

Taylor squeezed her eyes shut. How could this have happened? She thought they were careful. Three weeks? That means she got pregnant the first night they were together. God, the first time she had sex. Was he going to blame her? She didn't even know if he wanted children. This wasn't part of her plan. This was unfixable. Pregnant and unmarried. Her parents would have been disappointed.

As she sobbed, her body shook, sending more pain down her arm. She couldn't stop it. What was she to do? She couldn't face him now. She slid off her engagement ring and held it in her hand. She wept at her irresponsible actions. The door opened, and she tried to turn away from the unwanted visitor. The movement caused her to gasp aloud.

"Taylor, are you in pain?" Joe whispered as he approached the bed.

"Yes," she sobbed.

"I'll get the nurse," he said, turning toward the door.

"No."

He leaned over and wiped her face with a tissue. "You're hurt because of me."

"No," she said, wishing the pain meds would hurry up and kick in to knock her out.

"I thought about a hundred other ways we should have done it," he whispered. "I'm sorry. I let you down."

"I don't think that," she said, sniffing her nose.

He wiped her cheek with another tissue. "The nurse said you don't want to see him. Why?"

She started to feel less pain in her arm. The meds must be working. "Joey, I'm so ashamed," she mumbled as the tears fell. She weakly lifted her hand to give him the ring.

"Hey, you were fearless. You have nothing to be ashamed of," he said, looking at her engagement ring in his hand.

"He'll think I trapped him into marriage. He won't want me when he finds out," she whispered. Thankfully, her mind started to drift.

Joe leaned in closer. "Taylor, when he finds out what?"

She sighed as her pain and heartache quieted. "I'm three-weeks pregnant," she muttered.

STUART PACED OUTSIDE THE DOOR as the nurse and attendant rolled Taylor into the room. During the four hours of surgery, he and Joe had remained silent even when Reese joined them in Eva's room. Eva had been frustrated that she couldn't do anything to help.

Peter took charge of the Amber-Bebe mess. He said she had killed another agent to gain access. Peter had tried to lock down the floor, but it was too late.

When the nurse exited Taylor's room, he and Joe stood in front of her. "How is she?" Joe asked.

"Can I see her?" Stuart asked, starting to pass the nurse for the door.

"She's upset and doesn't want to see you right now," she replied, blocking his way.

Stuart stopped. "What?"

"Can I see my sister?" Joe asked.

The nurse nodded and left with Taylor's chart. Joe entered the room. Looking through the doorway, Stuart saw her sobbing. Why didn't she want to see him? *Because you almost killed her, you idiot.*

He ran his hands through his already messy hair. He'd beg her to forgive him, that's what he'd do. It couldn't end like this. He waited and paced the hall. After a few minutes, Joe carefully shut her door and stalked toward him.

"You son of a bitch," Joe seethed. He punched him in the jaw.

Stuart staggered backward against the wall. Joe held up Taylor's engagement ring and shoved it at him. He felt his stomach drop as he reluctantly took it.

"What's happened?" he whispered, but he knew the answer.

"She trusted you, and you took advantage of her," Joe said through gritted teeth.

"I tried to protect her. You know that," he replied,

staring blankly at the ring in his hand. He couldn't breathe.

Joe stood within inches of him. "That Perfect Plan of hers—the one she's had since before I knew her—has gotten her through the deaths of both parents and kept her from falling apart from the stress. In a little more than a month, you've destroyed it and her. Her reality has frayed, and that's why she doesn't want to see you."

He opened his mouth, but nothing came out. The pain of hurting her was unbearable. "But I love her," he finally said.

Joe shook his head. "You wanted her, so you threw away all responsibility."

He blinked. He didn't understand. "What are you talking about?"

"She's ashamed and probably feels like she let her parents down." Joe narrowed his eyes. "My sister is three-weeks pregnant."

"What? That can't be right. We used protection," he replied, stunned by the news. He looked again at the ring in his hand. "Even so, we're engaged to be married. We'd just be starting a family sooner than we expected."

"You don't get it, do you? Her plan is organized in a systematic way. That perfect plan is now out of order."

Stuart groaned. Was that what she meant by not out of order? What had he done? Was there still hope for them? "But it doesn't matter," he replied, clutching the ring in his hand.

"You and I know that, but she's having a hard time getting her head around it. If you love her, you make her understand that it's not the end of the world."

He rushed past Joe. "It's only the beginning," he mumbled, opening the door to her room.

Stuart quietly pulled a chair closer to the bed and watched her sleep. He had disrupted her entire life from the danger of his death threat to her pregnancy. How could he fix this? Thanks to Taylor, his nightmares were finally subsiding. Her calming voice and nearness gave him the support he needed to get his demons under control.

He couldn't lose her now. How could he make her understand how much she meant to him? Holding her left hand, he slid the ring back on her finger. After saying a silent prayer, he cried with desperation. When she finally opened her eyes, she immediately teared up again.

He held up her hand, showing her the ring. "You accepted my proposal. You aren't allowed to take it off, ever."

"Joe told you?" she whispered.

He nodded.

She looked away from him. "I didn't mean for it to happen."

"I didn't either, but it doesn't change the fact that I love you."

"Do you want this baby?"

"Yes," he replied with a smile. "It's the ultimate gift."

"Everything is happening at once," she whispered.

His lips pressed against her fingers. "Let's get the chaplain in here right now to marry us."

She smiled through her tears. "It wouldn't be much of a honeymoon."

He laughed for the first time in a long while. "You have a point. As soon as you're up for it, we're heading for Vegas."

She frowned. "What will your parents think about

you having to get married because I'm pregnant?"

"First of all, we're getting married because we love each other. The baby is a bonus. Second, the fact that you're fertile and pregnant already, my mom will love you more than me. What do you think she was saying in that message she left? She wants more grandkids."

Taylor blew out a breath, releasing her tension. He joked with her about their new adventure until she fell asleep peacefully. For another hour, he held her hand and watched her. She was giving him another chance, and he wasn't taking it for granted. He returned down the long hallway to Eva's room. Reese stood outside her door.

"Hey, I heard," Reese said, grinning.

"Her pregnancy doesn't change a thing."

"She's pregnant? I was talking about her drunken antics," Reese said.

Stuart growled and entered the room. Joe must have told Eva the news because they both glowered at him. Peter talked on his phone. Stuart winced at their glare and cringed at Peter's barking voice.

"Well?" Eva demanded from her wheelchair.

"She's resting, and we're getting married as soon as she's up to it."

She nodded as Peter swore at his phone.

"What now?" Joe asked.

Peter unsnapped his gun holster for better access to his weapon. "Cindy disappeared from the mental health facility. Somehow, she heard about Eva's hit and run accident and Amber's death. She knows Taylor's here. Her psychiatrist says she's out for blood," he replied, already moving to the door. Stuart and Joe beat him to it.

In the hallway, Matt Connor limped toward them. "Is David with Eva? I can't find him."

"We haven't seen him," Joe replied as a nurse and doctor joined the group.

"Ms. Valentine is gone from her room," the nurse said.

Using one hand and her good leg, Eva erratically rolled out of the room behind them. "What do you mean she's not in her room?"

"One of our volunteers saw a nurse in gray scrubs roll her and the bed out of the room. She told the volunteer it was for tests," the nurse replied.

"I didn't order any tests," the doctor stated behind her.

"It can't be that hard to find a woman in a bed wandering the halls," Reese said.

Stuart moved quickly past him. "Joe, call security and lock down the hospital."

"I'll look for David," Eva said, slowly maneuvering her wheelchair away from the men.

IN A SEMI-RECLINED POSITION, TAYLOR opened her eyes and became nauseated. The walls moved and the smell of stale plastic filled the air. Blinking through her drugged fog, she realized an oxygen mask covered her face and someone pulled her bed backwards down a hallway.

"Where am I going?" Taylor whispered against the plastic.

"I'm taking you to a more comfortable room."

With her right arm in the sling, she lifted her left to remove the stifling mask. When her hand wouldn't move, she glanced down to see the strap against her wrist. *Why was there a restraint?* For a brief second, she saw Stuart and Joe at the nurses' station with their backs to her. They disappeared as her bed moved down another corridor.

"Taylor, where are you going?" young David asked, walking beside her.

"We need to run more tests," the nurse replied, pulling the bed down a dark, empty hallway.

"What?" Taylor whispered through the mask.

"I'll walk with you," David said.

"This may take a while," the nurse replied as the bed stopped.

"That's okay," he said, holding her left hand.

The fog in her head abruptly dissipated. "David, run. Get Stuart," she muffled against the mask. She recognized her voice.

Cindy chuckled. "He knows where we're going. Come on, David. You can watch me do the test."

As Cindy pulled the bed into the service elevator, Taylor saw Eva in her wheelchair coming around the corner toward them. Taylor tried to yell to her, but the damn mask blocked her voice from carrying. Still holding her hand, David waved with his other as the doors shut. When the doors opened, Cindy pushed the bed onto the dark floor and down another corridor through a set of double metal doors.

"This is where they do surgeries," David said, looking around.

"We're taking a shortcut," Cindy replied.

"Run, David," she said, sitting up.

"We're almost there," Cindy said, putting her hand on Taylor's bandaged shoulder pressing her back against the bed. The jolt of pain made her want to pass out.

"Taylor, it's all right," David said, staring at her.

Taylor shook her head, but even that movement caused her to moan. Cindy chuckled again and pushed the bed into one of the many empty surgery suites.

"Due to some construction, we have the floor all to ourselves for your thorough testing. We should be completely blocked from unwanted interruptions," Cindy said.

"What kind of test are you going to do?" David asked, looking around the room with equipment and monitors surrounding the perimeter.

Cindy stopped the bed in the center. "Come over here and see." She pulled a tray of surgical implements from the cabinet and set them on a small, rolling cart.

Taylor took a deep breath. "No. Stay on this side," she said, gripping his hand. He looked down at the strap.

"David," Eva said, huffing in her wheelchair from the doorway, "you are not supposed to be in here. Leave now."

"But the nurse said I could."

"I said leave," Eva said, using her left hand to roll into the room.

"Nobody's leaving," Cindy said as she passed Eva and locked the door.

Eva continued toward Taylor's left side until she was next to David. Relieved that he was safer, Taylor tugged at her restraint and watched Cindy turn back from the door. She froze at the sight of her nemesis. The blond curvy Barbie from that Civil War seminar had disappeared. This woman in baggy gray scrubs had short, dirty, spiked hair and heavy blue eye shadow. Her blood red lipstick expanded the edges of her mouth.

Taylor jerked David's hand slightly to get his attention. He looked at her, and she stared at her wrist restraint. He fumbled with the buckle while Eva distracted Cindy.

"Why are you doing this?" Eva asked. "You could have had any guy you wanted."

"I want Dr. Morgan. He's supposed to be mine," Cindy replied, gripping the scalpel tighter in her fist. "I should be engaged to him. That should have been me on TV."

"Your plan with Amber and those guys didn't work," Eva continued as David released the strap.

Cindy twirled the scalpel with her fingers like a baton. "Those guys in the laundry room couldn't do anything right."

"It was pretty smart to manipulate them into helping you," Eva said.

Taylor took the mask off her face. The fresh air filled her body with renewed energy. Cindy set her toy back on the tray. Picking up a hooked implement, she tested the sharpness with her finger and tasted her blood.

"I'll be with Dr. Morgan very soon," Cindy replied.

She incoherently mumbled and fussed with the tray of razor-sharp blades. Eva slowly moved her wheelchair toward the head of the bed closer to the medical equipment. David stayed frozen. Taylor could tell Eva had a plan when she mouthed to distract her. Gritting her teeth, Taylor slowly sat up and swung her legs over the side facing Cindy. She felt a draft in the back of her open gown as she scooted to the edge of the bed. Her chest and arm throbbed, but her mind became clearer.

"You're going to get caught," Taylor whispered.

"No, I won't. I can take my time and savor the moment. What can you do? You're shot, she's in a wheelchair, and he's a kid," Cindy replied, laughing.

Eva whispered to David. He nodded and moved behind the wheelchair next to the wall. Out of the corner of her eye, Taylor saw David lift the phone off the receiver.

WHERE THE HELL IS SHE?" Stuart yelled at the security guard at the nurses' desk on the third floor.

"We have the exits covered, so she can't leave the building," the guard replied.

"Where'd Eva go?" Matt asked, looking behind Reese and Joe.

"Shit, she was here a few minutes ago," Joe replied.

"I've called my agents to help in the search," Peter added.

As Stuart continued to grill the guard about the security cameras, they heard a crack in the overhead paging system. "What's he doing?" a voice said that they recognized as Cindy's whine.

"He's a young boy. We won't let you hurt him," Taylor's voice said. "If you let us go, you can have Stuart. He's bored with me already."

"Trace that now," Stuart demanded.

The guard talked into his walkie-talkie while the

rest listened for any clues as to their whereabouts.

"I knew he'd get tired of you. I'm a princess, and I always get my way," Cindy's shrill voice said. "I wonder how these rib spreaders work."

"Rib spreaders? As in the surgery suites?" Stuart asked.

"Did you know Stuart's only two floors above us?" Eva said.

"Let's go," he said, before racing for the stairwell.

CINDY SMILED AND SET THE implement back on the metal tray. Taylor heard a slight flip of a switch behind her. One at a time, Eva lifted the defibrillator paddles off the crash cart and lowered them to the floor. Eva murmured something to David, and he crouched down.

Cindy saw him on the floor. "David, what are you doing?"

"He's scared," Taylor replied. "Did you know that Stuart thought about you while he was with me?"

"I knew I'd win. I'm better with men. I know how to please them. I know what they really want," she replied, looking at her reflection in the cabinet's glass window.

While David crawled on the floor, Cindy took her lipstick from her pocket. When Cindy turned back, they saw her smeared clown lips. She sashayed to the table for the scalpel as if she were a model on a runway. Hearing the machine hum from behind Eva, Cindy moved around to the foot of the bed.

Keeping her upper body stiff, Taylor quickly swung her legs across the bed to stand in front of Eva, David, and the tray. The cold floor against her feet kept her alert. She willed her bare legs steady.

"You can marry Stuart, but I won't let you hurt them," Taylor said a couple of feet away.

Like a cobra, Cindy struck out her arm and stabbed Taylor's bandaged shoulder with the scalpel. She twisted it and tried to shove it in farther. With her left hand, Taylor grabbed her wrist. Cindy's sickly sweet smile angered her more than the shock of the pain.

"Bitch," Taylor gritted, backing up to pull out the knife.

In no hurry, Cindy smiled as she held the bloody scalpel in her hand. Taylor stumbled backward around the tray. David pulled Eva's wheelchair behind the bed to the other side.

"No, I need to stay," Eva replied.

"You're doing a good job, David," Taylor said with her hand on the tray to keep it between Cindy and herself. "Keep Eva away from this wacko."

"I am not a wacko!" Cindy screamed.

"Taylor, you don't understand," Eva said.

"I do," Taylor replied, focusing her energy to her voice. "Cindy's a psycho for thinking I would just let her have Stuart. He is mine."

"Not if you're dead," Cindy replied, stepping closer.

Blood soaked her hospital gown while more of it dripped on the floor from Cindy's scalpel. Taylor weakly pushed the tray at Cindy, who easily stopped it with both hands. Cindy didn't see the paddles twisted around the lower metal bars.

"Is that the best you got?" Cindy asked with a

laugh.

"No, this is," Taylor replied, flipping the defibrillator's manual switch on the crash cart.

The shock dropped Cindy to the floor. She convulsed in the smeared blood from the scalpel. Stuart, Joe, and Matt broke through the doors before David could unlock it. Matt hugged his son and checked on Eva. Joe stood over Cindy's twitching body, and Stuart rushed to Taylor.

"I don't feel so good," she whispered, slumping to the floor. Blood poured from the gaping hole in her shoulder.

Weak and dizzy, she remembered Stuart picking her up. What seemed like a minute later, she heard voices. Afraid at first, she relaxed at the sound of Stuart and Joey's banter. Opening her eyes, she saw Matt pulling Eva's wheelchair closer to his chair. David sat on his lap. Half asleep in another chair, Peter had his head tilted back against the wall. Joe leaned on the closed bathroom door while Stuart paced at the foot of her bed. Seeing her awake, David grinned.

"It's only been a few hours. She'll be groggy," Eva said. "The pain meds won't hurt the baby, but it'll make her extremely tired."

"Hi," Taylor whispered, smiling at David. "You were so brave."

"I saw your bare butt," he replied. The group laughed.

Eva ruffled his hair. "He's our hero."

"Why did you make me punch those numbers into the phone? Nobody was there."

"The overhead page carried our exchange over the whole hospital," Eva replied.

"Oh, I get it." David looked at Joe. "Then what took you guys so long?"

"The conversation wasn't exactly helpful in pinpointing your exact location," Joe replied, shifting his stance against the door.

"That zap was cool," David said.

"If David hadn't unbuckled my wrist restraint, we wouldn't have had a chance," Taylor whispered as Stuart held her left hand.

"I'm proud of you, Son," Matt added.

David walked to the bed. "I'm glad you and your baby are okay," he whispered into her ear. "I'll make you a card, too."

"I have a feeling you will be getting a truckload of video games for Christmas," Stuart said. "Thank you, David."

"Awesome," he replied, grinning.

"Where's Cindy?" Taylor whispered as David returned to his dad's side. Eva shook her head as Matt set his hand on top of hers. "Can we share a room?"

"I'm officially a visitor now. I checked out earlier," Eva replied.

David frowned. "We won't see you anymore?"

"I'll be around," she said, smiling at Matt.

"I will be, too," Stuart said. "I'm sleeping here tonight."

Peter roused himself from the chair. "With this mess finally over, I need a detailed report. Joe, guess what? You're writing it."

Taylor's finger weakly tapped Stuart's hand. "Honey, go ahead. I'm tired. Besides, Eva's room was full of flowers, mine's bare."

"Just because you were shot and stabbed, you

expect flowers?" Joe smiled. "I'm going broke."

"We'll let you rest, and I'll see you first thing in the morning," Stuart said, kissing her forehead.

Joe waited for the rest to leave. "You need to pace yourself with all this excitement. His heart can't take it." He frowned and touched her finger. "Mine can't either. I'll share you with him if I have to, but you've got to stop doing shit like this."

"Oh, Joey," she said, sliding her hand into his. She cried as he gently squeezed her fingers. "I will always love you."

CHAPTER
twenty-four

A NOISE FROM HER HOSPITAL bathroom woke her. Taylor couldn't focus her eyes, but she heard mumbling. Something wasn't quite right. She lay still and reached for the call button with her left hand, but she couldn't find it. The light flipped on in the bathroom.

Without moving, she tried to see. A figure suddenly stood at the foot of her bed. The light partially outlined the person as she squinted.

"Good, you're awake. I found your clothes," the voice said. "I'll help you dress. We're leaving."

"No," she whispered, feeling nervously for the call button. "Why are you here?"

"I'm here to take care of you. Now sit up." He came around the side of the bed and unhooked her IV.

"I can't."

"I'll help you," he said, flipping back the sheet.

Smiling, he slowly slid his hands down her naked thighs and swung her legs around. She had no energy to fight. *Why was he doing this?* Pain shot down her arm. Why didn't she make Stuart stay?

"Please don't hurt me," she whispered, feeling a deep rumbling panic.

Loren Johnson, her former massage client, shook his head. "I saw your chart. I know a guy who'll make it go away." He yanked her sweatpants up under her hospital gown.

"No." She tried to ignore the pain as he roughly put on her boots. She couldn't let him hurt their baby.

"When are you going to realize that this is his fault?" Loren asked, putting a coat over her shoulders. "He hurt you. You were shot and stabbed because of him. I'm here to take care of you."

Weak and confused, she didn't know what to do. "He loves me," she whispered.

"He doesn't. He used you. Let's go." He tugged her left arm, sending pain throughout her body.

"Stop touching me." The demand exhausted her. She needed to conserve as much energy as she could for Stuart's baby.

"Sorry," he said, stepping back. "I know it hurts."

Her body shuddered and her legs wobbled. *If they left this room, someone would see them, right?* Maybe she could make a noise.

As if she spoke aloud, Loren reached into his pocket. "I have a knife. Be quiet or I will kill that thing right now."

How could this happen yet again? By the door, she waited while Loren looked down the hall. Glancing at the back of her left hand, she felt the IV stint. He had unhooked the tube but left the needle in place. Biting her lip, she pulled it out with her right. Letting her hand dangle, she dripped blood on the floor. Maybe she could leave a trail. *Focus, Taylor.* She would stay calm and trust that Stuart would find her again. In the wee hours of the morning, she took a deep breath, hoping to clear her jumbled thoughts. In a few hours, Stuart would realize she was gone and start looking for her. She needed to stay safe until then.

Loren shoved her the few feet to the stairwell at the end of the hallway. With her room away from the front desk, they could easily leave the floor undetected. She looked at her hand hoping it left a bloody trail. It trickled. She was having no luck at all. With pain searing through her shoulder and right arm, she slammed the back of her left hand against the doorframe, hoping to smear some blood. It bled, and she moaned. At least, with the throbbing in her hand, her shoulder didn't hurt as much.

Loren held the door open to the three flights of stairs. Each step jarred her body. She thought of other things. Her mind flashed to a comforting arm draped over her waist in that visitor's apartment the first time she and Stuart were together. On the night they conceived their baby.

After reaching the first floor landing, she leaned on the wall to catch her breath. The haze in her mind refused to clear. She rubbed her bloody hand on the wall and could feel wetness soaking through her shoulder bandage. She was a mess. She had to keep the panic down until Stuart could find her.

She took another deep breath. "Where?"

"You'll see. And before you know it, he'll be out of your life."

"He'll find me," she whispered, sapping more of

her energy.

Loren opened the outside door of the stairwell. A rush of cold air hit her face. It helped her nausea but immediately chilled her to the bone. She shivered and clenched her teeth as he grabbed her left arm. He ushered her to a rusted, maroon Monte Carlo parked along the curb. Huge flakes fell across her body as she staggered through the new inch of snow along the sidewalk. A foot and a half piled high along the walkway. If she got into that car, how was Stuart going to find her? She glanced around the empty, well-lit parking lot. She was having a shitty night. She put her left hand on the backside window to smear blood before he roughly sat her in the passenger seat.

"Why?" she whispered as he started the car.

"I told you why. I can take better care of you than he can. Besides, I asked you to marry me first. Nobody will find us. I've been very careful."

"Stuart will find me."

He stabbed his four-inch hunting knife in the air next to her. "No, he won't! When will you figure out he's put you in danger?"

Focus, Taylor. Keep it together for Stuart and his baby. Her right arm burned as blood flowed down her hospital gown. She wasn't going to have any blood left.

Trembling, she realized Loren wasn't joking all those months. He's insane, and here she was bleeding, pregnant, and ready to faint. Stuart would come for her, somehow.

BACK AT BOB'S HOUSE, DORIS fixed a late supper then left them to work on a complete account of the last few weeks. In the living room, Stuart sat back and listened to Peter dictate to Joe, who scrambled to write everything down. Reese helped himself to his third bourbon.

Two hours later, Peter looked over Joe's handwriting and nodded. "I think this will tie up all the loose ends. I'll get it typed," Peter said, grinning.

"Take credit for now. Soon, I'll be your best agent," Joe replied.

"You're pretty sure of yourself," Reese said.

"I know what I want," Joe replied.

Peter stood and said his goodbyes. "Bob, it's been swell. Please, thank your wife for her hospitality. Stuart, good luck with your Lightning Bolt Theory, and, Reese, stay out of trouble. Joe, I want you in my Detroit office on January fifth before I send you to Quantico."

Joe grinned. "You betcha, Pete."

Peter stopped and glared. "What?"

Joe winced. "I'll be there first thing in the morning, Director Bingaman."

"That's better," Peter replied as the others chuckled.

After Peter left, Joe leaned back on the couch and flexed his fingers from his writer's cramp.

"I hope you didn't forget to put in that report that I was a hero, too," Reese said, stretching out his legs.

"Since when?" Joe asked.

Stuart leaned back. "Yeah, where were you when I was getting shot two different times in the parking lot and when Lindsay Brant pulled out a knife?"

"I dragged you from the smoke," Reese replied,

"and I came to Taylor's rescue at Bob's shindig."

"What was that about anyway?" Joe asked.

"Taylor said the guy's a professor and her client," Stuart said. "He was upset that she might say something about his treatment."

"I don't think so," Reese said. "He asked her who she was with. It seemed more personal, like he was jealous."

"Who was it?" Bob asked.

Reese shook his head. "He didn't give his name, but he had slicked black hair, kind of dweebie like George McFly."

"That sounds like Loren Johnson. He teaches math at Western," Bob replied.

Joe sat forward on the couch. "I know that name. Taylor told me he proposes after every weekly session."

"You're kidding?" Stuart said.

"Taylor laughs it off as a joke. She always replies that she's not ready to settle down," Joe replied.

"I don't like the sound of that," Stuart said, standing.

"Do you think he saw your TV proposal?" Joe asked. Stretching out on the couch, he stifled a yawn.

"Everybody's seen it," Reese said with a laugh.

"I'm going back to the hospital," Stuart said.

"Wouldn't you be more comfortable here?" Bob asked.

"I'll sleep better next to Taylor."

"In the morning, I'll check that guy out," Joe replied, yawning.

Before Stuart got to Taylor's hospital room, he could tell something was very wrong. Two nurses and a chubby security guard stared at the floor. He ran and saw the smeared, bloody trail that led to the stairwell from her empty room. *God, it was a lot of blood.* Feeling lightheaded, he flashed to all the blood in the Afghan sand but quickly forced himself back to the present. Taylor needed him. Their unborn child needed him.

Stuart inhaled slowly. "Who found this?" he demanded.

"I did, five minutes ago," a nurse replied.

"When was the last time you checked on her?" Stuart asked.

"I changed her IV an hour ago," the other nurse said.

Groaning, he followed the trail down the stairwell while the useless guard huffed behind him. "Any cameras aimed down this area?" Stuart asked, seeing the smeared blood on the wall.

"No, not in the stairwells," the guard replied.

Stuart clenched his jaw and rubbed his head. He opened the outside door to a parking lot. The blood trail stopped at the end of the sidewalk. Snow covered any distinguishing tire tracks.

"Shit," Stuart said, looking around. He pointed to a security camera at the corner of the building. "Let's check that one." In the security room, he stood behind the guard as they scanned the tape. "There." He pointed to Taylor, covered in blood, and Loren Johnson, holding a knife.

After telling the guard to alert the police, he ran from the room. They could be anywhere by now.

LOREN JOHNSON DROVE DOWN THE snowy streets. His windshield wipers worked overtime as an icy layer formed around the frame of the window. The heater on high made her queasy. She had no energy to speak, much less move.

He turned into an apartment complex and parked behind a dumpster. "You won't deny me anymore. My cousin is a certified minister off the internet."

What had she done to bring this on? She had always been professional, hadn't she? Still holding the knife, he opened the passenger side door and swung out her legs. Helping her stand, he absently pressed it against her arm. Shiny and pointy, she watched it fly around her as she staggered. She looked down at her big bloody mess. These sweats will never come clean.

The large parking lot had one light at the entrance and many cars thick with snow. The fresh layer made the parking area less dingy. It was too bad they were stomping all over it with red snow. She struggled to stay upright as they approached the building. She almost fell, but he grabbed her tighter around the waist with his left hand.

Into the darkness, Loren yelled, "Stop right there! Don't come any closer!" Although she didn't see anyone, she did feel the knife, poking into her neck.

A figure stepped out from the shadows. "I want my wife back." Stuart aimed his gun at them.

She smiled. She knew he'd find her. Feeling blood trickle down her neck, she tried to hold steady, but she was so tired. Loren lowered the knife from her neck to her abdomen.

"She isn't your wife!" Loren yelled.

"We were married last night," Stuart replied.

They were? She couldn't remember. She hoped they recorded it.

"She's mine! Drop the gun or your bastard baby's dead!"

"Do not hurt my wife," Stuart replied, slowly lowering the gun to the snowy pavement.

"Don't call her your wife!" Loren screamed. "Now, back away."

She felt the point push past the hospital gown into her skin. Loren stepped closer to Stuart's weapon. She looked at Stuart and pleaded for his help. She tried to use ESP to send him a mental note to be careful. *Whoa, Taylor, keep it together a little longer.*

"I will hunt you down," Stuart said.

Her husband looked so upset. They were supposed to be happy on their wedding day. He needed a hug. Laughing, Loren lessened the knife pressure and leaned over to pick up the gun. He let her go. Without the support, she slumped to the ground. From behind, Joe dropped Loren, pressing his face against the packed snow.

"Dude, you don't mess with this family," Joe said with his knee jammed into Loren's back.

She saw his Hardballer next to Loren's ear. Joey's still her protector. He'll be the best agent Peter will ever have. Joe slid the other gun and knife away from Loren while Stuart knelt beside her. She smiled at him. She asked if he wore his black tuxedo, but she didn't think he understood what she said.

"Oh God. Honey. Stay with me."

She tried again to tell him that it was okay now with him and Joey working together, but she didn't think her voice worked. Stuart frantically stripped off his coat and put it against her shoulder. She worried he'd catch a cold without it. She tried to protest.

"Come on, Honey. Hang in there," he whispered. "Please, don't leave me. I need you."

She blankly stared at the large flakes, falling from the sky. The pain wreaked havoc within her body as her mind grew numb to it. *Was that a good thing?* She vaguely remembered the police and ambulance arriving and being strapped to a stretcher. Joe hauled Loren to his feet and shoved him toward the police. Stuart climbed into the ambulance next to her. She started to cry; she couldn't remember anything about their wedding.

CHAPTER
twenty-five

FRIDAY

ONCE AGAIN, SHE WOKE TO a room full of family. Matt and David sat close to Eva. Taylor had a good feeling about those Connor boys. Joe paced while Stuart held her hand. The doctor stood beside her IV machine. She felt more relaxed with the fragrance of flowers. She remembered now that they weren't really married yet. She smiled when she thought about Stuart calling her his wife. She liked the way it sounded.

"Merry Christmas," David sang out. He held his partially unwrapped video games on his lap.

"What?" Taylor whispered.

"Hey, Honey. Welcome back," Stuart said.

"Where did I go?"

"You've been in a drug-induced coma for the past three days."

Dismissing his unfunny joke, she smiled at her brother. "Joey, when did you become so stealthy?"

"I've practiced sneaking up on people ever since

you and Eva started hounding me."

"Thanks, Joe," Stuart said quietly. "We may have to name our first born son after you."

"Sweet," Joe replied, grinning. "And you can have her. Trying to protect Taylor is becoming a full-time job. You give it a shot for a while."

"Has this family always led such exciting lives?" Matt asked.

"I don't need any more excitement. Can we live a boring life together?" Taylor asked.

Stuart leaned closer, so only she could hear him. "Everything but the sex," he said. "It's time for a new plan with new rules.

Continue the story with *The Kindred Code.*

THE AUTHOR
christina thompson

As a former holistic practitioner with a science background, Christina Thompson enjoys writing about the physical science, the emotional workings of our mind and heart, and the spiritual energy that taps into our passions.

Her degree in biology from Nazareth College in Kalamazoo gave her a love of science and a background into the physical realm of the body. Her diploma in Traditional Chinese acupuncture from Midwest College of Oriental Medicine taught her that the mind and spirit affect the body in powerful ways. The healing power of LOVE is incredibly profound.

She currently resides with her husband, Kraig, in Michigan.

For more about Christina Thompson,
visit her at:
www.ChristinaKThompson.com

Like her Facebook page:
www.Facebook.com/TheChemicalAttractionSeries

Enjoy this sneak peek of the second book in
THE CHEMICAL ATTRACTION SERIES

THE KINDRED CODE

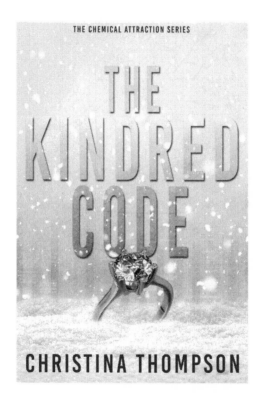

CHAPTER
one

FRIDAY, JANUARY 2ND

IN HIS CLUTTERED HOME OFFICE in Ann Arbor, Michigan, Professor Stuart Morgan frantically searched through last semester's lecture notes piled high on his desk. He stuffed a few files into his briefcase as his fiancée, Taylor Valentine, watched from the doorway. In a rush, he scrubbed the back of his head, messing up his wavy blond hair. Sighing, he glanced around the room.

Two of the four bookcases held textbooks and more binders of his lecture notes from every class he's taught. Military books about the Civil War, WWI, WWII, and the Korean War lined the third. Sci-fi books packed the fourth bookcase. As unorganized as he was, he thought he had a method to his madness. *Apparently not.*

"Have you seen my daily planner?" he asked.

"This one?" she said, wiggling the thick five-by-seven leather-bound organizer in her hand.

With her light brown hair in a ponytail, she puckered her lips as he neared her. Ignoring her gesture,

Stuart snatched it and shoved it into his briefcase. He darted out of the room without a word. Rubbing her abdomen, Taylor followed.

"Your driver will be here at ten to take you to physical therapy. His name's Franklin," Stuart said.

Over his black suit and tie, he slipped on his dad's old Navy peacoat—still in good condition—and was comforted by the heavy wool. He needed the protection from the elements, both the external physical ones and the internal mental ones.

Taylor nodded and absently massaged the area just below her right collarbone where she had been shot and then stabbed. Her bright red wound had healed into a pink puckered scar.

Stuart groaned at the constant reminder. That bullet was meant for him. She had inadvertently gotten in the way ... literally. During her hospital stay, they had been surprised to learn of her pregnancy. Taylor wasn't as thrilled about the news as he was. It had taken her a while to process the changes to her life's plan.

Now, he needed to protect her and their unborn child better than he had before. *Better* as in no more shootings or stabbings. The doctor had said any further strain would be detrimental to her overall recovery.

Stuart slowly exhaled. The relaxation technique didn't help ease his stress. He headed back to the University of Michigan for his departmental meetings today, taking him away from Taylor. Classes would start next Wednesday.

He hugged her. "My mom's flight arrives later tonight. I'll stop by after my meetings then we'll pick her up together," he said, inhaling her lilac scent, his new favorite flower.

"Okay," she whispered against his chest.

He stepped back and looked at her. He couldn't believe how much he loved her. A natural beauty, for sure, but she had an empathetic way about her. He craved it. Looking past her lush lips and thick eyelashes, he recognized her tell of worry as she bit her lower lip.

"Hey," he said, "my mom's going to love you, and she's only staying for a few days. A couple of those, she'll be visiting her sister, my Aunt Tecky. Mom wants to make sure you're all right, especially since our business has been televised."

Boy, that was a loaded noun. Our Business had been on the news for the last three weeks. He had strayed from his rigid rules, and all hell broke loose. Taylor had been assaulted by thugs, shot by his stalker, stabbed by her rival, and then abducted by a lunatic. The doctor had put her in a drug-induced coma for three days to help her and their unborn baby heal.

Good God, all of this upheaval because he pursued her while she was his student. *Why is she still with me? She could easily leave.* He tensed at the thought.

"You better get going. More snow's on the way," she said, stepping back farther.

She wouldn't look him in the eye. They needed to reconnect without distractions. He grabbed his briefcase on the way out the door of his two-bedroom apartment. After scraping the three inches of snow off his Mustang, he started up the car and put it in reverse. His tires spun.

"Shit. What else can go wrong today?" he mumbled.

Rocking between reverse and forward, he finally made it out of the unplowed parking lot. After a treacherous drive, he slipped and slid into the history department's brick building with fifteen minutes to spare.

If he hurried, he could drop off his coat in his office before the first of the three meetings. Savoring the smell of a fresh pot of coffee, he entered the reception area of the history department that connected four offices for the professors. He stopped short.

Unruly reporters surrounded their secretary, Kay Miller. Their uber-organized, elf-like assistant helped with class scheduling, faculty meetings, and students. When the reporters saw him, the noise level rose one hundred decibels, as loud as the roar of a Marine Huey. Any higher and his ears would bleed.

He didn't understand a single one of the questions hurled at him, just the chaotic yelling of reporters trying to be heard over the others.

"Kay, call security," he mouthed.

She nodded and handed him a stack of messages as he maneuvered through the mob to enter his office. He quickly locked the door behind him. Leaning back against it, he blew out a long breath and looked around. He hadn't been here in weeks.

With all of the students' reports and papers from last semester gone, his tiny office was less cluttered than usual. He noticed the binders of teaching notes stacked on his desk. Two of his grad students had returned them after teaching the second half of his semester because … well … because of this mess he created.

Sitting down behind his desk, he scanned the messages Kay had given him. Two local TV stations and a national show wanted interviews. He wadded those up and pitched them into his empty wastebasket. He also had a message from his lawyer to call him and another from the university president.

With a groan, he used his personal cell to call his lawyer. He wanted to be extra cautious and keep private conversations off his work line. Yes, he was becoming paranoid. He thought having a lawyer sift through all the chaos would be less stressful for Taylor. Although in self-defense, he had shot a woman and Taylor had electrocuted another.

On hold, he heard a knock on his door, then Kay's voice. He hurried to unlock it.

"Security escorted them out," she said, nodding toward the empty reception area. She handed him another post-it note. "President James has demanded a meeting with you in forty-five minutes. I tried to tell him that you have meetings, but he was adamant."

He looked at his watch. "Where?"

"His office," she replied.

"Across campus? Great. It'll take me that long to get there. Thank you, Kay."

"Stuart? Stuart, are you there?" his lawyer, Calvin Waters, asked through the cell phone.

"Yeah, I'm here. Did you get my retainer?" he asked. Stuart had to tap into all of his savings. *How am I supposed to provide for a family?* Dismissing that question for now, he listened.

"Yes, and the court dates are in the process of being set. Taylor's assault case, her abduction case, and your stalker case are all separate and will have their own hearing," Calvin said.

Stuart groaned. "And none of that was our fault."

"I'll take care of them. When do you start teaching?"

"Next Wednesday. I have meetings for most of today. And a crucial one with President James within the hour." Glancing at his watch again, he grabbed his coat and briefcase.

"Can you reschedule it, so I can be there with you?" Calvin asked.

After leaving his office, Stuart set a fast pace down the hallway. "No, he's adamant. I have a feeling I'm going to get reamed then fired. Tenure will only get me so far."

"Unfortunately, it's not as permanent as most people think. Don't admit to anything. Basically, keep your mouth shut and I'll handle it. He can't fire you without presenting evidence that you were incompetent or behaved unprofessionally."

"I dated a student," Stuart whispered as he left the building.

"Only after that Civil War seminar you guest lectured at, which was at a different university. Listen, Stuart ... Western Michigan may reprimand you over that but Michigan can't. We have some leeway with the rules that can work for us. Keep your mouth shut. Don't let anyone bait you into saying something they can hold over you. Call me after the meeting and we'll figure out our next steps."

After slipping and sliding in his car across campus, he hoofed it up the staircase for the president's office working up quite a sweat. He finally stood before President Jim James's secretary with thirty-one seconds to spare. Narrowing her eyes as she looked at the clock, the grandmotherly secretary pursed her lips and pointed to a chair. Pretending he didn't have a care in the world, he smiled, sat, and crossed his legs. He really needed coffee though, and his stomach growled loudly.

Stuart was used to people disliking him. He had graduated from Michigan with a PhD in history at nineteen. He joined the U.S. Marines soon after. With his background in strategy and tactics, he became a lieutenant under the tutelage of General Daniel Bingaman. Stuart was hated by those under him and above him for favoritism and not paying his dues by moving up the ranks like most officers do.

After his tour in Afghanistan, he returned to U of M to teach. Because of his military service and awards, he was offered tenure at the start of his teaching career. Professors disliked him for not having to go through the usual seven-year probation period for a tenured position.

President James thought the tenure committee preferred Stuart's accomplishments over the other professors. Stuart thought it was more about the money. He brought in government grants for his papers on innovative military tactics and strategies. The military wanted to hoard his ideas, not share them. It also irked James that the students loved Stuart's classes. Hoping for low attendance and a reason to fire him, James sat through the first few days of all of Stuart's classes every semester for an entire year. Every lecture hall had been filled to capacity since Stuart started teaching five years ago.

Stuart kept his Post-Traumatic Stress Disorder quiet. Although medication helped many, he didn't take any because he didn't want that to be an issue with his job. Unfortunately, it would give the university president more ammunition against him.

Many vets with PTSD refused to seek medical help, Stuart included, because of the negative connotation of perceived violence. Working out at the gym aided his mental and physical therapy. His night sweats and nightmares had subsided since he met Taylor, but he still had panic attacks about the thought of her leaving him. Taylor was carrying their child as well as his sanity.

Twenty minutes later, President James opened his office door and grunted. Stuart entered the enormous room and set his coat and briefcase in one of the chairs before sitting in the other. Four of Stuart's offices could fit inside this one.

Law books on the heavy oak bookshelves took up two walls. The regal desk, large enough to seat twelve as a dining table, spoke volumes about the pompous ass sitting behind it.

Stuart smiled at the picture of James with the Vice President prominently displayed on the other wall. He wouldn't bring up the fact that Stuart had his picture taken with the President and numerous generals. Stuart's medals and ribbons were impressive, not that they mattered much now. He'd give them all back for a good night's sleep.

James smiled with contempt. "You've really stepped in it this time, Mister," he said, steepling his fingers with his elbows resting on his desk.

Stuart remained silent, annoying the hell out of the president.

CHAPTER
two

AS SOON AS STUART SHUT the apartment door behind him, Taylor burst into tears. Her chest hurt, not because of her shoulder injury, although it ached, but because of her broken heart. After waking up from her coma, she started having intuitive experiences about her best friends, Joe and Eva, and Stuart. In a brief flash, she would see them and feel their emotion, whether it was anxiety, anger, or sadness. Last week, while in the hospital, her mind saw Stuart sitting in his car in the hospital parking lot. She had felt his mental anguish, which brought tears to her eyes.

He wouldn't open up to her. She was trying to be patient, but her own prenatal emotions swung sporadically in all directions. As much as she wanted to blame her pregnancy, the drastic changes to her life also pushed her to the edge. Except for this baby she carried, she felt more alone than ever before. The thought frightened her. The rigid plan for her life had crumbled.

That list—the one her deceased parents had instilled in her since kindergarten—was no longer in the order they had intended for her. A child had moved to the top; a career had completely fallen to the bottom.

The buzz of the intercom brought her back to the present. She pressed the button. "Hello?"

"Good morning, Ma'am. I'm Franklin, your driver."

"I'll be right out." She rubbed her abdomen. "Come on, Little Flower. Your mama has work to do."

She grabbed her brown winter coat and shoulder bag then locked the door. Passing Mrs. Bradbury, Stuart's nosey neighbor, in the hallway, she tightened a smile. Mrs. Bradbury had been interviewed twice on TV about Stuart. The gossipmonger loved the attention.

Outside the lobby door, Franklin waited. The polite young man in an oversized black suit coat and chauffeur cap offered his arm on the snow-covered sidewalk. With a smile, Taylor linked her arm with his. Tall like she was, he led her to his sleek black car.

"How are the roads today?" she asked.

"A little slick. *I am the tortoise. Slow and steady wins the race.* And I'll still get you to your physical therapy session on time," he said, flashing a smile.

Taylor laughed. "My father used to say that."

"A smart man," he replied, opening the back door.

"Yes, he was," she said. "Thank you."

During the quiet ride, she contemplated her life with Stuart, their unborn baby, and the love she felt for them, but she still struggled with the recent adjustments to her mindset. And when her abduction and assault crept to the forefront of her mind, she lost sleep from the terror of it.

Wiping her eyes and sniffing her nose, she suddenly

felt an electrical jolt of alertness followed by a vision of Stuart surrounded by reporters. His despair took her breath away. Was Stuart changing his mind about her? He liked his rules and order, and she was causing so much chaos in his life. Her breakfast churned and rose up and into her throat.

"Pull over," she cried out.

Franklin turned into an empty strip mall parking lot. Before he stopped completely, she opened her door and vomited the morning's toast and orange juice. She didn't feel much better. While she heaved a second time, Franklin turned back and set a box of tissues on the seat next to her. He waited.

"Sorry," she said, wiping her mouth with a tissue.

"Not a problem. Thanks for spewing outside the car and not in it," he replied, smiling in the rearview mirror. "Are you okay?"

"Yeah, just morning sickness," she said, searching her purse for some gum. Not finding any, she sighed.

"Are you ready to continue?" he asked.

"Yes," she said, leaning back. The mixture of stomach acid and orange juice burned her throat as she tried to swallow it away.

Franklin finally stopped in front of the Ann Arbor Physical Therapy Center. She opened the door.

"Ma'am," he said, before she slid out, "it's my job to help you."

Taylor waited while he jumped out and offered his hand. In his other, he held out a peppermint candy. She took it and then his hand.

"Thank you, Franklin," she said. "Your sweet gestures will reflect handsomely in your tip."

He laughed. "My pleasure, Ma'am."

"Please call me *Taylor*."

Holding open the door to the center, he chuckled. "I'll be waiting next door at the coffee shop. You can text me when you're done." He handed her his business card as she entered.

With an elderly couple in line ahead of her, she waited and popped in the peppermint, which immediately soothed her raw throat and upset stomach.

At her fourth visit to PT, she already knew the stretching routine. She had to relearn the small things—shaving her legs and armpits, washing her body, and even combing her hair. Getting dressed had gotten better although it still took a while. She worked hard to strengthen her arm and felt frustrated by her slow recovery. She worried she wouldn't be able to take care of her baby, much less hold her.

During a brief break, she rubbed her abdomen. "I'm working hard for you, my Little Flower," she mumbled.

Distracting herself from the pain of lifting the weights, she thought about Joe and Eva. When her parents died while she was still in high school, Joe and Eva had become her family. Now, her family was moving on without her.

Eva stayed in Kalamazoo to start medical school. Taylor suspected Eva wanted to stay close to Matt and David Connor, too. She and Eva talked often. Joe had visited her every day while she was in the hospital in Kalamazoo, but since arriving in Ann Arbor, she had only talked to him briefly on the phone once. She could feel him distancing himself from her.

Tears stung her eyes as the three-pound weight in her hand dropped to the floor. A sharp pain shot down her right arm into her fingers. For the thousandth time, Kenneth, her bald, bodybuilding therapist who looked like Mr. Clean, lectured her that strengthening was a process. She nodded and wiped her eyes with her sweatshirt.

Before texting Franklin that she was finished, she sat in the reception area and dialed Eva and then Joe, getting both of their voicemails. Isolated from her family, she felt a panic attack coming on. She was pregnant with no car and no job. *What am I going to do?* As she headed to the door for fresh air, doubt seeped into her mind about every decision she'd made since she first laid eyes on Professor Stuart Morgan.

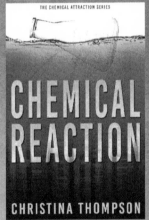

Made in the USA
Columbia, SC
24 October 2017